Thirteen Award-Winning Stories
take you to places you've never been before

You are invited...

To a future where a cop's performance depends upon the quality of his illegal brain-enhancing drugs.

To the home of Jack, who is troubled by a misbehaving pet Death God name Zu'ar.

To the planet Hesperidee, where one girl is on the brink of becoming something other than human.

To hop between doomed planets...and celebrate each one's apocalypse.

There is a world where...

Mankind's sins must be forgiven, lest it be doomed.

The spirit in Abe's magical book makes big promises, but will only deliver at a tremendous cost.

The mobsters in Vinh Quang hope to purchase freedom for entire families—if they can just avoid the cops.

One young man's hallucination might be a ghost—or the key to survival.

Meet the neighbors...

A girl named Elizabeth is haunted by ghostly echoes from her past.

A person whose genetic upgrades let him speak only in five-word sentences.

The kids at Kessington House—a dorm for the psychomorphically unstable.

A writer gets to see what he could have created, if he'd only found the courage.

You think you have problems?

In the seaside resort of Summerland, a young artist struggles to complete a mural, and mend broken spirits.

Daniel's neighbors want your life—but only because they need it to get your soul.

Sam is trapped on a refinery in space and his fusion reactor is about to blow—and that's just the first of his problems.

It seems that our sun has just exploded.

What has been said about the

L. RON HUBBARD

Presents

Writers of the Future

Anthologies

"Always a glimpse of tomorrow's stars..."
— *Publishers Weekly* starred review

"Not only is the writing excellent...it is also extremely varied. There's a lot of hot new talent in it."
— *Locus* magazine

"A first-rate collection of stories and illustrations."
— *Booklist* magazine

"I really can't say enough good things about Writers of the Future.... It's fair to say that without Writers of the Future, I wouldn't be where I am today...."
— Patrick Rothfuss
Writers of the Future Contest winner 2002

"The book you are holding in your hands is our first sight of the next generation of science fiction and fantasy writers."
— Orson Scott Card
Writers of the Future Contest judge

"If you want a glimpse of the future—the future of science fiction—look at these first publications of tomorrow's masters."
— Kevin J. Anderson
Writers of the Future Contest judge

L. Ron Hubbard PRESENTS
Writers of the Future

VOLUME 31

L. Ron Hubbard PRESENTS

Writers of the Future

VOLUME 31

The year's thirteen best tales from the
Writers of the Future international writers' program

Illustrated by winners in the Illustrators of the Future
international illustrators' program

Three short stories from authors L. Ron Hubbard /
Kevin J. Anderson & Rebecca Moesta / Larry Niven

With essays on writing and illustration by
L. Ron Hubbard / Orson Scott Card / Bob Eggleton

Edited by David Farland
Illustrations Art Directed by Bob Eggleton

GALAXY PRESS, INC

CONTENTS

Preface

When Daedalus of Greek mythology first stretched his makeshift wings to soar toward the heavens, humanity was able to tell a story. It was a story of striving for something new, something greater than the fulfillment of a single life.

It was the story of reaching for the heavens, for what was above.

For thousands of years, the tradition of storytelling has breached the canopy of the sky on wings of imagination, despite the fear of repeating Icarus' fiery crash....

To tell a story is to embrace our spirit, our essence, our heart and our soul—it is to speak the language of dreams. For eons, that tradition went uninterrupted, spoken from generation to generation and painted on every possible surface. Then came canvas and the printed page, and with them, a new era of storytelling. The speed of our achievement began to match the pace of our dreams. The industrial revolution, which so shrank our world, also changed the nature of the stories we told. Daring adventurers stretched the limits of science and art, pursuing the dreams of the Creative, and humanity flew.

A single story could be shared with millions. Storytellers like Dickens, Verne, and Wells paved the way for Steinbeck, Mann, and Hubbard to lay a literary foundation for the Golden Age of Storytelling—a road map to the future. McCaffrey, Bradbury, Heinlein, Herbert, and a wave of far-seeing, almost prophetic, writers of the human condition created a new world for the modern novelist such as Kevin J. Anderson, Rebecca Moesta,

Larry Niven, and Orson Scott Card to create in. In turn, these storytellers have found the bright torch of creation to be one that can be passed along to the next generation of great creators.

But a curious thing has happened...for a score of centuries, humanity strove to catch up to the impossible dream of Daedalus' flight, and in the last eighty-five years, we caught up to the future told in the stories of those who wrote such far-fetched dreams. The current judges and winners of Writers of the Future live in a world where jet packs are real. Google is testing the self-driving car. Sony has created robots that look like humans....

As the torch of imagination is shared with this newest group of Writers and Illustrators of the Future winners, we can only imagine what wonders they will discover as we come full circle into the New Golden Age.

Introduction

BY DAVID FARLAND

David Farland is a New York Times *bestselling author with over fifty novel-length works to his credit.*

As an author, David has won many awards for both his short stories and his novels. He won the grand prize in Writers of the Future Volume III *for his story "On My Way to Paradise" in 1987, and quickly went on to begin publishing novels. He has since won numerous awards for his longer works, including the Philip K. Dick Memorial Special Award, the Whitney Award for Best Novel of the Year, the International Book Award for Best Young Adult Novel of the Year, and the Hollywood Book Festival Book of the Year Award—among many others.*

Along the way, David has written a number of bestsellers, designed and scripted video games, such as the international bestseller StarCraft: Brood War, *acted as a greenlighting analyst in Hollywood, and worked as a movie producer.*

*David has long been involved in helping to discover and train new writers, including a number who have gone on to become #1 international bestsellers—such as Brandon Mull (*Fablehaven*), Brandon Sanderson (*The Way of Kings*), James Dashner (*The Maze Runner*), Stephenie Meyer (*Twilight*), and many others.*

David currently lives in Utah with his wife and children, where he is busily writing his next novel, teaching workshops and judging entries for L. Ron Hubbard Presents Writers of the Future, *Volume 32.*

Introduction

Each year I get to read thousands of stories for the L. Ron Hubbard Presents Writers of the Future Contest. It's a bit like looking for perfect little diamonds among the tailings from a mine.

Sometimes, I'll start reading a story and find just a gleam of talent. The story may show promise, but the author might need to do more work.

Other times, the gleam is strong and undeniable. I have a good story, but when I look at it from a certain angle, it seems to have a flaw or two.

Then there are those rare stories that are perfect gems—gleaming and flawless.

The stories that you're about to read are some of those perfect gems. Once again we have winners from around the globe. What's even cooler is, one of these writers will win the grand prize for the year. Which one? I don't know. There are four first-place winners here, each so good that much will depend upon the tastes of our illustrious judges.

This year marks the 75th year since L. Ron Hubbard launched his first writing competition, "The Golden Pen," on radio station KGBU while wintering in Ketchikan, Alaska. It was the genesis for the Writers of the Future, designed to create a level playing field for newcomers. "Anyone but professional writers may participate." That was the rule.

The spirit of that competition flourishes today as we celebrate our 31st year of L. Ron Hubbard's Writers of the Future Contest—

making this one of the longest-running writing competitions in the world, and it is also one of the largest. For the Illustrators of the Future Contest, this ends the 26th year of our competition.

I vividly recall being a new writer poring through Volumes I and II of the anthology, trying to figure out what it would take to win. If you're a writer, and you want to know what it takes, look at the stories here: I genuinely was delighted with every story in this anthology.

Each year, we see growth and changes in the Contest. The number of submissions continued to increase in the past year, and the Contest is taking on more and more of an international dimension.

When I read a story, I look for three things:

1. Is the concept fresh and original? By that I mean, is there something here that is unique?

2. Is the form of the story developed well? In other words, are the characters believable and interesting? Is their world well-realized? Does the character need to struggle repeatedly to deal with significant problems? Does the story touch upon themes that have broad implications for the rest of humanity?

3. Is the story told beautifully? Does the author write concisely, with power, and use the language well?

If the answer to those three rather broad categories of questions is yes, then I've got a story that is worthy of a prize. And in this anthology, we have thirteen worthy stories.

In addition, we have classic tales from L. Ron Hubbard, Kevin J. Anderson, Rebecca Moesta and Larry Niven.

Each year thousands of authors send stories from around the globe, at no cost for entry. I then judge these stories blind, not knowing who the authors are.

My goal is to find great new writers who are worthy of recognition. Many of our winners have gone on to gain fame as writers, winning awards and becoming international bestsellers, and as you read the biographies for the writers here, you'll find that many of these authors are already selling short stories and getting novel contracts, while our illustrators are on their way to their own illustrious careers in books, comics, and film.

Just as our writing contest has grown, the Illustrators of the Future Contest has also blossomed. It too has taken on an international flavor, and our winners have come from all over the world. The works that they're producing are so gorgeous, that once again we're presenting them in full color so that you can appreciate the magnitude of their talent.

Along with our stories and illustrations, we have insightful articles by author L. Ron Hubbard, author Orson Scott Card and artist Bob Eggleton.

So I invite you to join our writers and illustrators in some grand adventures. We'll supply the book. You can supply a comfortable chair, a quiet place to relax, and perhaps a cup of hot cocoa....

Switch

written by

Steve Pantazis

illustrated by

DANIEL TYKA

ABOUT THE AUTHOR

Steve Pantazis knew he wanted to be a writer after purchasing The Hobbit *with his allowance money when he was eight. A lover of all things Tolkien, he emulated the author in a number of stories throughout his young adult years. He got the opportunity to pay homage to his hero by penning a spoof on a rejection letter to the author, published in the* Writer's Digest *November–December 2013 issue.*

When he is not dabbling with words, Steve runs a small software firm, set in sunny, warm San Diego. He enjoys exploring the great outdoors, and using his culinary skills to create feasts for his better half, who has affectionately named him "Love Chef."

Steve has written four novels, the latest set in the same universe as his short story, "Switch." He believes this is a stepping stone toward getting his sci-fi novel, Godnet, *published. He hopes to someday entertain the masses with his love of the craft.*

ABOUT THE ILLUSTRATOR

Born in 1983 in Warsaw, Poland, Daniel Tyka was raised with the smell of oil paints, as his father was a painter. It was a difficult time, when Poland was ruled by communists; Tyka didn't have fancy toys or computers. To fill his time, he could either go outside to play with other kids or draw.

In high school, Daniel loved art, but instead of art school, he followed a path into the financial industry where he lost nine years trying to fit into the financial corporate life.

Then, eight years ago, inspired by a website called "CGSociety," he began watching free tutorials on the net and studying by himself.

With a little push from his friends, Daniel decided to quit his job and spend all his time drawing. He began spending sixteen hours per day working on his laptop. After a year he began getting his first jobs, which enabled him to slowly make a living. From then on, art has been a wild ride until now.

The decision to take art seriously was the best decision in Daniel's life. With all of the resources on the net, he didn't think that art school was necessary anymore.

Today, he is living his dream. It's a great honor to be in this Contest, and he considers himself a winner already.

Switch

The teenager is sprawled by pump number five, multiple gunshot wounds to the chest, the word "deceased" hovering over his body through the projection in my retinal overlay. We're in the middle of a crime scene at a gas station in Jackson Heights, Queens just after sunset, where the decedent expired during a shootout with police. One officer was hit in the face, pronounced dead on site, the other two in the neck by return fire, now at a nearby hospital. I pray they make it.

The June humidity makes me want to tear off my clothes. Instead, I let my blazer bunch up around the elbows as I squat by the body. We have the station taped off and the street blocked on either end with a couple of cruisers.

Lieutenant Briggs is on his way, and at some point we'll talk to the media. There's a crowd of hungry spectators beyond the barricade, along with several news vans. I'm not going anywhere for the next few hours.

My partner, Detective Ed Mullins, holds up an evidence bag. He's sweating worse than me. "Three casings, nine mil."

"Where are the rest?"

"That's it."

"What, he got lucky or something?"

Mullins shoves a stick of chewing gum in his mouth. "That's what I'm saying. I checked the mag on his Glock. You can count the bullets yourself, if you want."

I peer at the teenager with fresh eyes while Mullins chomps his gum. The suspect is a good-looking kid, Puerto Rican with an athletic build, ocean wave-style trendy haircut and gelled sideburns. He's wearing a plain, bloodied white T-shirt and expensive jeans and sneakers. Doesn't fit the profile of a sharpshooter.

"How many shells from our side?"

"Eleven." Mullins pops a bubble. "Our ME says this one took four to the chest. He must have been on something, 'cause he didn't drop until after our guys went down."

I didn't take the kid for a user, but then again, you can't assume anything these days. We ID'd him as Kurt Rodriguez, seventeen, address from the nice part of Forest Hills. His head is cocked to the left. I part the hair above his ear, exposing the port of his temporal lobe implant. There's a designer enamel grommet clamped on, Chinese characters around the ivory-colored rim. Kids love to mod their TLI ports with all kinds of stuff. This is pretty conservative considering what I've seen.

Twelve feet away is a splotch of blood soaked into the grime from where Officer Nolan Yee bled out, numbered markers left in place of his body. Part of me wants to plant the heel of my shoe over Rodriguez's skull and cave it in.

Yee and my younger brother Tommy graduated from the academy together. I remember Yee and his girlfriend coming over to the house at our big Super Bowl party where we shared beers while barbecuing out in the cold. Yee was a smart kid, with aspirations of making detective. His girlfriend was pretty, and I could tell he was crazy about her, from the way he kept his hand on the small of her back to the goofy I'm-in-love smile tattooed on his face. Such a freaking shame. He wasn't a close friend of Tommy's, but they were rookies together, paying their dues on patrol. I can't imagine how Tommy will take the news, but it pisses me off just thinking about it. Rodriguez won't even get a chance to stand trial for what he's done. Son of a bitch!

The stench of gasoline is heavy. Mullins steps closer, blocking the bright gas station canopy lighting with his two-hundred-twenty-pound frame, belt swooping below his enlarged gut as if holding back a storm. He points at the body. "I'm still picking up a TLI broadcast."

"Me too. Should have quit with brain death, but something must still be firing."

Every few seconds, I get a discovery ping from Rodriguez's temporal lobe implant, which flashes red in my overlay. Usually, you set your TLI on discovery mode if you want another device to find you over the Mindnet. Some neural activity must have triggered the response, but I'm no doctor, so I don't bother dissecting it.

Our blood spatter analyst corroborates the stories from a couple of eye witnesses that gave their take on what went down at the gas station, including the attendant: Rodriguez had walked over to Yee, who was buying a bottle of water at the kiosk, and shot him point blank in the face, without provocation.

According to Dispatch, two officers in a squad car heard the gunshot from down the block and zipped over in their cruiser. They engaged the suspect and squeezed off a number of shots before Rodriguez fired back, just twice, taking down each officer from about fifty feet away after being critically wounded. The crazy part is that the suspect made no attempt to run or hide.

Mullins shares my sentiment. "He just stood there and picked them off. I'm telling you, he was on something."

I search the kid's pockets, turning them inside out. House keys, cash card, mini flashlight, and a packet of breath-freshening strips.

Mullins squats next to me. "Nada, huh?"

I want to agree, but I pop open the plastic dispenser and hold it up to my nose. It smells of cinnamon and cloves and something else I can't quite place, but I'm positive what we're dealing with without needing to wait for results from a lab. I lick my lips, imagining how it would taste, dissolving the wafer-thin strip until only the exotic oils remain on my tongue.

Mullins calls my name, but I don't respond until he says it a second time. "Parker!"

I snap the dispenser closed. "Yeah, just thinking."

"Well, think out loud."

I hold up the blue plastic case. It's half the size of my thumb. "Homegrown."

"You sure?"

"Smell." He does, but his face clouds over, like he's trying to wrestle with the fact it's not something you buy at a 7-Eleven. He wrinkles his nose. "What kind of product, you think?"

"Switch."

He nods slowly, getting it. "Told you he was on something. They usually come in pasty dots, printed on paper ribbon, or in clear tabs. Haven't seen this form before."

But I have.

Sublingual delivery is by far the best way to get it into your bloodstream. Dots, tabs, strips—doesn't matter. Stick one under your tongue and say goodbye to foggy thoughts. It's big with the underage crowd because they love to surf the Mindnet in long marathon sessions. Rat race junkies enjoy the extra boost when they have to pull eighty-hour workweeks. Athletes have been accused of taking it, but there is no mandatory testing yet in the sports community. Same with military and law enforcement.

The best way to describe the experience is to imagine a massive caffeine high. You get that awesome rush, that laser focus, that burst of euphoria, like who cares if it's Monday morning at the office with a ton of shit to do. Nothing matters at the moment because your brain has turned off all your concerns, all the pain, all the problems of the day—everything. What you're left with is your subconscious mind taking over; and you just go with it. Switch does that. It gives you a mental edge over those around you. You think better, you work better, you fight better. You *are* better.

Unfortunately for the enthusiast, it's illegal, and you don't just get a misdemeanor for possession these days.

"Well, it explains a few things." Mullins waves a hand over the scene. "But it doesn't explain why he snapped and went on a killing spree."

Mullins is wrong, but I don't say it. He's never had a taste, so his only experience is what he learned during morning briefings, and on the Net. This is cutting-edge, psychotropic-grade product, and the scientific community is just starting to discover its true potential. In my mind, this stuff is a game changer.

I hold the dispenser between gloved fingers with newfound respect, almost reverence. So small, yet a powerhouse of mind manipulation. I place it in an evidence bag and resign it over to Mullins. "See if your guy can get us an expedite on this. I want to know how much is in our susp's system."

Mullins holds the bag up to the light. "I'll see what I can do."

I come to my feet, and the blood returns to my cramped legs. We need to finish processing the crime scene. "All right, chief, let's get a move on."

It's almost midnight by the time I crawl into bed. I'm so exhausted I can't sleep. We made a statement to the press, buttoned up the scene, and tried to interview the murder suspect's mother, who was in pieces over her son's death. Then I had to spend almost thirty minutes on a call with Tommy, trying to calm him down. The whole evening was a mess.

My wife Suzie's eyes flutter open when I turn on the lamp. She looks over at the clock radio on her nightstand and frowns. "So late. Everything okay?"

"It's just work. I'll tell you about it in the morning, sweetie. Go to sleep."

She yawns. "Caitlyn asked about you. I wished you would have called."

"I know." Our four-year-old loves to hear my voice at least once before she goes to bed, even if I'm on the job. It's not like me to miss the opportunity. If I had even the briefest moment alone...

I give my wife a cursory kiss on the cheek and let her roll onto her stomach, covers pulled up to her neck. She tells me in her drowsy voice that she loves me.

"I love you too, babe."

Thirty seconds later, she's asleep. I watch the soft rise and fall of her back and the dark-brown tumble of hair lying across her shoulder blades. I've been married twelve years, and I still see the same twenty-one-year-old, that fragile girl who defied her parents to marry a cop.

Caitlyn is the spitting-image of her mother. She's incredibly smart and uses the Net better than anyone I know. She was born into the Mindnet generation. I was sixteen when it became commercially available, touted as the "Internet for the mind," and twenty-nine when I got my temporal lobe implant. I used to the think the Internet was the end-all-be-all, as a kid. Then the Mindnet came along, and all of a sudden, we were using wearable prosthetics that could connect our brains to banks, retailers and social networks. TLIs followed, replacing cell phone calls, e-mails and texts with thought-enabled communications. My parents would laugh, recalling a time when a networked computer was a marvel. Now it's the brain, and little Caitlyn will think of the Mindnet as I did of its predecessor, and how she never knew a time before it existed.

I shut off the lamp, but I still can't sleep. I'm smelling cinnamon and cloves and . . .

Cardamom! That's the spice I couldn't think of!

I connect to the Net through my TLI and quickly pull up a wiki on Switch. It appears in my retinal overlay as a semi-transparent page against the room's darkened background. There's a complete on-screen breakdown of the history of Switch. It started as an accidental offshoot of a popular antidepressant, found to increase memory retention and response time in rodents. The pharmaceutical name is Duoxatane, but it was never approved for human trials. Still, somebody came up with the brilliant idea to package it into digestible form and put it on the street. The Cardamom masks the bitter taste of the active ingredient.

Thoroughly awake, I log into the precinct portal and pull up the case file for today's homicide. A thumbnail of each page is tiled across the bottom of my overlay. I select the first one and start at the beginning. Some of the information on the expired suspect has been updated, but it will be at least tomorrow when the lab work comes back. I remember Alicia Rodriguez crying her eyes out, wondering how her son could have shot anyone.

There were similar reactions from the father and younger sister, who swore Kurt Rodriguez, track and field star of Forest Hills High School, was incapable of perpetrating the murder of one police officer, let alone three. Wait until they find out how much Switch was in his system.

I get out of bed and peek in on Caitlyn. She's asleep, thumb in her mouth, with the covers bunched around her feet, same long, dark hair as her mother. She's got my wide-swept ears though. I feel bad about missing our nite-nite chat. I pull her blanket over her shoulders and tell her how much Daddy loves her. She snoozes on. I wish I could sleep like that.

I go down to the basement, my man cave. I'll never get the smell of cigars out of the carpet, but it's comforting to me, and this is where I do my best thinking. There's a workbench by the water heater, with an old, rusted vise mounted on the side, and a bunch of small tools I use for my hobby work. I rest my palm on the vise for a moment. It was my father's. He was a tool-and-die worker, and spent most of his career at a ball bearing manufacturing plant in Philly. He always wanted me to find an honest job, and stick to it; and all I wanted to do was make my old man proud.

I take a deep breath and ease open the plastic organizer that holds the assortment of nails, screws, washers and bolts. There's a box of matches underneath a dozen ten-penny nails. It doesn't have any matches in it. I turn on the bench light and open the box. Like precious bars of gold bullion, the wafer-thin strips glint in the light. I'm greeted by a fresh burst of apple and hint of cardamom. There are only three strips left, and a slight panic settles in. I usually do a strip before breakfast, but on a night like tonight, especially when my conscience is weighed down, I'm tempted to do a second. That would leave me a day to restock. Suzie doesn't know about my secret habit. I could never tell her.

A pang of guilt floods my innards. I imagine what my father would have thought of my stealthy enterprise. What would I say to him—that I started because of the long hours at work; that it helped me cope with the Nolan Yees of the world; that I kept going to deaden my nerves any time I came upon a teenage tragedy like Rodriguez's? My father wouldn't buy any of it.

I reach over and give the vise a good pat. Thank goodness the old man's not around to witness this. He had that sixth sense, the kind that kicked in anytime I did something wrong, no matter how good I thought I was at hiding it. Tommy, on the other hand, seemed to get away with everything.

I dislodge a paper-thin sheet from the matchbox. It adheres to the moisture on my fingertip. I hold the see-through amber film up to the light, marveling at how such a thing could have driven Rodriguez to murder. I can understand the elevated aggression with higher and more prolonged doses, but the same could be said of alcohol. Was the Switch enough to make a star athlete snap?

I have a lot of questions percolating through my head. At the top of the list is finding out what drove Rodriguez to murder.

I place the strip on my tongue. It dissolves in seconds. Immediately, my head is clear, my concentration restored. I can feel the heat from the light, the faint scent of glue from the applicator across the room, the electrical pulse of my TLI firing packets of data out into Mindspace.

I am not the man I was a minute ago. I am not like my partner, whose mind is dulled by everyday living, nor like the honest working man I aspired to be. I am something else entirely. Free. Evolved. A new category of species. My unamplified self would condemn my actions. But in my enhanced state, I am exactly who I need to be.

We're in our cubicle farm at the precinct, a little after eight in the morning. Mullins distracts me with his nasty habit of biting his nails. Forty-three, divorced with five kids from two different marriages, and alimony payments to both wives, he's a perpetual ball of nervous energy. I thank my stars Suzie and I have stuck through thick and thin and waited until I made Detective before we had Caitlyn. Mullins was fresh out of the academy when he had his first kid. He looks like an old man, with deep rings under the eyes on his puffy face. I feel sorry for him, but not as sorry as I do for his children. My parents divorced when I was seven, so I know about shitty deals.

The second dose from last night kept me going until dawn. Even though I started out the morning feeling like a zombie, I've had two cups of coffee on top of my usual strip, so I'm a little more wired than usual. I don't like to dose in the evenings for exactly this reason, but I needed the extra perk to keep my mind from racing in random directions, which would have kept me up anyway. With my cleared thoughts, I was able to contend with the culpability of using, of being a deceiver who classified Rodriguez as a criminal when I wasn't much better.

But then again... I hadn't shot Yee in the head.

Mullins stops gnawing long enough to speak. "I don't get it. He was being interviewed by scouts from two top-ten universities, with the chance at a sports scholarship. He had his whole life ahead of him. What's wrong with this generation?"

I've asked myself the same question a million times.

As expected, the lab test came back positive for Duoxatane. We'll have to wait four weeks for the full toxicology report, but at least we have a preliminary finding that supports my suspicions. Rodriguez had twenty-two milligrams of the drug in his system, a lethal quantity. There were also markers indicating cumulative dosing. It means he was an experienced user, and that he knew what he was doing when he dosed up. Now I'm really irked. And the more I think about it, the more I want to know where he purchased his product. There aren't too many dealers that supply Switch in the strip form. Could it have been my guy? I give it a few seconds of serious consideration before I dismiss it as coincidence. It could have been anyone—a close friend, a family member, or someone at school.

Mullins pops open a can of soda and slurps loudly. "I've been doing a bunch of medical research on Switch." He pauses to belch. "It doesn't just amp you up; it interacts with the same neuroreceptors that our TLIs use. I've been thinking about how our suspect took just three shots and hit every target. He struck each of our guys above the neckline. You know what kind of skill you need for that in a firefight? How about the fact he didn't hit them in the Kevlar, like most suspects would? See—this shit is different." He crosses his arms, smug, as if he's telling me something I haven't already figured out.

I flick his can with a finger. "I guess you ruled out paramilitary training, or that he might have been an experienced marksman with a handgun."

Mullins knots his forehead, not getting my joke. He uses a nail clipping to floss his teeth. It bugs me to no end. "Do you have to do that?"

He frowns, then wipes his saliva on his sleeve, and shrugs. "All I'm saying is that this stuff is potent."

I grab my jacket.

Mullins looks up. "Where are we going?"

"To get answers."

Look, I don't know where he got it. I already gave my statement. You think I would have let him take that crap under my roof?" Mr. Luis Rodriguez is angry. He's clutching a white handkerchief embroidered with his initials in his left hand while seated on a bourbon-tinted leather armchair.

We're at the Rodriguez's three-bedroom co-op in Forest Hills. It's upper middle class like the rest of the neighborhood. Mr. Rodriguez works for Delta Technologies in Manhattan, a maker of smart furniture. Supposedly the leather couch I'm sitting on can sense when my back is aching and offer oscillating stimulation to pamper me. It doesn't feel any different than the other overpriced couches I've sat on.

I read over the hand-written notes on my yellow pad. We've already spoken to deceased's mother, sister, track coach, last girlfriend, next-door neighbor, and a former coworker from where the young Rodriguez caddied at a golf course last year. His father is the last stop on a day of zero leads, and I'm hungry. It's half past four, and the last thing I ate was a bagel with cream cheese first thing this morning. Mullins is sitting next to me, probably ravenous from the way he's massaging his belly. We're no closer to getting any answers than before we left the station. The only thing of interest came from the coach who said Kurt Rodriguez had smashed the state record in the hundred-meter dash about a month back.

I give Mr. Rodriguez a few seconds to settle down before I ask the next question. "What about his behavior? You must have noticed something different."

Mr. Rodriguez's tone is less confrontational. "Not really."

"Nothing at all?"

He scratches behind the ear. I examine the body language, but it doesn't look like he's covering up for his son.

"I guess the only thing that jumps out at me is that he was studying really hard before the summer break," Mr. Rodriguez says. "He stayed in his room a lot."

"Is that unusual?"

"Kurt used to hang out with his buddies after track practice every day. His sister said he stopped doing it altogether and complained he was in his room all the time, playing loud music. I'd always come home late from work, so I didn't notice the change, and I didn't think a lot about it."

I tap my pen against the scribbles on my notepad. I'm surprised the sister didn't say anything to us about her brother's newfound seclusion. "How do you know he was studying when he was in his room?"

Mr. Rodriguez looks at me oddly with his tired, sunken eyes, either surprised or offended by my question. "His grades were the best I've ever seen. His GPA was always in the high twos, low threes. He got a 4.0 his last marking period. He even scored a perfect hundred on his Math Regents exam. He'd never gotten more than a C in math. So, yeah, I assumed he was studying in his room."

I want to write something down, but the information is unremarkable. "What about changes in mood? Was he happy, mad, irritated, depressed?"

Mr. Rodriguez glances off to the side. Any hostility he felt toward me is replaced by sadness. He presses his fingertips into the hollows of his eyes while holding up his other hand. I give him a moment. When he opens them, tears roll down his face, and he quickly wipes them away.

"Mr. Rodriguez, I'm sorry, but we need to ask these questions."

He nods rapidly. "It's just that—" He clears his throat. "I mean, there are all these calls I have to make. I have to arrange the—you know—the funeral and—" His voice catches. He rubs the stitched initials on his handkerchief with his thumb, and then notices me looking at it. "Kurt gave this to me a week ago for Father's Day. He had it personalized. See?" He turns it over, and the stitching reads, "To the best father in the world. Love, Kurt." The anger returns in his voice. "You think he would have done that if he was messed up on that stuff?"

We sit for a moment. I give Mr. Rodriguez the space to collect himself. Mullins is impatient, tapping his foot annoyingly. I shoot him a quit-it look and he stops. I resume my questioning.

"Mr. Rodriguez, do you know what Switch does to the central nervous system? It rewires it. It affects judgment, restraint, motor skills, focus and attention. If you're doing bad in math, it fixes it. If you think you're weak, it changes that. If you're feeling aggressive, it amplifies the sensation. It does a lot with just a little. And when the high is off, the craving hits you, because feeling normal just isn't good enough anymore." I hit a high note with the last part, my sermon fueled by confession. Mullins looks at me strangely, but I ignore him, and continue.

"Mr. Rodriguez, it's not that we don't hear what you're saying. No one wants to think their child uses. But do you think nothing was wrong when he shot those police officers?" I'm surprised at my own flare of anger.

Mr. Rodriguez brandishes the handkerchief. "He wasn't on it when he gave me this! I know my son. He must have taken it for the first time yesterday. Or someone drugged him. Why aren't you looking into *that*?"

Kurt Rodriguez was an addict, pure and simple. His father can't recognize the signs. "We found quite a bit in his bloodstream. There were indications he was dosing regularly. No one drugged him."

Mr. Rodriguez perks up. We're not allowed to share lab specifics during an investigation, especially before the official report comes out, so I leave it at that.

I try to get back to obtaining a meaningful answer. "What about new associates? Did your son meet any new people, either outside of school or over the Mindnet?"

"None that I was aware of."

"What about his feelings toward authority? Any changes in his views on religion or politics or the government?"

Mr. Rodriguez throws his hands up. "Look, I already told you I don't know anything. I hardly saw him as it was, and now..." He swallows. He's on the verge of crying. His voice comes out chaffed. "And now, I won't get to see him again."

I sigh inwardly. We're spinning our wheels.

I thank Mr. Rodriguez for his time. He barely acknowledges me. We leave him in his armchair, handkerchief clenched in his hand, tears of defeat streaking down his face.

Back at the precinct, we go through the items seized from Kurt Rodriguez's bedroom. The little shit had to have been OCD, because everything was arranged and aligned perfectly on his desk and drawers—his socks, underwear and T-shirts folded and pressed, his other clothes hanging in the closet, hangers spaced evenly apart.

I recognize the pattern. Switch makes you do things like that. You get all this energy, all this creativity, and you have to use it or you get antsy. Suzie would always ask me how much coffee I drank whenever I'd redo our cupboards, making sure every label on every can or box faced forward, all stacked and sorted neatly, and dust-free; or when I'd work on the lawn for hours, snipping the edges with a scissor, on my hands and knees.

Rodriguez's room was a total disaster by the time our team was done tearing it apart. The only computerized device they found was his digipad, loaded up with meaningless, hand-drawn sketches and the notes he took during his junior-year classes. The problem these days is that anything of merit is on the Net, and since people use their TLIs instead of old-tech computers for just about everything, you have to go to the cloud if you want anything.

Mullins and I review the panoramic photos taken of the kid's room, looking for additional clues. The one facet of interest is on the north wall where Rodriguez had meticulously pasted a few hundred blank sticky notes in straight rows and columns, each sticky equally spaced apart.

Mullins shakes his head. "You mean to tell me his father didn't notice *this*?"

Thinking about the pattern gives me an idea. I rub my hands together. "You know what we need to do, right?"

"What, get something to eat?"

"No, we need to tap into his last memories."

Mullins tents his eyebrows, forehead creasing in puzzlement. It takes him a few seconds to get what I'm suggesting. Then he smiles big. "I'll get us the warrant."

It's called a cerebral trace, and it requires an okay from a judge. I'm not a big fan of digging into a person's private memories, even when they're dead, but it's helped us in the past, like when we scanned the last memories of a murdered rape victim a few months back to find a serial killer before he struck again. I honestly think we saved lives, because we weren't anywhere near catching the bastard. Privacy advocates argue the technique violates Fourth Amendment rights, and in a way, I see their point. With a pending case at the Supreme Court, we'll see what happens. Until then, we keep doing our job.

Mullins and I race over to the Office of the Chief Medical Examiner in Manhattan, warrant already forwarded. We meet with Dr. Sanjay Parekh, a neuropathologist certified in cerebral traces. Time is of the essence, considering the decomposition of the brain after death, so I'm happy to see Parekh already at work in the autopsy room. Rodriguez's blanched form is lying upright on a metal table, the body covered with a sheet below the collarbone, a probe jutting from his skull where I imagine Parekh drilled into it only moments ago. It's a good thing too because I get a little queasy seeing drills and bone saws in action. Plus, I hate the odor. Mullins always jokes that it smells like corn chips.

Parekh plugs the other end of the electrode into a beige cylinder with a monitor affixed to a mobile cart. "Almost there," he says, as he continues to set things up.

Mullins chomps noisily on his gum. "Hey, I got a question about the autopsy report." He attempts a bubble, but the gum flops over his lower lip. He shoves it back into his mouth. "You mentioned something about his right shoulder tattoo being animated. I thought those things stopped postmortem."

I'd noticed the oddity too, but hadn't thought much about it. Rodriguez had a black-and-white tattoo of a Bengal tiger with bared teeth that transformed into Chinese characters when animated—nothing fancy or useful in my opinion.

Dr. Parekh checks the monitor while adjusting the cranial probe. The screen is grainy, a dark sea of shimmering speckles. "It's rare, but not unheard of. Skin cells can survive for days. Animorphs—animated tattoos—function as long as the cells sustain them."

"So, it'll work now?" Mullins asks.

Parekh moves over to Rodriguez's left side. "Take a look." He presses a gloved finger firmly into the stiff muscle of the shoulder. The Bengal tiger dissolves, changing into a pair of Chinese characters, and then back to the original tiger. "See? Animorphic transformation. Pretty cool, actually."

Mullins lifts his eyebrows. "Huh. What d'ya know?"

"Stand back, please." Parekh motions for us to not make contact with the cadaver. I maintain a safe distance.

The doctor taps an icon on the side of the monitor and Rodriguez's body convulses for a split second. The speckled screen dissolves into a blob of gray and black gradients, expanding and contracting like heated wax in a lava lamp. Parekh rotates his finger over a shaded dial in the sidebar menu, and the screen's contrast brightens. He adjusts several more controls, and the blur sharpens into an image that looks exactly like the canopy lights at the gas station. "It's the last thing he saw," Parekh explains. "We call it residual retinal burn. Let's see if we can get anything else."

He taps the screen. The body shudders again. We see fractured images, glimpses of a school locker, a crowd of students in a hallway, a few flashes of different parts of the Rodriguez household—boring scenes, although I'm quite impressed that we're actually seeing what Rodriguez saw when he was alive. I've been through this process before, but it amazes me every time.

The on-screen image changes. We're looking at what I imagine to be a Mindnet page showing an online store, followed by a chat session with a succession of static images representing a conversation. I'm thinking we're going nowhere until I spot the familiar packet of strips. I assume our suspect is holding the dispenser when it turns out to be someone else. The dispenser gets handed off to Rodriguez, but I glimpse a y-shaped scar on the knuckle of the tanned individual before it disappears from view.

"Wait, go back!" I jab my finger at the monitor.

Parekh freezes the frame. He tries to retrieve the last scene, but now we're looking at a bowl of cereal and Rodriguez's brown fingers moving a spoon around in circles, not bothering to eat. "Sorry, I can't go back. Don't worry, it'll be on the recording."

The scene continues with Rodriguez still not eating. Something must be bothering him. "Any idea how far back this is?"

"Probably the morning of the incident, or the day before," Parekh says.

"Not earlier?"

"I've never seen any memories older than seventy-two hours. This is pure visual cortex feedback. It's always short-term."

Rodriguez slams the spoon down on the table, splashing milk everywhere. There's no sound with these memories, just raw imagery. Someday, I hope the technology improves so we can get audio. Rodriguez removes his dispenser from his pocket and empties out all the strips. He stuffs the entire wad into his mouth. There had to be at least ten strips in the bundle! Mullins and Parekh seem unfazed. Am I the only one who noticed?

The better part of a minute goes by with Rodriguez sitting

at the table. He takes the spoon and bowl and neatly moves them to the side, wiping up the spill with his napkin. Whatever agitation was coursing through him seems to be gone. We watch as he calmly leaves the table and goes up to his room and locks the door. It's bizarre as he walks in a circle, round and round. He finally stops, and lifts up his mattress. He grabs a handgun resting on the box spring.

Mullins snorts a laugh. "Hah, there's our murder weapon!"

I ignore Mullins' outburst and continue to watch as Rodriguez takes his firearm over to his desk. He removes the magazine and makes sure the chamber is empty. He then disassembles the rest of the gun—slide, recoil spring assembly, barrel, pistol base. Each piece is carefully placed on the desk. It's as if Rodriguez is creating an exploded diagram from an engineering schematic. He retrieves a cleaning kit from a drawer, and proceeds to clean the components with obsessive detail. I recognize the precision in his movements, the need to clean. He's amped, a fully-charged human turned into a purpose-driven machine.

From there, Rodriguez picks up the pace. He does at least a hundred push-ups on the carpet of his bedroom, runs up and down the stairs two at a time, assembles and disassembles his gun faster than anyone I've seen. The tasks are repetitive, the mind trapped in a continuum of exacting execution. The next scene shows Rodriguez running on the sidewalk. He glances at his body once. It confirms he's wearing the clothes we found him in, establishing a time frame. He hops a chest-high chain-link fence like it's nothing, dodges cars in a frantic burst across a busy intersection. He then runs past three young males in front of an apartment building. They're perhaps a little older than him. I catch a sneak peek of their stereographic tattoos. Gang glyphs, visible only through a retinal overlay. Rodriguez stops and turns around with near inhuman dexterity. The largest of the three is goading him, making obscene, taunting gestures. The other two laugh, but in a blink, Rodriguez is on them. He smashes the first in the side of the head with his fist, the second in the Adam's apple, the third in the side of the neck. It's something I picture a Navy seal doing to enemy combatants. They're down in an instant, squirming.

I'm getting an adrenaline high watching the action. I want to deny it, but I can't help but revel in Rodriguez's ass-kicking abilities. I want to mimic his superpowers, to become invincible like him.

The thrill ends the second I recognize the gas station. Rodriguez is running at full steam. Without missing a step, he pulls the Glock from his belt. A second later, the kiosk comes into sight. Officer Yee is holding a bottle of water, ready to pay the cashier behind the glass. He looks over to Rodriguez, mystified expression. Rodriguez slows to a walk. My heart is beating crazy in my chest. I know this feeling, this anticipation. The animal wants the prey to engage him. Yee holds off a moment longer, as if trying to rationalize what he's seeing. He then goes for his duty weapon. Rodriguez blasts Yee in the face. The three of us gasp, Mullins adding in a "Holy shit!" I want to turn away, but I can't. I'm captivated by Rodriguez's inhuman display of savagery.

Rodriguez takes a long moment to stare at his reflection in the kiosk glass. I feel like I'm looking at myself, carriage heaving to suck in more oxygen, a predator ready to maul his next victim. I clutch my chest. My heart is thumping like it's going to explode. Mullins looks my way. "Parker, you all right?"

I have to get out of this room. I need air.

I'm becoming Rodriguez, mirroring his animalistic breathing, a hair trigger from snapping at anything that touches me or comes too close. I think Mullins senses it too, because he leans away.

We let the rest of the scene play out—the arrival of the police cruiser, the shootout with the other two officers, the suspect's violent death. It ends with the first image we saw of the canopy lighting, then speckled blackness. We're all quiet, as if waiting for the end credits to the horror movie we just saw.

Mullins is the first to say anything. He turns to Parekh. "You get all that?"

"Everything. My God!" Parekh is obviously shaken.

"'My God' is right." Mullins wipes the sheen of perspiration from his forehead. "I swear, if that SOB weren't already dead…" Mullins knots a fist, then relaxes his grip. He looks my way. He raises his hand, like he wants to place it on my shoulder, but drops it quickly. "You okay, partner?"

"Fine," I say. But I'm anything but fine.

This is crazy, you know it?" Mullins has his jowls pushed up on his left hand, fat folds in his face bunched like a shar pei's. He's on his third can of energy water, the other two empty and crushed into pucks.

We've been going over Rodriguez's recording for almost four hours. Everyone on our floor has gone home for the evening, leaving the rest of the cubicle farm dark and quiet, except for us.

Mullins is playing with his bowl of microwaved popcorn, circulating the kernels endlessly, his nervous energy eating away at my resolve. He points a greasy finger at the screen. "I mean, who gets this kind of front-row seat into a murder's craziness, huh?"

I replay the scene showing the dispenser hand-off between what I imagine is the drug dealer and Rodriguez. We've already run the still image against our biometrics database, searching through the collection of tattoos, scars and birthmarks. Fifteen potential matches were returned, not a single one quite like the knuckle scar in the still. The only thing we were able to determine were generic traits: male, late thirties to mid-forties, approximately five-nine in height, medium build, possibly Hispanic.

Mullins downs the last of his water and burps. "Hey, I gotta go. Sandy is driving me crazy. She keeps pinging me to pick up Kevin."

"I thought this was *her* week to watch him."

"It was." Mullins heaves himself out of his chair and grabs his blazer. He sighs heavily, the weight of life showing in his weary eyes. I don't envy his situation. Both his exes can be a pain in the ass.

"You'll be fine," I say. "Just think: you can knock back a couple after Kevin goes to bed."

He jiggles his big belly with a smile. "Yeah, that's what I need."

I shove him playfully. "Go on, get out of here!"

He tosses a goodbye hand wave and disappears, leaving me with the video of our dead suspect. My smile fades when I see the frozen image of the dispenser in the dealer's hand. It not only reminds me that we're no closer to figuring out who's moving product on the street, but that I'll be out of my own supply tomorrow evening. I begrudgingly turn off the monitor, sinking into a cesspool of disgust, most of it aimed at myself. What would happen if I were to just go on empty? It's not like I'm addicted to the stuff.

I catch myself licking my lips again.

I bang the desk, angry. I need to fix this. And the only way I see how, is to do exactly what I'm not supposed to do.

I park on Sutphin Boulevard, about a block from the Jamaica Long Island Railroad station. A little after eleven, and the streets are still teeming with pedestrians. It's a shithole of a neighborhood, as mixed as a melting pot gets, mostly low- to middle-income, depending on which side of the block you're on. My beat-up SUV is fine where it is. I push through the mangle of people walking by toward the subway and stores at the end of the street. I hear the L train in the background as I turn down an alley. I'd ended up going home after Mullins left, only to head out after reading Caitlyn a bedtime story and telling my wife that duty called. In a way, it's not too far from the truth.

I ring the bell to Apartment Fifteen on the steps outside a rundown tenement. I'm wearing a nondescript tee, jeans and sneakers, with a Mets baseball cap, brim pushed down over my forehead to keep a low profile. I'm mindful of the pair of gang members sitting on the stoop two buildings over. I can tell they're tracking me as they talk to each other. They're both wearing wife beaters and shorts that extend down to the ankles. I recognize the stereographic tattoos projecting in front of their chests, burning sigils of circles with exes for eyes. These guys are *la hermandad de fuego,* Brotherhood of Fire, a Dominican gang that controls this part of Jamaica; and judging from their dot rankings above the circles, I'd say low-level enforcement.

DANIEL TYKA

The lanky one doesn't even bother covering up the handgun with the taped grip peeking out from his waistband. He turns my way, and I sense a pingback through my retinal overlay. It's a discovery ping, a way of saying, "Who are you?" I ignore him; don't even move an inch to let them know I'm aware of what he's trying to do. If I were on the job, I'd do my own active pingback, and pull up his rap sheet through our NYPD portal using the electronic signature from his own temporal lobe implant.

The buzzer sounds just in time. The lanky one stands and whistles at me. He just wants to see my face. I quickly push through the door, pretending like I didn't hear him, and make sure it locks before heading up the stairs.

The building reeks of trash, and the hallway walls are filled with graffiti. How can anyone stand living in a place like this? I knock once on the metal door of Apartment Fifteen. Reggie opens the door, but leaves the chain on. His one visible eye is looking at me, red-glazed, pupil dilated. He's getting skulled, I'm sure. It's a cheap high, requiring a Mindnet app you download to root the firmware of your TLI. The TLI fires a pulse every few seconds, flooding the brain with alpha waves. Stupid in my opinion, because you can get stuck in an endless loop, and eventually, a coma.

Reggie wipes the dribble dangling from his lip. "Hey."

"You going to let me in?"

He waves a catatonic hand. "Pockets."

It's the same ritual every time. I turn my jean pockets inside out and lift my shirt to show him I'm not packing. He's too stupid to ask me to lift the cuff on my pants. I've got a .22 handgun concealed in an ankle holster. Not much use against the guys downstairs though.

"Okay." He unlatches the chain and lets me in.

I hate the routine—going inside, smelling that rotten Chinese food stink that never goes away, seeing the disarray of clothes, wrappers and dirty dishes everywhere. I've asked him a number of times to exchange product for cash at the door, but he wants me to wait on the dirty couch as he tries to remember where he stashed his supply of Switch. This time, I'm glad he let me in. I've got to talk to him.

"Have a seat." He points at the couch as he teeters toward the kitchen. I don't bother sitting.

Reggie is an odd-looking creature, real narrow head, with a leather-brown Columbian complexion, early thirties, although his compulsive drug use has him looking much older. He was a certified informant for us a couple years back, paid to report on local gang activity. He helped me make a buy, and that's where I got a sample of the good stuff. He's no longer on payroll, but he's still my go-to guy.

After a few minutes, he staggers back in. "Yo, I can't find it."

It's not what I want to hear. "You can't remember where you put it? Maybe it's in the bedroom, like last time, or the closet."

His drowsy face twists into a frown. "You telling me how to run my shit? I"—he yanks his hand haphazardly—"Yo man, I know what I'm doing. Don't tell me how to run my shit, okay?"

I let him go through the motions. Part of my brain says I've made a mistake coming here, the other part knowing this guy's track record. He's always come through for me. I've used other sources in the past, but Reggie's stuff is hands-down the best, even if he's out of his mind.

His expression clouds over. Then he starts giggling like a child, snot bubbling from his nose. "Wait!" He snorts his way into a laughing fit. He catches his breath and then settles into a massive grin. "The bathroom! Yeah, it's there."

He weaves out of sight, returning a minute later, waving a plastic dispenser with a Listerine logo, carrying a few more in his other hand. He tosses me the one with the logo. "Hope you like grape."

I exchange money for product, taking possession of the five dispensers, a hundred strips total. I've asked for more in the past, but Reggie claims it's all he has.

I click open each dispenser, examining the contents, making sure I'm getting a full supply per unit. The cardamom scent is subtle.

"What, you don't trust me?"

I ignore him and shove the collection into my jean pocket. I pull out an equal sum of money as I gave him a minute ago, along with a folded printout from my back pocket. He looks at me and just blinks. "What's this?"

"I need to find someone. Here, take the money." He palms it, still blinking in confusion. I show him the blowup image of the knuckle with the y-shaped scar. "I'm looking for a guy who deals, Hispanic, with a scar like this on his hand."

He holds up the printout and squints. He looks at me, then the printout, and darts his eyes back and forth several times. He stops and tosses it on the floor, along with the money. Bills spill over the dirty carpet. Damn!

Reggie points harshly at me. "You crazy, man? What's this all about? What do you want? I don't work for you anymore!" He rocks back and forth, anger blossoming into mental discord.

I hold up my hands neutrally. "Slow down, Reggie. I just want to know who he is, that's all."

His rocking gets more pronounced. "What do you want with the Candyman?"

The name rings a bell. A big-time street dealer with an even bigger ego, if memory serves me correctly. "I want to meet him."

Reggie grunts. "That's crazy talk, 'cause he don't want to meet *you*."

He gets his shoulders into the back-and-forth swing. Spittle flies from his lips. I'm worried he's going to flip out on me and do something stupid.

"You know him, Reggie? You know the Candyman?"

He shakes his head manically.

I keep my hands raised, a peace offering. "It's okay, Reggie. Calm down, buddy."

The manic jerking continues. "No!" He keeps his eyes fixed on the sprawled printout between full shoulder swings.

I should leave, cut my losses. But he acts like he knows the guy. I pump him for information. "You see this money? It's yours. Just tell me who the Candyman is."

He snorts, getting his chin into the swing. "Candyman's crazy. Yessiree. Crazy."

"You sure he has a scar on his knuckle? Did you see it yourself?"

Spit dribbles down his chin, and his eyes are wide, as if in a trance. It reminds me of what a voodoo shaman from Haiti might look like.

"Reggie?"

He stops abruptly, gaze leveled my way, drool leaking from the corner of his crooked mouth. His voice turns gravelly. "You're too slow for the Candyman, white boy." He opens his mouth in a lunatic grin, revealing a missing front tooth. "Craaaazee slow."

He's not making sense, but I need to see where this leads. "Why am I too slow, Reggie?"

"Why?" His gaze wanders off, lost in the mess of his apartment. He drops his voice to a whisper. "Why."

"Yeah, Reggie, why?"

He almost sounds lucid as he speaks the next couple of sentences. "Because he's got the mojo, that's why. The best mojo, not like yours."

"And how to do I get a hold of this mojo?"

He flicks his eyes at me, insanity restored. "You gotta go down the rabbit hole, white boy. You gotta go deep. And when you get there, the Candyman will be waiting. Yessirree. And when he catches you, he's gonna snap you in half, 'cause that's what he does when you're too slow." He cackles, gap in his teeth wide and ugly.

He's speaking gibberish. Pure, worthless trash. I bend down to retrieve the printout. He can keep the money, but there's no way I'm going to leave the photo.

Reggie shouts at the top of his lungs, scaring me stiff. "Don't touch that!"

I unclench my body. "Just grabbing my paper, Reggie. Money's yours, okay? That was the deal. But this I'm taking."

He shakes his head like a rabid dog. "I don't care. You're leaving it. Get out!"

"Look, Reggie, I'll just take the paper and—"

He grabs what I imagine is a paper bag stuffed with garbage from the ratty credenza behind him, but when I see the gun, I know better than to make a move. I swallow, watching his hand tremble with the revolver pointed at my chest. It's a .357, enough to put me six below. I don't have my vest, so there's no point questioning whether it's loaded.

"Okay, Reggie," I say in a surrendering tone. "I'm going to leave, all right?"

"Yeah, you need to go." He jabs the air with his gun. He's got his index finger tugging on the trigger. You have to put some effort into pulling it, but I'm not taking any chances. My thoughts filter over to Suzie and Caitlyn, and I imagine them, for a split second, crying in the hospital room as I lie on a bed with a respirator.

I back away. Reggie keeps pace with a jagged twitch to his carriage. He then tosses his head back and talks to the air, in Spanish. *"Sí. El blanco hombre sigue aquí."* He laughs his twisted laugh, and it chills me to my core. My panic button goes off.

Who's he talking to?

You can do anything through the Mindnet without the other person knowing. Reggie definitely contacted someone, either through a thoughtlink or M-text. The fact he spoke aloud just confirms it.

I'm out the door in a flash. It rattles closed, muffling Reggie's hyena laugh. Down below, I hear heavy footsteps reverberating off the treads of the stairwell, and voices. I peek over the railing and see the Dominicans, guns drawn. One spots me and points. They break into a run. Shit!

I sprint up two flights of stairs to the top landing and slam open the door to the rooftop. The gravel on the flat roof crunches as I scamper for cover. I duck behind the industrial cooler as the door shuts, and take out my .22 pistol. The one thing in my favor is that it's dark, with the only strong light source behind me, by the door I exited. Ahead, the roof's ledge rises a couple of feet, blocking some of the city lights, aiding in my concealment.

I hurriedly scan my surroundings. I'm sandwiched between two apartment buildings. The rooftop of the closer one is about a half flight lower. I might be able to outrun these guys and get to the door on the other side. It'll either be open, or I'm screwed. Calling for backup is out of the question.

I get ready to launch, quickly estimating my jump and landing. The door swings open before I take one step. I hear the familiar whistle of the lanky Dominican. "Hey *blanco*, oh *blanco*," he calls out in a singsong voice. He claps, then makes kissing noises. From the sound of their footfall, I can tell they're splitting up. They know I'm hiding, and I know they're hunting. I can fire a warning shot to buy more time, perhaps create a standoff. Except, when they realize I'm using a small-caliber weapon, it will be for naught, and I will have wasted a precious bullet.

"Hey, *blanco*, come out," the lanky one says. "We just want to talk." The other one laughs, giving away his position. They're closing in from either side, covering all angles of escape.

My heart is racing. How the hell did I end up here? Again, my thoughts turn to my family. No hospital room this time, just an image of my bullet-riddled corpse being scraped off the concrete sidewalk below. I won't even get an honorable burial. This isn't getting killed in the line of duty. Not even close.

I'm swelling with anger. I had no business coming here. There was a reason my supply of Switch was almost out. There was a reason why I witnessed what it did to a teenager with no priors. And there was a reason why my gut told me to leave Reggie alone and head home.

All the signs; yet I didn't pay attention to any of them.

I yank the bundle of dispensers from my pocket. I'm tempted to hurl them toward the edge of the roof. Or better, try to barter my way out of this predicament. The product has street value, although I doubt my stalkers would be interested. As I squeeze the collection of plastic dispensers in frustration, one pops open. Reggie's cackling fills my thoughts, and his accusation: *You're too slow for the Candyman, white boy.*

Too slow.

Craaaazee slow.

My fingers go to work, hinging on a ridiculous idea. I wedge the .22 into my belt and rip the plastic sheath open. I drop the rest of the dispensers on the ground. I grab the whole stack of strips from the open container and bite down. I chomp furiously. The Dominicans are maybe eight or ten paces away. In a few seconds, they'll have a clean shot. Saliva mixes with film, and my mouth is awash in grape and cardamom. I slosh around the shreds, feeling bits churn into a paste. I chew frantically, trying to get the mixture to dissolve in time.

Within a couple of seconds, my cheeks warm. Two more, and my face flushes.

Then something inexplicable happens.

Time slows, as if each frame of the film reel in my vision is moving a tenth of its normal speed. Yet my mind accelerates in a hundred different directions.

My eyes dart around, picking up the minutest details: bird droppings along the ledge, peanut shells in the gravel, the hoarse breathing of my pursuers, the step of each foot, the position of their bodies, and the intention of each movement.

My .22 is no longer useful, I realize. I rest it on the ground and crouch, leg muscles bunched to spring. There's a clarity in my thoughts so bright that I could count the strands of hair on my head and still have time to measure my next move. My other senses kick in, and I pick up the scent of unwashed skin, the change in air pressure, the tang of foreign sweat.

I scoop up two large pieces of gravel, and transfer one to my throwing hand. The lanky one clears my line of sight first, just as I hurl the rock. It strikes him in the left eye, and he staggers sideways.

The second guy appears on the other side, momentarily distracted by his partner—enough for me to hit him squarely below the Adam's apple. He drops his .38 and clutches his throat, wheezing as he steps back.

Everything is happening in slow motion.

I'm after the lanky Dominican, predator urge unfettered.

He fires a blind shot, ricocheting off the ground where my foot was a moment earlier, his good eye blinking reflexively and tearing. A second shot rings out as I dodge to the right. I shift all my weight, calculate the distance to close on him, and spring, taking to the air.

My fist catches his jaw with an audible crack, dislocating it. He shrieks as I land opposite him, grabbing his wrist and wresting his pistol in one fluid motion. He loses his balance, sprawling to the gravel, crying out in pain, neutralized.

His partner is gasping, trying to recover his breath while aiming at me. I'm moving again, a blur, faster than before. I run to the side of the cooler, concealed for little over a second, and skid, throwing up a shower of rocks.

He pulls the trigger prematurely, hitting nothing. By the time I appear on the other side, I'm on him. My brain computes a combination of fatal blows—strike to the temple, elbow to the summit of the nose, hook to the base of the cerebellum. The information is just coming at me, as if my brain has been transformed into a supercomputer.

I opt for a non-fatal blow, and shatter his clavicle instead, pile-driving my fist with agonizing force. It knocks him back into a screaming tumble.

I hold still, both assailants in my peripheral vision. My heart is pumping harder than it's ever pumped. I'm supercharged, and I know I can kill these men a dozen ways to Sunday if I want to. And I do.

But I need to resist the craving. I'm a vampire, fighting my nature to drain their lives. Thoughts even go to Reggie and what I might do to him. I clench my fists, try to remain rigid and block out the temptation. I'm not going to become a Kurt Rodriguez. I'm not going to indulge, even though I want to snap these creatures to pieces.

I straddle the chest of the second man, startling him. The doorway light catches the dread in his eyes. He's breathing fast, groaning from the agony of the pressure I'm placing with my knee squashed against his broken clavicle. He's mine.

I squeeze either side of his mouth with my fingers like a vise. "I'm going to ask you once, and if you lie, I'm going to rip your fucking jaw off. *Comprende?*"

He nods, scared out of his ever-loving mind.

My voice is a hiss, a venomous hiss. "Where do I find the Candyman?"

There is no coming down from a twenty-strip high, at least not in the first couple of hours. Before this moment, I had no idea what it was like to do more than two hits in a twenty-four-hour period. Now I'm worried the high will never end.

I've got the worst case of the jitters, and I'm holding my arms to keep from shaking, braced against an I-beam beneath the elevated transit line that ferries the 7 train to and from Manhattan.

Mullins picks up on the other end of my call. "Hey." He's barely awake. A second later and, "God, it's one in the morning. What's up?"

There are a thousand things I want to say, blistering thoughts competing at light speed in my overclocked brain. "Rodriguez wasn't a victim."

"Yeah, I know."

"He enjoyed every minute of his high. He wanted to kill those cops. You see, it's a dark side, Ed. It's a dark side that wants to control you. And if you don't have the strength, well, you're a goner."

There's a pause on the other end. Mullins' voice comes back dead serious. "Hey, is everything okay? This doesn't sound like you."

Mullins has it wrong again. It sounds exactly like me. The true me. The unleashed me. "You're a good guy, Ed. I know you've had it rough, but I'm telling you, it's going to work out in the end."

"Man, you're scaring me. You've been drinking or something?"

"Ed, I want you to listen for a second, okay?"

He keeps quiet on the other end.

"If anything happens to me, I want you to take care of Suzie and Caitlyn. It's a partner's oath. You remember that, right?"

"Of course." He sounds like he wants to say more, but he's afraid, I can tell.

"There's nothing to worry about, Ed. I've got something to take care of, and I'm going to follow the rabbit hole. I'm going to dig deep, real deep, and finish this."

"Finish what?"

"What we started. I'm going to close out the Rodriguez case. I'm going to make it right for Yee's parents, for the family of the other two officers that were shot, for my brother Tommy, for Mr. and Mrs. Rodriguez. For you, buddy, and the rest of the boys. I'm going to rip out the source and make it right."

"Jesus, Terry, what the hell is going on? Are you in trouble? Hey, man, I'm here. I'm here, you understand? So talk to me!"

He never calls me by my first name. It gives me a modicum of comfort. "I gotta go, partner. See ya."

"Wait, Terry. Hey—!"

I disconnect and block him from calling back. The L train grinds above me and I let go of my arms. The jitters wrack my body, and I vibrate to the rolling of steel wheels over the tracks. I'm a ball of bottled-up venom, every sedentary moment poisoning my blood a little more. I need to release it. I need to release all of it.

And that's exactly what I'm going to do.

It's a fifteen-minute drive to my destination. With each passing streetlight, the pressure builds. I want to uncork the pressure, to let it burst. But I have to hang on a little longer.

I park in the heart of Astoria, Queens, a twenty-four-hour nonstop mini-Manhattan of low-rise apartment buildings and single-story businesses. Spanish, Greek, Arabian and Brazilian clubs and cafés are hopping, showing off the neighborhood's multicultural personality.

The one I'm interested in is a club called *El Toro Loco*. My rooftop informant said the Candyman fronts as a legit businessman, using the nightclub scene to traffic product. He claimed he didn't know which club, but I followed the rabbit hole to its very depths. It's amazing what you can learn through the Mindnet when your neurons are ablaze.

Reggie was right about the "crazy" part. *El Toro Loco* translates to "The Mad Bull," or literally, "The Crazy Bull." I don't know if it was his rabid ranting, or he was trying to tell me the answer.

Latin dance music echoes out onto Broadway. Young twenty-somethings are clustered in line, waiting to get into the club while 3-D glyphs advertise drink specials that change in price as demand shifts during the night.

The bouncer at the door is big, like an NFL offensive tackle, close-shaved afro indicative of prior military experience. He's three hundred pounds easy, with very little body fat. My brain has already calculated six ways to take him down using nothing more than my God-given hands. I'm not dressed for the club, and he makes it a point to tell me to remove my hat and get to the back of the line. I do neither. The young crowd makes no attempt to hide their disgust for my older presence. I don't care about them. I want in.

There are nineteen people in line at *El Toro Loco*. A video camera above the door confirms that we're being watched. The old me would have flashed a police glyph, and the bouncer would have moved aside.

There's no room for the old me.

I step toward the bouncer.

"Sir, I'm going to ask you again. Please move to the back—"

Faster than he can react, I sock him in the windpipe. He claws his throat, bug-eyed. I follow it up with a knuckled fist to the kidney. His body flexes involuntarily, and he hits the ground, all three-hundred-plus-pounds of solid manpower, down for the count. I step over his mountainous carcass, leaving an astonished crowd behind.

The club is packed. Lasers, stereographs and booming bass thrills my senses. I see two men with the word *Security* across the front of their black T-shirts quickly pushing through the throng toward me. I've been made.

I shove sideways across the dance floor, toward the restrooms and staircase leading up to the catwalk and second bar. People are hanging out everywhere, laughing, talking, drinking and dancing. I don't want to alarm them. I just want to get to my prize.

I'm rough, pushing people aside, swimming upstream, trying to beat my pursuers. I hit the stairs a couple of paces ahead of them. I punch up the steps, zigzagging precisely between bodies. I'm four strides ahead by the time I catch the top step. It's less crowded up here, and I bolt toward the back area, past the VIP roped-off access and velour-cushioned lounge chairs, along the black walls toward the solitary door in the very rear. The door opens six paces before I get there. The suited, short Asian man that exits fires a stun gun at me. A pair of electrodes shoot out. Time slows again. I see the dart-like projectiles and conductive wires propel through the air. I bend sideways, eluding their trajectory. It forces me off balance, but my brain won't let me fall. It tells me to throw my weight into my right foot and push off into a leap. Airborne, I rain down, driving my forearm into the bridge of my assailant's nose, breaking it and knocking him to the ground with my momentum.

I waste no time getting my bearings. I grab the butt of his stun gun and wheel about, clipping the first bodyguard across the forehead with the carbon fiber grip. He knocks mouth-first into the wall, and pitches heavily to the side. The second guard tries to put me in a bear hug. I smack him upside the chin with the butt of the stun gun, snapping his head back. He's down a moment later, lights out.

I take an adrenalized pause to absorb my audience, frozen with their drinks in their hands. Their expressions vary from shock to sheer terror. They're seeing the venom released, the poison of what I've become. It triggers momentary remorse. A second later, and I'm ready to engage my prize, any notion of guilt extinguished and forgotten. I told Mullins I was going to finish this, and I am.

I toss the stun gun on the floor and enter the lion's den.

He's sitting comfortably behind the solitary wood desk in the small office, stained glass peacock lamp illuminating his face in a wash of yellow light. He's not some prizefighter, or Olympian, or martial artist or bodybuilder. He's ordinary, my age, Hispanic mixed with Caucasian, with a medium build hidden beneath a tailored suit. Behind the calm eyes is a storm I recognize, a tidal wave waiting to crash ashore. I wasn't expecting an amped welcome, but I'm not frightened by it either.

I lock the door behind me. There are no windows, no secondary exit, just the four walls of our cage. He could have chosen any place to wait for my arrival. But he chose here instead. One way in, one survivor.

He loosens his red silk necktie. I'm drawn to the crimson hue as it shimmers against the bright, recessed lights above, but more so by the y-shaped scar on his tanned knuckle. Air conditioning is piping in, blowing down on us. I can't feel the cool though.

"So, you're the Candyman."

"And you're Detective Sergeant Terrance Parker." He has an American accent.

I don't care that he knows who I am. Facial recognition technology in networked video cameras can easily pick up a name. They use it in casinos; why not a nightclub?

"I'm not here to arrest you."

His eyes are set on me, hungry, seething. "I know."

"Good. I just wanted to get that out of the way."

He pulls his tie off, folds it in thirds, and sets it parallel to the edge of his table, same as what I would have done in his place. His jacket comes off next as he remains seated. I'm surprised as he tosses it over his shoulder, letting it land sloppily atop the wastebasket in the corner. I notice the clothing hooks embedded in the cinder-block wall behind him. "Yes," he says, catching my gaze. "You would have hung it there."

He unbuttons his left cuff and rolls up his sleeve. My mind is parsing his comment, analyzing its meaning: why he tossed the coat; why he told me that I was expecting it; why he seems so relaxed while I'm nearly quaking from anticipation.

I launch an active pingback. It comes up empty in my retinal overlay. I check the signal strength of my Mindnet connection. It's at ninety-seven percent, almost perfect. Why can't I get a read on him?

"You won't find me that way," he says, starting on the other sleeve. His movement is steady, but I can tell his blood is boiling. "My name is Jean Le Vau. All you had to do was look up the owner of this club, and you would have found me. Easy."

I'm surprised that I missed that. Is the Switch finally wearing off? I had left the other dispensers behind on the rooftop of Reggie's building. I've got no backup. It's just me and the chemical substance in my bloodstream.

Someone bangs on the door. "It's all right," Le Vau says loudly. The banging ceases. "Sorry about that."

"You look Honduran," I say. "I wouldn't have guessed French."

"My mother was Nicaraguan, my father French. But you didn't come all this way to figure me out, did you?"

"No, I came to kill you." I'm surprised to hear myself say it. It sounds like a line from an old James Bond film. Maybe I'm not crashing after all. I can feel the surge of excitement, the tingle in my face, the need to put this man to his end. I quickly remind myself that I'm a police officer. I'm *not* going to kill this man. Am I?

Le Vau takes off his watch and places it next to the tie. Everything he removes lightens the load, allows him to be more nimble in a fight. I should be considering my own outerwear, but I'm already stripped down to a T-shirt and jeans. I remove my baseball cap.

"Feel free to toss it," he says. He points at his jacket.

I want to throw the cap, but I need to place it neatly somewhere. I center it on the cushion of the chair facing him. He smiles politely, hateful beast masked by a level of control I can't comprehend. How does he do it?

Le Vau offers me a seat. "You can always put your hat over there." Again, he points at his jacket.

"I'll stand."

I'm evaluating his physicality, considering all the ways I can take him down. He will have his own brand of tricks, enhanced by heightened senses. *Dig deep,* I tell myself. Reggie's advice.

"How long have you been using?" he asks, removing his gold wedding band, which I had failed to notice. I expect him to toss it on the jacket, but he surprises me again and sticks it in the drawer. I would have put it next to the tie.

"Two years. And you?"

"Five."

I had no idea Switch has been around for half a decade. Hardly anyone knew what it was when I stumbled upon it. Even the wiki didn't date its origin back that far.

Le Vau responds as if reading my mind. "Yes, it's been that long. The first generation product was terrible. Liquid drops. It caused violent mood swings. We replaced it with clear tablets, but the stomach acid destroyed a lot of the positive effects, so we went to coated tablets, and even those didn't do the job quite right." He unbuttons the top of his blue dress shirt. Curly chest hair spills out. "Your generation has been around three years. It's very good, but it also has its limitations, as you well know."

My generation? He makes it sound like there's something else. I've encountered plenty of variations in the form, quality and efficacy of the product. Is Le Vau alluding to that?

"My condolences, by the way," he says. "I heard about the shooting at the gas station."

His comment makes me mad. If we're going to fight, what is the point of being polite? I examine the desktop for anything I can turn into a weapon. A pen to the eye, a letter opener between vertebrae, a paperweight to the philtrum, that area between the upper lip and the bottom of the nose. There are plenty of choices with these ordinary objects. Again, I'm thinking of killing, not wounding him. I amend my thoughts and consider a blow with the stapler to jostle the cerebral cortex. That might do the trick.

"My generation, however, has none of the side effects of yours," he continues. "We're experimenting with the dosage. If all goes well, we should start FDA trials next spring and get our approval fast-tracked. We've got some good people working on it. A much better business venture than the street has to offer."

My mind tells me not to believe him, that he's trying to placate me into thinking he's working for the greater good. I'm not going to fall for his guile. Yet I'm stuck on the "we" reference. Who's "we"?

He lifts the stapler. "Of course, I'm not all about the legal dosage for recreational use. If you're going to save the best champagne for the best occasion, why waste your time on the cheap stuff, right? You go for the gusto!"

He switches the stapler to his left hand. His dominant hand.

"The good news about your generation of product is that it will be off the market once ours hits the pharmacies. No more psychotic episodes, no more cop killings, no more psychological addiction. You get a prescription for that attention deficit disorder you've been complaining about, and you're good to go."

He's feeding me a line, but I'm keen on his game. I think his silver ballpoint pen is the best weapon to use. I come up with eleven methods to paralyze him without even thinking about it.

"You know, that's a pretty good story," I say. "I'm sure someone will buy it, but not me. So how about we cut the bullshit?" I step toward him. "Why did you deal to Kurt Rodriguez? Was he an experiment to you?"

Le Vau rolls back in his chair, leaving the stapler on the desk at a strange angle. The compulsiveness in me wants to nudge it just a little so it's even with his tie. Again, he appears in control of his emotions. Not a blink at the mention of Rodriguez's name. "That boy had potential. I was just curious to see how far he would take it. I had no idea he'd go all the way."

"So he *was* an experiment. And you, what, coached him?"

Le Vau is smug in his response. "He had that spark. I simply opened his eyes."

Le Vau makes it sound as if he was a benefactor. As if he were helping Rodriguez. Rodriguez wasn't some kind of loner or misfit or abandoned child. He was well-liked by his friends, and loved by his family. All he wanted was a way to distinguish himself from the ordinary. It's funny how you find what you want if you really seek it. Le Vau happened to own the candy store, evangelizing the merits of his product. One strip, and studying becomes easier. A second, and you can run faster. Up the dose again, and maybe you'll make history. Keep going, and you'll become God.

Le Vau is nothing more than a preacher, spreading his infected gospel while hiding behind a club to pursue his true proclivity.

"You could have stopped him."

Le Vau stands and pushes in his chair, bringing it flush with the edge of the desk. "I could have done a lot of things. How about you? Who did *you* stop?"

He wants to make me out to be a hypocrite, and maybe I am. My selfishness hasn't made me a better husband or father. It hasn't made me a better partner to Mullins. And it hasn't helped kids like Rodriguez stop themselves before it was too late. Right now, my nerves are frayed to the point where I'm not sure of what I am. But I know this: our encounter is going to end with one man standing.

Le Vau walks calmly around to the front of the desk and perches himself on it. It's a disadvantageous position. He'd have to go on the defense to fend off my attack. Why would he do that?

He pulls a clear plastic sheet from his pant pocket. He lifts it up, exposing a two-by-five set of gel-like buttons, also clear. He pops one square off the perforated sheet. There's a single button in the middle of the square. He pockets the rest of the sheet. "One of these is better than thirty of your strips. Except you don't pop it in your mouth. You apply it to the skin, like this." He places the square flat against his wrist and pushes the button. It pops inward, squeezing out a gel that reminds me of hand sanitizer. He tosses the empty square on the table and rubs the gel into his wrist. "See? It absorbs almost instantaneously. The rest evaporates, with no residue. It's pharmaceutical grade quality. The good news is that it hits twice the neuroreceptors as the old product. That means you're firing on all cylinders."

I'm painfully aware that I just let him dose up in front of me. I think my senses are dulling. Are the strips finally wearing off?

He answers my next question before I even ask it. "It's my second application today." He folds his hands, scarred knuckle on top. "Normally, I do one but, you know, special company and all."

He's blocking the pen by sitting on the desk. And all the other implements I was considering using. He's outmaneuvered me before I realized it. Even though I don't feel afraid, I'm starting to get this sick feeling in the pit of my stomach.

"Well, there you have it," he says with a smile.

I can't resist asking, "So, what happens now?"

Le Vau slides off the desk. He shrugs, still smiling. "Now, I kill you."

He comes at me before I have the chance to duck out of the way. His knee connects with my stomach, propelling me backward. I stumble three steps before righting myself, the wind nearly knocked out of me.

Instant nausea rises up my throat. I suppress my gag reflex. It costs me an elbow to the face. I barely deflect it, taking the brunt of the blow with my shoulder, the rest with my cheek.

I collide with the wood casing adjacent to the door. It's a hard knock to my scapula, pain surging up my back.

Le Vau throws a kick. Somehow, I manage to sidestep it. His foot demolishes the Sheetrock to my right instead of my sternum.

When he removes his shoe from the hole he created, I'm already to his left, near the desk. Pieces of drywall chip off and cascade to the floor. He stamps the dust from his foot. The whole bottom part of his pant leg is coated with Sheetrock debris. It seems to infuriate him, but only for a moment.

"You're good," he says, shifting the weight to his left heel. "Nice to see you actually remember your combat training as a police officer."

There are equations firing in my brain. Some are telling me that my odds are greatly improved using one of the desktop implements available to me. The others are telling me that I have a one in five chance of surviving, period, based on the amount and quality of product in my system. I need something better to even the fight.

"It's right here." He pats his left pocket, again reading my mind.

One gel would do it. But I'd never last long enough to get one.

I lunge for the pen, snap it up, and roll across his desk, knocking over his expensive lamp. It crashes to the floor. The glass and bulb shatter, but I'm on my feet, desk between me and my foe, my only safety net.

He steps around to his right as I circle back. I expect him to grab the stapler, but he's going to use his bare hands.

He hops oddly on each foot toward me, like some kind of wound-up toy with springs for legs. I wait for his bounce to reach one body length and then swing the metal pen to stab him in the carotid artery.

I'm mid-swing when he alters his step, ducking below my thrust. I can't block his punch to my groin. Pain explodes from my testicles.

I double over and lose the pen, along with my balance. He follows up with a kick to my solar plexus, sending me skidding into his coat-covered waste basket.

I land on my back, cushioned only by his sports jacket. I try to use my leg as leverage to stand. I manage to get one foot on the floor. I cry out as the pen I've dropped is driven through the top of my sneaker.

"Ouch," he says. "That must hurt."

I've never experienced agony this intense. I'm unable to get up. The waves of crushing pain are radiating upward from my foot. I'm seeing stars.

"Anyway." He peels me off his jacket and onto the floor. My face strikes broken glass. It cuts into my skin. The pen is sticking out of my sneaker, punched through the tendons in my foot, gnawing at my nerve endings.

Le Vau ties the arms of his jacket together around my throat, lifting me up. I instinctively pull at the hangman's noose, try to breath.

He slams me onto my side in the middle of his shattered lamp, knocking my skull against the brass base. My head throbs, but the air rushes back into my lungs. I'm left gasping, a dab of blood rolling down my cheek.

He reaches across for something on his desk. I should take advantage of the split second his midriff is exposed above me, but I can't do anything. My autonomic system is misfiring. He pulls back, standing over me with an object in his left hand. It takes me a second to focus, and when I do, I'm seeing that silly stapler.

I actually laugh. It's funny, although I don't know why. Maybe it's the idea of Mullins reading my cause of death in a report, crying and cracking up at the same time.

Le Vau laughs too. "I know, who would have thought: a stapler!" He hefts it. "It's made of resin, fabricated by a 3-D printer. I'm guessing part of it will disintegrate when I drive it through your skull. What do you think?"

I keep laughing, not because it's funny, but because I need to buy time. There's a moment in any life-and-death situation where you know whether you're going to make it or end up with a headstone. That's when you need that FM, that f'ing miracle. It happened to me once, when I was rookie, during a shootout with an armed robber in a convenience store. My duty weapon had jammed, and all the junked-up kid needed to do was take me out with his pistol. Instead, the clerk did what she wasn't supposed to do: engage the suspect. The pepper spray to the face bought me my second chance. Now I need that same kind of FM. Too bad no one's around to save my ass.

I feel glass beneath my right hand. A couple of pats, and I find a shard about four knuckles long. I grab a hold of it. I fix my sight on Le Vau's left thigh, right where his pocket is. If I can just get myself into a sitting position...

"Let me ask you something." It's a last-ditch effort to gain a few more precious seconds. I push myself up onto my elbows, knuckles down, shard hidden. I prop my back against the wooden leg of his desk. "If you had the new generation of product available, why didn't you sell it to Rodriguez? Why give him the old stuff?"

He rotates the stapler with one hand, the other ready to wield it if I flinch wrong. "I think you already know the answer."

I do, and it sickens me. Le Vau is a sadist, pure and simple. He wants to create an army of flawed super humans to watch them destroy and combust. The new product isn't any better. It's the same maker of monsters, except the user will think he's in control, when in fact, he will end up changing into the very thing Le Vau has become.

He gives the stapler one last twirl and then holds it up. I know he's faster than me. I know he's stronger than me. I also know that I'm dead sitting here. If I make it out alive, they'll probably take my shield away, and that's okay. I've gone down the rabbit hole, and I don't like what I've turned into. But the most important thing is that I don't want to leave my daughter a legacy of a loser father who threw his life away chasing a drug high just to feel "normal."

In slow-mo, I watch the grip in Le Vau's left arm tighten. I can tell he's going to be dramatic and go for the overhead blow by the way he's arching back, emboldened by my injury and compromised position no less. It'll take him a half second longer to execute, but the payoff will be as grandiose as he had hoped.

His thigh is within arm's reach. I don't need theatrics for what I have to do.

I pivot the weight to my right hip. With all my strength, I lash out with my glass dagger. I anchor the point three inches in from his hip flexor, sinking deep and dragging down with a ripping motion. He yelps, losing momentum.

With my other hand, I reach for his torn pocket. I snatch the bloodied sheet of plastic tabs from the fabric, tearing away three gel squares in the process. Reflex drives Le Vau backward to recover from my stabbing. I smash the torn sheet against the floor, popping the gels with my fist, slathering my skin with clear liquid and blood. His eyes widen, a notion of fear and recognition on his pain-tortured face.

I feel my skin electrify as I yank the pen from my foot. I'm hit with a major endorphin rush as it falls from my hand. Every synapse and neuron awakens. I'm slowing time more than I ever could with just the strips.

A second goes by, and I'm on my feet. I know there's pain in my foot, but I reroute the signal, and block it off. I'm thinking faster, multitasking processes normally handled linearly, going deeper than I've ever gone.

Instinctively, I've got my hands gripped on the lip of the desk, assessing weight, size and mobility. I don't even think through the shift in power to my lower body. I just do it.

Le Vau swings into action. He knows what I'm about to do.

But I'm faster. I redistribute power to my hands and forearms and flip the wood table up. I anticipate his angle of attack and thrust hard. The desk smashes into his torso. I throw all my momentum into the push, crushing his body into the cinder-block wall. There's no yield to the masonry's ruthless surface. The desk breaks apart from the force of the collision, two of the legs prying loose, splinters flying.

Impact complete, I grip the side of the damaged table and toss it. It lands loudly a few feet away, upside down. Le Vau crumples to the ground, blood streaked along the wall from where his head made contact.

I collapse to my knees next to him, winded. He looks at me, head cocked oddly, neck vertebrae damaged. "I can't feel my hands," he manages to say, alarm in his voice. Something's wrong with his mouth too because his speech is slurred. "Go ahead," he prompts. "Finish it!"

There's nothing more in the whole world that I want. I conceive eighteen different ways to sever his spinal column. It's what a Roman gladiator would have considered with a fallen adversary in the arena. I look around the disaster of the office. There's no emperor to give me the go-ahead. The decision is mine.

"No." I pat him on the shoulder, my way of saying, "You're not getting out of this easy, pal." The reality reflects in his horror-stricken eyes. I imagine he's scared shitless of going to prison as a cripple after facing an unforgiving jury. I don't care what he thinks.

45

I try to rise to my feet, but something's wrong with my motor functions. It's like the wires have been disconnected from the battery, leaving my limb muscles unable to contract voluntarily. I push back against the wall with what little strength I have.

Time begins to return to normal. With Le Vau incapacitated, my thoughts shift to home. I want to crawl into bed so badly, to hold Suzie close and confess everything, and ask for forgiveness; to promise her my selfishness is over, and that I will be the father and husband she deserves.

The door bursts inward. Knob and lock smack the vinyl floor. I glimpse a portable battering ram being retracted.

The first police officer aims his submachine, shouting, "Don't move!" He's wearing ballistic armor and goggles. He gives an "all clear" and two more team members enter, followed by a most unexpected sight: Mullins, in jogging pants and a striped polo shirt a couple sizes too small.

Mullins glances at Le Vau, and takes a knee beside me. "Hey partner, what the hell, huh?" He looks me over. "Jesus H. Christ. What have you gotten yourself into?"

It's a damned good question. I lean my head against the cinderblock. "I know." I don't bother asking him how he found me. I'm sure my subconscious mind wanted this. I thumb in Le Vau's direction, pointing out his scarred knuckle. "Arrest him."

Mullins registers a sliver of surprise and nods his head slowly. He motions to the element leader. "Read him his Miranda rights, and then get someone with a backboard in here." The SWAT member goes about his task.

I feel my brain baking under a torrent of neural activity. I'm crashing, and I'm crashing hard. My eyes close for a moment, electrical pulses firing across my retinas.

Mullins snaps his fingers. "Stay with me, buddy. I've got EMS on the way."

I reach out, my arm blurring into three. How fast is my pulse racing? Mullins takes my hand. "Easy there, stud."

I try to keep from fading. "I've done a bad thing." My throat is suddenly dry. I'm parched and there's no water to be found. "Real bad, Ed."

"Yeah, I know. It'll be fine." To me, "fine" amounts to rehabilitation, maybe incarceration. I do appreciate Mullins not being a jerk about it. He adds, "You can give me the details over a beer." He shakes his belly for emphasis, and grins.

We both know it's a joke. I eke out a smile for him. "Yeah, that's what you need."

I'm fighting to stay awake. I want to sleep, to pass out so badly. I can't help myself.

I slip into the shadows, drift toward the dark.

It fades to white, and I see my wife sleeping next to me, chest rising and falling as I watch her peaceful form. I get up and go to Caitlyn's room. She claps when I offer to read her a bedtime story. She snuggles next to me as I start on her favorite book, giggling at the way I act out the characters in the pictures. She's barely awake by the time I finish. I tell her that I love her with all my heart. She says she loves me too. She wants to know if I'm going to be around to read to her tomorrow night. "Of course, sweetie. Daddy's not going anywhere."

It's a nice dream.

The God Whisperer

written by

Daniel J. Davis

illustrated by

ALEX BROCK

ABOUT THE AUTHOR

Daniel J. Davis was born and raised in Massachusetts. He developed an early love for science fiction and fantasy by staying up late and watching movies. The stories on screen fired his imagination. Soon the ones on screen weren't enough, and Daniel was creating his own stories.

He only brings this up because his teachers always told him that TV would rot his brain. He would like to point out that they were wrong.

Daniel doesn't hold it against them, however. He also learned to read from some of those same teachers. Without them, he would never have discovered some of the amazing and fantastic worlds inside his favorite books.

They were still wrong, though.

He is a veteran of both the US Marine Corps and the US Army. In civilian life, he's been a machinist's apprentice, a security guard, and a building maintenance worker.

He lives in North Carolina with an amazing wife, two dogs, and several piles of unread books. Writers of the Future is his first professional sale.

ABOUT THE ILLUSTRATOR

Alex Brock is twenty-three and an art student attending his last semester at the University of Arizona. He loves all things fantasy and creepy. He's been drawing since he was a kid, but what really got him into art was Dragon Ball Z. *The majority of his drawings from fourth to sixth grade were muscly guys with huge hair. He was really inspired by video games like Zelda and Oblivion, along with the awesome characters from* Super Smash Bros. *and* SoulCalibur. *He was also inspired, consciously and subconsciously, by reading such books as* The Chronicles of Narnia, The Lord of the Rings, A Song of Ice and Fire, *Harry Potter, H.P. Lovecraft's work and more.*

After his younger brother got a tablet in 2009 and Brock saw all the awesome stuff his brother was able to do in Photoshop, Brock got his first tablet. He became very interested in fantasy art shortly after discovering DeviantArt, and later CGHub. He tried his best to get on par with everything he saw on those sites, and now (while still trying to get on par) he is working on finding and creating his own niche.

With his work, he strives to bring things that don't exist in our world into reality, doing his best to imagine what they would actually be or look like. He aims to imagine settings and scenarios that would make his jaw drop if he ever saw them in person. Yet he still finds himself inspired by many of the old master painters from 1850–1950.

Today Brock is taking his work very seriously. He is really excited to explore the darkest depths of his imagination on his journey through art.

The God Whisperer

When Jack got home from work on Thursday, he found a pyramid made of bird skulls in his flowerbed. Zu'ar—ancient god of death, strife, and war—must have gotten out of the yard again.

"Ugh," he said.

More than anything, Jack just wanted to collapse in front of the TV. He wasn't in any mood to deal with this right now.

The carnage didn't end at the flowerbed. Scattered across his lawn were more than a dozen freshly-skinned chipmunk carcasses. The pelts were strung up in his holly bushes, drying in the sun.

This was getting out of hand. It was even worse than that time he'd owned a cat. At least the cat would just kill them cleanly, and bring them home as "presents." But Zu'ar had these barbaric little rituals he had to observe.

Instead of going through the front door, Jack walked around the back of the house. More death and carnage was strewn through the shrubs along the side yard. And sure enough, he noticed a small hole underneath the fence. He'd have to remember to put a trashcan there tonight, until he could get to the store for a bag of gravel.

He decided to leave the back gate open behind him. If Zu'ar was prowling the neighborhood, Jack wanted it to be easy for him to get back in. He went inside and put his laptop bag down on the kitchen table. He got himself a glass of ice water.

"Zu'ar!" he called. "Zu'ar are you here?"

Jack didn't hear him running around. He wasn't sure if that was a good sign or not. He went into the living room, afraid of what kind of destruction he'd find.

51

The end table next to the couch lay on its side. One of the legs was broken off and missing. Worse, his grandmother's old lamp had been smashed into pieces.

Jack sighed and rubbed his eyes. He could clean this up later. First he needed to take care of the mess out front, before the neighbors complained.

Two hours later, just as Jack was placing a spiked rabbit's head into a trash bag, he felt a dark and terrible presence behind him. The air grew cold. The wind took on the distinct smell of fire and decay.

"Hello, Zu'ar."

He heard the rumble of the god's voice inside his head.

"Greetings, Cowardly Weakling."

"I wish you wouldn't call me that," Jack said.

"I call you that because that is what you are," the god thought. *"My followers would have used you for chattel in their day."*

Jack made a mental note to look up the word *chattel* tonight.

"Look, you can't keep going out and doing this." He waved his arms around him, indicating the front yard and the flowerbeds. "I already told you that you could kill whatever comes into the backyard. The inside of the fence can be your realm of terror. I don't care. But you have to leave the front yard alone. That sounds like a fair compromise, doesn't it?"

"Zu'ar does not compromise with mortals, Weakling. Mortals beg him for mercy."

Jack turned. Zu'ar stood before him defiantly, with his muscular legs spread apart. He glared at Jack with bone-yellow eyes. His beard was the color of blood. He was wide, powerfully built, and just a few inches taller than a Barbie doll.

Zu'ar was wearing one of Jack's old sweat socks as a shoulder bag. The bag-sock was filled with tiny spears. He had apparently carved their shafts out of the missing table leg, and used the broken lamp to make the tips.

The smell of fire and decay intensified. The little guy was obviously due for a bath.

"You really need to stop destroying my stuff. That lamp was an irreplaceable antique."

"I laugh at your sentimentality, Weakling. I was old before the mountains were young. My followers were among the first men to climb out of the Living Mud that spawned your kind.

"Your 'antique' bauble was less than one hundred years old. That time is not even the blink of an eye in the span of my existence."

Jack studied Zu'ar. He stared straight at him, meeting his tiny gaze head on. One second ticked by. Then two. Then three. On the count of fifteen, the god blinked.

Jack laughed to himself. "The 'blink of an eye,' huh?"

"I was attempting to put it in terms your feeble mind would understand, Weakling. Perhaps I failed."

Jack sighed. "Right. I don't suppose you'll help me clean this up, huh? I've had a long day at work. I'd really just like to get this over with so I can relax."

"You do the work of children and wet-nurses, Weakling. I exist for greater things."

He watched Zu'ar go to the corner of the yard to relieve himself, before proudly walking through the gate and into the backyard.

Jack woke with the sun shining through the shades. He rolled over sleepily and looked at the display of his alarm clock. It was blank.

Jack shot bolt upright. What time was it? He stumbled out of bed, dragging half of the sheets with him. He fumbled in his pant's pocket for his cell phone.

He flipped the phone open and read the time: 10:37. He was more than an hour late for work.

Jack swore. He looked back at his alarm clock. The power cord was gone. It had been ripped completely off.

"Zu'ar!" he yelled. "Zu'ar, where are you?"

"I am here, Weakling." He walked into the room, carrying the wound-up cord in one of his tiny fists. He held up the frayed end with an evil smile. *"I have created a scourge so that my enemies may know pain."*

"You destroyed my alarm clock!"

"Time is a human contrivance. I have no use for it."

"But I could lose my job!"

"Fear not. I am confident that your sniveling ways will earn you another master to grovel before."

Jack rushed to his closet. He hurriedly started laying out his work clothes. "You aren't going to think this is funny when I don't have any rent money this month."

"On the contrary, I believe it would strengthen your character to live beneath the stars and fight for your food."

But Jack was already more worried about what he would say to his boss when he got to work.

The boss had chewed Jack out when he arrived. He gave him a speech about responsibility, commitment to the company, and work ethic. Jack took the lashing like a whipped dog. He said "Yes, sir" and "No, sir" in all the right places. In the end, he'd escaped with his job. Now Jack was enjoying a very late, very short lunch break in the cafeteria.

"Have you tried obedience school?" Cory asked.

Jack popped a potato puffer into his mouth. Cory was the company's IT wizard. He'd been solving Jack's tech problems for years. He'd also been listening to Jack's personal problems for a large chunk of that time.

"I was going to," he said. "I signed up for the class and everything. But Zu'ar ended up fighting with one of the other gods. It got so bad that the trainer asked me to leave."

"That bad?" Cory asked.

"You have no idea." Jack remembered the woman's shriek of horror as Zu'ar strangled her precious little love goddess with a leash. He remembered the awful looks he got as he carried Zu'ar out of the store.

"I don't know," he said finally. "Maybe I'm just not cut out to be a god owner."

"Well, what about in-home training?"

Jack gave him a quizzical look. "I don't know. Isn't that expensive?"

Cory shrugged. "No more expensive than replacing all that stuff the little guy destroys on you."

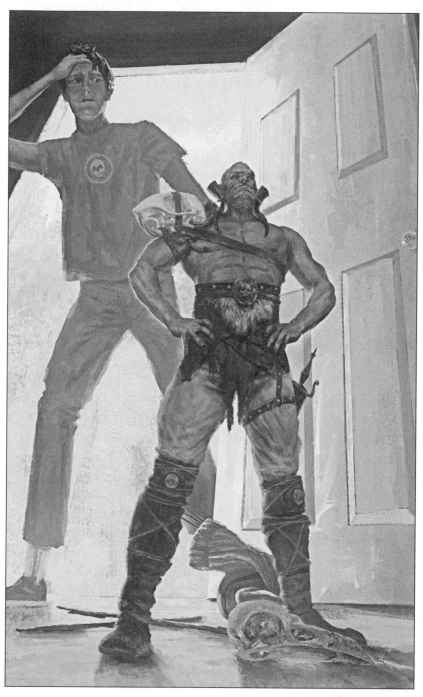

ALEX BROCK

Jack thought about it. Maybe Cory was right. He popped another potato puffer into his mouth, and chased it with a sip of Diet Pepsi.

That night, he did an online search for in-home god training. There were several trainers in the area. He wrote down the number of the one that seemed the most promising, a woman calling herself "The God Whisperer." He'd call from work tomorrow.

And how long have you had this god in your home?"

Doris the god trainer sat on Jack's couch. She was a friendly, big boned woman, with dark hair that she wore teased up into a beehive. She had both the breath and the voice of a lifelong smoker.

She'd need to interview Jack first, she'd said. Get a feel for Zu'ar's living situation. Once she identified the problem areas with the god's behavior, she'd be able to figure out what training steps were needed.

"Um, I adopted him about six months ago."

She scribbled on her notepad. "Did his aggressive behavior start right away? Or did it develop over time?"

"No. He was always pretty aggressive."

"Mmm-hmm. And I'm sorry, but I don't have my notes from the phone call in front of me. Did you say he was a rescue?"

"That's right. I got him at the humane society."

She was in the middle of asking how much exercise Zu'ar normally got, when the tiny god stalked into the room.

"Who is this woman, Weakling? Why is she in my house?"

Doris wrinkled her nose. "Does he always bring that burning and decay scent with him?"

"Yes."

"Answer me, Weakling. What does this woman want? Why does she ignore me when I speak into her mind?"

"That's actually a very common sign of dominance with war gods," Doris said. "They use it as a way to mark their territory. The scent is supposed to terrify more passive gods and mortals into submission. Have you ever tried to get him to stop?"

"No, I mostly just ignore it."

Doris nodded. She scribbled a few more notes into her pad.

"I will see this woman's bones bleach beneath the sun, Weakling. Tell her I will not be ignored. Tell her she will hear me, or she will suffer the consequences.

Jack swallowed. "Um, he says..."

The trainer held up her hand. "No. Don't pay any attention to him when he's sending prophesies of doom into your mind. When you acknowledge that kind of behavior, it just encourages him to keep it up. You should only give him attention when he communicates in benevolent prophecies."

"Okay."

Doris closed her notepad. "Look, I'm going to be honest with you, Mr. Foster. War gods are some of the most difficult deities to care for. Their owners have to be assertive and in control at all times. They aren't inherently 'bad,' but they only respect strength and ruthlessness. Their behavior can get out of control if you don't prove to them that you're the strongest member of the household. Do you think you're ready to do that?"

Jack looked at Zu'ar. He remembered how small and defenseless he'd looked in the cage all those months ago. Zu'ar had been sitting by himself in his little corner, while all of the other gods played and performed miracles together.

He was alone. He had nobody. That was why Jack had taken him home. And now Jack couldn't imagine putting him back in that situation. He loved the little guy.

"Yes," he said. "I'm ready."

"Do not make me laugh, Cowardly Weakling. You will never be stronger than me. My followers were feared all across the ancient world."

Jack turned to say something. But he caught the trainer's look out the corner of his eye.

"Do not ignore me, Weakling. You will come to regret it."

Jack didn't answer him. In a rage, Zu'ar kicked the wall. Then he stormed up the steps. A few seconds later, Jack heard him slam the bedroom door.

"Good," Doris said. "Now I'd like to ask you about his eating habits."

Jack came home from work to a pile of bloody pigeon feathers on the front walk.

"Oh, no."

The training sessions had been going well. Zu'ar hadn't slaughtered anything in weeks. He was even beginning to listen when Jack told him to do something. Things were actually getting peaceful around the house for a change.

Now this.

"Zu'ar? Zu'ar where are you?"

"I am here, Weakling."

"I told you not to call me that," Jack said.

Zu'ar looked at the ground and slumped his shoulders, adopting a submissive posture. *"I am sorry. I meant no offense. That is how I have named you for so long, I merely forgot. Please, forgive me."*

Jack pointed at the pile of feathers. "What is this? I thought I told you, no more killing things in the front yard."

"I know. I am sorry I broke your edict."

"What are you holding behind your back? Give it. Give it here."

Zu'ar held up a small necklace made of twine. Two fresh birds' feet hung from the loop.

"The eagle's claw was a status symbol among my people, Mortal. I wanted to make you a similar gift."

"That's touching. Thank you." It was also a little gross. Jack was very careful to hold the necklace by the loop.

Zu'ar peered up hopefully. *"Is the Wise Woman coming to the house today, Mortal?"*

That was his name for the god trainer. "She is," Jack said. "She'll be here in a few minutes, in fact. We should go inside."

"The Wise Woman has much strength and authority. You should ask her to bear you some children. She would raise them into fine warriors."

Jack shook his head. Gods. What could you do with them?

"I think she'd prefer a check," he said.

Stars That Make Dark Heaven Light

written by

Sharon Joss

illustrated by

CHOONG YOON

ABOUT THE AUTHOR

The daughter of a college biology professor, Sharon Joss was born in Oregon and raised in central California, where she learned at an early age to identify many different species of birds and desiccated road kill. She has worked as a waitress, bartender, and operating system software programmer for the space shuttle Columbia before earning a master's degree in Management of Technology.

At an early age, the novels of Rudyard Kipling, Andre Norton, and Ray Bradbury inspired her lifelong love of speculative fiction. As a child, she dreamed of speaking to animals and the magic of flight. Although she wrote (and illustrated) her first book at the age of nine, she did not begin to write seriously until 2009. Since then, she has written five novels and more than a dozen short stories.

After living in upstate New York and Idaho, in 2012 she decided to return to Oregon, where she now lives amid a thicket of blackberry vines and writes full-time. Although she made her first professional short story sale in 2013; Writers of the Future marks her second professional publication.

ABOUT THE ILLUSTRATOR

Choong Yoon was born in Anyang, South Korea and moved to Seoul at the age of ten. He loved drawing animated characters and copying comic book panels, which helped him make friends in the new city.

But drawing became more than just a tool to make friends. His interest and passion for it grew until eventually his parents had to take him to a private atelier near his home so he could learn academic art at a young age.

Academic art lessons naturally led him to apply to an art high school. Studying art in high school naturally led him to pursue art in college. He studied fine arts in Seoul National University. In the art school, he was able to meet many people from different departments who were just as passionate about the craft.

His love of comics and animation never faded even though most students in the fine arts department were into gallery work. He was fascinated with the arts that involve narrative storytelling, scenes with characters and drama, so he transferred to the School of Visual Arts in New York to study illustration and learn how to tell stories with images.

After graduating SVA in May 2014, Yoon began working as a freelance illustrator in New York and he is developing a short animated film with his friends.

Stars That Make Dark Heaven Light

1

"Multiply, vary, let the strongest live and the weakest die."
—Charles Darwin, *The Origin of Species,*
Posted in the communal dining hall
of the grounded SS *Dominion*

A dull pounding at my temples told me to take a break. The rich oxygen mixture inside the colony's greenhouses usually gave me a headache after a couple hours, but I was reluctant to quit just yet.

I liked being here. Diffused sunlight filtered through the translucent ceiling, and regular misting kept the air moist; a blessed relief from the arid climate. I stroked the pollen-laden hairs of my brush against a spray of brackenberry flowers. Unlike the younger kids, I enjoyed the quiet solitude of my daily hand-pollination chores; it was the only time of day I was free from looking after the children.

The rich scent of loam at my feet mixed with the sweet essence of the berry blossoms in my hand, a heady blend made richer in the still air. I stretched my neck, wiped the sweat from my forehead with the back of my hand, and resettled myself on the low stool among the vines.

From outside, I heard the pounding of running feet and clatter of excited voices coming closer, and knew immediately that I was back on duty again. I stood and slipped the pollen brush into the pocket of my apron.

Layfe came tearing into the greenhouse, shouting at the top of his eight-year-old lungs, a baby lapid clutched in each grubby hand. "They've hatched, Auntie Ettie! Look, they've hatched!"

Behind him, Gehnny, the youngest at five, shrieked with excitement. "Hurry up, Ettie! Or they'll be gone!"

I grinned and grabbed a handful of coarsely woven sacks from the drying shed. We never knew exactly when to expect the baby lapids to emerge from their unmarked nests beneath Hesperidee's surface, but when they did, every kid in the colony joined in the hunt.

No one ever tried to locate the nests ahead of time, as a midnight encounter with a broody female stone scorpion was almost always fatal. Lapids could inflict venom with both pinchers and two massive stingers carried scorpion-like above their armored backs.

But the big-eyed babies were adorable, and until their armor hardened, harmless. The other kids were waiting for us in the paved area between the children's dormitory and the ship. I handed everyone a sack; then Layfe, eager to show us the way, led us screaming outside the Dominion's barricades. The first day was always the best collecting day; by the third or fourth, the babies had either managed to scuttle off and hide amid the larger boulders out on the range, or had died of extended exposure to sunlight.

He led us to The Cliffs, an area about a mile from the colony, where an outcrop of crumbling boulders as big as a mountain jutted up through the planet's crust. The rough surface of Hesperidee stretched around us in a stony plain, broken only by grey-green clumps of woody firebite bushes, so named for the blistering effect their oily leaves had on bare skin. Overhead, yellow clouds scudded across skies of palest lavender. In the middle distance, a series of gradually ascending plateaus marked the rims of distant craters.

The cartilage instead of bones in our skeletons necessitated that us kids spend at least six hours each day exposed to the light of the twin suns, Tesla and Newton. After the dry tutelage of the instructional archives and our shifts in the greenhouses each day, we were always eager to be freed from the confines of the colony.

"Got one!" Mia held up her prize.

Nearly all the dangerous predators on Hesperidee were nocturnal, so as long as I was there to supervise, we were allowed to roam anywhere within sight of the ship and barricades.

I clutched my sack to my chest as I scanned the broken surface beneath my feet, searching for the slightest movement. Mottled yellow and grey, the leathery shellbacks of newly hatched lapids exactly mimicked the stony surface that covered so much of the land close to the colony. The hatchlings' instinct to get out of the sun kept them moving. Sometimes the very shapes of their bodies betrayed them. Their still-soft shells weren't quite as sharp as the surrounding rocky soil. But usually, it was a plump segmented leg, waving as it searched for a foothold among the scree that caught my attention. *There.*

"I got one, too!" I called.

I picked up the lapid and grinned. About half the size of a ping-pong ball, eight maroon little legs waved at me in helpless lapid fright. A lovely yellow stripe ran around the outer edge of this one's shell. I'd never seen a striped one before. I shoved it into my sack and kept hunting.

After the initial excitement of collecting, we headed back to Dominion and settled all three hundred and twelve of the babies into shallow bins meant to simulate their rocky habitat in the raising room of the children's dormitory.

For the next few weeks, they'd be fed a crumbled mixture of soybeans, clippings from the gardens, and local lichens; which would accelerate their growth. After they entered their second pupal stage, we'd move them into the freezers aboard the SS *Dominion,* as the eight-pound pupae provided the colony's only source of animal protein for the entire year. The sweet meat had a light flavor and texture.

But before we placed the babies into their bins, Gehnny and I, like every other kid in Dominion, each got to pick out one baby lapid as our very own pet for the season. Sometimes we traded amongst the other kids, but not this year.

This year, I chose the one with the lovely yellow stripe. I had no idea how much that one decision would change my life.

2

"All children are a gift of great value.
No child shall be favored over another."
Posted in the communal dining hall
of the grounded SS *Dominion*

The excitement of the lapid hatchlings paled against the announcement made by Mother Jean at dinner that night in the colony's communal dining hall. She stood, tall and sere, her hand resting lightly on her twelve-year-old birth-daughter's shoulder, until everyone stopped talking.

"I am proud to announce that Daughter Rae has begun her first cycle. She has become a woman. The *first* of her generation to do so."

She stared right at me when she said that last part.

The announcement hit me like a physical blow. I blushed furiously. At seventeen, I should've been a woman, and a mother, twice over already, but my body hadn't shown the slightest signs of puberty. My chest was as flat as a boy's, and I stood no taller than kids half my age.

The whole room applauded, and I joined in, but my heart wasn't in it. Rae basked in the attention, as each adult in the room spontaneously came forward to kiss her cheek and offer congratulations. Our leader, Father Isaac, announced that Father Lyle would begin immediately to build a new dormitory to house the adults of the next generation.

Resentment flooded through me. In a few months, Rae would be artificially inseminated and move into her new quarters. She'd have her choice of work assignments. As a birthmother, she would have more prestige and a voice in colony decisions. It wasn't fair.

It should have been me.

Gradually, the hubbub died down and the usual hum of dinner conversation took over.

Mother Bekke, the silver-haired woman seated across from me, leaned over the expanse of the long steel table between us and grasped my hand.

CHOONG YOON

"Don't look so sad, Henrietta." Her five pale fingers curled lovingly around my brown, syndactyly-melded three. Among the adults of Dominion, Bekke was well-regarded as a pattern-maker and seamstress. To the children, she was our former full-time nanny and caregiver until five years ago, when the responsibility passed to me. "We have decided to celebrate your womanhood at the coming equinox as well."

I sat back in my seat, relinquishing her tender touch for the rough pockets of my linen jumper. As the eldest of the first generation of children conceived and raised on Hesperidee, I knew my responsibilities.

"B-but I'm not a woman, yet."

The excitement on Bekke's face faded somewhat. "Father Isaac has recently discovered that everyone's hormone levels seem to be dropping, possibly due to the environmental conditions here. He thinks that's what may have happened to you."

I glanced at the head table, where Father Isaac sat. He was the oldest man in Dominion and the colony's geneticist. He'd been born on Earth, and was the last survivor of the original colonists.

"Why didn't anyone tell me?"

"When we lost power to the cryo unit last summer, no one fully appreciated what the loss of the sperm and egg bank would mean to the colony. But he thinks once you are bonded with a partner, your hormones will wake up. We simply cannot wait any longer."

I clutched the wadded cloth napkin in my lap for dear life, unable to believe she was serious. All my life I'd looked forward to the day when I'd be declared a woman, with the right to choose artificial insemination or a partner. I'd already decided to choose artificial insemination for my first child or two. In a few years, I'd marry one of the boys. Layfe or maybe Simon, as soon as they were old enough.

This wasn't how it was supposed to go. I felt the walls of the crowded dining room closing in on me.

I looked around the room, searching for the truth in everyone's face. The unnatural yellow light from the ship's power source gave everything a sickly, jaundiced cast. Every one of the colony's ninety-six adults looked old and tired; most of the men and all the women had grey or silver-shot hair. Even before the loss of the cryo unit, no children had been conceived in several orbits. Gehnny, the baby of the colony, was now five.

The SS *Dominion* and the dining room in particular were showing its age too; a fact which couldn't be blamed on the lighting. After forty years, the portraits of Charles Darwin, Thomas Jefferson, and the great space explorer, Beroe Dunmore had faded; lost their intensity. Less formal, but equally dingy and yellowed inspirational plaques admonished us to remember our priorities:

You cannot escape the responsibility
of tomorrow by evading it today!
Where there's a will, there's a way!
We're all depending on YOU!

"But none of the boys are men yet, either," I pointed out. The oldest boys, eight-year-olds Layfe and Simon and seven-year-old Kole were too young to father children.

Father Isaac approached our table.

Bekke's husband, Father Torov, took a deep breath, as if he needed to brace himself for what he had to say. He nodded to the two men sitting next to him. "After testing all the men, Father Isaac says Robert and Lyle have the most viable sperm. You may choose whomever you prefer."

Both men stood and bowed, red-faced. Stooped and sallow Father Robert, who worked in the ship's power plant, and slab-faced Father Lyle, the builder. They smiled at me uncertainly.

Father Isaac stood between them, smiling broadly; his mahogany skin crinkled in deep creases around his eyes and along well-worn smile lines in his ancient face. "The important thing is that you spend time with them. Allow them to compete for your affections."

I fought unsuccessfully to suppress a shudder. The room had gone eerily quiet.

The fourteen other children in the room stared at me in

wide-eyed silence. The whole room was watching me. The adults must've already known about this.

The sign on the wall above Bekke's head shouted at me.

BE THE EXAMPLE!

They were depending on me to accept this. I did want to be a mother; I wanted children. If dating two men old enough to be my grandfather was what it took to wake up my hormones and become a woman, I had to try, no matter how queasy I felt about it. The future of the colony depended on it.

It had to work. I *had* to go along.

It took all my effort to smile, but when I did, the tension in the room seemed to evaporate.

Mother Bekke patted my arm. "Good girl."

I had never felt so alone.

The rest of the evening passed with interminable slowness. I couldn't eat. I shoveled beets back and forth across my plate, unable to make eye contact with anyone, least of all, well, anyone. Bekke watched me like a hawk—so did all the other kids.

During dessert, Father Isaac announced that I didn't have to address Robert and Lyle as "Father" any longer, since they were now suitors for my affections. Kind and well-intentioned as Father Isaac was, he was not a child of the colony. He hadn't been raised on Hesperidee. He couldn't possibly understand what I was going through.

I'd known both Father Lyle and Father Robert all my life. The adults raised us to treat *all* the men and women of the colony as our parents, whether they'd birthed us or not. One big happy family. Considering either of them as a romantic partner was... unthinkable.

Would I be expected to kiss them? *Oh god.*

If I thought my humiliation for the evening was complete, I was wrong.

I sat, frozen to my seat as Robert bowed and presented me with an ancient book on Desalination Engineering. Not to be outdone, Lyle kissed my hand with his whiskery stubble and offered me a sun-baked bit of clay he'd modeled into the shapely figure of a woman. Not the head or legs; just the body.

I thought I would die of embarrassment.

I thanked them for their thoughtfulness, but couldn't think of anything else to say. Bekke came to my rescue, and let them know I'd be pleased to spend time with each of them on alternate evenings here in the dining room.

I was finally able to slip away by saying the oxygen saturation in the room was making me dizzy. Bekke knew I was heading outside and said she'd come with me.

After she suited up, she followed me back through the dimly lit grey corridors leading outside while the rest of the colony remained in the dining room, playing games and telling stories to the children.

"Talk to me, Ettie. I realize now that tonight's announcement must have come as a bit of a shock," she began. "But we thought it was time. You're certainly old enough."

I didn't say anything.

"Isn't this what you wanted? To join the adults?"

"Yes, but it feels wrong." *In so many ways.*

I waited for her to put on her oxygen helmet. Only four of the adults in Dominion colony had gills; Bekke and Lyle both did. But as children, they'd slept onboard the Dominion in oxygenated quarters, and their lungs never fully adapted to hydrogen, so although they could venture outside for short periods without an oxygen mask, they couldn't function well, and would die if deprived of supplemental oxygen for more than twenty minutes.

The adult's dependence on oxygen kept them separate from us most of the time. As frozen embryos intentionally infected with an aggressive transmutation gene virus, Bekke and her peers had been transported to Hesperidee from Earth to help subsequent generations adapt to alien environments at an accelerated pace. The entire mission of Dominion and other space colonies was to pioneer settlements of the human race on other planets.

In contrast, I and all the rest of the kids who'd survived infancy had been born with gills and two sets of lungs, which also enabled us to breathe the hydrogen-rich atmosphere on Hesperidee. None of the children of our generation born without gills had survived more than a few days. Dozens of Dominion's children had died in infancy before the adults learned this lesson. Father Isaac predicted that all future generations of humans born on Hesperidee would have gills, and no one would think us any different for having them.

We'd been taught to celebrate the differences between us. It was a good thing, which would ensure the survival of the human race. Father Lyle and his crew built the children's dormitory outside the ship to encourage our bodies to adapt to this planet's atmosphere, rather than Earth's.

We looked so different. Sometimes, like now, it was hard to believe we were the same species.

"I know my responsibilities to the colony. I get it. Survival of the human race and all that." I pushed the panel to release the inner door lock. "But I always thought I'd marry Layfe. Or Simon. They're more like me."

She nodded, her expression pained behind the mask.

"I thought so too." The mask muffled the tone of her voice, sapping all the emotion from her words. "But Robert and Lyle are good men."

"How can I possibly look at Father Robert or Father Lyle *in that way*? It can't work." I shook my head. "It's sick. *They're my parents!*"

"Technically, Robert and Lyle are not your parents. Yes, we're to blame for encouraging all of you to think of us that way. Given our current situation, that was a mistake. And I'm sorry for that. But I'm afraid you'll just have to get over it. You kids are our future, the future of the human race. We're teetering on the edge of extinction here, Henrietta. There's no guarantee the boys will mature in the timeline all of us expected. I mean, look at you—"

"Why can't I just go with artificial insemination?" The thought of one of them touching me, or seeing me naked, nauseated me.

"Honey, don't you think we've already considered that? Your body needs to mature first. Father Isaac thinks you've spent too much time around the kids. He thinks the courtship rituals will expose you to male testosterone and put you back on track. Get to know them as real people. This is hard for them, too. You don't want to disappoint them, do you? The whole colony is depending on you."

I swallowed my revulsion and nodded. Bekke knew how to get me to agree to almost anything.

"And you need to eat more soy and animal protein. Are you getting enough sunlight?"

3

"It is not the strongest or the most intelligent who will survive but those who can best manage change." —Charles Darwin
Posted in the communal dining hall
of the grounded SS *Dominion*

This is Dawah," Gehnny announced the next morning. Like me, she had chosen a lapid with a yellow stripe. She didn't want to let poor Dawah out of her hands for even a moment, so already the creature only had five legs remaining. Based on Gehnny's sole previous attempt at animal husbandry, Dawah would likely not survive his first molt.

We were seated in the girls bunk room in the children's dormitory; a squat, one-story structure made of local stone, cement, and salvage from the Dominion. The building housed separate boys' and girls' sleeping and bathing quarters, a communal living room set up with video ports connected to the SS *Dominion*'s instructional archives, and a number of spare storage rooms, one of which had been converted into the raising room for the baby lapids.

From her perch on the top bunk, Rae eyed my baby lapid with barely concealed contempt. "I can't believe you're keeping another one of those blasted things this year."

Blasted was not an adult-approved word, but I didn't say anything. Now that she was officially a woman, Rae seemed determined to rub my nose in it. I cuddled the creature protectively against my chest. "What's wrong with them?"

She whiffled her throat gills with no little scorn. "When are you going to grow up, Ettie? You are so immature. The only reason they're letting you participate in a womanhood ceremony is because you're so *old,* they don't know what to do with you."

The truth in her words echoed the sting I'd felt the previous night; I could only hope the rest of the colony didn't think the same.

"You're not a real woman, and you never will be. They feel sorry for you, but I don't. I can barely stand to be around you anymore." She heaved herself off her top bunk and stomped out.

I stared after her, shaking my head. If anyone was immature, it was Rae. She'd always been snippy. I'd often had to bite back a retort of my own, knowing that if I said a cross word to her, she'd run off in tears and grab the nearest adult, usually Bekke or her birther, Mother Jean, and claim I'd been cruel to her.

Bekke would frown and tell me how *disappointed* she was in me. Disappointing Bekke, or any of the adults was something I never wanted to do. I cherished my role as the responsible one. Bekke trusted me with the children; the whole colony did.

But sometimes, being the example wasn't easy.

"What is his name?" Gehnny asked.

After Rae's comment, I briefly considered putting him back into the group bins, but decided against it. I wouldn't give her the satisfaction.

"I'm still thinking."

The lapid's stubby digits tickled across the palm of my hand. At this stage, the body was rubbery soft; not much more than a carapace, liquid brown eyes, and sticky feet.

"Ask him." Gehnny cradled Dawah between her cupped hands and danced across the bunk room to me. "He'll tell you, if you ask."

"No, that's just your imagination."

"It's true! Dawah talks to me!"

Gehnny often blurted out such fantasies. No one believed her, of course. Until she reached her name-day, nothing she said carried any weight. But I'd been taking care of her since infancy, and she sounded so certain. I could usually tell when she was making up a story.

"He barely has a mouth. How can he talk?"

She squeezed herself into my lap, her soft brown curls nestled against my neck.

I cuddled her closer.

"Like this."

She closed her eyes, held the tender creature to her lips, and kissed it. "I love you, baby lapid. Tell me your name. *Mmmmm.*" As she hummed, the lapid seemed to clutch at her chubby chin with its remaining limbs, as if to return the embrace.

So cute.

She held him close to my cheek, so I could feel a gentle vibration emanating from the creature's carapace.

She opened her eyes, a smile spreading ear to ear. "See? I told you, his name is Dawah!"

Nona, an impressionable seven-year-old who'd just witnessed Rae's rude behavior, snorted loudly. "He didn't say anything, you ninny!" She tossed her head and stormed out of the bunk room in a perfect imitation of Rae. "And Dawah is a stupid name!"

Gehnny's mouth pursed into a frowning pout.

I kissed and rocked her, soothing her wounded pride. "It's okay, Gehnny. I believe you. And I think Dawah is a fine name."

She cradled the vibrating lapid against her neck. "You can do it too, Ettie. Try it."

I wanted to give my lapid a nice name. Names were important. Last year, it had been Mercutio. The year before, Juliet. Not Romeo; Rae would never have let me hear the end of it. Something more grown-up. Like Shakespeare, maybe. Or Navarre.

Gehnny stared at me with such an expression of yearning, I just couldn't disappoint her.

"Oh all right. Do I *have* to kiss him?"

Her whole face lit up. "No. You just have to hum your question at him through your lips. At least for the first few times. Until they learn to speak our language."

I held my palm up to my chin. The yellow-striped lapid stared at me with what could only be a terrified expression. "Like this?"

Gehnny curled my fingers forward, forcing him closer to my mouth.

"Breathe out softly," she said. "And close your eyes."

I obeyed.

The creature seemed to relax. It settled into the palm of my hand.

"Now, say something nice to him."

I cracked an eye open to see if she was teasing, but she looked as serious as I'd ever seen her.

The lapid tensed.

I closed my eyes again. "It's okay, little lapid. I won't hurt you. I love your yellow stripe."

Velvety toes inched across my palm. So close, I could feel his warmth not-quite touching my lips.

"Now ask him his name in your mind while you hum."

Mmm. What should I call you, little lapid. Who are you?

The answer came almost immediately, ringing in my brain as clear as if Gehnny herself had spoken.

Vox! Vox. Vox, Vox. Who?

My jaw dropped in amazement. His eyes met mine, and I recognized the intelligence behind his sweet expression.

Gehnny bounced excitedly. "What did he say?"

I stared at him. "He said Vox. I think he wants to know my name, too."

I pulled him close and hummed against his rubbery skin. *Mmm, I am Henrietta.*

Etta?

Mmm. Yes.

Like the kiss of a firebite, I felt an immediate bond with Vox. His questions were simple—not words so much, but I could understand his intention. And like a child, persistent.

What place this?

Is safe?

Is food?

He was so curious and had such a quick mind. The more we "spoke," the faster he learned English. His questions quickly grew more sophisticated, and within a few hours, his vocabulary improved enough so we could mind-speak in conversational English, as long as we stayed in contact with each other.

He liked being held. The humming vibration he emitted represented a contented and receptive state of mind for him.

The other children insisted that they could mind-speak to their lapids too, but Vox was adamant that he was not lapid. He was Tok. And Gehnny's Dawah was Tok. And Layfe's Botto was Tok. But lapid was not Tok.

Only the three yellow-striped Tok seemed able to communicate, and even then, only with the child they'd bonded to. We checked the raising bins for more of the yellow-striped Toks, but found no others.

Vox mind-speak to Etta. Botto mind-speak to Layfe. Dawah mind-speak to Gehnny. All Tok mind-speak to each other. 'Umans no mind-speak except to mind-bond Tok.

This was huge. I couldn't wait to tell Father Isaac and the rest that we'd found intelligent life on Hesperidee after all this time. It was fantastic! I could imagine standing next to Father Isaac as he made the announcement at dinner. He'd have his arm around me. This would be bigger even than Rae's womanhood announcement.

Rae would go nuts with jealousy.

4

"We hold these truths to be self-evident: that all men are created equal; that they are endowed by their Creator with certain unalienable rights; that among these are life, liberty, and the pursuit of happiness" —Thomas Jefferson
Posted in the communal dining hall
of the grounded SS *Dominion*

In all the excitement of communicating with Vox, I completely forgot about my new standing in the colony until dinnertime.

Most evenings, us kids walked over from the nursery block as a group and were given our table assignments after we cleared the air locks. This ensured that all of us kids got equal time and attention from the adults, and vice versa. After being served at the buffet, we would take our assigned seat at one of ten tables for dinner.

But when we arrived for dinner that night, a new table had

been added to the room. A small one, covered with a white tablecloth and just two chairs, one of which was empty.

As soon as he spotted me, Father Lyle rose from the other chair and hurried over to offer me his arm.

"Good evening, Henrietta. You look, um, quite vigorous tonight."

My eyes searched the room, frantic for escape, but there was none. Behind me, I could hear the giggles of Gehnny and Layfe and the others, while the adults all smiled and nodded encouragingly. White-haired Father Isaac even gave me a thumbs-up.

"I will be your dining companion this evening. Allow me to escort you to the buffet."

Ohgodohgodohgod.

Dazedly, I took his proffered elbow, which brought squeals from the kids behind me.

Father Lyle led me to the buffet table. He must've been worried about my stunned silence, because he leaned close and whispered into my ear.

"Actually, Robert and I drew straws on who would get the first date with you, and I won. Tomorrow is his turn. Hope that's okay. We can switch, if you want."

He smelled strongly of the herbal soap Mother Anne made of yucca, sage and rosemary. Everyone was watching us. I didn't want to hurt his feelings. "No. It's fine. I guess I'm going to have to get used to it."

The meal passed at a glacial pace. I kept my eyes on my plate, as every time my eyes met the gaze of my dinner companion—or worse, glanced around the dining room—I was met with broad smiles.

Just as I thought dinner had finally come to an end, Gehnny announced that we'd found something new among the latest crop of lapid hatchlings. Talky-Toks, she called them.

"Is this true, Henrietta?" Father Isaac, had instructed us kids to bring any new plant or animal discovery to him immediately. I should have told him before dinner.

I stood. "Y-yes, Father Isaac. I meant to tell you." Again, I felt the weight of everyone's stare. "I'm sorry. I forgot." I explained how Gehnny discovered their ability to communicate telepathically.

"They call themselves Tok. They were left behind as dormant eggs long ago, timed to hatch when planetary conditions improved."

Rae tossed her hair over her shoulder and rolled her eyes.

"That's ridiculous," Mother Jean said.

"No, it's true!" Layfe shouted. "We can prove it!"

The last pink fingers of sunset were fading from the evening sky by the time the adults finished donning their environmental gear and assembled in the main courtyard outside the kid's dormitory. Not everyone came, but more than half the colony showed up.

Layfe, Gehnny, and I were excited to show off our new pets. I showed Dawah a pebble I had hidden in my hand and Gehnny correctly guessed the color. Then Father Isaac tried it with other hidden objects between Layfe and Botto, and Vox and me.

When we explained how each Tok mind-spoke to only one of us, nobody spoke. I don't think they believed us.

Father Isaac didn't seem convinced, either, although he probed and petted the creatures for quite some time.

"Hesperidee's stone scorpions have been studied for decades. They've never demonstrated any signs of telepathic ability. Most likely, those abilities are coming from you kids. I'm not convinced there's anything special about these lapids." He took a few scraping samples of their skin and handed them back to us. "I'll check the DNA, just to be sure."

"I knew it had to be a trick," Rae said.

"No, it's true," I protested. "They do speak to us. They're from an advanced culture. They're more intelligent than we are, even."

"It's getting late." Father Isaac said.

Gehnny grabbed at his suit. "Ask us to ask them something else. We'll show you."

Mother Jean and most of the others began to drift back to the ship, shaking their heads.

"Please, at least let us prove their intelligence," I begged. "Ask them something you know we don't know."

He sighed. "Very well. What is the specific gravity of water on Hesperidee?"

Vox had no answer to that, and Layfe and Gehnny both shook their heads. My heart sank.

"I see." Father Isaac rubbed the top of Gehnny's head. "Perhaps we're asking the wrong questions. Let me think on it a bit. In the meantime, I'll analyze these samples to see if I can find anything new."

The rest of the kids followed the quiet adults back to the ship for the usual after-dinner stories, but Layfe, Gehnny and I headed back to the dormitory.

Layfe cupped his hands protectively around Botto. "Why don't they believe us, Ettie?"

The idea gnawed at me. Admittedly, we'd brought them a pretty fantastic story, and maybe hadn't thought out the best way to demonstrate the Tok's abilities. But I hadn't expected the hostile reaction in the dining hall or the tension among the adults in the courtyard when we gave our demonstration.

And what if they *had* believed us? What would they have done?

They'd have taken them away from us.

Vox trembled in my hand. All three Tok seemed agitated by their encounter with the adults. They already thought we were huge. I could only imagine what they thought of the giants in their bulky environmental suits and helmets; or Father Isaac as he poked and scraped at them.

"They do. Sort of. Or, at least, Father Isaac does. They just don't understand what it's like."

Having only known Vox for a few hours, I'd already accepted his mind-speak as the most natural thing in the world. Maybe not believing wasn't such a bad thing, after all. We settled into the common room. Me, on one end of the sofalounge, with Layfe on the other end, and Gehnny on the floor between us.

Vox, are you real? Are the Tok real? Or am I imagining you?

What is imagine? Vox was so curious about everything.

Imagine is wanting the stones beneath my feet to be soft, and thinking it is so.

Stones are 'ard.

Yes. Real stones are hard. Are you real, Vox. Or am I wanting you?

Vox is real. Tok are real. Etta is real.

That night, we spoke, mind-to-mind until dawn. I asked him about the Tok, and he explained that 'Esperidee, which in his language was referred to as a word I couldn't pronounce, had been just one of many planets settled long ago by his people, who then evacuated after a meteor shower devastated the planet. They left behind several clutches of eggs timed to hatch at intervals after climate conditions improved.

He asked me about the adults, and especially, Father Isaac. I explained that, no, he wasn't my father. My father had died on Earth, long before I was conceived. I then had to explain the whole human reproductive cycle, including artificial insemination and in vitro fertilization, which, to my own embarrassment, seemed to fascinate him.

When will you molt?

Humans do not molt.

You do not look like adults. When will you molt?

I blushed. *No. They birthed us, but our bodies are different. We are born helpless, but as we grow, we change and evolve by growing, not molting. We have two pairs of lungs for respiration. We have gills to breathe the atmosphere on Hesperidee and a nose to breathe oxygen of our home planet, Earth. The adults have smooth, thin skin of many colors, while our skin is thick and brown, which protects us from the suns. The hands of the adults have a thumb and four fingers, while our hands consist of only a thumb and two fused fingers. We are small and fast; and in this gravity, our bones have remained soft. The adults have birthed many other children, but only those like us survived. We are human, but we are new humans. We have evolved beyond our birthers.*

Tok also evolve, Vox told me. *The first molt is the first evolution. After first molt, you will see Tok are not lapid. In the nymph stage, I will gain much in stature and be able to access more of the ancestral memories of my people. After the second molt, I will become my final form. I will be adult. I will communicate with Tok people and they will come for me.*

I fell asleep with Vox cuddled up beneath my neck and dreamed of golden palaces with spiraling towers and handsome sun-browned, men and women.

5

"Man selects only for his own good:
Nature only for that of the being which she tends."
—Charles Darwin, *The Origin of the Species*
Posted in the communal dining hall
of the grounded SS *Dominion*

The next morning, I slipped Vox into the pocket of my jumper. Like Gehnny, I could not bear to let go of him. With baby lapids and Tok to care for, we needed to obtain fresh food every day. At this stage in their development, the baby lapids preferred the grey lichens which grew in good quantity near The Cliffs.

Dawah, Vox, and Layfe's Tok, Botto, couldn't chew the tough dry lichens as well as the lapids. We had to pre-chew the leaves for them, instead of chopping them. The dry grey, leathery leaf fronds tasted a bit odd at first, but it was a flavor that all three of us quickly became accustomed to. A bit peppery, but not at all unpleasant. Once chewed, we'd spit the leaf/saliva mixture into a small bowl and our new charges gobbled it up.

Rae had already moved out of the girl's dormitory and into one of the storage rooms, which Lyle had converted into private sleeping quarters, just for her, until the new adult residential annex was built. Since neither Rae nor any of us kids could tolerate an oxygen-rich environment for more than a couple of hours, the new adult residence would have dual environmental controls.

At dinner that night, Rae was allowed the same free seating privileges as the adults, while I was again seated at my "private" table in the middle of the dining hall, this time with Robert.

After dinner, Father Isaac announced that he'd completed his preliminary analysis of the yellow-striped hatchlings.

"Based on both the physical and genetic comparisons done between the normal grey *Lapidis Laruae* hatchlings and the yellow-banded variety, I have determined their DNA to be a 95% match. Physically, at least from the outside, they appear identical except for a minor color variation.

"And while there may have been some minor psychic capability demonstrated, I'm not certain as to the practical value of this ability to us. However, in all fairness, I will continue to give this matter further consideration."

Layfe looked as embarrassed as I felt, but I don't think Gehnny understood. Robert chided me for my childish fantasies about talking animals. Bekke caught my glance, and I wondered if the others all thought the same thing.

Fine. I decided to keep all my conversations with Vox to myself.

Over the next few days, the excitement around Dominion Colony gradually settled into a new normal. By day, I tended to the children and our studies, worked in the greenhouses, and in the afternoons, set out with the other kids to gather fresh lichens for the baby lapids.

In spite of what Father Isaac had told us, Gehnny, Layfe, and I refused to believe that the Tok weren't anything other than what they said they were: descendants of a great civilization whose people would return for them once they were old enough to make the journey back to their homeland. And like all babies, they needed our help to survive.

Father Isaac retested the Tok and the lapids several times. He even had us run them through a series of mazes. The Tok performed so much better than the lapids, even Father Isaac conceded that their problem-solving capabilities far exceeded that of the lapids, but still didn't fully accept what we told him about their ability to mind-speak.

Once we began adding greens from the garden to the lichens, the lapids and Tok grew quickly. Twelve turns after we found them, the lapids stopped eating and went dormant. We couldn't help but notice how much larger and plumper our Tok had become compared to the lapids. Four days after the lapids pupated, Vox, Dawah, and Botto each curled into a tight little ball and went dormant as well. We couldn't even reach them through mind-speak.

6

After sleeping with Vox curled into my neck every turn for the last two weeks, I detested the sudden isolation, but I had little time to think of him. Robert and Lyle had taken the whole courting thing to heart, and seemed intent on claiming my every spare moment.

With our afternoons now freed up from lichen gathering, I'd expected to spend them supervising the kids by hiking and playing games. But now I also had Robert or Lyle as my constant escort, a daily reminder of my responsibility to procreate for the sake of the colony, and to set a good example for the other children. Rae had taken to her new status with a confidence and sense of purpose I secretly admired. She seemed to be looking forward to her coming pregnancy and new living quarters. Why couldn't I?

I quickly grew to dread the time I spent in Robert's solemn company, even though our time together was limited, due to the long hours he put in at the power plant. Dinner conversation topics were technical in nature, generally focused on the latest problems in the plant. After dinner, he preferred to sit next to me and hold my hand throughout story hour, when a rotating group of adults read stories to the children.

Lyle, on the other hand, took an entirely different approach. Unlike Robert, Lyle had flexible work hours. Every afternoon, as we emerged from our lessons, I'd find him waiting for me.

"Come with me. I want to show you something." He tucked my hand into his arm.

Minutes later, I'd be strapped into the passenger seat of one of the colony's two solar-powered Personal Local Transport Vehicles, and Lyle would take me wherever I wanted to go. I don't know how he got permission to take the restricted-use hovercraft out on joyrides with me, but he did.

Every day we went someplace different.

I loved it.

We visited the impact crater fields, some twenty kilometers from Dominion Colony. I'd seen pictures of them in the instructional archives, but never by hovercraft. Lyle took me up, up, over the lip and we hovered above the massive impact site for as long as I wanted. He flew the ship parallel to the steep-sided walls, and when I asked, he brought the little craft to rest on the crater floor so we could get out and explore.

That first time, I collected bits of melted glass and broken chunks of meteor created by the impact. Other days, we'd go fossil hunting, or discover the desiccated remains of some predator's previous meal. Every trip was a new adventure; we never knew what we'd find in the next crater, or over the next ridgeline.

Lyle even taught me how to pilot the hovercraft, which was without a doubt the most fun I'd ever had. It was complicated, but once I got the hang of it, not at all difficult. Sometimes, he'd let me pilot it the whole afternoon.

For an hour or two, I was excused from tending to the children.

It felt strange, at first. Almost as if I'd forgotten something. But as our trips took us farther and farther afield, I began to view these escapes as brief glimpses of freedom. I wanted to know more. To see more.

I searched the instructional archives, looking for the topological surveys for Hesperidee done by the original settlers. I wanted to find evidence of the lost Tok civilization Vox had described. I pushed Lyle to take us beyond even where he had ever ventured before. There was so much I wanted to see.

Even hampered by his oxygen suit, Lyle seemed to enjoy these excursions as much as I did. It became a regular thing for us. And on the nights we dined together, we talked about what we'd seen and found and where we'd go next.

Sometimes, I'd catch the other adults nod knowingly as they watched us make out plans over dinner. I wanted to say, *no, it's not like that—we're just friends,* but I just couldn't.

Nothing was ever going to happen between me and Lyle.

Even without saying it, I think we both understood that. But even I had to admit, we'd become friends. Good friends.

7

"A scientific man ought to have no wishes,
no affections—a mere heart of stone." —Charles Darwin
From the instructional archives
of the grounded SS *Dominion*

Gehnny was the first to get sick. Within hours, her entire body puffed up like an overstuffed sausage. Tiny blood vessels in her eyes burst; her bloody tears stopped only when she slipped into a coma.

Mother Flor, the physician, could do nothing for her.

Within days, we were all sick to varying degrees. The symptoms started with a fever accompanied by severe body aches and nausea, followed by vomiting and diarrhea, ending in coma and death.

Jonahs, who at six, dreamed of piloting a spaceship like the SS *Dominion;* and Mia, a sweet darling of a girl who ran faster and could jump farther than anyone, died within a day of the onset of the first symptoms.

Mother Alora, the first adult to die, was followed within hours by Bekke's husband, Father Torov.

Father Isaac and Mother Flor immediately isolated all the sick, but nothing they did contained the virus. Ten days later, twenty-one adults and six children were dead, including my beloved baby Gehnny, who died in my arms.

I thought I would die of heartbreak. How could I live without her? An orphan like me, I thought of her as my own child. Every time I closed my eyes, her sweet face came to me.

For weeks after, the ghostly voices of dead children called to me in my sleep. I'd wake and rush to them, only to be confronted by the fresh misery of their empty bunks.

A sense of doom settled over the colony. As if the emotional loss was not enough, the virus left a lingering weakness and ache in our joints.

Gradually, as our mobility improved, our grief began to abate. The colony began to return to a slowed-down version of normal. Us kids recovered more quickly than the adults, and returned to our studies. The water and power plants came back online. The laundry and kitchen reopened. Lyle and his men buried the dead in a mass grave a good distance from the colony, and posted bio-hazard signs around the perimeter.

The evening meal, once a cheerful experience for one hundred and eleven people to come together and enjoy each other's company, now hosted a silent, hollow-eyed group of seventy-five adults and nine children.

Grey with fatigue, Father Isaac reminded us of our duty.

"We cannot allow something like this to overwhelm us. Yes, the loss of our families and friends is painful and disheartening, but our imperative has not changed. Think of Jamestown and the early colonies of North America. Those settlers faced similar disasters, and their colonies rebounded and thrived. We are not done here. We will persevere because we must."

Mother Jean stood. "It's those damn Tok. They're the cause of all this. They're the only thing that's changed around here."

More than a few heads nodded in agreement. Layfe gave me a stricken look. I knew exactly what he was thinking.

But Father Isaac came to our rescue.

"I do not believe the Tok are the source of the illness. Their biology is too dissimilar from ours, and they've been dormant for quite a while. The source of this virus could have come from almost anywhere, even from within our own cells. Every one of you was born infected with the HRV2211-A virus, which was designed specifically to mutate aggressively and vigorously. The generational effects of that virus are unknown, and it is possible that a variant of that virus is the culprit here. Or it could be something airborne, in the soil, or simple transference from an infected surface. We may never have the answer."

But I didn't like the doubtful expression on Mother Jean's face. I excused myself early, saying I wasn't feeling well, and headed back to the dormitory, with Layfe right behind me.

We checked the cupboard where we'd placed the Tok pupae.

Two of the pupae were elongated, heavy, and thicker around than my calf, the third had shriveled like a raisin.

"It's Dawah," Layfe said.

It happened to the lapids sometimes. The body inside desiccated into nothing more than a leathery bit of tissue instead of developing. The process took several days, but nothing could be done. Dawah must have died on or near the same day as Gehnny.

I choked back sobs, missing Gehnny all over again. I didn't think my heart could stand any more losses. Any more death. I thought of the expression on Mother Jean's face and knew the Tok weren't safe. I couldn't lose Vox, too.

"We've got to hide them. If anyone wants to take them away from us, this is the first place they'll look," I said.

We moved them into a storage closet in the basement furnace room, concealed behind a stack of empty bins. It was clean, dark, and dry, even if not quite the same environmentally as the cupboard in the climate-controlled dormitory.

8

"It's often just enough to be with someone. I don't need to touch them. Not even talk. A feeling passes between you both. You're not alone." —Marilyn Monroe
From the instructional archives
of the grounded SS *Dominion*

After three weeks of dormancy, the lapids emerged from their cocoons.

At this stage, the lapid nymphs had morphed into something that might have looked like a distant relative of a soft-shelled crab on Earth. The rounded torso had flattened out to the size of a dinner plate. Their eight legs had lengthened and sported four distinct segments. They moved slowly, using the back four of their eight legs for locomotion. In the front, the first pair of legs was used to shove food into their mouths and the second pair, which were tipped with tiny pincers, used to pluck at vegetation.

Their large expressive eyes rested atop retractable eye stalks, and their hatchling shells, while still soft, had developed a more leathery texture. In color, the nymphs remained a pale, mottled grey. Their bodies would not harden into the distinctive mahogany armor of the adults until their final molt.

Grown too large for the raising drawers, they roamed free on the floor of the raising room, fed on a diet of lichen, weeds from the greenhouses, and whatever other vegetation we could find.

Layfe and I checked the Tok pupas several times every day, but there was no change. After three days of waiting, we were both on pins and needles. What if they didn't emerge? What if the furnace room was too warm? Or too dry?

Finally, on the fifth day, we were working in the greenhouse, and Layfe heard Botto's summons. "Come on, Ettie—it's time!"

We dropped our baskets filled with green beans and raced to the dormitory furnace room.

Botto lay panting on the concrete floor. Her gills fluttered from her recent effort, her skin glistened with moisture.

Vox's pupae had a long horizontal split in it, and I could see his back pulsing gently as he pushed himself clear of the stiff leathery husk. I wanted to help him, but didn't dare interfere. With a final effort, Vox shoved himself out and away from the stiff outer covering. Blindly, he struggled to untangle his folded limbs, and when he touched my hand, suddenly he was in my mind again. I gasped with relief.

"'Ello, Etta. I am 'ere. What do you think?"

"Oh my God, you can speak!" Not clearly, but understandably, and their speech was undeniably English.

Layfe and I could hardly believe it. The other kids crowded into the cramped furnace room, eager to say "'ello" and touch their caramel-colored skin, so like ours.

They looked so different. For one thing, they had faces.

Each had evolved a somewhat triangularly-shaped head, a proper human jaw, and two auditory slits where ears might be perched atop a single thick neck stalk about three inches long. New eyelids framed their beautiful brown eyes, and while not particularly expressive, their faces appeared undeniably humanoid.

They'd also developed a trunk-like, golden-brown torso; rigid enough to allow them an erect posture. Their hindmost legs had lengthened and jointed in places that mimicked our human legs. Their leg joints and proportions at the hip, knee, ankle, and ball of the foot mirrored those of us kids. Twenty minutes after emerging from their old husks, they could walk on their hind legs. Both Vox and Botto stood about as tall as a three-year-old child. Their two middle pairs of appendages dangled shrunken and useless from the sides of their torso, while their first pair of appendages jutted from their shoulders and ended in a rubbery, two-fingered pincer.

I sent Simon to get Father Isaac and the adults, and we all trooped out into the courtyard to see what the Tok could do with their new bodies.

They could do a lot.

They could run and climb and walk almost as well as we could. When Father Isaac and the others arrived, they were just as astonished as we had been. No one in Dominion Colony could possibly believe that the Tok were lapids anymore.

Father Isaac spoke to them and they were able to understand and answer him. They readily asserted their names, and demonstrated their obvious intelligence by answering as many questions as quickly as Father Isaac and the others could ask them. It felt great to finally be believed, even as I realized what being believed might mean for the Tok.

Some of the adults, like Mother Jean, seemed openly hostile, while Father Isaac appeared overly concerned about the rest of the "Tok Horde" as he called it.

In particular, he asked about what kind of ships and weapons the Tok possessed, what kind of technology they possessed, whether or not they planned to invade Hesperidee, and what they wanted from us.

"Tok cannot answer all 'uman questions at this stage," Vox answered. "Botto and Vox not yet adult Tok. When Botto and Vox emerge from final pupal stage, we will be fully adult and able to communicate with Tok universal mind. Only then will we be able to summon our people to return for us. Only then will we 'ave answers to the questions you ask."

This caused a stir among the adults, and I began to get nervous. Father Isaac didn't seem to notice. He wanted to know more about their biology and adult forms.

"Tok can adapt to any form," Vox said. "We chose 'uman form to improve communication with 'umans. We 'ear now to improve communication with 'umans. We change our form to match 'umans."

Not everyone in the Colony liked the idea of the Tok evolving to match humans. Many of the adults, including Mother Jean still blamed the recent deaths on the Tok.

The courtyard had quickly become crowded with adults in their silver enviro suits and plastic helmets, hemming us in. Everyone was talking at once, and the tension was making me uncomfortable. I could feel Vox's terror, and some of the children were getting upset.

With a quiet word, I instructed Layfe to take Vox and Botto into the raising room with the lapids and get them fed. I then charged Nona and Simon to get the rest of the kids back to the greenhouse to finish up their chores.

I don't think the adults even noticed when they left.

Someone asked, "So what do we do with them?"

"Stick 'em in the freezer," Robert said. This suggestion elicited chuckles from some and horrified looks from the others.

I couldn't believe he could even joke about such a thing. "They're just babies! You can't mean to hurt them!"

"They aren't human, Henrietta," Bekke said. "They don't belong here, and I certainly don't want them in with the children. We don't know what they're capable of."

"No, no." Father Isaac held out his hand for calm. His face bore deep lines of worry. "You're right. We can't just let them wander around inside the compound."

"You can't take them away from us," I said. At that moment, I felt as if the whole colony had turned against me.

Lyle spoke up. "How about they stay in one of the storage

sheds? We can set something up so they'll be comfortable in there, and we can lock it from the outside."

He held my gaze and I nodded, smiling.

Father Isaac agreed. "That'll work."

9

*"Intelligence is based on how efficient a species became
at doing the things they need to survive."* —Charles Darwin
Posted in the communal dining hall
of the grounded SS *Dominion*

Father Isaac suggested we treat the undeniably intelligent Tok as guests, saying we had much to learn from each other.

For now, interaction was necessarily limited, as the colony was still struggling to recover after the loss of so many, particularly in the power plant and the greenhouses.

With the adults so busy, they rarely visited the dormitory. The door to the shed was kept unlocked during the day so the Tok could be fed. At this age, much of their waking time was spent eating. I couldn't see any reason why they couldn't be fed in the children's common room during class periods. So I took them there and began showing them the instructional archives.

They were both eager students, and had an ability to absorb new information with startling speed. I started with a timeline of Earth and moved forward through the different eras, biological classifications, and the evolution and major civilizations of man. The evolution and diversity of our architecture in particular, fascinated them. They seemed particularly drawn to the minarets of eastern Europe, the ziggurats of Mesoamerica, and the grandeur of ancient Rome.

Within two turns, they were able to manipulate the archives' computer terminals themselves and direct their own searches. Along with architecture, Vox's interests ran to Earth's technology, and biology.

And space.

Using a map of the solar system, he pointed out the galaxy

where the Tok now lived. The instructional archives referred to it as Kepler 4406.

Although some aspects of Tok biology and technology mirrored that of humans on Earth, their universe contained different and diverse elements; and neither Vox nor Botto were able to explain the details of their culture's technology—not at this stage of their development.

The mind link they shared with their people at this point in their life cycle was one-way. They had access to their own history and culture, as if the events of the past were part of their own memories, but they would not be able to actually converse live with their group mind until they emerged from their next molt as adults.

Father Isaac gathered new DNA samples from each of them and shared his findings one night at dinner.

"I have completed a general analysis of tissues gathered from the Tok creatures after their molt and discovered significant changes in their DNA. In the first sample, the comparison between the *Lapidis Laruae* hatchlings and the Toks indicated their DNA to be 95% identical. But when I tested the samples taken after the metamorphosis, the similarity between the DNA profiles had dropped to about 60%. The DNA conclusively proves the Toks assertion that they are not lapids."

The few nods of acceptance around the room were far outnumbered by stony-faced frowns.

"So what are they?"

"What do they want?" asked Rae.

"After spending a good deal of time with them, discussing what they are willing or able to share with us about the Tok, I believe these intelligent creatures are what they say they are: orphans of a past civilization which once thrived on Hesperidee, forced to flee when meteors struck the planet. In addition to their intelligence, they are highly adaptive, and claim a history which predates man. Surprisingly, they seem to have only an ordinary curiosity about us, as merely one of many intelligent species they've encountered. They are understandably most concerned with their own safety and survival until they can rejoin their own people."

Gratified by Father Isaac's findings, I gazed around the room, but wasn't convinced everyone else had the same reaction. Some, like Rae's mother Jean, and my would-be suitor Robert, seemed to find the idea distasteful.

"Until we encountered the Tok, man has never encountered a life form with the ability to alter their own genetic code at will. On a whim, I decided to compare their DNA to some human DNA samples. And while the early sample shared only a 40% match with human DNA, this latest sample is an astonishing 90% match with us."

A collective gasp filled the room.

Father Isaac nodded. "Yes. They are altering their DNA to match ours."

Mother Flor, the physician, asked the question everyone was thinking. "What does this mean? For us?"

Father Isaac shook his head. "I've asked them individually what they want from us, and they both have the same answer. Their people are a multitude of different physical forms, located on countless different planets, united by a single consciousness. Based on my conversations with them, they seem to consider themselves more advanced than humans. They say they mean us no harm, and ask only for our hospitality until they mature and their ship arrives."

Robert jumped to his feet. "Why should we trust them? What if this ship is carrying an invading army? We could all be killed. Or enslaved." He shook his head. "I don't like this. They're a danger to all of us."

Everyone started talking at once. Father Isaac asked Mother Bekke to escort all the minors back to the children's dormitory. I didn't want to go, but neither Rae nor I were allowed to stay.

10

After I tucked the children into their bunks, I started to tell Vox what had happened.

"We are mind-bonded, Etta. I experienced everything that happened through our bond. Your people fear what they do not understand. 'Umans are no different than other cultures in this regard."

Ever since they'd developed the power of speech, both Vox and Botto usually chose to speak their thoughts aloud, even as they were also speaking to us within our minds.

"I'm worried for you, Vox." I wrapped my hand around his leathery pincer; not so very different from my three-fingered hand. "I want everyone to love you like I do, but I'm not sure it's possible."

His liquid brown eyes held mine. "The Tok are not enemies of 'umans. Your Father Isaac understands this. You understand this. Some of the others understand this, too. In time, all the 'umans of Dominion Colony will understand. Do not fear."

We lay on the grey sofa-lounge in the common room, watching a documentary on Greek architecture from the instructional archive. Vox had curled up comfortably beneath my arm. When the subject of Greek theatre came up, the video panned over the ruins of the famous theatre of antiquity, the Odeon of Herodes Atticus.

"What is fiction, Etta? Is it true or imagination?"

He'd asked me this question several times previously. The concepts of fiction and drama were aspects of human culture the Tok had trouble understanding. With the history of their civilization stored in their memories, they had no need to tell stories. *They remembered.*

They understood facts, history, science, and even art, but the idea that a recorded event was intentionally not true seemed beyond their grasp.

I tried a different approach. "Fiction is a story. Story is narration about things that might have happened about people who might have once lived. A story can be used as an example to illustrate a lesson or evoke an emotion. It may or may not be true, but it feels true. It feels real."

"So, fiction is imagination."

"Well, yes, but it's more than that." I had a sudden inspiration. I instructed the archive to bring up Shakespeare.

"Ah yes. The playwright."

I nodded. "A play is a fiction told by actors. It illustrates a story through their actions." I sat up, excited to share my most secret pleasure with him.

"This is *Romeo and Juliet*. It is one of Shakespeare's most famous plays, and my favorite." The archive contained dozens of performances, some recorded centuries earlier. I'd seen them all, many, many times. I knew all the scenes by heart.

Fearing he might not understand the original dialog, I selected one of the modern interpretations.

He watched the video in silence, only occasionally glancing at me.

"Why are you crying, Etta?"

"I always cry in this part." I wiped my eyes with the back of my hand. "He loves her so much; when he thinks she is dead, he would rather die than live the rest of his life without her. And then, when she wakes and finds him dead, she feels exactly the same way." I sniffed. "It is beautiful. It is a tragedy. I cannot imagine loving anyone that much."

"But this is not true. This is fiction."

"Yes, but it *could* happen. It might have happened. It's a dramatization. Fiction mirrors life. It is a story you *want* to believe is true. It feels true, and I believe there are people who experience that kind of love. I wish, I mean, sometimes I wonder what that would be like. To love someone like that."

His face held little expression, but I sensed his inner struggle to understand. "You would die for love?"

I shook my head. "For me, something like that could never happen. Dominion Colony is my here-and-now. My life is already set in place. I accept that the love I experience will be that of a mother for her children. My responsibility is to preserve the human race through my children. But on Earth, in that time or some other time, yes, it might happen."

"And that love makes you sad?"

I thought of Gehnny and the other children who had died, and how much I missed them, every single day. "If I could have given my life to save Gehnny's, I would have. The love for a child is unending."

"I feel you yearning for this other kind of love. The love of Juliet and Romeo. Yet you say it is fiction."

"To love someone so completely that you would give up everything, and to have that love returned with equal passion, is a beautiful idea. I cannot imagine a romantic love as powerful as the love between a mother and child, but this story moves me. It makes me believe it is possible. I think most humans who see this play feel the same way. That is the power of fiction."

"Show me more. I want to understand why 'umans want fiction. What is this fascination with what-might-be-but-is-not?"

We viewed *Midsummer Night's Dream, Hamlet,* and then he wanted to see *Romeo and Juliet* again. This time, I selected a version which preserved Shakespeare's original dialog. To my surprise, he gripped my hand tightly in the most moving scenes. Afterward, he seemed subdued.

"What's the matter?" I asked.

"Who do you love, Etta?"

"In Dominion, we're taught to love everyone equally." I said the words lightly, but my throat caught. No one had ever asked me that kind of question before. "We love each other and are dedicated to saving the human race, which is more important than romantic love. It's more important than anything. Nothing else matters."

"I think it matters to you."

I blushed. I had no secrets from Vox. "Maybe. Yes. But that's just wishing."

11

"We are always slow in admitting any great change
of which we do not see the intermediate steps."
—Charles Darwin, *On Natural Selection*
From the instructional archives
of the grounded SS *Dominion*

The next morning I went to see Father Isaac. The humming of the DNA purification and extraction units, which I recognized

95

from my previous visits, sent gentle vibrations through the floor as I passed them on the way to Father Isaac's office.

His lab, two levels above the communal dining hall, was easily as large as the children's dormitory. The entire space was contained within a single open room. Clear partitions divided the lab into six separate work areas, several of which held an intent scientist conducting experiments or recording their results in the instructional archive.

In his office, I perched on the edge of my seat, our knees almost touching. One wall was covered with built-in, now mostly defunct electronic displays and equipment, once used to monitor atmospheric conditions in space, now repurposed to monitor the weather conditions in the Colony and its surroundings. In one corner, a model of a double helix DNA strand twisted its way toward the ceiling.

"Good morning, Ettie. I don't often get a voluntary visit from one of you kids. How can I help you?"

"I want to know why I was asked to leave the discussion last night."

"We didn't want you to be unnecessarily upset. We all know how you kids feel about Vox and Botto. People expressed their opinions, but no decision has been made. Nothing for you to worry about."

I sighed. "You announce that I am a woman, but then you send me from the room when the discussion is about something which affects me the most."

He pressed his lips together, but said nothing.

My pulse pounded in my ears. I'd been wanting to ask this question for a long time. "Am I sterile? If I am, I have the right to know."

"I wish I had the answer for you, Ettie." He sounded reluctant to say more. "I believe something in the planet's flora or in the soil is the cause of the divergence in your blood work. I'm working to isolate the culprit and remove it from the environment. Hopefully, it's only temporary. We'll have to wait and see. I'm sorry."

Divergence. The word sent a stab of fear into my heart. "Why isn't it affecting Rae? What if I'm sterile?"

"We don't know that for certain yet. Don't worry, Ettie. You've done a fine job taking care of the children. I don't see why anything would have to change."

He leaned forward in his chair and patted my knee. "Conception is only one small part of the equation. We don't know if any of you kids will be able to conceive, much less deliver a healthy child. We've celebrated more than a hundred pregnancies over the last twenty-five years." He shook his head. "But so few of you survived infancy."

"There are only nine of us now. It's not enough, is it?"

"That's why it's so important for you to continue your bonding efforts with Lyle. If there's any possibility...."

"I don't have those kinds of feelings for Lyle. It's not going to work. You've got Rae now, anyway. What do you need me for?" I hadn't intended to sound so bitter.

"Don't give up, Daughter. It's only been a few weeks. That virus threw us all for a tumble. I do believe that the presence of male testosterone will eventually make a difference. We must make sure we pursue every avenue. I realize you're not very happy about Lyle courting you, but the whole colony is depending on you." He touched his finger to the tip of my nose. "Be the good example we all know you to be. The future of humanity is depending on you."

12

"Is love a tender thing?"
—William Shakespeare, *Romeo and Juliet*
From the instructional archives
of the grounded SS *Dominion*

Later, when Lyle asked me to go exploring with him, I told him I didn't feel well.

"Nothing serious," I assured him. "Just a stomach ache."

Which was true, but it wasn't as severe as I'd made out. My lower back had been bothering me: I felt bloated and uncomfortable. But instead of spending the afternoon on my bunk, I wanted to take the hovership out on my own.

The very idea thrilled and terrified me. Six months ago, I never would have considered touching any of the colony's equipment without permission. Of course, six months ago, there had never been a reason to ask such a thing, but I couldn't stop worrying about Vox.

Both of the Tok had grown a lot in the past few weeks. Vox now stood almost to my shoulder, and Botto was only slightly smaller. They'd gained girth as well, and both weighed close to sixty pounds.

The lapids had gone torpid two days earlier, a phase which generally lasted about a month. If allowed to emerge from their cocoons, they would be fully formed, poisonous and nasty-tempered adults; incredibly dangerous, and hard to kill.

Instead, after two weeks, we would humanely move them into the freezers onboard the Dominion. Lapid meat was considered by many to be a sweet, light-tasting delicacy, rich in protein.

I worried about what might happen when the Tok went dormant. Robert and Mother Jean especially had been outspoken in their desire to add the Tok pupae to the freezers as well. Robert kept telling people there was no way to tell how the Tok would evolve in this dormancy period; they could very well emerge every bit as dangerous as the lapids.

Even though Father Isaac assured me that the Tok would not be harmed, I thought it might be safer to take them to the site of their ancestors' ancient city. That way, they'd be safe while in their most helpless state, and once they emerged, they'd be able to call their people from far enough away to avoid risk to the Colony.

But Layfe had different ideas. We'd argued about it earlier that morning, when we were alone inside the largest of the colony's six greenhouses. We were propping up the heavy fruit-laden branches of the avocado trees. He wiped his sweaty face on his sleeve and glared at me.

"You heard Father Isaac. Nothing's going to happen, Ettie. They're depending on us to take care of them. I'm not going to abandon Botto out in the middle of nowhere. She could get eaten. Or freeze to death. Or dehydrate."

Layfe and Botto had been as inseparable as Vox and I. Now that they could speak, the other children completely accepted Vox and Botto as odd-looking distant cousins. Only Rae kept her distance, although she wasn't really one of us anymore.

"Vox says that we can place them in a cavern or bury them. It will keep them safe from predators and the elements. They'll be fine. You can't watch her every minute, Layfe."

A stubborn expression I knew well came over his face. "You can't tell me what to do anymore, Ettie. Botto wants to stay here with me."

So that afternoon, with Vox strapped in the seat beside me in the hovercraft, the two of us raced across the rocky terrain, past the weathered cliffs, soda marshes, and craters I'd explored with Lyle. In minutes, we'd traveled farther from Dominion than I'd ever been. He'd never been to the site itself, but he retained a memory of its location.

He seemed completely relaxed. Surprising since this was his first trip in a hovercraft. I could feel him purring in my mind.

"You're not scared."

"The sensation of air travel is a shared memory." He directed me east, toward the lip of the largest crater we'd seen yet.

We flew in a slow spiral up and parallel to the outer walls, our eyes riveted to the top. As the ship crested the rim, I marveled at the sheer size of the impact footprint. According to the ship's sensors, the diameter of the crater spanned more than a mile. There was nothing to indicate a city of half a million Tok had once lived here.

He gasped.

I reached for his hand. "Oh Vox, I'm sorry."

"My memories of this place are of how it looked when my people lived here, and the pain they felt as they left this world behind."

I scanned the floor of the crater, all the while feeling his despair build. Layfe had been right. I couldn't leave him here. Not like this.

"Let's go back. There are caves much closer to Dominion which would keep you safe, and I'll be able to look in on you."

He nodded. "Thank you, Etta. I am afraid the shock has accelerated my need for dormancy. I must sleep soon."

I turned west, back toward Dominion. I knew of a crevice in the cliffs near the lichen fields which was big enough. I could seal up the front with stones and he would be safe.

"Tell me, Etta. Will you mate with Lyle? Your mind is not clear on this."

My heart skipped a beat. "What? Why do you ask?"

"When I wake, I will be an adult. I will call my people and they will come for me. You are my mind-mate. I would bring you too." His voice sounded strained. His mind, a whirl of undecipherable thoughts.

I grinned at the idea of traveling across the universe to meet the Tok. To live among them and—

No.

I shook my head. "I'm sorry, Vox. I'm not Tok. Dominion is my home. My responsibilities are with the Colony. When I become a woman, I will bear the children of the next generation. The Colony is depending on me."

"That is what you have been taught. But you are not capable of bearing a 'uman child."

"Don't say that! Father Isaac thinks I can." My hand went to my swollen abdomen, which had been sore to the touch for days. I'd been praying it was going to happen, that I would get my period. That I would *finally* be a woman. *This had to be it.* "Why would you say such a thing?"

He fell silent; but I felt the pain in him, and regretted my anger.

"I'm sorry. I shouldn't have lashed out at you."

"I understand." He closed his eyes and was quiet for the rest of the trip. I tried to mind-speak with him, but he refused to respond.

By the time we arrived at the crevice, I recognized the signs of his impending dormancy. A dull glaze covered his eyes; his skin had begun to thicken and darken. His limbs were stiff, and he was heavy now, only a little lighter than me.

All around us, sheer cliffs rose some forty vertical feet above our heads, shading the crunchy gravel beneath our feet. The twin suns had already passed the halfway point of midday, but the narrow vale retained the suns' heat long after suns-set.

I took him to a particularly narrow place where a horizontal fissure had developed in the cliff face. There was a natural shelf about shoulder height with an opening some five feet wide, two feet high and more than a dozen feet deep. The opposite cliff face was only a few yards away here, so it had a very safe and secluded feeling. I hoped the peppery scent of the abundant lichen growing on the rocks would help him feel at home.

After helping him into a comfortable position deep inside the dusty crack, I began to build up a wall of flat stones and gravel to disguise the entrance. Already, I could feel his mind withdrawing from mine; fading. He was leaving me. I felt a lump rise in my throat.

I wiped my nose on my sleeve. I was being silly. Getting this choked up about Vox going dormant was ridiculous. He was safe and that was all that mattered. And it was only for a few weeks.

Just before I closed off the crevice and sealed him in, he twisted his head blindly toward me one last time.

"I love you, Etta."

My lips trembled, and I fought the strange, competing emotions welling up within me. I wanted to laugh and cry at the same time.

I could feel his love for me, even as Gehnny's voice echoed in my head. I could not remember when I'd heard those words from anyone but the children, but there was a different tone to this declaration of love from Vox.

One that made my heart race.

In all our time together it never occurred to me to ask him if the Tok loved, or whether love was a uniquely human emotion. They must, certainly. But here he'd confessed his feelings to me aloud and I didn't know what to say. I didn't know how to respond.

And then it was too late. His beautiful brown eyes grew opaque and he was gone. I was alone and empty as a shell.

"Sleep well, Vox." *I love you too.*

13

"The smallest worm will turn, being trodden on."
—William Shakespeare, *Henry VI*
From the instructional archives
of the grounded SS *Dominion*

Two weeks later, we moved the lapid cocoons into the walk-in freezers onboard the Dominion. I worried that the adults would insist on moving the pupae of Botto and Vox into the freezers as well, but Father Isaac assured me that we still had much to learn about the Tok and promised they would be perfectly safe locked inside the storage shed.

I didn't say a word. Not a lie, exactly. If they thought Vox was safely locked in the shed, and that made them feel better, who was I to spoil things? I felt better knowing he was hidden in that crevice near the lichen field. Everyone was happy.

The whole colony was involved in making preparations for the upcoming womanhood celebration for Rae and me, and the building of the new private dormitory.

I secretly hoped to join Rae in the ranks of true womanhood before the party.

My lower abdomen felt bloated, just as Rae and the other women described. And although no one had mentioned it being lumpy, mine definitely was. And tender to the touch. I didn't want to say anything until I knew for sure. I wanted my announcement to be as big as Rae's had been. I tried not to think about it too much, afraid that if I did, it wouldn't happen.

I was in the greenhouse, pollinating pepper blossoms when Layfe came running up, out of breath.

His face was sweaty, his eyes wild. "Did you take Botto?"

My heart skipped a beat. Something had happened. Something bad. Instantly my thoughts went to Vox. I fought to keep my voice calm.

"No. I haven't even looked in on her since she went dormant. What's wrong?"

His expression hardened. "She's missing."

"Maybe one of the kids moved her."

"No. She was too big for the cupboard, so Simon helped me put her in one of the empty bunks with a blanket over her. She's too heavy for one of us kids to move without help." He began to tremble. "What do we do?"

"Come on, let's talk to Father Isaac."

We hurried to his lab, and found Robert, Mother Jean, Bekke, and several other adults already there, observing Father Isaac's dissection of Botto's pupated corpse. Their guilty expressions said it all.

As soon as Layfe saw Botto, he gave an anguished cry and buried his head into my shoulder.

The sight of Botto's lifeless body spread out on the cold steel of the examination table like some laboratory science project sickened me.

"Why?" I tried to finish the sentence, but the words would not come. I had never leveled an accusation against the adults before. I was the good one. I did as I was told. I was the example for others. I tried again. "What have you done?"

Chunks of white tissue, floating within clear glass containers, filled with preservative, stood in neat rows on the counter behind Father Isaac.

"What should have been done as soon as we saw what they were!" Robert's face held the high flush of righteous indignation. Mother Jean stood rigidly beside him.

"It was already too late to do anything." Father Isaac smiled sadly. "It was dead when they brought it to me. As it happens, I have to agree with their decision to destroy the cocoon. Where is the other one?"

His face, always so sincere and so caring, was a lie. Bekke's too.

I shook my head. "I don't understand. You said yourself that they're intelligent, advanced beings."

"They're mimics. The young can change their bodies to adapt and blend in with the dominant species. The DNA of the creature in this cocoon is almost a genetic match to a human."

"An abomination!" Mother Jean's eyes bored into mine.

Robert stepped around the table. "We cannot allow them to contaminate the gene pool."

I held up my three-fingered hands, spreading my fingers wide. "Look at me! Look at Layfe! We're different. Would you kill us too?"

"It's not the same," Bekke answered. "You are our own children. The differences between us are the result of the genetic virus."

"All our lives, you've told us that the future of the human race depended on us, on our differences and ability to survive and adapt to the conditions on Hesperidee. The Tok have already mastered that ability. If they can make themselves into a genetic match for us, why can't they be considered human too?" My voice cracked. "What makes us human and them not?"

I blinked rapidly, trying to fend off tears, as the adults stared down at me in silent judgment. "All those DNA samples you took from me. From all us kids. With all our adaptive mutations, we're not really human anymore, are we?"

The kindly expression disappeared from Father Isaac's face. "That's enough."

Then the realization hit me. My voice came out a croak. *"Or is it just me?* Maybe there's a reason I'm not a woman yet."

Anger flickered in Father Isaac's eyes. "Where is the other pupa?"

I chewed my lip as I backed toward the door. "No. You can't ask me to do this."

Robert, who was closest to me, made a sudden lunge. He grabbed at my wrist, but I twisted away before he could catch me. I hit the double doors of the lab with both hands and was out of there.

I heard Father Isaac telling him in a cool voice, "Let her go. She's got nowhere to run."

I didn't care.

I raced down the corridors until I reached the air locks, tears streaming down my face. I slammed the doors open and sped out into the heat, even as I knew they could not pursue me without oxygen suits.

Once outside, I kept running—past the dormitory, past Lyle and his men in their enviro-suits, working on the new residence, past the cement barricades and through the front gate to the wide stony plain.

I forced myself to turn away from the lichen fields, where Vox's pupa was safely hidden. Instead, I sprinted toward the soda lake where Lyle and I often walked. Beneath the delicate fronds of silver-grey lichen trees, where the afternoon heat wasn't so intense.

I made my way to a flat-topped boulder that made a natural bench overlooking the pond. I sat with my arms wrapped around my knees, staring across the shallow yellow-green water.

They'd killed Botto. *How could they do such a thing?* They'd cut her into little pieces and dissected her because she was *almost* human. It didn't matter that she was intelligent, or childlike, or had been living among us for four months.

And then there was the other truth, the one I couldn't quite believe. That I wasn't human, either. The genetic virus experiment had worked a little too well on me.

I rocked for what seemed like hours, my mind numb. What would happen to me now? What about the other kids? Or was I the only one?

I fell asleep, or maybe I just passed out. I woke moaning, lying on my side in a fetal position.

I examined my hands. So ugly. My thick, rubbery, dark skin. I wanted to tear it off. None of the adults had skin like mine. *If I'm not human, what am I?*

Vox had been right. Somehow, he'd known I would never have children. A feeling of inconsolable sadness washed over me.

I thought of Gehnny, and how much I missed her.

There was nothing I could do about it. I remembered Father Isaac telling me it didn't matter. I was part of the Colony, and always would be. He'd also said that no harm would come to the Tok, but look what he'd done to Botto.

Would they cut me up, too? How could I have ever believed him?

Vox wouldn't lie to me. The Tok were incapable of lying. No one who hadn't experienced their mind-speak could possibly understand that. Yet the Tok would never be accepted into the Colony. They were *other,* and not to be trusted.

I didn't know what to do.

I couldn't go back. I'd made a big scene, and refused to give them Vox. If I wasn't part of the Colony anymore, where would I go?

I heard the hovercraft approach, and moments later, Lyle set it down beside the marsh. When he gave me a wave from the cockpit, relief flooded through me.

Lyle appeared calm and took his time, strolling along the edge of the lake until he reached me. He motioned to me to scoot over and squeezed himself next to me on the boulder, his silver suit crinkling as he made himself comfortable.

"You all right?"

Even through the breather, I could hear the authentic concern in his voice. I nodded. I didn't trust myself to say anything.

"Father Isaac told me what happened. I know you're upset. Everyone is. What Robert and Jean did." He shook his head. "Well, that was wrong. I think. But I don't know. And that's the whole thing of it, Ettie. Nobody really knows for sure what the Tok's intentions are."

I picked at a bit of lichen from the boulder we were sitting on and twirled it between my fingers. The Tok had been such adorable babies. No one cared that they were different then.

"They wouldn't hurt us. I know it."

"The fact is, we can't take the chance. We're barely hanging on by our fingernails here. We need every person pulling in the same direction. And as long as the Tok are here, they're a distraction. A misdirection. A risk."

He held his hand out for the bit of lichen and I gave it to him. He held it up to his face mask to sniff and I laughed, even though it wasn't really funny. *Old habits die hard.*

106

He flicked it into the water, where it floated, creating the barest ripple across the surface. "Yeah, okay, maybe they're great and more advanced than humans will ever be. But they aren't *us, and they never will be.*"

"But if they're just like us—"

"The idea to destroy the pupae was all Robert and Jean's. But now that it's done, people are kind of relieved, to be honest. We don't want them in the colony." He put his arm around my shoulders. "We want you. We need you back, Ettie."

I leaned into him as I stared out across the still, green-grey water. It was so quiet here. Peaceful.

I didn't say anything. I couldn't. I wanted things to be the way they had once been. Before the lies. Before they killed Botto. Before I found out I wasn't human enough.

"Layfe said you took Vox out to one of the craters. You don't have to tell me where, just let me know if he's gone."

He was trying. Even through the bulky enviro suit, I could see that. Maybe that was why I'd gravitated toward him instead of Robert. It wasn't attraction. Bekke was right; Lyle was a good man.

I nodded. "He's gone. When he wakes up, he'll call his people and they'll come for him. He asked me if I wanted to go with him."

"I'm not sure I like the sound of that. Your place is here with us."

My hand slid to my stomach. So tender. Something had to be happening. If only I could be sure. "I might not ever be able to have children. I might not be . . ." I couldn't finish.

He took my hand in his. Even with all three of my fingers spread wide, it wasn't as big as his gloved palm. "I'm not a scientist, but it doesn't mean that what I do isn't important. In my opinion, having children is a bit like that. It's important, but it's not the only thing."

I stared at him. "That goes against our mission."

He waved his hand dismissively. "Our mission is survival. We all saw how hard you worked with Mother Flor when everyone got sick; especially with the children. And whether you can have kids or not doesn't make you any less one of us. All children are a gift, Ettie. We can't afford to lose any of you."

"I'm not a child anymore."

"You're right," he admitted. "But you are part of Dominion. We're not complete without you. Whatever the Tok are, they aren't us, and they never will be.

He was right, too. I loved the *idea* of Vox and the Tok, but Dominion was my home. The only home I'd ever known. My future was here. To think differently was pure fantasy. Time to put away those childish thoughts.

14

"How silver-sweet sound lovers' tongues by night"
—William Shakespeare, *Romeo and Juliet*
From the instructional archives
of the grounded SS *Dominion*

*E*tta. *I am 'ere, Etta. Where are you?*

Vox's voice in my mind woke me from a sweat-soaked dream in the middle of the night. I hadn't been sleeping well. The angry, lumpy skin of my lower abdomen had become enflamed; swollen so tight that I thought it would burst. I'd put off telling Mother Flor or anyone for weeks, thinking it was just the sign I was about to start my period. Now I wasn't so sure, but couldn't bring myself to say anything.

I sat bolt upright in my bunk, my hand cradling my stomach. I answered, *Stay there, Vox! I'm coming!*

I threw a robe over my nightgown and slipped outside, a blanket from my bed wrapped around my shoulders to keep off the night chill.

Hesperidee's trio of moons shone brightly between banks of scudding clouds, casting flickering shadows across the courtyard. Vox's cocoon was hidden among the cliffs bordering the lichen fields. In daylight, it was an easy run, even for the youngest children, but I couldn't even consider such a thing in the dark. Night was no time to be outside the walls of Dominion; all the planet's major predators were nocturnal.

I raced to the hoverport.

Minutes later, I was airborne in the two-seater, flying low and as slow as I dared over the stony plains toward the cliffs, as I could not see beyond the lights. I caught glimpses of an armored hunting worm and three large, adult lapids scuttling away from the lights, their venom-tipped tails arching aggressively over their broad backs. None of the landmarks I knew so well looked the same at night, and I did not know how to use the navigation system to pinpoint my destination.

I only had Vox's voice in my head.

I recognized the wall of cliffs in front of me, and angled the hovercraft, searching for the familiar gap.

There.

I set the agile craft down on the hardpan, as close as I dared to the scree at the foot of the cliffs. After grabbing a headlamp, blanket, and a sonic bangstick from the ship's weapon cache, I turned on all the ship's exterior lights, hoping they would keep any predators at bay, and at the same time show me where I needed to go.

The gravel crunched loudly beneath my feet as I faced the cleft. I paused when I reached the gap. "Vox? Are you 'ere?"

"Turn out the light, Etta. It 'urts my eyes."

The walls of the cliffs rose steeply around us, but overhead, the moonlit sky offered plenty of light. I turned off the headlamp and waited for my eyes to adjust.

A moment later he stepped into the moonlight, and my whole world changed.

15

"To breathe such vows as lovers use"
—William Shakespeare, *Romeo and Juliet*
From the instructional archives
of the grounded SS *Dominion*

Gaunt as he was from his prolonged dormancy, Vox's face appeared as handsome as any Romeo's, at the same time uniquely his own. An angular face, with broad cheekbones and a high, intelligent brow. No hair, but when he smiled at me, white, even teeth glowed like pearls behind full lips.

His beautiful dark eyes had not changed, and when they caught mine, I shivered.

"What do you think, Etta?" His voice had changed as well, dropping to a lower and more pleasing register. I sensed his nervousness, and something else. *Excitement.*

My heart pounded. "Is it really you?"

He was my height now, darker-skinned, with broad shoulders, narrow hips, and well-formed, muscular legs of human proportions.

When he reached for me, I stepped willingly into his arms.

He didn't just touch me; he somehow came *into* me. Into my mind. The essence of him filled my senses with the scent, breadth, and depth of him.

It wasn't just mind-speak, it was a complete melding of our inner selves into each other. I could feel his emotions, like electric sparks across my skin. His sensations were mine, richer and more powerful than any I'd ever known. I had never felt so alive.

And just as he was now fully embraced by the collective consciousness of his people, so was I.

So many different life forms! So many languages, ideas, likes and dislikes, while underneath it all there was this unifying feeling of *connection*. Like a universal family. I could see it now.

All different, yet all the same. Bound together by a common, never-forgotten history that seemed so vast as to be eternal. Beautiful.

I now understood his confusion about storytelling and fiction. His people had no need for fiction, yet I could see how he'd already brought it to them. Romeo was already there. Juliet, too.

And me.

I was there! They knew me. Welcomed me. Accepted me. I bit back a sob.

His three-fingered hands mirrored mine. His lips, where they pressed against my skin, were as soft as anything I'd ever felt.

He pulled me closer, breathing me in, so focused in memorizing my scent I could taste it. The smell of him was intoxicating. My entire body throbbed with the beat of his heart, which pulsed in perfect synchronicity with mine.

We pressed against each other, tentatively at first, then with more familiarity. My swollen abdomen seemed to contract and harden with the contact. I never wanted the moment to end. This was where I belonged. I ached to get even closer to him.

I pulled my nightgown off over my head. Naked, we pressed against each other, his abdomen hard against mine. An irresistible tension began to build within me.

"What do I do?" My voice sounded breathless. Hoarse.

"Kiss me."

I obeyed. Not only with my lips, but my mind and body and every part of me, as if the last door between us had flung wide open.

"Your eggs are about to erupt through the top layer of skin on your abdomen. When I release my sperm onto your belly, the skin will dissolve, and your eggs will be fertilized. They will harden quickly."

He showed me in his mind what would happen. The logic and simplicity of the Tok's reproduction stunned me. Freed from the responsibilities of parenting, they dedicated themselves to improving their collective mind and advancing their culture. What an elegant alternative!

There would be pain, he promised, but pleasure also. Once hardened, my marble-sized eggs could be buried safely. In time, they would hatch, when conditions were best for our children's survival.

Our children. Mine and Vox's. Unique in the universe; offspring of two people who had evolved to be each other's perfect match. Independent and able to care for themselves from birth, only the fittest and most clever would survive. As opposed to human children, the Tok required only a season to mature, and would return to us as adults.

I could see the future now.

I wanted it. All of it.

I gasped as spasms shook my whole body. He held me close and murmured into my ear until I came back to myself. The Tok pair bond for life, he told me. We are bonded now in body and mind.

Yes.

There would be more clutches. More children. More chances to preserve humanity, our version of it, into the distant future. But more than that, there would be more love. We were one now.

He didn't have to ask, and I didn't have to say a word. He already knew my answer.

Oh my sweet love, yes.

16

"Parting is such sweet sorrow"
—William Shakespeare, *Romeo and Juliet*
From the instructional archives
of the grounded SS *Dominion*

By the time we'd buried our eggs, the sky was growing light above the horizon. Time for us to leave. The Tok would soon arrive at the crater site.

We were making our way back to the ship. In the light of the coming dawn, I couldn't help but admire his naked beauty. Like a Greek god.

He sensed my thoughts and grinned. He kissed me, and again and again until I pushed him away, breathless.

His glance flicked to the sky behind me.

The other, larger hovercraft from Dominion Colony streaked toward us. Lyle sat in the pilot seat with Father Isaac beside him.

I gave Vox my robe and asked him to put it on. I didn't want them to see my beloved's nakedness. They landed next to the one I'd taken, and after they got out, Mother Bekke emerged as well. All three walked stiffly; all three wore sidearms.

"What are you doing?" Lyle asked.

I had never seen him so tense. Gone was the easygoing man I thought I knew. He wouldn't even look at me. His eyes were glued to Vox.

"I'm taking Vox to the rendezvous spot."

Father Isaac shook his head, his expression a dark scowl. "Lyle tells me that creature wants you to come with him. I can't let you do that."

"'Is name is Vox."

"He's not one of us. You are," Father Isaac said.

I shook my head. "Your definition of 'uman is based on a number, and as you said yourself, my numbers don't add up. You think that's why I'm sterile, but that's not the right answer. The truth is that I'm not 'uman anymore. I'm something new."

"You sound like *him* now." Bekke said. "What have you done, Ettie?" She looked furious.

My face grew hot, but I said nothing.

"It doesn't matter to me." Lyle protested. "I'll marry you, if that's what you want."

"Why do you want to marry me?"

He looked away. "If you want..."

Lyle didn't really want me, not any more than I wanted him, but I hadn't anticipated this. Leaving Hesperidee might be more difficult than I expected.

Vox put his arm around my shoulder. *I am 'ere.*

I leaned into him, savoring his touch. Nothing would change my mind about him, but I had to ask. *If I asked, would you stay with me? On 'Esperidee?*

He wiped a stray wisp of hair out of my face. A simple act, yet so full of caring. His eyes were soft as he gazed into mine. "You are the stars that make dark 'eaven light for me, Etta."

My breath caught in my throat. That line from Shakespeare touched me in a whole new way. In Vox's eyes, I was a beautiful woman. *I am Juliet.*

Oh my sweet love. I put my hand on his soft cheek.

To Isaac, Bekke, and Lyle, I was the little brown girl who took care of the children. Their estimation of me would never change, and nothing I could say would convince them to let Vox stay. I turned to face them. "I've made up my mind. I'm leaving with Vox."

"He's nothing but a mimic," Isaac said. "This is what their species does. You've manufactured some romantic notion of him, but it's all a lie."

"And what about the children? How can you stand to leave them?" Bekke edged closer. "I know how much you love them."

113

I thought about the beautiful clutch of nine fertilized eggs Vox and I had buried. Our children. I loved them too. They would hatch when conditions were right. And when they reached maturity, they too, would enter the shared mind of the Tok, and I would know them. Maybe next year, maybe in another millennium.

I said softly, "This is a different kind of love. Vox and I are bonded." His hand felt comforting in mine.

Isaac drew his gun, his expression cold. "You're about to make the biggest mistake of your life."

I choked back a gasp. *This can't be happening!* In spite of all his assurances about treating the Tok as guests, he really wasn't much different from Jean or Robert. Or any of them.

"No!" I quickly stepped in front of Vox, shielding him with my body.

"Get away from him, Ettie."

Vox twisted himself around and stepped in front of me. "No. Whatever you want, I'll do it. Don't 'urt 'er."

"Put down the gun, Isaac." Bekke said. "Ettie, you know you belong with us."

"I said, get away from her!" Father Isaac shouted.

"No!" I clung to Vox, refusing to let him go.

It's all right, Etta. I won't let them 'urt you.

No! I don't want to lose you. I couldn't bear it. Please, Vox. Please trust me.

I whirled to face them. "If I stay, your plans to save 'umanity mean nothing! By your own definition, I'm not 'uman anymore, so I have nothing to contribute to Dominion. Vox, has given me—" I stopped. *No.* I wouldn't tell them about the eggs.

"Vox has evolved to be a genetic match to me. And my body has changed to match 'is as well." I felt myself blushing. "Even without the DNA test, you must you know I'm right, Isaac. If I am 'uman enough for Dominion, so is Vox. If Vox isn't 'uman enough for you, then neither am I."

Isaac's gun hand began to tremble.

I eased toward the hovercraft, Vox arm-in-arm with me at every step. "What kind of example are you setting by taking away my freedom? If all children are a blessing, then so am I. Dominion was never intended to be a prison."

Isaac's hand dropped. "Please don't do this."

"You've got the wrong idea," Bekke protested. "We would never try to hurt you—"

Lyle took the gun from Isaac. "Go, on. I won't let anyone stop you. I don't understand your reasons, but I agree that you've got the right to choose your own path."

"Thank you, Lyle." *'E really is a good man. Just not the one for me.* "Good luck."

I gave a final glance at Isaac, deflated now, and Bekke, who seemed to have finally accepted my decision to leave. I thought about the rest of the colony and Rae and her upcoming womanhood ceremony. I would miss it, of course, but no matter.

I'd already 'ad mine.

17

We stood together on the dusky gravel floor of the suns-baked crater, Vox and I, 'olding 'ands as the bronze-colored spacecraft arrived to take us to *Volkjaryn-ko*. Whatever fate the future 'ad in store for us, for good or bad, we'd face it together.

The Tok who greeted us at the bay doors were bigger and stranger-looking than either of us had expected, but they sensed our nervousness, and welcomed us aboard with thoughts and expressions of unabashed joy. When it came to getting to really know someone in a 'urry, 'umans could really learn a lesson from the Tok.

I considered leaving a message on the 'overcraft about the eggs. Not that I was worried; our children would be self-sufficient at birth. They would adapt and thrive or perish, just as Darwin 'ad so famously observed centuries ago. Only the fittest of any species would survive.

Maybe the fittest were the 'umans of Dominion Colony.

Maybe the fittest were the Tok.

Or maybe the fittest would 'ave a little bit of both of us. I liked that thought the most. In the end, I decided against leaving a note.

Better to let nature decide.

Art

BY L. RON HUBBARD

During a remarkable life, filled with adventure, new discoveries
and meaningful accomplishments in an array of professional fields,
L. Ron Hubbard mastered numerous artistic skills as an avid
photographer, an experienced cinematographer, musician, poet and
songwriter.

But of all the arts, writing, for Ron, was always first and foremost.
He wrote in a myriad of genres including adventure, western, military
and war, mystery, detective, romance, and of course, science fiction
and fantasy. During a long and distinguished career spanning more
than fifty years, and with international bestsellers and sales of some
fifty million translated into better than thirty languages, he is among
the world's most enduring and widely read authors.

Then, too, he is legitimately credited with helping to reshape
whole genres and laying the foundation for much of what we know as
modern speculative fiction.

As author and critic Frederik Pohl stated: "There are bits and
pieces from Ron's work that became a part of the language in many
ways that very few other writers imagined."

Not surprisingly then, his belief in, and respect for, the artist can
be found in this all-encompassing statement:

"The artist has an enormous role in the enhancement of today's
and the creation of tomorrow's reality. He operates in a rank in
advance of science as the necessities and requirements of Man. The
elevation of a culture can be measured directly by the numbers of
its people working in the field of aesthetics. Because the artist deals
in future realities, he always seeks improvements or changes in the
existing reality. This makes the artist, inevitably and invariably, a
rebel against the status quo. The artist, day by day, by postulating
the new realties of the future, accomplishes peaceful revolution."

His studies, and his involvement in the arts, led him to compose
helpful essays on the subject, including the following article titled
"Art."

Art
The Fundamentals of Art

Basic Definition

ART is a word which summarizes THE QUALITY OF COMMUNICATION.

It therefore follows the laws of communication.

Too much originality throws the audience into unfamiliarity and therefore disagreement, as communication contains duplication and "originality" is the foe of duplication.

TECHNIQUE should not rise above the level of workability for the purpose of communication.

PERFECTION cannot be obtained at the expense of communication.

Seeking *perfection* is a wrong target in art. One should primarily seek communication with it and *then* perfect it as far as reasonable. One attempts *communication* within the framework of applicable skill. If perfection greater than that which can be attained for communication is sought, one will not communicate.

Example: A camera that shoots perfectly but is not mobile enough to get pictures. One must settle for the highest level of technical perfection obtainable *below* the ability to obtain the picture.

The order of importance in art is:

1. The resultant communication
2. The technical rendition.

Two is always subordinate to 1. Two may be as high as possible but never so high as to injure 1.

The communication is the primary target. The technical

118

quality of it is the secondary consideration. A person pushes 2 as high as possible within the reality of 1.

A being can take a lot of trouble with 2 to achieve 1 but there is a point where attempting 2 prevents 1.

If the ardures of 2 prevent 1, then modify 2, don't modify 1.

Perfection is defined as the quality obtainable which still permits the delivery of the communication.

Too much time on 2 of course prevents 1.

It is usually necessary to lower a standard from absolute perfection to achieve communication. The test of the artist is how little it is lowered not how high it is pushed.

A professional in the arts is one who obtains communication with the art form at the minimum sacrifice of technical quality. There is always some sacrifice of quality to communicate at all.

The reduction of mass or time or impedimenta or facilities toward the ability to render a result is the exact measurement of how much technical perfection can be attempted. The rule is if one is being too perfectionistic to actually achieve a communication, reduce the mass, time, impedimenta or facilities sufficiently low to accomplish the communication but maintain the technique and perfection as high as is reconcilable with the result to be achieved and within one's power to act.

No communication is no art. To not do the communication for lack of technical perfection is the primary error. It is also an error not to push up the technical aspects of the result as high as possible.

One measures the degree of perfection to be achieved by the degree of communication that will be accomplished.

This is seen even in a workman and tools. The workman who cannot accomplish anything but must have tools is an *artistic* failure.

"Art for art's sake" is a complete paradox as a remark. "Art for the sake of communication" and "Attempted perfection without communicating" are the plus and minus of it all.

One can of course communicate to oneself, if one wishes to be both cause and effect.

One studies art only if one wishes to communicate and the search for artistic perfection is the result of past failures to communicate.

Self-improvement is based entirely on earlier lack of communicating.

Living itself can be an art.

The search for freedom is either the retreat from past failures to communicate or the effort to attain new communication. To that degree then the search for freedom is a sick or well impulse.

Searching for and discovering one's past failures to communicate an art form or idea about it will therefore inevitably rehabilitate the artist.

How much art is enough art? The amount necessary to produce an approximation of the desired effect on its receiver or beholder, within the reality of the possibility of doing so.

A concept of the beholder and some understanding of his or her acceptance level is necessary to the formulation of a successful art form or presentation. This includes an approximation of what is familiar to him and is associated with the desired effect.

All art depends for its success upon the former experience and associations of the beholder. There is no pure general form since it must assume a sweeping generality of former experiences in the beholder.

In any art form or activity one must conceive of the beholder (if only himself). To fail to do so is to invite disappointment and eventual dissatisfaction with one's own creations.

An artist who disagrees thoroughly with the "taste" of his potential audience cannot of course communicate with that audience easily. His disagreement is actually not based on the audience but on former inabilities to communicate with such audiences or rejections by a vaguely similar audience.

The lack of desire to communicate with an art form may stem from an entirely different inability than the one supposed to exist.

Professionals often get into such disputes on *how* to present the art form that the entirety becomes a technology, not an art, and, lacking progress and newness of acceptance, dies. This is probably the genus of all decline or vanishment of art forms. The idea of contemporary communication is lost. All old forms become beset by technical musts and must-nots and so cease to communicate. The art is the form that communicates not the technology of how, the last contributing to the ease of creating the effect and preservation of the steps used in doing it. A form's reach, blunted, becomes involved with the perfection alone, and ceases to be an art form in its proper definition.

A communication can be blunted by suppressing its art form. Examples: bad tape reproduction, scratched film, releasing bits not authorized. This then is the primary suppression.

On the other hand, failing continuously to permit a nondestructive communication on the grounds of its lack of art is also suppressive.

Between these two extremes there is communication and the task is to attain the highest art form possible that can be maintained in the act of communicating. To do otherwise is inartistic and objectionable.

These, therefore, are the fundamentals of ART.

When Shadows Fall

written by

L. Ron Hubbard

illustrated by

GREG OPALINSKI

ABOUT THE STORY

Originally published in July 1948, this timeless story communicates as well, if not more so, today as it did upon its first publication.

"When Shadows Fall" is set far in a future when Earth faces the prospect of slow environmental death, or more immediate destruction by the fleets of the colonial civilizations spawned by Earth among the galaxies.

Played out against a barren and destitute landscape, the story reveals the supreme power of words and art to not only create new civilizations, but bring them to heights not yet envisioned.

ABOUT THE ILLUSTRATOR

Greg Opalinski began his artistic journey the way many others did. As a child growing up in Poland, he loved drawing, which contributed to many notebooks being filled with doodles and cartoons.

In grade school his skills were quickly utilized by his classmates who requested drawings of their favorite characters from the television show Dragon Ball Z *and others. Greg quickly realized that getting paid for drawing would be a great life.*

However, it wasn't until he came to the United States and attended the School of Visual Arts in New York City that he realized that there are people who actually do that. There he discovered old master painters, as well as contemporary illustrators who inspired him to take art seriously and commit to a life of creativity.

Greg was a winner of the Illustrators of the Future Contest in 2012 published in Writers of the Future Volume 28. He is currently working full-time as a freelance illustrator for various companies and exploring personal projects during free time.

When Shadows Fall

And then there came a day when Earth lay dying, for planets also die. About her crept a ghost of atmosphere, the body eaten full away by iron rust and belching smoke until the plains, stretching wide, were sickly red, and no green showed from range to range and pole to pole.

Red as Mars.

Dead, or nearly so, with the broken tumble of her cities peopled with the lizard and the wind. And the spaceports, which had given birth to the empires of space, were charred and indistinct upon the breast of Mother Earth.

So thought Lars the Ranger sitting in the window of the Greater Council Hall, so he saw from this eminence above the world and the red plains.

He too was getting old. Strong and young he had voyaged far on dangerous ways to bring the treasure back, but now he voyaged no more. Science had prolonged the beating of his heart a thousand years beyond his time, but now he was old and stiff and the Council chamber was cold.

The voices were thin behind him. They echoed oddly in this reverberant tomb. Seats were here for all the Council members of full six hundred systems. But the seats were empty now and their metal threw back the reedy whine of the clerks who called them all to order, reading names which had been gone these seven hundred years, all formal, all precise, and noting that they were not here.

Mankin, Grand President of the Confederated Systems, sat hunched and aged upon his dais, looking out upon his servants, listening to the threadbare rite.

"Capella!"

Silence.

"Rigel Centaurus!"

Silence.

"Deneb and Kizar and Betelgeuse!"

Silence.

And onward for six hundred names.

Silence.

For they were mighty there in the stars and Mother Earth was old. They were thriving across a mighty span of ten thousand light-years. And Mother Earth had no longer any fuel. They had taken the oil from her deepest springs and the coal from her lowest mines. They had breathed her air and forged her steel and taken their argosies away. And behind them they had scant memory.

Earth had no power of money now, no goods, no trades, no fleet. And the finest of her strong young men had gone this long, long while. The lame, the halt, these and the dimmest of sight had stayed. And now there was nothing.

"Markab!"

"Achernar!"

"Polaris!"

No one there. No one there. No one there. No one.

Lars the Ranger stood and stiffly shook out his cloak. He couched the ceremonial space helmet in his crooked arm and advanced formally to the dais. He bowed.

He might have reported there in the ritual that the fleets were ready and the armies strong, that as General of Space he could assure them all of the peace in space.

But he was suddenly conscious of who they were and how things stood and he said nothing.

There was Greto, once a wizard of skilled finance, sitting chin on breast in an advisor's chair. There was Smit, the valiant warrior of five hundred years ago. There was Mankin, tiny in his robe, crushed down by years and grief.

About Lars swirled, for an instant, the laughing staff of centuries back—young men with the giddy wine of high risk in their hearts. About Lars thundered the governing mandates of Earth to Space, to System Empires everywhere.

And then he saw the four of them and the clerks, alone here on a world which was nearly dead.

He broke ritual softly.

"There are no fleets and the armies have melted away. There is no fuel to burn in the homes, much less in the cannon. There is no food, there are no guns. I can no longer consider myself or this Council master of space and all that it contains."

They had all come there with a vague hope that it would break. And it had broken. And Greto came to his feet, his wasted body mighty and imposing still.

There was silence for a while and then Greto turned to the dais. "I can report the same. For fifteen long years I could have said nearly as much. But I admit this now. Earth is no more."

Smit lumbered upright. He scowled and clenched a black fist as he looked at Lars. "We have our fleets and our guns. Who has been here these last decades to know that they are without fodder? Bah! This thing can be solved!"

Mankin hunched lower, opened a drawer and brought out a tablet which he took. As he set down his water glass, he belched politely and looked from one to the next, bewildered, a little afraid. He had been able to handle many things in his day.

He fumbled with his reports and they were all the same. People were old and children were few. The food was gone and winter would be cold.

He cleared his throat. Hopefully he looked at Smit. "I was about to suggest that some measure be taken to remove the few thousands remaining here to some planet where food and fuel are not so dear. But I only hope that I can be advised—"

"You could remove nothing," said Greto, thrusting his hands into his pockets. "You could take nothing away. For there's not fuel to lift more than twenty ships from the surface of Earth. The cause may be lost, but I am not lost. Earth is no longer tenable as she is. I propose that, with credits long past due, I force the purchase of atmosphere manufacturing equipment and other needful things."

"Credits!" said Smit. "What do I know of credits? If this thing is at last in the light and the need is desperate, I can give them the promise of guns in their guts. Need they know?"

Mankin looked from one to the other. He was heartened a little, for he had begun to see these fabulous men as little more than companions of his desultory chess games. But he did not heed them too much.

He turned to Lars.

"What says the General of Armies and Admiral of Fleets?"

Lars the Ranger laid his helmet on the clerk's table. All semblance of formality fell from him as he took a pipe from his pocket, loaded it and lighted it with his finger ring. He looked from Mankin to Greto.

"My fleet," he said, "has not fired a jet in so many years that I have quite forgotten how many emergency charges were left aboard. I do know that mechanics and even officers have long since used all reserve atomic fuel for the benefit of lighting plants in the cities and our few remaining factories. At the most, on all our five continents I seriously doubt whether or not we retain enough fuel for more than two or three hundred light-years. That is, of course, for one of our minor destroyers. Hardly enough for an extended cruise of space.

"At the old Navy yard at the Chicago spaceport I daresay there may be four destroyers in more or less workable condition. Certainly there are enough spare parts in the battleships to complete them and make them usable. In our service lists we have a handful of technicians who, though they may be old, still retain some of their touch.

"We could probably beg enough food in the way of voluntary contributions to provision the trip. Perhaps we are just dreaming.

We may be at best only old men sitting in the sun and thinking thoughts much better carried out by young sinews. But I for one would like to try.

"Today I walked through the streets of this city and an illusion gripped me. Once more I was a young man returning from a colonization in the Capella system. The sidewalks were lined with people, the unbroken pavement glittered before me thick with roses. Young boys and girls darted in and out amongst the crowd adding their shrill cries. I knew how great, how strong, Earth was. And then, the illusion faded and the pavement was broken and the roses were thorny weeds, and an old woman whined for bread at the street corner. I saw but one child in half a hundred blocks of walking, and he was ill.

"An old man is old and has nothing but memory. It is youth which plans, endeavors and succeeds. Frankly, gentlemen, I have but little hope. But I cannot stay, while even a few years remain, and know that Mother Earth which I served for all my thousand years is dying here, forgotten and unmourned."

He sat looking at them a little while, puffing his pipe, swinging an ancient but well-polished boot, not seeing them but remembering.

Smit blustered to his feet. "We are speaking of dreams. I know very little of dreams but I demand to be told why our friend desires to beg for food? Are we still not the government? Must we dig in garbage cans to provision our government's expeditions and crawl in dung heaps for a few crumbs of combustium? The first right of any government is to enforce its will upon the people.

"I highly approve of the expedition. I demand that I be allowed to take one section of it. And I desire, if this matter be agreed upon, that all necessary writs and manifestos be placed in my hands to create it a reality."

Mankin looked nervous, took another tablet and washed it down. It had been three hundred years since an expedition of any major import had been planned in this chamber. All the major expeditions formed on Centauri now where food, fuel, and crews were plentiful. The bombastic tone of Smit had battered Mankin. He looked at Greto.

Greto was aware of the eyes upon him. He shifted his feet nervously. Hesitantly he said, "I approve of this expedition even though I have little hope of its success, for it will be very difficult to attend to the financing here. Our funds are in an impossible condition. Our currency is worthless. I take it that at least two units, perhaps four, will be sent. I myself would like the command of a unit. But how we are to finance the voyageurs is a problem I cannot readily solve. One Earth dollar can be valued no higher than one-thousandth of a cent on Capella. This means I must assemble millions." He rubbed his thumb against his forefinger. "They like money out there in those systems."

"Print it," said Smit. "Who'll know the difference? And if you are to command one of the units, then my advice is to print a lot of it."

Mankin coughed, he looked at the three of them and knew that it was he who must make the decision. A small flame of hope was leaping up in him now. He thrilled to the thought that Earth might once more prosper and send forth and receive commerce and trade. The strangely renewed vitality in Smit's voice gave him assurance.

"Gentlemen," he said, "you give me courage. Unless one of you has some objection to offer, I hereby decree that, if possible, three units be dispatched singly on this mission. They will progress as far as possible through the empires of space and the outer worlds and will return with whatever succor or tidings each has been able to obtain. This mission would be worthwhile even if you return with no more than a few hundred pounds of Element One Hundred and Seventy-Six. There must be some way, gentlemen, there *must* be some way."

Lars the Ranger stood up. "I shall order the preparation of three destroyer units and do what I can to provide them with fuel and food. If it is your will, I shall command one of them and place two at the disposition of Smit and Greto."

He about-faced and approached the door, where he turned. "I can hardly believe, gentlemen, that we have at last decided upon a course of vigorous action. Who knows but what we shall succeed?" The door of the Grand Council Chamber shut behind him.

Rumors spread far and wide across the planet and hope attended by many doubts turned people's eyes to the night skies where the stars blinked strong and young. A few broadcasting systems expended hoarded ergs of power to announce the departures of the expedition. Several old-time glass-paper editions of the newspapers in Greater Europa were given over exclusively to accounts of the various explorers. Smit was cited as the commander most likely to succeed, and his boasts at the spaceport before he took off were quoted as the purest truth.

A week after Smit's departure much space and talk was devoted to the fabulous Greto whose reputation as a financier had been founded fifteen hundred years ago with the Capella exploitation. They neglected the fact that it had been his further speculations which had impoverished him. They placed their hopes in his ability to "flimflam the money moguls of the greater empires."

When it came the time of Lars the Ranger to depart most of the news value of the expeditions was gone. Lars the Ranger had very little to say at the port. No one questioned the mechanics or remarked the fact that he had prudently taken weeks to groom his ship and to choose his crew. But old officers came and offered this one a map, that one a chart, and another a handful of bullets. And men who had ranged far and knew were on hand to bid him Godspeed and good luck amongst the spinning suns, the comets and dying stars. They toasted him in farewell and Lars the Ranger was gone.

Earth, only half remembering, waited and starved. Winter came. Frugal of their power, the expedition ships transmitted no messages. And Mankin, day after day moving thin-worn chessmen idly about on his board, bided his time.

GREG OPALINSKI

The plains and mountains lay red, the thin air moaned bitterly cold about the towers of the government building. Sand drifted across the char-marks on the rocket field. Then spring came, and summer came, and were gone again, and another winter lay coldly dusty upon Earth's breast.

And one bitter morning a battered and rusty *Mercy,* which had borne Greto, came to rest on the government field. The instant it was sighted each man thought of his rank and vied at the doors of the Council chambers to give welcome to Greto. But it was no smooth and wily treasurer who came up to the big black doors. Greto hobbled, tired and bent, his space clothing ragged and out of repair. He was worn by hunger and all the bitter hardship of space. He did not need to push through the crowd, his appearance alone was enough to compel it back.

The doors opened before him and he entered. Mankin was about to mount the dais in formality when he saw Greto.

He stopped. Tears of sympathy leaped into his eyes. He came forward, arms outstretched. "Oh, my friend, my old friend," and he quickly seated him in a chair and brought him wine.

"Where are your officers and crew?" said Mankin. Greto did not need to answer. His eyes remained steadily on the floor. He turned over one hand and let it drop.

"From hunger when we had no food, and from sickness for which we had no medicine. I am ashamed, Mankin. I am ashamed to be here."

Mankin sat on a small stool and folded his hands in his lap. "I am sure you did what you could, Greto. Nothing can tell you how sorry I am. Perhaps things do not go so well with them."

Greto shook with sudden anger. He lifted his worn, starved face. His eyes glared up through the ceiling and at the unseen stars.

"Things go well enough up there. They are fat, they are wealthy." He grasped Mankin's hand. "They hate us. They hate us for the rules and mandates we put upon them. They hate us for the taxes that once we levied. They hate us for the wars we fought to stop. They hate us for the centuries we depreciated their currency to uphold the value of our own. Pluteron in the Alpha Draco Empire laughed at me when I came. He laughed with hysteria and was still laughing when I left. There was no mirth in that laughter. There was only satisfaction. They hate us, Mankin. We shall get nothing from them, nothing!

"Cythara of Betelgeuse took a collection amongst the officers of his court to put a wreath in orbit about our sun after we were gone. I have been driven by laughter, by scorn."

He sat for a little while, chin on his breast. "Help me to my house, Mankin. I am afraid I have not long to live."

But it was Smit's return which spread the blackness of gloom across the world. For Smit was neither starved nor weary. Hate stood like a black aura around him through which cracked the lightning of his voice. Feet planted wide apart, he stood in the spaceport. He met all who came to him with such a tirade concerning the ungratefulness of the children in space that the world was shocked into hopeless rage.

He had gone the length of space, stopping everywhere he deemed it expedient. Everywhere he went he had met violence and suspicion. He had crossed the trail of Greto several times. He spoke of the Greto Plan to stabilize the currency of all space, with Earth as the central banking house, and the brutality with which the scheme, quite feasible, had been everywhere rejected. He told how Greto had sought to borrow a sufficient amount to rehabilitate Earth, and the outrageous interest that had been promised and how the governments which Greto had approached had fought Smit with the plan on his arrival.

But this was not the seat of bitterness with Smit. He told them of space fleets equipped with weapons more deadly than those that Earth had ever known. One governor had given him a slingshot and had ordered him to fight a soldier equipped with a magnetic snare. And Smit had spent two weeks in a foul prison for driving in the governor's teeth.

He had been refused food, fuel, water, and medical attention for his men. He had been scorned and spat upon and mobbed from Centauri to Unuk. He had been insulted, rejected, scorned and given messages of such insulting import for Earth that here, delivering them, he seemed about to burst apart with rage.

The story of his return journey was one of violence. He had brought back his men but in the progress of returning need of fuel had forced him to loot the government arsenal at Kalrak. He had left the city burning behind him. Smit preached war, he preached it to old men, to rusted and broken machines, to tumbled and moss-grown walls.

Mankin opened the government radio for him and for four days Smit vainly attempted to recruit technicians and scientists to reconstruct the weapons that would be necessary to fight. Immediately after a broadcast in which he had attempted to stir up interest in an ancient and long-unused idea of germ warfare, an old officer of the republic's fleet barred his way as he attempted to leave the broadcasting building.

Smit, still affecting the dress he had worn on his return, filthy and ragged and seared as it might be, was offended at the clean, well-mended gray uniform.

"If you would help me, what are you doing here?" said Smit. "I have ordered all men to repair to the military arsenal if they wish to forward this campaign."

The old officer smiled, undaunted by the blunt rage of Smit. "General," he said, "I have no ideas and I doubt that you would listen to any from me, but I was at the arsenal this morning and I do not think that we could do anything without fuel, weapons or the materials with which to make them. But I do not come here to advise you to abandon your idea. It will fail of its own accord. I came to ask you news of Lars the Ranger. Certainly if you found Greto's track, you must have news of Lars."

Mankin and several others were coming up the steps and Smit grasped at them as an audience.

"Yes, I have news of Lars. He had been in three places before I had arrived; he had said nothing, he had done nothing."

The old officer looked incredulous. "General, I am not of

your branch of service and I would not argue with you, but I believe you play carelessly with the reputation of one who, if he commanded it could have audience wherever he went."

Smit was stunned. "Yes, certainly, audiences he did have. But he was given nothing. This I know."

Mankin was interested. "Did you learn nothing of him?" he asked Smit.

"All I know is that when I received audience after him I was heard coldly. My requests were refused, my demands were laughed at, and I was personally insulted. I know but little of this, but I can tell you this certainly, that you can expect nothing of Lars the Ranger."

The old officer turned away and, as he went down the steps, was seen to be laughing to himself.

For more than two months the campaign of Smit's raged feebly across the worn, arid surface of Earth. Where he had recruited, no army stood; where he had built, only junk could be seen. The waning efforts of technicians and bacteriologists finally stopped. Earth fell once more into an apathy, and at night men no longer looked hopefully at the stars.

In the first days of spring a mutter of reports came from the spaceport, and people wandered toward it in surprise to find a destroyer there, polished hull carefully repaired and a crew "at quarters" while the commander disembarked. An officer rushed from the crowd and grasped the hand of the voyager.

"Lars," he cried. And at the shout, several men in the crowd ran across the field to form a group around the newcomer. But the greatest number turned away. Two expeditions had arrived and the dream was spent, the hope was gone.

"What news?" said the old officer. Lars shrugged tiredly, he had aged on his voyage. "Little enough, my friend. They are vastly busy with their own concerns out there, but here I have brought at least some packets of food." And the quartermaster behind him signaled that the presents be brought down. When they were distributed, Lars walked toward the city.

Mankin heard of his arrival but did not go forth to meet him, for two disappointments were all that he could possibly bear. He had been sitting in the chill of the Council room when he received the tidings from his clerk. He just nodded hopelessly.

Lars entered the chamber and stood for a little while, feeling the coldness of it, looking at the withered Mankin in his chair. Lars came forward and put his helmet down upon the table.

Mankin spoke, "You have been gone for a long while, Lars."

"What of Greto and Smit?"

"They have both returned. Greto, I am afraid, is dying. He is sick rather with insults than with disease. Smit for some time was a man deprived of reason and he wanders now about the countryside speaking to no one, eating only what is thrust into his hand. He is a beaten man, Lars. This expedition was ill-starred. It would have been better that we had died at least with our dignity rather than to beg for crusts and make fools laugh. As the iron has eaten our air, so has this expedition drained the last sparks of vitality from the two who went before you. It was ill-starred, Lars."

Lars was about to speak, but Mankin again held up his hand.

"No, do not tell me. You have brought back your men, you have brought back your ship. Perhaps you have begged a little fuel, perhaps you have a little food. But you have nothing with which to save Earth. This I know."

Lars shook his head slowly. "You are right, Mankin. I have brought nothing. I did not expect to receive anything, since I did not beg. I did not threaten. In some places I heard of Greto's schemes. They hated him because they hated the financial control which Earth in her power exercised over the outer empires. In all the immensity of space there is not a man who would give a plugged mean coin to save a single child on Earth, if it meant the restoring of the financial tyranny which once we exercised."

"I know this," said Mankin sadly. "We hoped for too much."

Lars again shook his head. "No, Mankin, we were greedy for too much. Perhaps I have failed, perhaps I have not failed. I do not know."

"What did you tell them?" asked Mankin, not wanting hope

137

to rise in his heart. "What did you tell them that you dare believe they might help us?"

"I did not tell them very much. And I thought first of how I might gain their goodwill. I found immediately that it could not be purchased or begged. I am afraid, Mankin, that I have amused myself at your expense."

This shocked the ancient president. He leaped to his feet. "You had better explain that, Lars!"

"I dined with them," said Lars. "I looked at their fleets, I admired their dancing girls, I saw their crops, and had the old battle places pointed out to me. And I told them stories. And this, reminding them, stimulated many tales. I asked for nothing, Mankin. I did not expect anything. I hope for nothing now. I am sorry that this is the report I must render."

"You had better go," said Mankin quietly.

For a month Lars, nearly ostracized, lived at the Navy yard in the improved destroyer, receiving old shipmates, giving presents from his frugal stock but going unaddressed in the streets. He heard nothing but condemnation for "the man who did not even try."

And then, one morning the town was shaken by a terrible roar and with certainty that vengeance had been their return for the expedition, the populace tumbled from their beds to find six great gleaming spheres on the spaceport landing. They were larger than any other space vehicle these people on Earth had ever seen. From them came tumbling young men, well fed and laughing. Then they began to unload equipment.

No one dared to address the newcomers. With a hysterical certainty that they were about to be enslaved, the people of the capital, taking what little food they had, began to stream out of the far gate. A radio message from Asia was broadcast to the effect that fourteen huge vessels, unidentified, were landing troops. Greater Europa reported being besieged but said that no overt act had been made and all was being done to evacuate the population before bombardment.

Mankin received the reports in terror on his dais. He called together his cabinet. Noteworthily omitting Lars, he spent some fruitless six hours in feeble and frightened debate on measures of defense. No one came to him from the enemy forces and he felt, at last, that he must surrender before lives were lost.

When he and his staff went forward from the palace, they found that nineteen new vessels lay in the plain beyond the city. And that an encampment was being hastily constructed.

He was met by four boisterous young officers, each one from a different empire, all in working dress. The first of them, caught by the dignity of the cabinet and the president, and recognizing them as people of authority, quickly turned to his friends and sent one of them racing back toward a nearby sphere.

Mankin took a grip on his courage, he had never looked for the day when he would have to surrender Earth to an attacking force. But now that he saw that it could not be helped, he could only try to carry it forth with dignity.

He was somewhat amazed at the courteous mien of the young officers, who did not speak to him but respectfully waited for a sign from the large spaceship.

In a moment or two, hastily pulling on a uniform coat and adjusting his epaulettes, a large middle-aged man strode toward the group. He stopped at a distance of five paces from Mankin, identified the chest ribbon and the ancient robe of office and then spoke.

"You are President Mankin?" he said politely.

Mankin stiffened himself and answered. "Yes. Whom have I the pleasure of addressing?"

"I am General Collingsby," he said. With a crisp military bow, he extended his hand. "It is an honor to meet you, sir," said Collingsby, "I am sorry I occasioned you the difficulty of having to come to the port. I am ashamed at my own discourtesy in not having called on you immediately. However, command has its responsibilities and, as these are supply forces, there has been considerable trouble in establishing consignments and in distributing our various fleets over the surface of the earth."

He coughed. "Excuse me, sir, but by Jupiter, your air is certainly thin here! My blood pressure must be up off the meter.

But here, permit me to invite you into my cabin where it is more comfortable, and we can talk at leisure."

Mankin straightened his shoulders. "Sir, I thank you for your courtesy. I can only say that I hope that you will observe the various usages of war and that you will treat your prisoners without inhumanity and that you will occasion as little suffering as possible."

General Collingsby looked startled and then embarrassed. It was easily read upon his face that he had no clue to the meaning of Mankin's statements.

"My dear sir," he stammered, "I do not understand you. Has not my own governor, Voxperius, contacted you concerning our arrival?"

"General," said Mankin, "the ionized beams of communication between Earth and her former colonies have been severed for more than seventy years. I am afraid we have not had sufficient power or even need to continue them in operation."

Collingsby looked at his staff in round-eyed wonder and then at Mankin. He looked beyond the group before him and his face lighted. "Perhaps this gentleman can clarify matters."

Mankin turned to see Lars the Ranger, with a small group of officers, approaching.

Collingsby eagerly grabbed Lars by the arm. "My dear fellow, would you please acquaint your president with the true complexion of affairs. By Jupiter, I had not thought of it before but it certainly does look like an invasion. Oh, I am ashamed of this, Lars! I am ashamed of it! What a panic we must have caused. But I was certain that my government and the other governments had contacted Earth. Didn't you know, Lars?"

Mankin was bewildered. For the first time he had a clear look at what was poured into the encampment. He saw huge machines being unloaded. He saw that they were already at work with some of them. Beams were playing across the plains and at each place one struck, puffs of smoke rose. Others were drilling into the earth and sending up high plumes of exhaust. Mankin suddenly realized that they must be reoxygenators replacing humus, injecting heat under the crust. A faintness came over him. He could not believe what he saw and he could not hope.

Lars turned to him. "I could not tell you, I could not promise you. But truly, I did nothing."

Collingsby interrupted with a sharp, "No, he did nothing. He came and sang us old ballads and told us the hero tales of Earth; he reminded us of the heritage we had behind us; and of what we owed the mother planet. She was drained of her blood for our sakes. He made us see the quiet ocean and the green hills where our fathers lived. And then, having shrugged and said it was no more, he moved on.

"He went all through space and told his tales. In the empires everywhere school children formed subscriptions, governments formed expeditions, scientists worked, on what had to be done—but here, certainly, President Mankin, you can see how this would be. After all, Earth is the 'Mother' of all the stars. And somewhere in the heart of every man in the empires lurks a fondness for the birthplace of his race. For our histories are full of Earth and all our stories, all our great triumphs, contain the name of Earth. Should we then let her die?

"And so we have come here, these combined forces, to make the old land green again, to replace the oceans, to rebuild an atmosphere, to make the rivers run, to put fish in the streams, and game in the hills.

"We'll make this place a shrine, complete and vital as once it was, where Inter-Empire councils may arbitrate the disputes of space. Here we can meet on the common ground of birth and, in the halo of her greatness, find the answers to our problems. For in the long run the problems and the answers change very little. All the fundamental questions have been asked and solved on Earth before; and they will be again.

"But come," said Collingsby. "We have less than a week to repair all. It is," he asked Lars, "just a week to July fourth, is it not? And that was the anniversary of the launching of the first expedition to Earth's moon, wasn't it?"

"But come into my ship where we can have some refreshments.

There will be time enough to stand around in the sun when all these fields are green."

They looked at Lars and he smiled at them. Mankin swallowed back a lump of emotion in his throat.

"Lars, why didn't you tell me you had saved Earth with a song?"

A Revolutionary's Guide to Practical Conjuration

written by

Auston Habershaw

illustrated by

SHUANGJIAN LIU

ABOUT THE AUTHOR

Auston Habershaw has always wanted to tell stories, and so he always has, for as long as he can remember speaking. The only question was what kind of stories he ought to tell, and that was settled by fate: on the day he was born, Skylab fell from orbit. It was pretty much destiny that he found himself writing science fiction and fantasy.

In his quest to be a professional writer, Auston has worked as a lifeguard, swim teacher, dog walker, video game tester, slum lord minion, office temp, theme park performer (he dressed like a pirate), coffee barista, waiter, SAT tutor, and pedicab driver until eventually settling on English professor. Now he teaches at Massachusetts College of Pharmacy and Health Sciences.

Auston has published stories in Analog, Stupefying Stories, Sword and Laser Anthology, *and other places, too. His debut fantasy novel,* The Iron Ring, *was released on February 10, 2015 by Harper Voyager Impulse. Its two sequels will be following along shortly. You can stalk him on his blog if you are thusly inclined. It's okay—he likes attention.*

Auston lives, writes, and works in Boston with his wife and two children.

ABOUT THE ILLUSTRATOR

Shuangjian Liu was born in 1992 and raised in Guangzhou, China.

At eighteen, he moved to California and started college. He loved playing video games, so he played them a lot, and as he did, he gained an appreciation for the wonderful computer graphic illustrations in them.

So, when he went to college, he started to teach himself how to draw digital art, and got his first freelance drawing job while in school.

He's always excited while drawing because as time passes, he gets to see the picture grow more and more vivid. He enjoys creating new art from abstract ideas. Even though he has been working and studying toward this career for many years, Shuangjian still loves it and hopes to create his own video game.

A Revolutionary's Guide
to Practical Conjuration

The man with the crystal eye could peel the skin off a camel with his glare, and Abe struggled to meet it. He couldn't determine which eye to look at. The crystal one was alien, yes—it glowed with a sort of half-light, as though a candle flickered somewhere in its glassy depths—but for all that it was inanimate. Looking at it felt like gazing at a lantern, and the idea that it peered back was unsettling. The other eye—the man's human eye—was dark and sharp, like a bird's, and it didn't blink as it darted up and down Abe's body. It wasn't an improvement over the crystal eye at all. Abe tried to hold still.

"You are not a practitioner of the High Arts," the man announced finally. He took up the mouthpiece to a water pipe and took several introspective puffs.

Abe glanced over his shoulder reflexively. Nobody in the tooka-den seemed to have noticed the man's comment. It was late, and the evening shadows were deepened by the sweet, heady smoke that bunched around the ceiling lamps. The other patrons, scattered about on deep pillows and separated by muslin curtains, were too deep into their own smoking to even look up.

"Relax, boy. I would not have chosen this place if it were dangerous."

"How do I know I can trust you?" Abe asked, hands balled into fists.

The man laughed, his bird eye never wavering from Abe. "You do not. You cannot know; this is life. Please sit...or run. Whatever you do, stop acting like a spooked rabbit."

The man motioned to a chartreuse cushion across from him, and Abe sat. The cushion practically swallowed his bony frame, pulling his feet off the floor. A sickly sweet perfume—a mixture of tooka smoke and stale sweat—puffed up around him. Abe gagged.

The man with the crystal eye nodded. "Much better. Now for introductions: I am Carlo diCarlo, and you are?"

Abe tried to prop himself upright in the huge cushion, but couldn't quite manage. "I'd rather not tell you my name."

Carlo sighed. "Obviously not, but you *could* make one up. I just did, after all."

"You did?"

"You didn't seriously think my name was Carlo diCarlo, did you? Come now, I need something to call you besides 'boy.' Spit it out."

Abe spat the first thing that came to mind. "Oz—call me Oz."

Carlo nodded. "So far, so good. Now, Oz, would you like any refreshment? They don't serve drinks here, but perhaps some food? Tooka? Ink?"

Abe pulled himself to the edge of the cushion. "I'm no ink-thrall." He growled.

Carlo puffed his pipe and shrugged. "You didn't have the look, but you never can tell. It's only polite to ask."

"Do you have what I need?" Abe said, putting a hand on his purse.

Carlo shook his head and closed his real eye. The crystal one glowed more brightly. "You aren't accustomed to having illegal dealings with black marketeers, are you? Never mind—a silly question—of course, you don't. When I received your message, I assumed you were some Undercity alley wizard looking for an edge, or perhaps an alchemist or thaumaturge looking to expand his business down semi-legal avenues, but I see now that you're just an angry young man with an axe to grind."

Abe frowned, trying to fashion his stare into something icy. "You don't know the first thing about me."

Carlo tapped his crystal eye. "I see a lot more than you realize, Oz. Now, to answer your question: yes, I have what you need. To answer your second question: you cannot afford it."

Abe tossed his purse on the carpet before Carlo's feet. It clanked loudly. "There's 50 marks in silver crowns. I can get more."

Carlo sighed. "What exactly do you think this peculiar eye of mine *does,* anyway? I *know* how much silver you have in that purse—I counted it when you came in. I am telling you that you don't have enough and that I find it unlikely that any additional amount of money you can secure will be sufficient. You're out of luck, boy—go home. Honestly, I'm doing you a favor."

Abe felt his face flush. "I *need* that book, Carlo. I'll pay anything."

"Go home, Oz. Get a job, if you can. I recommend thievery—you appear to be good at it, judging from that robe you are wearing that you clearly couldn't afford, and all those coins which are *not* the product of your diligent scrimping. Forget you ever came here and live a much longer, happier life."

"You don't understand! My life...*all* our lives are..." Abe stopped and took a deep breath. "I will pay anything—*anything,* understand? I need that book."

Carlo puffed his pipe for a few moments and began to blow smoke sculptures. Birds and serpents swirled out of his mouth and danced with each other in arabesque patterns until they vanished into the cloudy ceiling. It was a simple glamour, nothing more. He supposed Carlo was doing it to prove something, but he didn't know what. The black marketeer, for his part, simply watched the creatures unfold from his lips in some kind of tooka-induced trance before finally speaking. "Very well, boy, I will make you a deal."

"What kind of deal?"

"One you will have to accept, of course. It goes like this: I give you the book, but under a particular condition. In ten days I will find you and, at that time, you will give me two thousand marks in gold."

Abe stiffened. "That's impossible! I could never—"

Carlo held up his hand. "You will have the book, remember? Don't think I am unaware what you wish to do with it; two thousand marks seems a reasonable sum. Now, if you do *not*

147

have the money in ten days, I will reclaim the book and go on my way. This is the deal."

"What makes you think you'll be able to get the book back from me?"

Carlo shrugged. "I strongly believe that you will be dead in ten days, so it should be a relatively simple matter. Do we have a deal?"

"I have a counteroffer."

"Not interested. This is the deal, take it or leave it."

"But—"

Carlo's face narrowed into a glare. "If you are as desperate and angry as you appear, you know as well as I do that you are going to say yes, so stop wasting my time, please. I am running out of patience."

Abe sighed. "Deal."

Carlo pointed at the floor. "Spit."

Abe spat.

The black marketer spat as well, then sighed. "There—was that so hard?"

"The book, Carlo."

Carlo diCarlo shook his head, muttering about Illini manners, and produced a large, leather-bound book wrapped in string from a belt pouch obviously too small to contain it without sorcerous interference. He extended it towards Abe and Abe snatched it. It was heavy and smelled like mildew and stale air.

Abe fiddled with the knots holding the string around it until Carlo slapped his hand away. "Fool, boy! Don't open that here! Do you want the mirror men on us? Go, go—begone! Back to the wretched Undercity with you, understand?"

Abe nodded. "Thank you."

Carlo snorted. "Don't thank me, Oz. I've just killed you."

"See you in ten days." Abe shot back. Taking the rejected bag of silver and tucking the book under one arm, he walked into the smoky recesses of the tooka den. When he glanced back, he saw no sign that anyone had been there, let alone anyone named Carlo diCarlo.

The strangest thing to Abe about Illin's Upper City was the street lamps. They were ten feet tall and made of iron, their heads glowing with sun-bright crystals the size of large melons. Even now, in the dead of night, they cast sufficient light on the broad, white streets that Abe could read the numbers on the houses from twenty paces away. One of those crystals would fetch enough money to buy a large house in Abe's neighborhood, yet none of them had been stolen or damaged. Abe found himself glaring at them as he made his way to the public lift terminal. "Lousy toppers."

As Abe got close to the edge of the Upper City, the houses and businesses gave way to defensive structures—minarets and parapets, trapezoidal barracks, and huge, black war-orbs hovering over pyramidal control loci. A patrol of ten mirror men, their mageglass armor gleaming beneath sunny streetlights, marched toward Abe in perfect formation, their firepikes bobbing and flickering as they reflected their bearer's even gait.

Clutching the book tightly to his chest, Abe looked at his feet as he shuffled to one side, letting them pass. He felt as if he were glowing somehow—as though their foreign faces were studying him as they passed. He tried to keep his breathing even, but his heart wouldn't cooperate. It pounded like a war drum, announcing to every part of his body that it could all end here. The mirror men just needed to ask "Say, what's a scrawny teen doing out alone at this time of night?" He'd be whisked into one of those trapezoid barracks in an instant; no one would ever see him again.

The men didn't stop, though—just marched past. They were just common soldiers, their sergeant more interested in keeping security than recovering contraband.

Heart still racing, Abe made it to the terminal—a small, colonnaded dome perched on the very edge of the Upper City, overlooking the Undercity beneath and the ocean beyond. A few mirror men gave him a cursory glance before letting him aboard the night lift. The basket, made of wicker, was large enough to carry perhaps four people—much smaller than the daytime gondolas that could haul dozens of people and livestock. Abe tipped the lift man at his winch for a speedy descent, then said goodbye to the white paved streets and well-lit avenues of the toppers' domain.

The basket plummeted from the edge of the terminal, causing Abe's stomach to flutter. His tip had been appreciated.

Almost immediately the darkness that blanketed the rest of Illin for most hours of the day swallowed the light of the Upper City. The Undercity was named so literally: it rested directly beneath the Upper City on a flat pan of dry ground in the midst of an endless maze of marshy reeds and slow-flowing estuaries that brought trade and disease from the troubled regions to the south. Though it was twice as large as the Upper City and was home to four times as many people, the Undercity was dark and seemingly deserted. Abe could see only a few fires from his basket—bonfires lit by gangs or religious fanatics or worse, all of whom used the night to gather numbers and strength.

The public lift terminal at the bottom was the vandalized, scorched mirror-image of its wealthier sibling. A group of cheap sellswords in worn black leather and rusty studs were employed to stand guard here, but really spent most of their time dicing and boasting in the guttering candlelight. They didn't even look up as Abe's basket landed, which was good. He didn't have any money to bribe them.

"Did you get it?" Krim's bony frame separated from a shadow and she fell into step beside Abe. She lit a candle with a match. "Let me see!"

"Not here." Abe hissed. "I'll open it at home."

Krim cuffed him. "Dummy! How'd you know you weren't cheated if you didn't open it, eh? You lost our money for nothing, betcha!"

"I've got it, don't worry—see?" Abe held the book up to the candlelight. It looked older and blacker than it had in the tooka den. Though without design or device, something about the cover made his skin crawl.

It seemed to have the same effect on Krim. In the dim light, Abe saw her dark eyes widen. She stepped back and made the sign of Hann on her heart. "I'll tell the others."

"Don't tell them yet. I still don't know if I can use it."

Krim scowled. "Don't give me that! You can read, can't you? Isn't that all it takes for books? Monda will bust your ankles if he gave up his purse for nothing."

"You don't understand—these things are very compli— "

Krim slapped Abe across the face. "No, *you* don't understand, Abrahan Anastasis! We're counting on you, and you don't get to let us down, right? You read the book, you work the spells, and we change the world—that's the deal."

Abe nodded. "I know, I know. I'm sorry, Krim."

"Should be. The topper take all fifty?"

"Uh..."

Krim cocked her head. "What's it?"

Krim was lighter than Abe, but he had no doubts about the danger she posed. He'd seen her cut a throat for a sovereign. "Yeah, he took all fifty."

"Somethin' else?" Krim's weight shifted to the balls of her feet. Abe saw a hand dart inside her tunic.

Abe shook his head. "No, just the fifty."

Krim waited, as though sniffing for a lie, and then relaxed. "Fine. Take the book back to your Mama and read or whatever. I'll call for you tomorrow, take you to see everybody and report, right?"

"Sure."

Krim vanished into the shadows like a rat darting into a bolt hole. The hairs on Abe's neck didn't relax. She was probably still watching him. The rumor was that Krim walked around with a shard of mageglass in her tunic wrapped in leather, sharp enough to cut right through bone. Cut a man's head open like a barrel-top once, or so Monda said. The image of her with blood on her face, her dark eyes grinning at Abe, kept him up at nights sometimes.

Still, without her and Monda and the rest, he would never have gotten the money and the book. And the book was the key.

In the pitch-black night, the Undercity changed from a confusing tangle of dead ends, alleys, and crumbled ruins into a deadly labyrinth. Abe's mother talked about how the streets had been clean and lit in the old days, before the war, but when the Kalsaaris had invaded they hadn't been gentle. The sewers were now filled with imps and lesser demons, the descendants of various weapons of war utilized by both sides during the Kalsaari occupation and subsequent Allied liberation of the city. Parasitic gremlins swarmed through most buildings, eating supports and ruining attempts to rebuild, while more dangerous things—unexploded brymmstones, trapped war-fiends, and worse—lay beneath every pile of rubble. All this, of course, didn't even include the dangers posed by the desperate survivors—people like Krim, lurking in the dark with a sharp knife and a keen ear for jingling coins.

Tracing a long-memorized route through the rubble in the dark, Abe arrived home. On the front steps, the candles in the small Hannite shrine burned low. Sighing, Abe bowed to it and slipped past to unlock the door and go in.

Before the war, the Anastasis home had been a three-story townhouse squeezed between a bakery and a church. Today the bakery was abandoned, playing home to a rotating cast of squatters and vermin; the church was merely rubble, destroyed by a brymmstone during the initial Kalsaari bombardment. The home itself was now only one-story tall, the top having burned when the church was destroyed, and the second story was half collapsed. Abe and his mother used the old sitting room as a makeshift bedroom, had access to the kitchen and the front hall, and stayed out of his father's old office, just in case the ceiling finally collapsed beneath the weight of the rubble upstairs.

Abe took the book into his father's office. The risk was there, true, but he trusted that if the ceiling hadn't collapsed in five years, it wouldn't likely collapse tonight. Also, there was no other place the book could feasibly avoid his mother's notice. On a cursory glance, if she found it here, she would likely conclude it was just one of his father's old ledgers or law books and leave it be—that, or command Abe to sell it, which put it safely back in his own hands. His mother couldn't sell his father's books without weeping.

Abe lit the only oil lamp his family had left and sat behind his father's hulking desk. Even atop its broad, bare expanse, the book looked menacing—a kind of curse made thick and dark and physical, like a clot of congealed blood. Licking his lips, Abe untied the strings and pulled back the cover.

The book sprang open and flipped itself to a random page, somewhere in the middle. Every available space on the yellowed pages was filled with a cramped, meticulous handwriting in deep maroon ink. Abe tried to turn back to the beginning, but every time he flipped a page, the page flipped back. Finally, growing frustrated at the enchantment (was this some kind of security feature? Perhaps...) he settled down to read.

If you are reading this, stop! You are unqualified to use this book, and any attempt to utilize its lore will inevitably end in serious injury, death, or worse. Return this volume at once to its place of origin.

Abe blinked—what a peculiar thing to say in the middle of a book. He pressed on.

Since you are still reading, the text said, *it is evident the above warning was insufficient to dissuade you from your self-destructive course. You are to be simultaneously scolded for your recklessness and commended on your bravery. Consider yourself both as of this moment.*

Abe grinned. A book with a sense of humor was not what he had expected. He skimmed the next paragraph but found the handwriting difficult to read without focusing, so had to go back to the beginning again.

If you expect to be able to skip ahead or skim your way to an understanding of the art of conjuration in a short time, it is evident that you are a fool and that, again, it must be stressed that your death is almost guaranteed. You are advised for a second and final time to close this book and get rid of it.

Abe sat back, eyes narrowing, and read the paragraph again. Was it... could a book be *aware* of him? Was that possible? "Are you alive?" he asked aloud, and then kept reading.

As has been implied, this book is an instructional manual designed to assist the experienced practitioners of the High Arts to gain facility in the art of conjuration in a relatively short period of time. As you are inexperienced

*in all magecraft, however, it would be advisable for instruction to begin at
the essential basics of magical instruction, since without these it is unlikely
you will be able to conjure anything at all except, perhaps, a splitting
headache. Tonight will involve an overview of what "magic" is, exactly,
since that is both the most important topic to understand and the only topic
simple enough to outline before your mother wakes up.*

Abe's finger shot back from the line he was reading, his eyes
wide. He slammed the book closed. "What the...what the hell?"

The house creaked above as his mother's bare feet touched the
floor in the one usable room upstairs. Her reedy voice trickled
through the dark. "Abe, dear, is that you?

Abe backed away from the book, staring at it as though it
might leap off the desk. He remembered what the old smuggler
had said: *"Don't thank me, Oz. I've just killed you."*

Gods, he thought, *was he right?*

Abe's mother insisted on fixing him something to eat, despite
how late it was and the paucity of their stores. She wiped the
very last vestiges of some sour grape jam from an old, crusty jar
and scraped them over stale crackers. Once she had laid it before
her son, she blew out the candle. They sat together in the dark.
Abe didn't eat.

"No sense wasting the food." His mother said. There was no
fight in her voice, though, no sense of warning or caution or
even admonishment. She said things by rote these days, Abe
knew. What was the difference if they wasted food, anyway?
They were going to starve sooner or later.

"I'm sorry I'm so late. I was busy." Abe said, picking up a
cracker and dipping it in a warm cup of water to soften it a bit.

"Did you earn any money?" she squeaked.

Abe wanted to tell her about the fifty silver coins still under
his stolen robe, but he didn't. That money couldn't be spent
without Krim and Monda finding out, and that would mean a
grisly death for both of them. Besides, if he dropped it on the
table, his mother would know he'd fallen in with thieves. That
would be the end of her, he guessed.

She waited for an answer, so he cleared his throat. "No...nothing today. No ships new in town, so nobody needed a copyist."

"Mmmm..." Abe's mother *tsked* between her teeth. "Forgetting all about us, they are. They used to clog the harbor, you know. Your father wrote the contracts to a hundred different ships every year; he wore a gold chain about his neck, and when he walked down the street..."

Abe could recite what followed by heart. His mother, conjuring images of a past so far gone he wasn't really sure it had ever existed. How every house had a sunstone they'd set out to soak during the brief daylight and then use it all the night to light their streets. A city of light and life and happiness—all that drivel. She blamed the Kalsaaris, of course, and Illin's western allies who were so quick to row back home once the city was "liberated," and the mirror men—the "Defenders of the Balance"—who had been left behind to clean up the mess. She didn't speak a word about the toppers, though, or the Prince and his Black Guard, or the thousand thieves and thugs and sellswords who prowled the Undercity, leeching off the dying corpse of Illin.

He used to argue with her, tell her they should do something about it, how they could work together to fix the city. How someday he could learn sorcery at the foot of a great mage and fix the broken streets of the Undercity with a wave of his hand. The arguments used to carry on for hours, his mother's voice growing steadily weaker in the face of Abe's anger. He didn't bother yelling anymore, though. Now all he did was listen.

When, at last, she'd gone to bed, Abe crept back into the ruined office and opened the book. It picked up right where it had left off.

Magic, as you probably are unaware, is governed by five elemental forces. In ancient times, people misinterpreted these forces and associated them with the so-called "elements"—Fire, Water, Air, and Earth—and had no idea of the existence of a fifth. These people were primitives and superstitious fools, and you should take care not to follow their example. Magic is far more complicated than that.

The five energies are the Lumen and the Ether, the Dweomer and the Fey, and the Astral ...

Abe yawned. When were they going to get to something practical? He kept on.

If you are growing tired, perhaps you ought to take a rest and come back another time. The study of magic is extremely taxing, both physically and mentally, and it would be a waste of your effort to attempt to master it while fatigued.

Abe sat up straighter. "You...you *are* alive. You can see me!"

Every use of these energies, known colloquially as "magic" or "sorcery," but more accurately as the High Arts (as distinguished from the Low Arts), involves the use of three elements.

"No!" Abe hissed into the pages, taking care not to make so much noise as to wake his mother. "I want to talk with you, book! I want you to explain some things to me."

The first of these elements is the energy to be drawn from the world surrounding you, known as the "ley." The second element is the incantation by which the energy is drawn, known occasionally as the spell or ritual. The third of these elements is the focus, or the physical entity through which the energy is to be channeled by the incantation. In the case of a spell, this is the sorcerer him or herself; in the case of the ritual, it is through the object used to channel the power. (1)

Abe frowned, and referred to the footnote. It read: *1) Pay attention, you insufferable little ragamuffin. This book is not in your possession to chit-chat, but rather to instruct you as a master teacher might a dull-witted pupil. You aren't even taking notes, so the likelihood that lessons will have to be repeated grows with each passing instant, and this narrative thread is already boring beyond description.*

Sitting back, Abe scowled. "Maybe I won't read you, then. How about that?"

Glancing back at the page, the book had not responded. It continued to drone on and on about magical energies, incantational postures, and channeling techniques. He read it as long as he could keep his eyes open, then dragged himself upstairs to sleep on the threadbare pallet beside his mother. He dreamed of Carlo's crystal eye, following him through the tangled ruins of the Undercity, the book clutched in his bloodstained hands.

The next morning, Abe woke late. The thinnest rays of sunshine were still slipping past the rim of the Upper City, casting just enough light through the gaping holes in the roof that Abe could see that his mother was awake. He guessed that he would find her out front, praying to the shrine while the light still held. It was a common practice among the widows of Illin, especially since the Kalsaaris had burned most of the churches during the occupation and the toppers had yet to secure funds to repair them. Abe's own mother refused to walk the mile to the nearest functional church, claiming that the women there lived too close to the docks to be of "clean reputation."

When Abe stumbled downstairs, however, he didn't find his mother out front praying, but rather sitting in his father's office, the big black book of magic open across her knees. "Mother! What are you doing?"

She shrugged her bony shoulders. "Just looking through some of your father's old books. You know, I never knew he had a cookbook before."

Abe felt as if his mouth were unable to form words. "Cook... book?"

She shrugged weakly. "Funny, really, that I should find it now that we haven't any food. Well, I'm off to the market. They say some mirror men will be passing out bolts of cloth later and the moths have been at the quilt again. Winter is never too far away, you know."

Abe watched her leave, wordless. When the door closed, he tore open the spell book.

It is strongly advised that this book not fall into the hands of individuals even less talented than yourself, as their piggish, ignorant eyes are harmful to this book's contents.

"That's my mother you're talking about," Abe growled.

The exact nature or relationship of the stupendous ignorami permitted to flap about these pages is immaterial to the original warning. This advice ought to be heeded, as the consequences are apt to be most dire.

"Now you're threatening me? Well, what if I toss you in a fire, huh? What about that?"

Furthermore, it is strongly suggested that no vandalism be done to this book, as its contents are too valuable to you, the reader, as well as to the world in general. However, given the vagaries of human free will, no action can or will be taken to prevent the destruction of this volume should it be deemed essential by the owner.

"Let's just say I won't find it essential if you leave off insulting my mother—how about that?"

Apparently satisfied, the book broke into more tedious magical instruction. *To continue with our lessons from the previous chapter, let us begin by explaining the nature of conjuration itself.*

Abe spent the rest of the day reading, huddled by the lantern, trying to glean some practical knowledge of how to conjure what he would need to in order to impress Mondo and Krim and the rest of the band. All he got was general information—history, basic theory, simple exercises and drills, but not a word about a single spell. He couldn't even conjure an ounce of gold or a thimble of water—he didn't even know where to begin. He couldn't skip ahead, he couldn't skim to find the good parts; he was a slave to the book's slow, methodical prose.

He had only ten days to get Carlo his money? It was impossible. He didn't know the first thing about what he was doing, and the damned book was no help. What could he do? What would he say to the gang?

Finally, during the brief period of light as the sun passed from its hiding place behind the Upper City to its hiding place behind the edge of the world, Abe came across something potentially useful. The book was talking about the uses of advanced conjuration, and it finished with a discussion of what it termed "pure beings."

Pure beings, or "Spirits," as they are sometimes known, are creatures of a particular pure energy type that, so far as arcane theory is concerned, exist in planes of origin parallel to our own where only one pure energy is in abundance. These beings have a myriad of applications, the most obvious being the war fiends conjured to assault enemy positions. Those specific entities are pure fey energy and, as such, are well suited to the vagaries of war and destruction (though they are disinclined to take orders). Accordingly, a wide variety of daemons and djinns, angels and fiends are used by sorcerers to accomplish tasks that would, otherwise, have to be executed by human beings. These spirits sometimes manifest themselves in obvious ways, but can also be found trapped within mundane objects.

Abe blinked at the words, and then read them a second time. "You mean...like in books? Are you saying that *you* are some kind of spirit trapped inside this book?"

Looking back at the page, only one sentence could be clearly resolved, burning prominently in the center of the page, like a subtitle:

You're finally learning something.

Krim found Abe just as true night fell. As usual, she slipped inside the house unnoticed. In the few months she had been coming to the house, Abe doubted his mother had ever laid eyes on her. This suited him fine; Krim wasn't fit to meet his mother.

"You ready?" She sat across from Abe in his father's old, dusty chair. She put her feet up on the desk. "Learned any good spells yet?"

Abe took a deep breath. There was a right answer and a wrong answer here; he picked the right one. "A little bit."

"Good. Monda is pissed a stupid book cost all fifty. C'mon." She sprung lightly to her feet and cocked her head, waiting.

Abe stood, suddenly aware of how tired he felt. The room spun a little as the blood equalized in his head. He slid the magic book into a knapsack and threw it over one shoulder. "I'm coming—just don't get too far ahead, okay?"

Krim's big dark eyes twinkled in the lantern light. "What's a matter, schoolboy? Worried somebody might steal your homework?"

Abe grimaced but didn't speak. The answer, though, was *yes.*

The Brotherhood of Light, as Monda's group called itself, met, ironically, in the very darkest part of the Undercity, almost directly beneath the center of the Upper City's crescent-shaped foundation. The Spire of Dreams, the great tower that had once connected Upper- to Undercity, lay crumpled like an abandoned ball gown across the blocks of ruined shops, burned-out homes, and crumbling government buildings. Blocks of violet marble the size of fishing boats, once inlaid with gems and inscribed with the names and faces of ancient Illini princes, sat like upended jewelry boxes in the midst of the devastated streets. Those jewels that had not been lost when the Defenders cast down the Spire had long since been pried away by thieves, and the names and faces of that long line of princes were now cracked, smashed, and otherwise defaced.

The Spire of Dreams' death was a literal representation of the death of old Illin, a fact which hadn't escaped Monda and his pack of thugs. Their meetings were held in an old antechamber of that fallen citadel, tipped sideways and sagging with the weight of all that stone, and yet still standing. Abe sometimes wondered how far it had fallen and how it had managed to stay intact. He wasn't wondering that now, however—there were too many eyes upon him. Angry, violent, expectant eyes, lit by greasy orange torchlight.

Two such eyes were burrowed deep in the haggard creases of Monda's face. All Abe knew about the man's past was that he had been in the war and, supposedly, served at the side of Prince Landar the Holy. Everybody believed it, but Abe didn't. There was nothing holy about Monda. He was earthy and feral, like a warthog, and just about as hairy. When he spoke, it was always in quick, clipped syllables, as though talking was a waste of his time. "Well, boy? Report."

Everyone waited. They were a haggard bunch, most either as young as Abe or older than Monda, but every one had a knife or a rusty bit of sword or a weathered crossbow. Abe needed to give them something to be satisfied with, or he wouldn't walk out of this meeting. "Well...uhhh...it's been slow-going."

"You've had all day." Monda folded his scarred arms across the bushy black forest of chest hair that poked through his open vest.

Abe licked his lips. Krim was just behind him, her breathing even but quick, like someone preparing for the start of a race.

"It's more complicated than I thought."

"He said he'd learned a spell." Krim said.

The assembly exchanged glances and muttered in excitement. Monda quieted them with a jerk of his hand. "Do the spell, boy."

Abe's mouth went dry. He looked at Krim, and she must have read his expression. "I'm helping you out, Abe. Give 'em something, right?"

Monda stepped aside and motioned to an open space at the center of the fallen chamber where a flaming brazier belched a thick fume of incinerated camel dung and scrap wood. Abe stepped between them, as their eyes bored into him. How many times would he be stabbed, he wondered, if he couldn't convince them he'd taken their money wisely? Would they return his body to his mother, or would it be just another son who never came home?

"Do the spell." Monda repeated, putting his hands on his hips. "Now."

Abe cleared his throat and opened the book. "Just give me a second—I've got to find it."

He looked inside.

Frequently practitioners of the High Arts find themselves placed in awkward positions vis-à-vis the common population. In instances where mobs of slobbering thugs and half-witted cutpurses wish to be given a show to demonstrate one's power, conjuration is a very useful and successful discipline to employ.

Sweat ran down Abe's brow. He flipped the page.

Unfortunately for yourself, even the most basic conjurations require months of training to accomplish with regular success, and years to master; as hitherto mentioned, the study of the High Arts is not an easy one, nor is it quick.

"Well?" Monda's thick eyebrows lowered over his eyes like a pair of bristling window shades.

161

"Just a second!" Abe said, flipping another page.

The book read: *What exactly did you expect? Did you honestly think you could open some book of magic spells and just make one happen, like baking a cake or something? Did you expect to be conjuring buckets of gold for local orphanages by lunch? Restoring infrastructure with a word by sundown? You'll need weeks more training before we can even get you to channel energies consistently.*

"You've got to give me something." Abe hissed at the book. "Anything!"

"What?" Monda looked around at the assembled. "What did he say?"

"He's talking to himself," Krim offered. "He was doing that when I found him."

Abe wiped sweat from his eyes, hands shaking. He flipped another page.

There is only one way in which an inexperienced sorcerer can expect to execute magical spells of sufficient strength to impress dullards and fools. This process, while discouraged by most in the sorcerous field as overly risky, involves establishing an accord with a spirit in exchange for a favor. The most practical variety of spirit to be utilized in this fashion are the creatures of the Ether, also known as "ghul" by the Kalsaaris. Well known for their intelligence and creativity, as well as their basic avarice, they are eager to deal and useful servants.

Monda's hand fell on Abe's arm like an iron manacle. He yanked the book from Abe's hand. "Can you cast the spell or not, boy?"

Abe nodded. "Uhhh...yes, yes—I can. Just, can I have my book back, I need to—

"*Your* book?" Monda pushed Abe to the ground. "This book belongs to the Brotherhood of Light, boy. It was *their* money that bought it, *their* blood that was spilled to earn that silver. We gave it to you because Krim vouched for you, said you could read, and were a good, loyal son of Illin. Said you would work a spell to kill the mirror men, topple the Upper City, kill the thieves that feed on us."

Abe rose slowly, eyes fixed on the book. "I do hate the toppers; I hate them as much as anyone."

Monda threw him the book. "Work a spell. Show us we haven't wasted our money. I want to see what you can conjure, boy, and it better be good." The assembled Brothers nodded solemnly.

Abe opened the tome, hands shaking. There, in a flowing, red script, were the words:

Shall we make a deal, then?

Abe took a long, slow breath. This was what Carlo was talking about—it had to be. He was in over his head, and there was only one way out—a way he knew was wrong. Still, what choice did he have? He looked at the words, nodded and flipped the page.

There, covering both pages of the book, was a detailed contract, indicating how the book would assist him and the price it would demand. At the bottom, beside his name printed in the same maroon ink, were the words "Sign Here."

"I'm running out of patience, boy." Monda growled.

Abe, throat dry, dragged out his words in barely audible croaks. "I need a pen and some ink."

Monda cocked his head. "What?"

"I'll get it." Krim darted into the shadows. Oddly, Abe found himself missing her presence. She was the closest thing he had to an ally here.

Monda pushed Abe by the shoulder, like a bully jostling a child around a schoolyard, "Why a pen and ink?"

Abe squared his shoulders and tried looking Monda in the eye. All he saw there was suspicion, pure and icy as the winter sea. Abe tore his gaze away and looked back at the contract. "I need one for the spell."

"What's the spell do?"

Abe buried himself in the complex language of the contract, remembering what his mother had always said about his father and legal documents—"He always read every word—every word—and that made him the best."

The ghul offered to destroy Abe's enemies in exchange for...for...

"Well, boy, I asked you a question!" Monda pushed Abe again, but Abe didn't notice. He was trying to parse the sentence: *In exchange for the services detailed herein to be completed by the signee, as defined above, the signer shall relinquish whatsoever claim, be it legal, emotional, physical, or mystical, he has heretofore established with the flesh whose reproductive proclivities led to his issuance in this time and place and transfer that claim to the signee immediately upon completion of said services.*

It took him another moment before he had it figured. When he finally had it, he felt as though he had just been punched in the gut.

The ghul wanted his mother.

"Got the pen." Krim announced, handing over a filthy quill and a greasy bottle of blue ink. "Get on with it."

Abe looked up at her, barely noticing as she backed away. They were all backing away—all except Monda. "I'd better see some magic, boy."

The pen felt hard and prickly in his hand as it hovered over the line. He could save himself or save his mother—the choice was his to make, right now. He knew what Hann would want him to do, and Prince Landar, but it was a hard choice. It was especially hard as it was different from what his mother would want. She hadn't suffered so much and so long to see her son murdered because his anger led him to this dark place surrounded by these dark men. If he died now, what difference would it make? Would his mother want to live without him?

"Let's have it, *boy!*" Monda snapped, drawing his knife.

Abe signed. The letters glowed and then erased themselves, as though unwritten—only Abe's signature remained. It was the only thing, he realized, written with real ink. He looked up at Monda, heart quivering in his chest, mouth dry as sand, palms sweaty. "You got it, Monda."

The torches darkened, dwindling to little more than flickers. The air grew stale somehow, as though robbed of its lightness and motion by…something. Something black and amorphous, crouching like a pile of black velvet in the center of the chamber. It had one, solitary eye—green and glassy, with a slit-pupil that rapidly scanned the assembly.

Monda stepped toward Abe, eyes wide. "What…what's that?"

Abe didn't say anything—he, too, was backing up, along with everyone else. The ghul grew from a squat pile to a pillar of pure darkness, twice as tall as a man. The cloying air was pierced by its laughter—dry and dead as leaves in the wind. *"So...like to pick on studious young men, do we?"*

"Treachery!" Monda snarled, and hurled himself at Abe, knife raised.

Abe put up his arms to defend himself, falling back onto the floor, but Monda's blow never struck home.

When Abe looked up, he saw leathery black tendrils wrapped around Monda's chest and arms. The ringleader's face froze in an expression of horror and shock, the color somehow leeching from his skin, his body hair sloughing off like so much ash. He opened his mouth to say something—a curse, a scream for help, a call to arms—Abe never knew before the tendrils pulled him back into the black pillar of the demon's body and Monda vanished forever.

The Brotherhood of Light turned and fled in all directions at once, their half-dead torches dropped and forgotten. The ghul's glassy green eye followed where they went and then fixed itself upon Abe. *"This will only take a moment."*

The ghul collapsed into a pool of shadow and flitted from the chamber as quick as blinking. In the darkness surrounding the fallen antechamber, Abe heard a chorus of screams rise from the tangled ruins of the Undercity.

Abe didn't wait for the creature to return—he scooped up the empty book and ran for his life, shooting through narrow alleys and ducking beneath half-collapsed buildings in the utter dark, tripping and stumbling, until he finally reached home. He didn't know how long it would take the ghul to find and kill everyone in the Brotherhood, but he doubted it would be long. He burst in the door, panting and out of breath, spots dancing in his eyes. "Mother! Mother!"

"In here." The voice didn't belong to Abe's mother—it was Krim's.

He raced into the parlor. Krim knelt on his mother's back, the glittering mageglass shard in her hand, pressed to the back of the old woman's head. Her other hand held a fistful of Abe's mother's hair, pulling her head up. Tears mixed with blood ran down his mother's face. Abe knelt in front of them. "No! Let her go!"

Krim's big black eyes were wild. "Call it off, first. Call the creature off!"

"Abe, dear . . . wha . . . what's happening . . . ?"

Krim smashed his mother's face into the floor. *"Shut up, bitch!"* Abe noticed strange, gray wounds along Krim's spindly arms—she had barely escaped. "Call it off, Abe, or the old lady gets hers."

Abe shook his head. "You don't understand—I don't have a choice. I can't call it off!"

Krim flicked her wrist, and a blood-red ribbon of flesh was stripped off his mother's cheek. She shrieked in pain. Abe felt jolts of electricity shoot down his spine, but remained still. "Figure out a way, schoolboy, or after I finish her, I come for *you.*"

Abe's hands balled into fists. "If you want me, leave my mother out of it!"

Krim snorted. "Noble talk, schoolboy, but you're no better than me."

"Is this what a daughter of Illin does to her own?" Abe scanned the room for a weapon—nothing. He wouldn't even have known how to use one if he found one.

"Do you really believe that crap, huh?" Krim laughed. "It's all nonsense, Abe—fairy stories. This is a dead city and we're the maggots. Maggots don't get to care what they feed on. Get it?"

"That can change!" Abe scooted closer, but Krim pressed the knife to his blubbering mother's throat. "With the . . . the book, I can change all that! I can force the mirror men to listen!"

Krim shook her head. "Poor little schoolboy, still buying into the Big Dream. Don't make me lau . . ."

Krim whooshed up through the ceiling with a sudden jerk. Abe glanced up to see the big green eye staring down from the gap in the roof. He heard Krim swear once, then scream, then a second later her polished bones fell to the floor.

Abe's mother, who had dragged herself upright, saw them hit and fainted dead away.

"Time to collect my payment, Abrahan Anastasis." The ghul announced with a hissing chuckle.

Abe stood between his mother and the creature. "No, it isn't."

"You read the contract—you know the bargain. You aren't going back on your word, are you?" It said, sliding down through the ceiling like heavy smoke, the lime-colored eye scanning his face.

Abe took a deep breath. "No, you are."

It stopped. *"What? Nonsense."*

"The contract calls for you to destroy my enemies, but you haven't done that yet."

A leathery tendril referenced Krim's skeleton. "This was the last of the so-called Brotherhood."

"They aren't my only enemies." Abe said. "You haven't destroyed the mirror men. When you're done with them, you need to go after the war profiteers and the collaborators and the traitors to Prince Landar's memory."

"If you insist..."

Abe raised his voice. "Then you need to fix the roads that destroy commerce. You need to repair the aqueducts that pollute our drinking water and do away with the barren farmland that keeps us hungry. You need to rebuild the ruined schools that keep us bereft of knowledge, and the ruined churches that destroy our faith. It won't be until the sun shines again in Undercity that you, demon, can be said to have destroyed my enemies. Can you do all that?"

The ghul's green eye turned yellow, then red. *"This is...this is preposterous. There was no indication that your 'enemies' were to be metaphorical and..."*

Abe pointed directly at the eye. "Then *you* should have included that stipulation in the contract. You didn't, did you?"

Dead silence. Abe's heart pounded—he felt as if he might drop dead right there, just from terror. One flick of those horrible tendrils, and he'd be only bones. At last, however, the ghul seemed to sag down to the floor. *"What are you, boy? How can you have beaten me?"*

"My father was a lawyer." Abe held out the spell book. "You are in breach of contract—back in the book with you."

And, in the twinkling of an eye, the ghul was gone.

Seven days later, Abe deposited a wheelbarrow full of bones at a post where the mirror men paid bounties on wanted criminals. It took them a few auguries to verify that the bones belonged to twenty-eight wanted murderers, thieves, and terrorists. They didn't ask too many prying questions, paid him in gold, and sent him away.

The next day, Carlo diCarlo appeared at his door. Abe invited him inside, but the smuggler shook his head. "So, you made it, did you? I see you have my money."

Abe kicked the heavy strongbox of gold in Carlo's direction. He also held out the book. "I don't want this anymore."

Carlo looked at it and chuckled. "Neither do I. The damned thing is more trouble than it's worth."

Abe gazed down at it—he hadn't dared to open it since the incident. The thought of those words swirling across the page had practically put him off books altogether. "What am I supposed to do with it, then?"

Carlo leaned over, a smirk on his face. "If you want my advice, I'd sell it to some idiot for a king's ransom."

Abe shook his head. "That's a death sentence."

Carlo scooped the strongbox up under one arm and began to stroll away. "That's funny, Oz—I once thought the very same thing."

SHUANGJIAN LIU

Twelve Minutes to Vinh Quang

written by

Tim Napper

illustrated by

QUINLAN SEPTER

ABOUT THE AUTHOR

*Tim Napper is an Australian from a quiet country town currently
living in the "City of Noise"—Hanoi, Vietnam.*

*In 2002, Tim worked for a year as a volunteer in Mongolia,
managing a project to support street children. International aid
work became his profession after this, and he spent the subsequent
eleven years living and working throughout Asia. He lived in
Laos for three years, implementing programs that provided basic
education to the poorest children in the country, and has also
worked in Burma, Indonesia and Papua New Guinea.*

*While a voracious reader of science fiction since he was a young
boy, Tim only began writing fiction two years ago. He is a fan of
Philip K. Dick, Ursula K. Le Guin, and Kurt Vonnegut, and has a
particular obsession with the movie* Blade Runner.

*Tim has eased back on his regular job to devote himself to
writing and to raising his three-year-old son. Sometimes they have
been known to dress up in Star Trek costumes and pilot the couch
spaceship on dangerous missions while mum is at work.*

ABOUT THE ILLUSTRATOR

Quinlan Septer was born in 1992 in Tucson, Arizona, and raised in the small town of North Muskegon, Michigan. His desire to experience more than what could be seen with his eyes led him to imagine worlds and characters that he now brings to life through illustration.

He went to college in Florida and soon after moved to Ohio to work with a small indie game development team. Then he returned to Michigan where he currently works as a freelance illustrator.

Most of his early inspiration came from immersing himself in video games and card games with his brother Ryan, as well as his oldest brother Christopher, who was the initial influence as they would draw together often while they grew up.

As Quinlan grew older, he sought deeper, more meaningful inspiration, which he found in the old master painters. Their work helped him to better understand technique and purpose in his own art and satiated his interest in the philosophical aspects of art and illustration.

Quinlan is honored to be a part of the Illustrators of the Future Contest and is looking forward to his next big step as an artist and illustrator.

Twelve Minutes to Vinh Quang

The restaurant smelled of anchovies and cigarettes. Lynn hated both, but still, it reminded her of home. Comforting and familiar. The anchovies in the sauce wouldn't be real of course, and the tobacco almost certainly illegal.

It was three in the afternoon, but the room was still pretty much full. Patrons sipped glasses of tea, shrouded in the smoke and dusk, mumbling to each other in low-pitched conversation. Blinds were down against the windows, the only light emanating from shaded red lanterns hanging from the ceiling, casting the faces around her in crimson twilight.

The only light, that is, bar a government advertisement on the far wall. The picture of a decaying wooden boat on the high seas, the inhabitants of which were anonymous splotches of yellow staring over a thin railing. The holotype glow of the deep blue ocean was overwhelmed by the intensity of the red block letters stamped over the picture:

ILLEGAL

Everyday, middle-of-the-road fascism: it just had no imagination.

A small bell above the door tinkled as it opened, spearing an unwelcome slat of white sunlight into the room. Heat, too, gusting in to swirl the smoke and swing the lanterns. A shadow filled the doorframe, pausing perhaps to adjust its eyes to the gloom within. Maybe just pausing for effect.

An ancient Vietnamese woman behind the back counter came to life, pointing a gnarled finger at the new customer. *"Má Mày. Dóng Cửa Lai đi."* ["Close that door. Your mother!"]

The silhouette shut the door, emerging from the light into a broad-shouldered man wearing an immaculate tailored suit, deep-blue necktie, and an air of contempt for the room he'd just stepped into. He removed the black homburg from his head and ran a hand over his gleaming, jet-black hair, combed straight back. As he did so, Lynn glimpsed a tattoo snaking up under his sleeve.

The man walked to the back counter. Lynn turned to watch as he did, adjusting her silver nose ring with thumb and forefinger. He spoke in hushed tones with the old woman, glanced back at Lynn, then turned and started speaking again rapidly. The grandmother waved him away before disappearing through a beaded doorway to the kitchen beyond.

He walked back to her table, hat in hand, face set. "Mister Vu?"

"Vu Thi Lynn." She paused. "And that's a *Miz,* Mister Nguyen."

He made a show of looking her over. Her hair in particular came in for close inspection, dyed, as it was, the hue of a fresh-pressed silver bar and molded into a spiked Mohawk. She sported a tiny black leather jacket and a pair of thin eyebrows that could fire withering disdain at fifty paces.

His shoulders were hunched, like a boxer's. "Is this a joke?"

"What are you having difficulty processing, Mister Nguyen? That I'm young, a woman, or," she waved at hand at his suit, "that I don't walk around with the word 'gangster' tattooed on my damn forehead?"

His eyes narrowed, lips pressed together. Then the flicker of anger was gone. "Perhaps you don't know who I am."

"All I know is you're late."

Mister Nguyen placed his hat on the table and played with the large gold ring on his index finger, looking down at her with a studied grimness.

Lynn stifled a sigh at the posturing. "Look, we have business to attend to, and I was led to believe you were a businessman." She indicated the seat opposite her. "Let's get to work."

열하나:쉰아홉

QUINLAN SEPTER

He nodded, as though to himself, scanning the room as he took his seat. Appeals to *business* usually worked with these people, imagining, as they did, that they were part of some traditional brand of professional criminality stretching back through time to the Binh Xuyen of Saigon or the Painters and Dockers Union of Melbourne.

"We doing this here?"

She nodded. "I've never been here before. There are a hundred places like this in Cabramatta. Neither of us need return here again."

He looked around the room once more and took a palmscreen out of his pocket. He mumbled into it, pressed his thumb against a pad on the front, and then pulled a thin tube from the top. It unrolled into a translucent, wafer-thin flexiscreen. Soft green icons glowed across its surface. He looked at her. "So, what's the rush?"

"No questions, Mister Nguyen."

He clenched his jaw. He knew he couldn't argue with this statement of professionalism either. "The transaction will take thirty minutes to complete."

"Thirty minutes?"

Nguyen drew a cigar from the inner pocket of his jacket, and set about clipping the end with a steel cigar cutter. "The government tracks every freewave signal going into Vietnam. Our transaction can't be direct." He put the cigar in his mouth, took his time lighting it with a heavy gold lighter. He snapped it shut and puffed out a thick cloud of smoke. "We relay through a few different countries first before ending up at a front factory in Laos, right near the Vietnamese border. My contact there gets word across the border to a small town on the other side: Vinh Quang." He pointed down at the flexiscreen with the end of his cigar. "The money for the equipment—that's easy, will only take a few minutes. Unofficially, the Australians don't give a shit about private funds going to buy weapons for the Viet Minh. The money for people is tougher to get through clean. You know—the whole refugee thing."

Lynn nodded. She glanced over at the government ad on the wall, red letters glowing fierce and eternal. Yeah. She knew.

Money, of course, was always an exception. Five million

dollars and you and your family would be granted a "business residency" in Australia. The government funneled the arrivals into Cabramatta and the nearby suburbs, very quietly, so the general public wouldn't get too heated up about it.

The rest who arrived by boat were thrown into internment camps for a few months before being returned to Vietnam, where inevitably they ended up in Chinese prisoner-of-war camps.

Nguyen placed the cigar cutter and lighter on the scratched tabletop. "You insisted on being here when the money went through. It takes thirty minutes."

"You know the saying," she said, "trust everyone, but cut the cards."

He shrugged. "Sure. I need to keep the line open, verify who I am, confirm we're not a part of some Chinese sting operation. If we miss a call, I fail to enter a pass code, they burn the link."

She nodded.

He puffed on his cigar like a man who believed he was in charge. "You said you wanted to move twenty million. Minus, of course, fifteen percent for my fee."

"You told me the fee was ten percent."

"That was before you criticized my clothes."

"You look like a cross between a pimp and a wet echidna. I think I went easy on you."

His eyes went hard. He glanced at her hair, opened his mouth to retort, then shook his head. "I did some asking around. Everyone has heard about you. High profile means a higher risk."

"You didn't even know whether I was a man or a woman before today."

"The authorities could be observing you."

"They're not."

He inhaled deeply on the cigar, blew the smoke directly into her face. She closed her eyes for a moment, felt her hand clench into a fist.

Nguyen was oblivious. "Your regular guy got done for tax evasion. I have the contacts. And you're in a hurry." He opened his hands and smiled. "The fee is fifteen percent."

Lynn glanced around the room. A couple of faces were turned in her direction. She shook her head, a small shake—one that could be mistaken for Lynn trying to get the smoke out of her eyes.

She looked back at him. "I want a business residency for two families. That's ten million. The rest goes to weapons."

"I assume these families are on an Australian government watch list. They'll need new identities?"

She raised an eyebrow in the universal signal for *obviously*.

"You know these people?" he asked.

"No."

"Then why are you getting them out?"

"You appear to be asking questions again. Now what did I say about that?"

He brought his hand down hard on the plastic tabletop, causing the condiments to chatter. He took a deep breath. "No respect."

Lynn sipped her tea, watching him over the lip of the glass.

He took a long drag on his cigar and returned the stare. Then he blinked away whatever he wanted to say and began manipulating the glowing symbols on the flexiscreen, whispering into it from time to time.

Unobserved, Lynn allowed herself a small smile.

Through the nanos attached to her optic nerves, the c-glyph could broadcast data and images that only she could see. Some people would have multiple freewave screens open all hours of the day. Watching the betting markets or reality television or point-of-view pornography. As a general rule, if you were in conversation with someone and their eyes glazed over, or even closed, they were finding some facile freewave feed more interesting than your company.

Lynn tended to keep her visuals uncluttered. At the moment all she had loaded up was the timestamp in glowing green numerals that appeared, to her brain, about a foot away in the top left corner of her vision.

15:33

She marked the time. Thirty minutes to Vinh Quang.

They waited. She turned and signaled the grandmother, ordered a late lunch. A soft chime sounded a few minutes later. Nguyen closed his eyes and put a finger to the c-glyph behind his left ear, listening as it whispered directly into his eardrum. He murmured a response, paused, and then mumbled again.

He opened his eyes a few seconds later. "The money for the equipment is through."

She nodded, touched her own c-glyph, fingers against the small circle of cool steel. "Anh Dung?" She listened to the reply, nodded once.

"Everything check out?" Nguyen asked.

"Don't worry, you'll know if it doesn't."

Nguyen slurped his tea and settled into his chair, content to watch the slow burn of his cigar. The minutes stretched out. Nguyen didn't try to engage her in conversation; the first transaction had gone through smoothly: things were going well.

Until the bell above the door tinkled again.

Two men entered. As the blinding light returned to the dusk of the room, she could see that they weren't from around here. White men with cheap fedoras, crumpled suits, and the empty gaze of detached professionalism. Government men. They scanned the room, their eyes stopping when they found Lynn.

She held her breath, moved her hand to her belt buckle.

They walked right up to the table, removing their hats as they approached. "Mister Nguyen Van Cam?" Lynn's hand stopped, hovering above the lip of her jeans, she breathed out slowly.

Mister Nguyen looked up. "Who wants to know?"

"I'm Agent Taylor, Immigration Enforcement Agency." He flipped out a badge featuring an Australian crest, emu and kangaroo glinting chrome in the red haze. He pointed to the man next to him. "This is Agent Baker."

Nguyen was silent, his cigar trailing an idle string of smoke to the ceiling.

The time glowed softly at the edge of her vision.

15:51

Twelve minutes.

Nguyen was struggling to conjugate a response when the grandmother appeared between the two agents. The top of her head didn't even reach their shoulders. She looked down at Lynn when she spoke. *"Hai thằng chó đẻ này làm gì `ở đây vậy?"* ["What are these two sons-of-bitches doing here?"]

Lynn's spoken Vietnamese was close to fluent, but she kept her translator on when she was working. Though less frequent, this part of town also echoed with Laotian, Burmese, and a hundred Chinese dialects. Smart to be tuned in to those wavelengths.

So the c-glyph whispered the old woman's sentence into her ear, coming through in English a couple of seconds later. It made it look like the grandmother was speaking in a badly dubbed old movie.

"They won't be here long. Can you get them tea?" Lynn asked.

"Bác bỏ thuôć độc vô luôn đuọc nha?" ["Shall I poison it?"]

Lynn smiled a small smile. "No. Just tea." The men were moving their hands to their c-glyphs. Apparently they'd entered the restaurant without their translators turned on.

Lynn indicated a couple of seats nearby. "Gentlemen, why don't you sit down? Drink some tea with us."

One of the agents answered. "No thank you, Miss. We are here to take Mister Nguyen in for questioning."

"Now?"

"Now."

Lynn leaned back in her chair, used her eyes to indicate the room they were standing in. "Here's the thing. You're deep in the heart of Cabramatta. Not the safest place in the world for an immigration enforcement agent."

They looked around the restaurant. Perhaps noticing for the first time the quiet that had descended on it. All eyes in the room focused on them, the atmosphere turning like a corpse in the noonday sun.

"Gentlemen," she said.

They looked back at her.

"Just smile, grab a seat, and conduct your business politely. You'll be out of here in a few minutes, no trouble."

The agents exchanged glances. One nodded. They dragged

chairs with faded red seat cushions over to the table, smiling strained smiles as they sat down.

Nguyen cleared his throat, a sheen of sweat on his forehead. "What's the charge?"

The official looked across at him with dead eyes. "People smuggling."

"Do you have a warrant?" asked Lynn.

He turned back to her. "Are you his lawyer?"

"No." She indicated Nguyen with an open palm. "He's my pimp. Can't you tell?"

Agent Taylor didn't seem keen on smiling. "People smuggling is a very serious offense."

Lynn nodded. "Yes, I've seen the advertisements. Very, very serious—imagine trying to help Vietnamese civilians flee cluster bombing and nerve warfare? China would be livid. And we couldn't have that."

The agents suddenly seemed a lot more interested in her. Taylor looked her over and then held out his hand to Agent Baker, who removed a palmscreen from his pocket and passed it to his partner. It looked a bit larger than a regular model, maybe four inches across by six long. The retina scanner he flipped up from the end must have been specially fitted. Lynn cursed inwardly.

"Would you mind if I did an identity check, Miss?"

She pointed. "What is that?"

"The retina scanner?"

"That model. That's official immigration issue isn't it? An expensive unit, I believe. "

"Miss. The scan please." The agent had one of those voices trained to convey authority. Imbued with one extra notch each of volume, aggression, and confidence.

"I'm afraid I can't agree to that."

His gaze rose from the adjustments he was making to the scanner. "It's the law. We're making an arrest. You appear to be an associate of Mister Nguyen."

"I'm Australian. You have no jurisdiction over me."

"Sorry Miss, but we don't know that until we test it."

"That seems a conveniently circular argument."

"If you've done nothing wrong, then you have nothing to worry about."

Lynn raised an eyebrow. "Ah, the mantra of secret police and peeping Toms everywhere."

The agent's professional patina didn't drop. Not surprising, a person in his position would be subject to a wide range of creative abuse on a daily basis. "Like I said—it's the law."

"I read an article about this once. If you run my retina prints, I'll be listed as present during one of your arrests."

He responded with a shrug that indicated that while she was right, he didn't really care.

"And I'll be flagged as a person of interest for immigration."

"I didn't design the system, Miss."

"Of course not. An empty suit couldn't design a system so diabolical; your only function is to implement it."

Still no response. Not a flicker. She sighed and pulled out an unmarked silver cigarette case from her jacket pocket. "Do you gentlemen smoke?"

Agent Baker let out a humorless laugh. "You think we can afford to smoke on a government salary?" He glanced around the room, at Nguyen. "In fact, I doubt anyone here can afford to smoke. Legally, anyway." He looked back at Lynn. "Do you have a license for those?"

Her fingers lingered in the open case. "I thought you were in immigration, Agent Baker, not drug enforcement. Haven't you gentlemen got enough on your plate for today?"

The man pointed at his partner. "He's Baker, I'm Taylor."

"You people all look the same to me."

He raised his eyebrows. "White people?"

"Bureaucrats."

The one on the right planted his elbow on the table, holding the palm screen up at about her head height. The other agent turned to watch the room, hand slipping under his jacket. The patrons, seeing a hated ID check underway, watched him right back. Lynn snapped shut her case, sans cigarette, and placed it on the table.

15:56

"Here, hold it steady." She placed both hands on the palmscreen and held her eye up to the scanner. A small, black metal circle with a red laser dot in the center. She looked into the beam. The red glare caused her to blink.

"Try not to blink, Miss. It just needs five seconds."

She put her eye in the beam again, counted to three, then blinked rapidly. A chime in a minor key emanated from the palmscreen.

The agent sighed. "Miss." Firmer this time. "Just place your eye over the beam. Don't blink. It's over in a few seconds."

She failed another three times, eliciting more sighs and even a curse. She smiled sweetly. The smile didn't feel at all natural on her face, but their displeasure was satisfying nonetheless. On the sixth attempt, she allowed it to work.

16:00

He looked at the results of the scan. "Miss Vu. I see you have full citizenship."

"I'm aware."

"But your parents do not. They are Vietnamese–Australian."

She sat in silence. Let the threat hang there for a few moments while she studied it. "What the hell does that mean?"

"Nothing." He snapped down the scanner, put the palmscreen in his coat pocket. His flat stare lingered on her. "I'm just saying they fall under our jurisdiction."

Under the table, she slowly slid her pistol from the small holster under her belt buckle. She moved it to her lap, hidden in the shadows, easing the safety off with her thumb. "My parents have nothing to do with this."

Again, those dead eyes. "If they've done nothing wrong, they have nothing to worry about."

The grandmother reappeared, placed a pot and two glasses on the table. She glanced down as she did so. From the angle she was standing, the old woman could see the pistol Lynn clutched in her hand. She leant down, whispered close to Lynn's ear. *"Bỏ thuốc độc dễ hỏn."* ["Poison would have been easier."]

Lynn gave her a small smile in reply.

Agent Baker took one sip of his tea before turning to Nguyen. "Time to go." He pointed down at the flexiscreen sitting on the table. "That yours?"

Nguyen puffed on his cigar. Like Lynn, he seemed to be figuring the best answer to that particular question.

"Mister Nguyen, is that your flexiscreen?"

Nguyen began to speak, but Lynn cut him off. "Yes. Yes it's his."

The agent started to rise from his seat. "You better bring it with you."

16:03

A soft chime emanated from the screen. The four faces at the table turned to look at it. No one spoke. A few seconds passed and the chime sounded again, the ideograms on the flexiscreen increasing in brightness, insisting on attention.

"Mister Nguyen," she said. He didn't respond. He just sat staring at the screen. Her voice was firmer the second time. "Mister Nguyen."

He started and looked up at her.

"Why don't you answer your call while the agents here show me that warrant."

He looked from her, to the screen, over to the agents, then back to her again. He wiped the sweat from his brow with the back of his hand. "Sure." He put a finger to his c-glyph and closed his eyes.

"Gentlemen." Lynn held out her hand. "The warrant." She felt surprisingly calm given she was responsible for a crime occurring three feet away that could get her thirty years in prison. She focused on her breathing.

Inhale.

Exhale.

Inhale.

Agent Baker glanced over at Nguyen, who was now mumbling responses to someone only he could see. The agent sighed and reached into his coat pocket, pulled out the palmscreen, and pressed his thumb to it. "Verify: Agent Baker, immigration enforcement. Display warrant for Nguyen Van Cam, suspected people smuggler."

He waited. Nothing happened. He pressed his thumb to it again. Still nothing. It was dead. No sound, no light, no signal. He handed it to his partner. The other man looked at the dead screen, then up at Lynn. "What's going on here?"

She slowly slid the pistol back in the holster, eyes on the two men. "You tell me."

The agent held the screen up. "All official communications are contained in this, including the warrant. It's a closed system. It was working fine a few minutes ago. Now it's dead."

She leaned back in her chair. "Well, I'd say you boys are shit out of luck."

"This doesn't change anything."

"I disagree. It changes everything." Lynn signaled for the grandmother to come over to the table. She did so immediately. "This is private property. Unless you're conducting government-sanctioned business, you should leave," she turned to the old woman, addressing her in the formal Vietnamese mode, "Right, elder aunty?"

The grandmother looked at the two men, her eyes sparkling. She found a phrase for them in English. "Piss off."

The agents rose from their seats. One reached under his jacket. The other looked around at the customers, at the faces staring back at him from within the red haze, coiled with silent anger. The agent placed a hand on his partner's shoulder. "Let's wait outside. Warrant and back-up will be here in fifteen minutes."

The other man nodded, still staring straight at Lynn. He let his hand drop, looked over at Nguyen. "Don't even think about leaving." Then he spun and walked out, his partner right behind.

Lynn turned to the old woman. "We need some privacy."

The old woman set about ushering the customers out the front door. No one needed much encouragement. It wasn't worth witnessing what was going to happen next.

Soon all that remained was the smoke and the scent of anchovies. That, and two of her men. They walked over from where they had been sitting, one stood behind Mister Nguyen, one next to Lynn. They were big men.

Nguyen glanced up at them, then back at Lynn. "We should leave, now." He started to rise from his seat, but a heavy hand fell on his shoulder and pushed him back down.

Lynn shook her head. "Not yet, Mister Nguyen, not yet." She indicated the door with her eyes. "Your men in the car outside have been sent away."

"What?"

She sighed and folded her hands on the tabletop. "You led two immigration agents to our first meeting."

"I didn't know they were following me."

"You led two immigrations agents into our first bloody meeting." She didn't raise her voice, but the steel was in it this time.

Nguyen said nothing, just bowed his head and looked at the burnt-out cigar between his fingers.

Lynn pointed at the cigarette case. "Fortunately I keep a dot scrambler on hand for times such as this. The one I stuck on the agent's palmscreen will wipe any record of my retina scan, and freeze the unit until a tech can sit down and unwind the scrambled code. And this," she pointed to her nose ring, "is a refraction loop. You know what this does?"

He shook his head.

"To the naked eye I looked normal. But when you take the memory pin from your c-glyph and play back this scene, the area around my face is distorted. The light bent and warped. They'll still have my voice print, but I can live with that."

She placed the cigarette case in her pocket.

"So I'm in the clear," she said. "You know the laws on human memory. If it doesn't come from a memory pin playback, it is inadmissible as evidence. What with the frail psychology of natural memory and all that. Those agents won't remember what I look like anyway. Not if I change my hair." She reached up, touching the spikes with her palms. "Pity. I quite like this style."

She sighed. "There is, unfortunately, one loose strand. I didn't activate the refraction loop until after you'd walked in. Those agents," she waved at the door, "could subpoena your memory pin."

He stared at her for a few seconds, processing what she was saying. "I'll destroy it. I'll give it to you even. Right now."

She shook her head. "It is more than that. You're sloppy, and that makes you a liability. You know the names of the families I just paid for, and—"

"—I'll wipe all my records. You can have every—"

"—Enough." Her eyes flashed. "Enough. You endangered my parents. This isn't business, this is personal." She paused, watching the man squirm under the heavy hands pressed down on his shoulders. "That's the secret, by the way, Mister Nguyen. This business we have chosen—it's always personal."

"What are you saying?" He struggled to rise. The man next to Lynn stepped forward and drove a fist into Nguyen's face, rocking the gangster's head backward. Nguyen sat there for half a minute, one hand clutching the table, the other over his eye. When he pulled his hand away blood trickled down his cheek, the eyebrow split and already swelling.

Lynn indicated the man who had struck him. "This is Mister Giang. How is your family doing, Mister Giang?"

A voice, deep and clear, answered. "Well, Miz Vu."

She kept her eyes on Nguyen. "They been out here some time now haven't they?"

"Nearly three years."

She nodded. She pointed at the man behind Nguyen's left shoulder. "This is Mister Lac. His family arrived only six months ago. Have they settled in well, Mister Lac?"

"Very well, Miz Vu."

"Did your younger sister get into university?"

"Yes. She will be a teacher." A note of pride in the voice.

"Good. If there are any problems with tuition, you let me know."

It was hard to tell in the shadows, but Mister Lac appeared to nod in reply.

Nguyen watched her now out of one eye, fear blossoming behind it.

"Mister Giang?"

"Yes, Miz Vu."

"Could you take Mister Nguyen out to the back room and put a bullet through his head?"

Giang moved to where Nguyen sat and grabbed him by the upper arm. He and Lac hefted him out of his seat. Nguyen stuttered. "Wait, What? You can't kill me." Spittle fresh on his lips, his good eye wet. "Do you know who I am?"

Lynn stood. "Yes I do. You're a mercenary," she said. "And I meet people like you every day of the week."

She nodded at Giang. He punched Nguyen in the stomach, doubling him over as the air expelled from his lungs, his cigar butt dropping to the floor.

That was the last she saw of him—bent over, unable to speak, being dragged from the room.

She turned to Mister Lac. "Get my parents. Right now. Take them to a safe house. If they argue—when my mother argues with you—just tell her that their daughter will explain everything in a couple of days."

Lac nodded and left.

The grandmother walked in as he was leaving, handed over a warm bamboo box. *"Cơm của con nè. Bác đoán là con muốn take away."* ["Your lunch, child. I guessed you wanted take away."]

The scent of rice, sharp chili sauce and aromatic mushrooms rose from the container. Lynn smiled a small smile. "Smells delicious, older Aunt. *Cám ơn bác.*"

Grandmother nodded. *"Con bảo trong. Con đi há."* ["You take care. You go."]

"You too. *Con đi đây.*"

Lynn straightened, fixing the ends of her hair with an open palm. She faced the front door. Twilight to heat, crimson to blinding white. Lynn hated the world out there.

She reached for the door handle.

Planar Ghosts

written by

Krystal Claxton

illustrated by

AMIT DUTTA

ABOUT THE AUTHOR

Tragically born with a mis-calibrated sense of humor, Krystal Claxton lived in nine US states before the age of thirteen. The combination of the two has left her with an oscillating accent and a habit of laughing at things that aren't funny. She currently lives in Georgia with her long-suffering spouse, a dog who thinks she's a cat, and a number of children that is subject to change.

Krystal started writing her first speculative fiction novel in third grade. (It didn't pan out. The four after weren't too great either.) By high school it was clear she was meant to be an author so she procrastinated by earning dual Associate of Applied Science degrees in Information Systems. She now works full-time as a level-two computer support technician—when she's not secretly writing fiction. (Please don't tell her boss.)

She enjoys breaking Heinlein's Rules and attending Dragon Con (and any other function she can get away with) in costumes of her favorite fictional characters.

Her short fiction has appeared in Fantastic Stories of the Imagination, Fireside Fiction Company, Daily Science Fiction, *and* Unidentified Funny Objects 3.

ABOUT THE ILLUSTRATOR

Amit Dutta discovered the creative urge as a wee entity growing up in the African nation of Malawi. Science fiction and fantasy literature were the first to capture his imagination. Since nobody he asked seemed to think that art could actually be a career, he trotted off to university in Canada and focused on astrophysics. It was very sci-fi, after all.

A series of events, otherwise known as life, left Amit entangled in what might loosely be called "a career in IT." It led to him wondering where he had misplaced twelve of his years. They weren't in the fridge, and he dared not look under the bed. Amit moved to New Zealand where the slumbering creative phoenix finally erupted into the bleary-eyed, caffeine-fueled, solitary autodidactic artist he has become. Over three years he obsessively developed his skills and successfully destroyed his social life.

He quit his daily grazing at the cubicle farm in early 2015 to dedicate more time to his art. The automated mortgage payment glares at him in outright suspicion.

Amit currently hermits himself in a remote bush valley north of Wellington. He feeds cat food to the family of eels living under the ford across the river. The cat isn't impressed.

Planar Ghosts

The walls around the town of Bootstrap are mostly old cars stacked one on top of the other and welded together. Outside Bootstrap, market stalls made from patchwork tarps and rusty pipes lean on either side of the wide gate. They are temporary places for the people who live inside to trade goods with the people stuck outside who need in.

People like Pup.

He looks up at the guard by the gate, who is thicker, but not much older. Probably grew up inside the walls. He looks as if he's been well-fed, even during bad years. His skin is sun-reddened and spotted along his cheeks and the high bridge of his nose.

Pup offers his frayed duffle bag to the guard. The man kneels to comb through it with one meaty hand. Inside is Pup's winter scavenge—a length of rope, a glass vial with lighter fluid, and three almost-full rolls of duct tape.

If this is enough to buy Pup in, he can work for water until summer is over. As the guard measures Pup's worth, the one good pocket of his cargo pants seems heavier. Inside is something he's not supposed to trade. He's not sure what it is. Some Before thing. Probably the guard wouldn't know what it is either.

Pup can just make out Ghost waiting a long way off, gazing longingly into the dying grasslands and the stark, cloudless, afternoon sky. She is a violet shade at the edge of the crowd, a soft see-through specter that no one but Pup will notice. She's uninterested in his business, has been distant all winter.

AMIT DUTTA

Driving him farther, faster than normal, and not at all interested in foraging. Even now, she wants him to keep moving, but he needs to find a place to hole up. Summer is coming and it will be too hot and dry to survive on the plains.

The guard stands to his full height, presses his thin lips together, meets Pup's gaze and returns the worn bag. "It's not enough."

Pup sighs. He'll have to walk to the next town, Washing, but if they're full, the fee will be no better. If Pup were a young woman, preferably pretty, the price would be cheaper. If his skin was lighter, the price would be cheaper. If he was heavier, more muscle and less sinew, the price would be cheaper.

But Pup is none of these things, so he shrugs into the strap and makes his way along the wall, past people swapping lentils for plastic fletchings, moonshine for unrusted screws, salt for bullets. The market is too loud for Pup. Though the crowd is small, trading is more urgent just before the season change. The air is thin and the scent of roasting peppers fights against a dry breeze coming off the plains.

He lingers at an open pit fire with a grill made from a bed's link spring. A woman who would have already been old during the Before time is tending sticks skewered with carrots and onion slices. A few even have hunks of brown meat. He knows that he should get moving, but this may be his last chance for a hot meal. He glances toward Ghost to see if she's tired of waiting for him, but she's not paying him any attention.

"Have something to trade?" the old woman asks. Her fingers are thin and dry and singed at the tips like the skewers. Gray dreadlocks hang past her frayed shawl. She's hunched, but Pup recognizes the sharp look in her eyes. There's a reason she's survived these many years.

Pup sits in the dirt at the edge of the fire to dig a loop of twine hanging around his neck from beneath his threadbare shirts, measures out two arm-lengths, and holds it up for her inspection. When she nods he pulls the small blade from his boot.

She passes him a skewer with a big enough chunk of meat at the same time he places the string in her palm. He should wait until it's cool, but the scent of spiced meat fills his head and his mouth turns watery. It's half gone, tender carrots and juicy meat—beef? lamb, maybe—settling warmly in his belly before he can stop long enough to savor the taste. He stares off to the southeast.

"Hope you're not headed to Washing."

Pup's head tilts down as he studies her. She's busy turning each skewer with a blackened, doubled-over length of stiff wire. He doesn't answer, but waits to see what she'll say.

"Heard they're full up already." She peers at him with one eye.

"Not much else around," he says.

"Not unless you're headed to Springfield."

"Thought that was further off." Pup's never been this far east before. Ghost keeps him moving. But he's careful to ask after where he's headed and what'll be waiting for him when he gets there.

"Couple hundred miles.... About a month walking—two if the weather's bad," she corrects herself. "That's a full moon or two."

"I know what a month is." Pup sucks the juices out of the stick, careful not to let either charred end ruin the meaty flavor. He'll wait until next winter to make that trip, may take him the winter after too, if there's trouble along the way: raiders, flash floods, coyotes. Pup had planned to stop in Salem next year.

"Isn't Salem closer?"

She's talking to herself, and hasn't heard him. "Unless you're going over to Base."

Pup tosses the stick in the fire. "What's Base?"

She takes a breath that seems larger than her skinny frame. "Back in the day, the military commandeered a power plant a bit over the state border, east of here. They moved in, and they're still there. More or less."

Pup stands, brushes dirt from the seat of his pants. "They have summer work?"

She fights with her wire to turn a skewer that has burned to the grill. "Nope. They recruit every now and again, but you don't leave in the winter if you sign on with them for the summer, if you get my meaning."

"Then I guess I'm headed to Washing."

She's peering at him with one eye again. "Reckon so. Good luck."

Pup stops at the edge of the shanty booths to stand beside Ghost, but doesn't look straight at her. When he was very young, he learned that it's better not to speak to her when other people can hear him. Since she doesn't talk and no one else can see her, they tend to think he's touched in the head.

Ghost is see-through in places and seems to glow without casting any light or shadow. She is a faint purple, like butterfly-bush blossoms, and her long hair floats about her as though she is always being caught in the beginning of a breeze. Her face is soft around the edges, and her feet don't quite touch the ground.

A scrawny boy, no taller than Pup's shoulder, too young to remember what it was like Before, veers around Pup and steps right through Ghost, unaware. She is not a hot or cold spot, like the old people tell him ghosts are supposed to be, and no one notices her unless it's to wonder what Pup is looking at, who he's speaking to.

Ghost tears her attention away from the plain to look up at him. When she smiles, her face glows a little brighter and he forgets that he shouldn't look directly at her.

A dust devil swirls to life at the horizon, playing against the waves of heat already building on the plains. She points, insistent, to the east. Whatever it is that's caught her interest will have to wait. Pup shakes his head and turns south. He's only got a few days to get to Washing before it'll be too hot to travel.

Dry grass pokes Pup through the wide weave of a blanket threaded together from strips of old fabric. The sky is a thick jumble of stars without a moon and the air is too brittle to hold daytime warmth, but he won't risk a fire. Not while the plain is dead and yellowed.

On nights like this, when Ghost isn't with him, Pup jerks awake often. He's not sure what business a ghost has to attend to, but she's gone more often than not these days. He wonders what she's found that's so remarkable, if one day it will keep her interest for good.

He drifts between awake and asleep, dreams of the world ending. The scorch, the grind of twisting metal, the pulse of his mother's heart as she squeezed his face against her neck, running, her cottony hair tickling his nose. She must have died, but he's never sure. She is there in some of his memories and gone from others.

When it was over, Pup was on his own. A boy on the plains. That's when he met Ghost.

Pup starts awake. The night is too still and he holds his breath, straining to hear. The crickets have all gone silent. Was it the dream of his mother that woke him, or trouble? Most big wolves have followed their food north for the season. It could be something small that won't bother him if he doesn't go looking for it. A fox maybe.

He unwinds from the ball he'd rolled into as he slept, lifts his head from the duffle bag to peer above the dry grass.

The bottom of a boot fills his vision and Pup rolls sideways, the kick grazing off his forehead.

He staggers to his feet but he's already surrounded, one man to either side and a third—the one who'd tried to bash his skull in—before him.

He knows this man, even by dim starlight, recognizes the spotted face: the guard who turned him away.

The attackers descend like bobcats fighting over a scrap of meat. Tear at Pup from every angle. Grab his arms. Weigh down his legs.

Hot blood pumps in Pup's ears over muted gasps and grunts. He's swinging his arms and thrashing his legs, but they have him.

Even as he struggles, meaty hands paw over him. Search for anything worth stealing. Rip the twine from his neck. Shred his one good pocket.

Pup's causing too much trouble and the guard untangles himself from the fray to rear back a thick fist. It lands soundly in Pup's guts and Pup folds.

The other two men let him double over for an instant. He takes the opening to leverage one knee at an impossible angle and when they pull him upright, he jerks a leg free.

The guard pulls back to punch again and Pup braces himself against the two men holding him. He kicks off the ground with his free leg. And just as the guard is leaning in toward Pup, the other two pull him back down.

With the force of their help, he lands the thick part of his brow on the guard's nose. Feels the other man's face crack.

The guard reels, and on instinct, the man holding Pup's right arm reaches out toward the guard.

Pup takes the opening, twists into the distracted man, pulls all his weight against the one still holding his left arm, and breaks free.

He runs.

Without his scavenge, he isn't worth the trouble to stalk and kill, but he keeps moving all the same.

When he no longer hears footfalls behind him, he drops low and keeps his breathing soft. Waits to see if they'll search him out.

They have an electric light, crank or solar he can't say, but he watches, belly to the ground, as it combs his small camp. They gather all of Pup's belongings and start toward town. Pup keeps still and silent long after their light has become a pinprick in the distance.

At dawn Pup is already walking south again, toward Washing. He shouldn't be. They won't take him. Not without something to trade. Food at the least. But his heart is beating too fast, his jaw clenched too tightly, the muscles in his hands too strained for him to get any rest.

Ghost appears beside him, a bounce in her floaty step, a good-morning smile on her face. Until she sees that his forehead is oozing blood.

She steps in front of him so he'll stop, and he does because she doesn't like it when he ignores her. She reaches out her not-really-there fingers and traces the line of his wound across his brow, around his eye. Her fingertips dip into him, but he feels nothing. Her eyebrows are crinkled together, her eyes wide, her lips turned down.

He tilts his head away from her not-touch. "Where were you last night?"

Ghost's arms fold over her chest and she seems to shrink.

"It doesn't matter," he says. "I've got a long way to walk and nothing to trade once I get there." He sidesteps her and starts forward, the plain ahead cast red by the morning glare.

She's in front of him again, her legs back-pedaling even though she seems to float half a hand length off the ground. Ghost points east, forms a tense line with her arm, gesturing with her entire body catty-corner past him into the wasted grassland.

Pup crosses his arms over his chest. He doesn't shout because Ghost is trying to help. She doesn't eat or sleep or get heat sickness, so she doesn't always understand him. "There are no towns in that direction. No wells, no food, no shelter."

He should go back to Bootstrap and panhandle at the market while it's still open, but he's not small and cute anymore.

Ghost waves away the concern. Like water is a minor setback. Gestures again, takes ten steps in the direction she wishes him to follow, steeples her hands before her face, begging.

Pups unfolds his arms to let them hang limp at his sides. Forces his hands to unclench.

The first time he met Ghost she was a little girl, smaller even than Pup had been. She was crying, alone, and she was so happy to see him that she helped him find his way back to civilization, such as it was, After the world ended. Since then she's grown with him, helped him find the best scavenge, warned him of danger, saved his life another dozen times.

I should follow her now, he thinks. Summer is upon him and he has no plan and no supplies to survive it. But something has changed. He doesn't understand what and she can't speak to explain it to him. She's never around anymore and he knows he wouldn't be here now if she hadn't pushed the pace over the winter. Ever since they scavenged...

"I don't have it anymore," he says.

Ghost quirks her head to one side.

Pup turns his palms up. "That Before box. You wanted me

to keep it out of the scavenge." He tugs at the scrap of fabric hanging from his pants that used to be a pocket. "It's gone."

She crosses the space between them, slowly. Studies his face in a way that reminds Pup of yesterday at the gate. Like she's measuring his worth. Pup's not sure what he'll do if Ghost finds him lacking too.

She holds her thin hand palm-up between them. Beckons him forward. Turns and leads him east.

Pup follows, squinting into the morning glare.

Pup's blood pumps thick and heavy through his temples. Sweat has soaked through his thinned, long-sleeved shirts and he's glad he doesn't have the heavy duffle bag to carry. His throat is dry and cracking, his mouth pasty, his vision wobbly around the edges.

The place where Ghost is leading him appears on the horizon as the last long rays of summer sunlight turn the edge of the plain golden. Pup can't see all of its features but the column towering over the sprawling, multistory main building tells Pup it's the power plant—the base—that the old woman in the market spoke about.

The field he's walking through is made up of reaped stubs of corn and wheat in rows as far as he can see in any direction, a haul big enough to feed an army. The road leading up to the entrance is patched with asphalt, some bits still black against the sun-bleached surface, laid this very winter. A fence, part cinder block, part chain-link, is punctuated by three guard posts. They are After structures, welded or stacked from scavenge, sturdy but sharp and ugly compared to the clean lines of the blocky building beyond.

The soldiers at the guard towers see Pup before he's come within a stone's throw of the entryway. A giant light, brighter than any solar light Pup's seen, swivels at the top of the tower nearest the main gate. Fixes on him, blinding and inescapable.

Pup holds up a hand to spare his eyes, to cast a shadow over his face. "Now what?"

A few steps ahead Ghost turns toward him. Then she fades away.

199

The soldiers are nearly in uniform. Most have only sand-colored short-sleeved shirts and cargo pants, but a few have button-up shirts with badges and patches. They march, not quite in step. All have boots in good repair. And rifles.

It's dark in large unused stretches and as they take Pup around the largest Before structure, he's not sure which direction would be best to run if he has to bolt. The fading sunlight is improved along the way with islands of electric light, but there are more guard towers farther along the perimeter that might make running a bad plan.

They pass a pair of silos that are each a few stories tall and look like they were transplanted from somewhere else; drag marks gouge the pavement around them. There are other soldiers, men and women, moving about with purpose. Some are old enough to have been soldiers in the Before time, but most are not. A few are younger than Pup, kids still.

They round a corner and Pup misses a step. A long ways off, toward a cinder block section of the gate, under a tent pole canopy, Pup sees a dozen sand-colored trucks. Each looks new, with huge undamaged tires, windows, headlights. Even the front grills are intact. They're a fortune, sitting there. Even without gas, he could live on a scavenge like that for years.

Pup slows his pace to gawk and one of the soldiers pokes him hard in the back with the butt of a rifle.

There's a metal stair with studded steps bolted into the brick sidewall of the main building. It ends in a single door with a window that lets off the bright glow of electric light. Soldiers behind take up spots at the bottom of the stairs. Soldiers ahead escort him inside.

The room is a collection of luxuries. Two overstuffed leather couches on top of a thick floor rug. Ceramic lamps with paper shades in each corner of the room and a fifth lamp with a green plastic shade craned over a heavy wooden desk near the far wall. A row of brightly painted clay pots house strawberry vines in bloom. Artwork in frames with unbroken glass decorate the freshly painted yellow walls.

There are two women in uniform in the room, but the one sitting at the desk draws Pup's attention. Her hair is sun-lightened brown, straight, and cropped cleanly to her jaw line. Her sand-colored shirt buttons up in the front and has more badges and patches than any other soldier Pup has seen so far, though she's too young to have been an adult soldier when the world ended. She appraises Pup from head-to-toe as though he is a scrap of too-old meat and she's trying to decide if it's worth the risk of food poisoning.

She asks, "This is him?"

The other woman is standing beside the desk and answers, "Yes, sir, that's right."

Pup forces himself to break eye contact with the woman behind the desk. Looks at his hands. To the woman standing.

Pup's mouth hangs open. The blood drains from his guts in an unpleasant whoosh and his fingertips go numb. He feels the ground tilt beneath his feet, though he's still upright.

The standing woman is Ghost.

Not see-through, or purple, or floating.

She has wavy, dark hair that rebels against the braid running like a spine on the back of her head. Her eyes are too small. There's a mark peeking out from under the collar of her sand-colored short-sleeved shirt that looks as if tea stained the skin of her neck and never washed out. With her booted feet planted on the ground, she's taller than him.

But it's Ghost. There's no mistaking her.

When she speaks again, this time under Pup's stare, her voice seems misplaced. It reminds Pup of a puppet show he saw at a town two winters ago that'd had very bad actors and he's too distracted to notice what she said.

"Does he speak?" It's the woman behind the desk. Everyone in the room is staring at him. She speaks again, slowly, her voice raised like he's standing farther away than he is, "What's your name?"

He closes his mouth. Locks his eyes on the shiny brass arm of the lamp on the desk. "Pup."

Her tone twists in annoyance. "That's not a name, that's supper. What's your real name?"

Pup swallows the bile wetting the back of his mouth. He hasn't had a drink since yesterday. He focuses only on the goal of getting some water from these people. He'll deal with everything else after.

He returns the woman's stare. "Pup's good enough. Who're you?"

The woman behind the desk sits up straighter, her eyes narrowed to look down her nose at Pup. He's said the wrong thing. "I am General Nass—the highest ranking officer still operating in the United States Army—and you'll show the proper respect."

Pup bows his head, tries to make himself look small, lets the rasp that's leaking into his voice come through. "I'm sorry, General. I didn't mean anything by it. I'm not thinking clearly. I haven't had any food or drink in two days."

General Nass taps her fingers impatiently on the glossy desk. To the woman who is and is not Ghost, she says, "Are you wasting my time with this shit, Alice?"

"No, sir."

Pup peers at his captors from under his brow. He does not look at the woman named Alice.

Nass sighs. Flicks her hand toward Pup.

A soldier passes Pup a half-full canteen. Pup takes his time. Drinks every drop inside, unsure of when he'll get more.

While he's sucking down the water, Alice says to Nass, "He's a scavenger. One of my anchors. And I saw the power plant. He salvaged usable components. I wouldn't have dragged him here for your inspection if I wasn't certain he would be useful to you."

Pup swipes the drizzle on his chin into his mouth with the heel of his hand. He can't tell if the wobbly feeling in his guts is from the sudden rush of water or because of what Alice is saying about him. Anchor. He doesn't like the sound of that.

Nass says, "You have some reactor component? Let's see it."

"Don't have anything from a reactor."

Her eyes shift to the soldier taking the canteen from Pup's hands.

"Not a thing on him when we picked him up outside, sir."

Nass makes a sound between a growl and sigh, then pinches the bridge of her nose. "So what is he good for?"

Alice hedges, "He's a good scavenger. He could help you relocate the other reactor to power—"

"I'm not seeing the proof to back up what you're promising."

"Perhaps if you let him stay over the summer—"

Nass pounds the desk with a fist and the lamp, the strawberry pots, and everyone in the room jumps. "You may have been a darling of the last command, but all I can see is that keeping you requires more and more maintenance. You need to make yourself useful. This," she holds out an open hand toward Pup, "is not useful."

"General—"

"No." To Pup, "I'm afraid Alice led you here for nothing. I decide who stays and goes."

Alice tries again, "Please, General Nass—"

The general fixes her in a glare that silences her. To the soldier standing beside Pup she says, "Lock him up."

Pup tries not to think, but he's been so stupid it's hard not to go over every mistake that led him here. Letting himself get robbed so close to summer. Traveling too far too fast to gather enough scavenge. Trusting the shadow of a girl when he knew something was off. But she was Ghost. His Ghost. How could she have led him here to this?

He pushes the image of the flesh-and-blood woman out of his mind. It's harder to forget her voice, speaking about him as though he wasn't standing before her.

It's cold in the holding cell. The room is made of unpainted cement that still looks new and smells somewhere between dust and bleach. There are no windows, but long tubes overhead cast sickly light and buzz with electricity. Every so often they dim or flicker. One set of bunk beds is bolted to the wall, and Pup can see that it's been torn away from somewhere else and remounted here. Scavenged.

Time passes strangely. The air doesn't change, the lights don't change, and Pup's not sure if he's hungry or if the hollow feeling wearing on his stomach is the fear that they won't remember to feed him.

The false lights overhead go out and it's beyond any blackness Pup's ever known on the plains. Like he's been buried alive. His breath comes fast and shallow. Sweat soaks the tattered collar of his shirts and the fabric sticks to his cold skin in clumpy wisps. No matter how wide he opens his eyes, he can't see.

If it's been minutes or hours, Pup can't say, but he's staring at the door when Ghost's head pops through. The door doesn't open—it's not the girl from upstairs—it's really Ghost: see-through and purple and glowing without giving off any light. Pup's heart beats so loudly that the soldier on the other side of the door might hear it.

Ghost looks over Pup and vanishes.

Pup sits up as the bolt groans in the wall and the door opens, yellow lamplight pooling in.

Alice moves the door only enough to let herself in. She's carrying a flashlight that could double as a club and wearing thick socks that make her footsteps a whisper against the concrete floor.

"Hello, Pup." Even though she's whispering her voice seems too loud, too real.

Pup glances at the door without meaning to. She didn't bolt it again. How far could he get before someone noticed?

"If I thought we could sneak out, I'd try. Nass has you locked down. That's why it took me this long to sneak in."

Pup angles away from her, crosses his arms over his chest.

She watches him, her too-small eyes wide, as she straightens her loose, short-sleeved shirt.

Pup opens his mouth to speak, softly so that the guard won't hear, but he's not sure what to say, "Look, Alice—"

"You can still call me Ghost. If you like." Her smile is a phantom of the one he knows. "I don't mind."

He grinds his teeth. She looks so convincingly like his best friend but is completely different in every way. "Fine. Ghost, then. I don't have the reactor part anymore. You're on your own."

"I didn't come for that."

"So what do you want?"

"To talk to you. After all this time, I can't believe you're here." She sets the flashlight down and crosses the room to sit lightly at the other end of his cot.

Pup puts elbows to thighs, massaging his forehead with the tips of his fingers so he doesn't have to look at her. "Funny, since you're the one who led me here."

"You were hurt, and I thought if I got you here, I could convince Nass—"

"I heard what you said to Nass. How I'm one of your marks."

"A mark? I didn't—"

"Anchor." Pup leans back against the wall. "Yeah, I got what you meant."

She folds her arms over her chest in that way that always made Ghost seem small. "I can project my mind outside my body."

It's not what Pup expected her to say, and the reply he has ready gets lodged in his throat.

"I can't go very far, maybe half a mile, but there's a machine that lets me go much further. I was part of a military experiment just before the Collapse. And when General Ackerman—a real general, not like Nass—lost contact with the outside world, he asked me and the others like me to scout for him."

Ghost holds her chin high. "I'm the youngest. And better at it than the others. A lot better. But the plane and the physical world aren't alike, and I hadn't learned how to control my projection.

"I got lost."

She's studying Pup now, like she's saying something he should understand. But he doesn't.

"My body was dying here while I was on the plane looking for something to latch onto. To get my bearings." Ghost is smiling in a way that doesn't suggest happiness. "And then you found me.

"You weren't like the others. I can make most people see me, but at that time it was chaos. I couldn't make a connection. When I reached out to you, you reached back. You were my *anchor*."

Pup is shaking his head.

"You saved my life."

"No," Pup's voice is thicker than he means for it to be. "I'd lost my parents and I didn't stand a chance until you found me. I'd have died of heat stroke in a day—I was just a kid."

"So was I."

"But I didn't do anything."

"You were there for me when no one else was."

It's all backward from what he knows. Ghost takes care of him; it was never the other way around.

"That's why I was always pushing you in this direction. I thought if I could get you here..."

Pup finishes for her, "They'd let me stay."

Ghost rubs her fingernails together, making little clicking noises in the silence. Her voice is too soft, "And then Nass came. She was a refugee. Smart. Gained support. And General Ackerman died." She swallows hard. "He was old but...It happened so suddenly. We were all devastated."

"But not Nass," Pup guesses.

She meets his gaze. "No. Not Nass. She named herself general. We lost a lot of our original people. Nass got rid of them, one way or another."

Pup asks, "Why didn't you try to get away?"

"I couldn't have found you without the machine. When we scavenged a reactor, I hoped that Nass might let you sign on. She wants to expand, has a salvage of factory equipment—if she can get the plant really running. But now it's all so messed up. This is my fault. I should've been with you last night."

"Why weren't you?"

She points to the dead overhead lights and spits out the words, "Power restrictions."

Pup imagines reaching out, touching her shoulder, feeling that she's real. "That's not really your fault then, is it?"

She looks away. "Feels like my fault."

Silence settles over the space. The cold concrete wall at Pup's back is leeching the warmth from his body and he's afraid that if he doesn't say the right thing, she will leave. "I thought you were really a ghost."

She smiles the familiar, completely foreign, smile. "Most people I project to can hear me. You're the least psychic person I've ever met. I could've hurt you, forcing my way further into your mind than your nature allows."

Pup takes a moment to consider that.

"Tomorrow," Ghost says, "Nass will decide what to do with you."

"Any chance I'll get to stay?"

"I doubt it. Nass... likes to be the smartest person in the room. She only keeps people she knows she can control."

Pup's not sure he wants to hear the answer, but he asks anyway, "How does she control you?"

"With the machine. She thinks I'm addicted to it. She doesn't know the real reason that I needed it was you."

"I'm sorry."

She blinks. "For what?"

"I didn't know," he gestures at nothing, struggles for the right way to say it, "that it took so much for you to help me."

She smiles her best Ghost smile, the one that always made her purple glow a little stronger. Only now, in the splintered light she's brighter than he's ever seen her.

"I should get back before they find me here. Nass is treating you like enemy number one while you're on base. Pulling extra staff to guard duty in this part of the complex."

"Wait." Pup's brow furrows. "Where is she pulling guards from?"

Ghost shrugs. "I'm not sure. Why?"

He's staring at the door, trying to remember the layout of the complex.

"Pup?"

"Sorry. Could you do me a favor?"

She tucks a lock of hair behind her ear, giving up on keeping it in the braid. "Anything."

It shouldn't make his stomach flip-flop to hear her say that. But it does.

Pup wakes when the glaring electric lights hum to life overhead. The soldiers don't offer him food or water. They lead him out of the depths of the base, through narrow corridors with well-maintained pipes overhead. The surface looks different in the daylight. Though Pup recognizes the spot where the trucks had been the night before, they're gone now.

Nass waits for him in the yard at the gate with more soldiers than Pup could possibly merit.

"Mr. Pup," she says with a hint of amusement that Pup takes as an insult, "you're free to go."

"Just like that?"

She shrugs. Standing, Nass is neither tall nor short, broad nor lean. She moves with absolute confidence, an ease about her that Pup can't copy with so many rifles at the ready. "I might believe that you found a reactor, Alice seems to, but without proof, you're not useful, so you're on your own."

"What if I want to sign on?"

Her eyes narrow for an instant. "You're not the sort of man I like to recruit."

"What happens to Alice?"

Nass's jaw muscles flex tight for an instant before she answers. "Alice is mine and none of your concern."

"If you send me out into the plains now, with nothing, I won't last the summer."

Her head wobbles from side to side as she weighs an answer. She motions one of the soldiers flanking Pup to step forward. Unbuckles his belt while he stands at attention. Frees a knife in a leather sheath. Tosses it to Pup's feet. "Tell you what, you bring me working scavenge from a real reactor—I'll pay you enough to buy you in anywhere." She smiles without humor. "But if my people catch you around here without something to show for it, you'll have more to worry about than summer heat.

"Cut him loose."

Pup barely manages to scoop up the knife before soldiers begin shoving him toward the perimeter.

Pup's careful to stay within half a mile of Base and the day is gone by the time Ghost appears. His muscles uncoil at her familiar image, though she seems too small to be the person he now knows. Her features are hard to make out, fuzzy around the edges, like a sun-bleached photograph. Her butterfly-bush purple flat and bland.

He asks, "How'd it go?"

She hesitates, nods.

Pup breathes out a sigh. "Okay, let's have it."

She bites her lower lip as she lifts both hands to mime the answer. Her fingers hang rigid in the air between them a moment and then she lets her arms fall back to her sides. She huffs noiselessly. There's too much.

"You said that you could push your way into my head. I need to know what you know."

Her form wavers, her eyes growing large before she crosses see-through arms over see-through chest.

"Do whatever you have to do, I'll be fine," his voice is even, but his stomach twists against itself.

Her lips press into a tight line and she shakes her head.

Pup grits his teeth. "Just do it."

Ghost looks to the sky as if she's looking for a way out, but there isn't one, so she extends a delicate hand toward Pup's forehead. When her not-really-there fingers brush against his face, Pup's world vanishes in a flash of blinding pain.

The inside of Pup's skull is on fire. His throat is shredded and his mouth is dry, tacky. His hands and feet tingle and his guts quiver. He opens his eyes one at a time and finds the world a bleary haze. He's on his back and there's something crusty coating his face. When the washed-out blue sky comes into focus, he lifts a shaking hand to scrape the film away from his nose, lips, chin. It's blood, sticky and flaking.

He sits up and the world spins. He doesn't remember walking, but he's not in the reaped field outside of Base anymore. Ghost isn't in sight, but the town of Bootstrap is. And he knows what he has to do.

Neither of the guards at the gate are the one from before, and Pup's not sure if they're the two friends that helped rob him on the plain. He doesn't have the time to wait until a shift change that might not see the guard he needs come on duty.

Pup lingers among the shanty booths, chewing his lip as he considers. The scent of roasted carrots and spiced meat causes his mouth to water, reminding him that he hasn't eaten, and if he had something to trade he could buy a skewer. A skewer...

The old woman.

He tears his attention from the gate to see gray dreadlocks hunched over a frayed shawl. She's holding the bit of wire but has stopped turning the skewers on the open-pit grill and they're starting to blacken on one side, char ruining the flavor hanging in the air. Her face is bowed down, but one eye watches him with that knowing stare that says she's survived in the After as long as he has and knows how to get by.

"You."

Her voice is dry, high pitched. She doesn't run. She's too old to escape him. "Care for a hot meal?"

"*You* told him where I was going. Which direction I was headed."

Her tongue darts over her flat lips. "I didn't—"

"I don't care. I'm not here for you. I just want to talk to him. He's got something worth way more than he knows, but he doesn't have a clue what to do with it. You tell him to meet me where we met last time."

"I'm not—"

"Just tell him." He glares at her until her jaw clenches and her features settle. She nods once. When Pup snatches a pair of skewers off the grill, she doesn't try to stop him, only watches as he makes his way onto the plain.

Pup sits in the glaring sun, wishing that he'd thought to say that he'd meet them in the shade of the market. At least here he can see them coming. The dry grass is crumbling in the heat and already patches of dirt show through. In a week or two, the dust storms will start.

He's expecting three men, but four figures appear in the distance. They're washed out to dusty pale by the high sun and flicker in waves of heat, ghosts on the plain.

As they draw near, Pup sees the guard who turned him away. He's the tallest not because of height, but because he carries himself upright. The other three are lean, hungry, prowling after their leader like coyotes.

The guard stops a few arm-lengths beyond Pup's reach and the others surround him, loose and snickering. The guard speaks first, "You wanted to see me."

His friends laugh.

"I have a deal for you."

The guard's spotted face angles toward the man to Pup's right, but he's still looking at Pup, a purple welt across his nose. "Dumb shit here thinks we're gonna give his stuff back. Whatcha think, guys?"

There's a chorus of grumbling threats that Pup interrupts, "You've still got that box from my pocket."

"'Fraid I traded all your crap away."

"No you didn't. Not this. No one will trade with you for it."

"And you will?"

"I've got a buyer." Pup pauses to let the idea hang in the air.

"So, what? I'm supposed to give it back to you and you'll let me in on the trade?"

Pup folds his arms over his chest. "No. You're going to give it back to me and while I've got General Nass and her soldiers at Base occupied, you're going to steal a working military truck with tread on the tires and a full tank of gas. Drive it down to Springfield and trade it for a small fortune."

It takes a second for them to realize what he's said, a brief silence before the three goons start to break down and laugh.

But the guard's not laughing. "Nobody steals from Base. Their patrol routes change, their guns are better, their supplies are never in the same place twice."

For the first time it occurs to Pup that for someone like this guard, stealing from the base would be a constant temptation. A dangerous one.

"I have someone on the inside."

"You have a friend on Base? You're some little shit scavenger. Who could you know?"

"My friend got volunteered. This is a once-in-a-lifetime opportunity, and I'm here to cash in."

"Then what were you doing trying to buy your way into Bootstrap?"

Pup shifts his weight and rolls his eyes up toward the sky as if he's annoyed with the guard's stupidity, but really he's taking a moment to pick the right lie. "I can't exactly do it alone, now can I? If I'm busy distracting, how am I supposed to steal a truck?"

The guard shakes his head. "You expect me to believe that was a test? That *you* were testing *me*?"

"You proved you've got the guts for thieving."

His response comes late, his voice even and softer than before, "You really didn't have enough."

"Doesn't matter now. You in or not?"

The guard sizes up his three friends, but none of them have a word to say. Too greedy, scared, or stupid to find a flaw in a plan that could net them such an impressive haul. Maybe they're as desperate as Pup.

The guard looks back to Pup. "What's the play?"

Pup studies him a moment longer. Wishes that Ghost was here.

He puts one knee to the dirt and pulls the knife from his boot. Cuts a line in the shape of Base's perimeter. Goes back over it and marks the important bits. "Right when the sun is highest in the sky, you'll be here...."

The room has wood paneling that soaks up the sickly electric light, leaving the space dim and small. There's a fold-out table in the center of the room with one metal chair. Along two of the walls are sturdy wooden shelves packed full of books, some not much more than scraps of paper bundled together.

As Nass leads Pup inside, a man old enough to have been an adult during the Before time starts and stands up straight. He's thin, too tall, and his graying hair is cropped close to his head. He's standing beside a long desk bolted to one of the book-free walls and stacked with electronic equipment in various stages of repair. If Pup were scavenging, he would have discarded most of it, except for the many gray and black cables that tangle and hang to the floor.

Nass hands the man Pup's Before scavenge while four of the soldiers follow them inside and the door clicks closed. The air grows heavy with the hot breathing of too many people for the space. They've taken the knife Nass gave him, and they're— every one of them—taller and heavier than Pup.

The man accepts Pup's scavenge with long fingers that are knobby at the knuckles. Squints at the shallow metal box in his palm and then pulls a pair of wire-rimmed glasses from his uniform's front pocket. He holds the glasses up without putting them on, inspecting the tiny metallic markings etched into the one green plastic side of the box.

Nass turns her attention back to Pup and holds out one hand toward the fold-out table and chair. A soldier claps a hand on Pup's shoulder and urges him into the seat.

The older man shakes Pup's scavenge next to his ear, but it doesn't make any noise. His mouth turns down as he nods in approval.

Pup exhales.

The man connects the part to some wires, presses a button, and the pile of equipment beeps. The room fills with its clicks and tiny fans wheeze to life.

He taps at a screen that casts his features in sharp shadows and blue light. He squints at the screen a long time, tap, tap, tapping.

All the while Nass watches Pup.

Then the man's eyes grow wide and he turns to speak too

quickly to Nass. "It's not corrupted. I can force it to mount, but the system won't boot to it. Still as a secondary drive I think I can trick the main system into thinking we've met the requirements of the security protocols and—"

Nass rolls her eyes, looking from one young soldier to another before interrupting the man's ramblings, "Speak English."

He blinks dumbly at Nass, licks his lips. "This," he points to the screen, "just advanced our efforts by ten years. Maybe more. If any of the other equipment is in this good of condition..." He doesn't need to finish. Everyone in the room understands. Even Pup.

Nass turns her attention back to Pup. Her eyes narrow in a way that Pup has only seen on wolves, circling, growling. She gestures to one of her soldiers without taking her gaze from Pup. The soldier unrolls a bundle of maps, kicking dust and the smell of moldy paper into the air.

Nass stabs the stack of maps with a finger. "You will tell me where you got this."

Pup fights against the wrenching hollowness in his stomach, swallows the tightness in his throat. "Let's see the reward first."

"You'll get it—"

Pup interrupts, "I'm not telling you anything, until I see the haul."

Nass's nostrils flare. She flicks her hand out and a soldier thuds a backpack onto the table.

The pack by itself would be a prize find. It has two nylon straps, wide and padded, and a dozen pockets with working zippers. Pup flips open the flap and loosens the unfrayed drawstring. He takes out each item, slowly, stretching out time.

Inside is as good as out: a clip-on flashlight with working bulb and batteries. Boots with unworn soles and laces. A dozen unrusted cans of meat. Two thick blankets finely woven from some synthetic that won't rot. Rope, pliers, sewing needles, army knife, a leather belt. All new.

It's enough to buy him into any town twice.

Nass is pacing between the table and the old man tapping at his Before equipment, but the general's eyes never leave Pup.

Pup packs everything back inside, it's a challenge to get it all to fit so that he can pull the drawstring closed.

"Now," Nass says, "the maps."

Pup slides the heavy pack aside to get at the papers. He only knows how to read a few words, so even though he remembers how he got from there to here, it takes him a long time to get his bearings.

Nass lurks always at the edge of Pup's vision, and Pup takes his time. He shifts through each map, looking for some way to decode the markings. Finally, he settles on one with less writing. It doesn't highlight the old, deteriorated roadways and abandoned towns as much as some of the others. Pup focuses on riverways he recognizes, though many were only dried-up beds by the time he encountered them.

Pup asks about the map. Nass explains the symbols. Gives him a red pencil, and Pup picks out his route, starting at Base and working backward. He marks the dangers he faced along the way and suggests what kind of equipment would be ideal for each leg of the journey. Nass quizzes him, trying to catch him in a lie.

Long after Pup has figured which point on the map Nass needs, he's still asking questions, pretending to narrow down the space, and Nass is eager to supply Pup with answers.

"Okay, I have it," Pup says when Nass is about to burst.

Pup is hunched over the table, and Nass leans in, intent on the map, her face only a couple of hand-lengths away from Pup's. Pup clenches his jaw, tightens his stance, and waits for Nass to meet his eyes. Waits a beat after he's locked Nass in his stare. Says, "If I give you this, you're going to let me walk out of here."

Nass doesn't answer right away, which makes Pup think she might be telling the truth when she says, "Fine. Yes. Now tell me."

Pup is trotting across the grassland at a pace he could never keep up during daylight with the heavy pack. But the air cools with the oncoming night. He's in too big a hurry to care about the stitch in his side or the spasm in his thigh.

He can't know if the guard and his friends were captured, if they did their part right, or if they left him behind. Not until he gets to the meeting spot.

The bottoms of his feet still tingle from when Ghost forced her way into his head. And he's beginning to suspect it might not stop. It's a small thing. A trade he'd make again in a heartbeat to get to stand face-to-face with her real-girl version even one more time.

He waits until Base is out of sight, far behind, before he fixes the clip-on light to the pack at his shoulder. His head is up and he's squinting into the darkness between the edge of his bubble of light and the orange glow of the evening sun burning up the horizon. He should be about there, but he doesn't see them. He's a little late, but not so late that they'd have gone on without him, right?

Pup's looking to the left when a pair of blinding headlights cut on directly in front of him. One pair. A single truck. Then they flicker back off and he hustles the rest of the way.

The guard is leaning against the sand-colored military truck, his elbow crooked over its hood like it's a pretty girl. He's showing all his boxy teeth in a grin that stretches his spotted face too wide. "Guess I gotta take back all that shit I said about you behind your back."

"What about all the shit you said to my face?"

The guard throws his head back and laughs, high on his success. There are vague shapes, darkened outlines, of people inside the truck. The guard's goons. Pup doesn't see Ghost. "How'd it go?"

The guard pretends to think about it before he nods, his smile settling into a sly grin. "It went."

Silence stretches between them. The longest moment passes while the guard considers him. "You have any more bright ideas, you let me in, yeah? You see I'm good for my part."

Pup shifts his weight, impatience leaking into his voice, "Haven't seen that you're good just yet, have I?"

"I did just what you said. Gave her a *'choice.'*"

The blood drains too quickly from Pup's face, leaving him lightheaded. "And?"

The guard shrugs. Bangs his fist on the hood of the truck.

The rear passenger door opens and out climbs Ghost. She takes her time crossing the space to stand beside him. Smirks when she catches him staring. Pup remembers to close his mouth. To breathe. Looks back to the guard.

He winks at Pup.

"Alright," Pup says to the guard, "I guess you are good for it."

The guard laughs again, throwing his arms out to either side, wiggling his fingers toward himself. "You see? Remember me now. I'm your man."

Pup doesn't commit either way as the guard climbs into his truck and starts the engine.

Ghost leans in close, smelling of soap. "We're not going with them to Springfield?"

"No," Pup says, quiet so the guard won't hear him over the even rumble of the engine, "if Nass is going to try and track us down, she'll start by getting the truck back, and I don't want to be anywhere near there when that happens."

Ghost considers this as the guard turns the truck about, laughter spilling out of the cab, into the night.

Ghost asks, "Where are we going?"

Pup waits until the red glow of the truck's taillights has faded into the expanse. When he's sure they've gone, he unshoulders the heavy pack and kneels, tossing back the flap.

Ghost lets out a low whistle when she sees the supplies inside.

He says, "We can buy our way into Salem with this, easy."

"Then?"

"We can work for room and water during the summer."

She raises an eyebrow. "What kind of work?"

"Whatever they have. I might be able to find something that'll get enough water for both of us. Maybe make something out of your projecting? Or if you could read a little bit—"

"I can read. And write. In English and Spanish."

Pup laughs. Harder than he means to. Harder than he has in a long time, and it reminds him of the guard's too broad smile.

He closes the pack and hefts it onto his back. "Know any percentages? Addition?"

She falls in next to him as he strikes out, heading south, giving him a side-eye like she can't tell what he thinks is so funny. "We had regular school until Nass took over. I know up to college Algebra."

"Of course you do. What's Algebra?"

"That's a few years after percentages."

"In that case, you won't have any trouble finding a job. Maybe *you'll* work for both of us."

She's quiet for a time while they walk. Then she asks, "What happens after summer?"

Pup's stomach flip flops unpleasantly. He's never had to think about more than surviving the next summer, but Ghost has been playing a long game their whole lives. She wants a real plan, and he's not sure he has one good enough for her.

"When winter rolls around, I'll head out. Find a good scavenge and go from there."

"Are you going to bring me with you?" Her voice is high, tight.

He grips the strap on his shoulder so that it bites into his palm, but doesn't dare to look over. "I can bring you, if you like."

"What if I decide I'm happy with the work in Salem?"

"Then I guess you'll stay."

Ghost slows to standing and Pup stops. He turns to face her, but keeps his head down.

She asks, "Will you stay with me?"

It's a moment before he works up the nerve to meet her gaze. The Ghost he knew was a sad shadow of the person before him. Her brown eyes bloom green at the center, like the plains at the start of winter. Her glossy hair is too thick for the military braids to contain. She is tall, educated, soft-skinned, and discerning.

Her brow unfurls, and whatever she sees on his face forces her across the space between them. She reaches for him and when she takes his hand, Pup's fingers tremble.

Pup answers, "I can stay. If you like."

Fiction without Paper

BY ORSON SCOTT CARD

Orson Scott Card is the author of the novels Ender's Game, Ender's Shadow, *and* Speaker for the Dead, *which are widely read by adults and younger readers, and are increasingly used in schools. His most recent series, the young adult Pathfinder series (*Pathfinder, Ruins, Visitors*) and the fantasy Mithermages series (*Lost Gate, Gate Thief*) are taking readers in new directions.*

*Besides these and other science fiction novels, Card writes contemporary fantasy (*Magic Street, Enchantment, Lost Boys*), biblical novels (*Stone Tables, Rachel and Leah*), the American frontier fantasy series* The Tales of Alvin Maker *(beginning with* Seventh Son*), poetry (*An Open Book*), and many plays and scripts, including his "freshened" Shakespeare scripts for* Romeo and Juliet, The Taming of the Shrew, *and* The Merchant of Venice.

Card was born in Washington and grew up in California, Arizona, and Utah. He served a mission for the LDS Church in Brazil in the early 1970s.

Besides his writing, he teaches occasional classes and workshops and directs plays. He frequently teaches writing and literature courses at Southern Virginia University.

Card currently lives in Greensboro, North Carolina, with his wife, Kristine Allen Card, where his primary activities are writing a review column for the local Rhinoceros Times *and feeding birds, squirrels, chipmunks, possums, and raccoons on the patio.*

Fiction without Paper

It was a hard mental transition, when I first started writing on a computer back in 1979. The first time I lost twenty pages of writing, I began rigorously printing out my work every few minutes. If it wasn't on paper, it didn't really exist.

Gradually, my mindset changed. Instead of printing everything out, I saved it on multiple eight-inch disks. I no longer looked at stacks of typed-on paper with satisfaction, unless the same text was also saved on disk. Otherwise, typed manuscripts represented writing I couldn't do anything with.

My writing didn't become "real" until I could manipulate it with my word processing software. Therefore, printed paper was pretty useless. Only when I had keyed a manuscript into the computer did it exist in any useful way. There were new pleasures, though. When the story or novel was complete, ready to send to the editor, I would issue the PRINT command, and the NEC Spinwriter would start to type away at a lovely speed, as if I had a fantastic typist preparing my manuscript for submission. I would eat dinner, play with my kids, or watch a TV show while hearing that untiring worker typing away in my office upstairs.

When it stopped, I would tear off the last sheet, then separate the fanfold pages of the manuscript on the perforations, until at last I had a tall stack of pages, which I boxed up, wrapped, addressed, and shipped off to the publisher. But I already thought of that pile of pages as a copy—the original, the true document, was the series of bits and bytes electronically and redundantly stored on multiple disks.

Now, more than thirty-five years later, I can't remember the last manuscript I submitted in a box. Now I attach an .rtf file to an email and poof, it's submitted. It never touches paper between my computer and the editor's machine.

And while books printed on paper are still selling well, there are alternatives now. Books are written on a computer, prepared for publication, and issued as ebooks without paper ever being involved, between the writer and the reader. You can find a book that looks interesting on a website, buy it, and download it immediately. Either in print or as an audiobook, you start reading or listening only moments after making the decision to buy.

Yet all these hastenings do not make the act of telling the story one whit easier or faster.

You still have to invent the characters and the things they do and the reasons they do them. You still have to create the milieu of the story. You still have to spawn the language that will help readers create the story in their own minds.

And we still have to find people willing to put forth the work to read. I do mean "work." Watching a story unfold on a screen is not a mindless process—when the camera skips around in time and space, we have to do the work of organizing the events in some kind of order in our minds.

But that is nothing compared to the work that readers do. Their brains decode the symbols on paper and transform them into words, which enter the brain through the aural centers of the brain, so that they process the text as spoken language.

Then they use those verbal cues to create their own visual and audible sequences. Some people visualize more than others, but they create in their minds the same level of visual reality that they use for their memories of real events.

Just as with the memories of eyewitnesses, the story that they hold in memory is not "what actually happened." Instead, they remember the story as edited by their perceptions, their world view, the way that these events fit into their previous understanding of the causal universe.

At the same time, the causality offered by the fictional story also adds to or alters their mindset, so that to the degree the story has changed them, it participates in changing all future stories—and all future real events—by adding new elements to the available vocabulary of causes and motives their minds will assign to them.

Put another way, reading fiction makes the reader a willing collaborator. Just as an orchestra performs the notes assigned to each instrument, and actors and technicians in a play recite the assigned dialogue and execute all the set and lighting changes, so also the reader performs all the dialogue, designs and builds all the sets, creates the sound effects, casts and costumes the characters, all while simultaneously acting as the audience for the performance.

This is quite a set of mental tasks for the reader to perform all at once. It requires immense concentration. Yet when it's done, the reader credits the author with having created all those effects in memory.

I've had readers accuse me of writing horribly explicit violence in some of my stories. The few times when I've had a copy of the story in question at hand, I've challenged them to find the passages where I wrote such painfully explicit events.

They never find them, because they aren't there in the text. Instead, my text invited them to imagine some awful things—but all the details were put there by their own performance of my story, not by the text I actually wrote. Reading is hard work. There is such a thing as a talent for reading, as well as an acquired skill. Many people never get good enough at it to derive much pleasure from it. Others simply don't find the resulting performance worth the work.

Especially when there are attractive, easy alternatives like television, films, and video games, reading becomes something that more and more potential readers put off until another time.

When you watch a movie, people are put up on the screen fully formed. There's the actor, walking and talking. If it's a movie star we've already formed an attachment to, or if the actor is personable, then we engage with him or her exactly as we would with a real person. It takes no imaginative effort.

222

When characters appear in a story for the first time, however, we don't know who they are. Their mannerisms can't be instantly likeable, even if the writer tells us that they are. It takes time and work to get to know them, and, lacking all the easy outward signs we've learned to use to evaluate real people, we only get to know them by the gradual process of coming to understand their motives and attitudes—how they view and respond to the world around them, and what they mean to accomplish by their actions.

Gradually, these characters insinuate themselves into our minds so that we believe in them as surely as we believe in the characters we actually see on the screen. In fact, we believe in them more deeply because we understand them from the inside, for fiction can take us where film can never go: inside the character's mind.

But the effort of getting to know a character on the page can become a powerful barrier to engaging in a new work of fiction. I think that's one reason why we begin to prefer big thick books as we gain more experience in reading. Even when the cast of characters is enormous, our investment in the learning curve keeps paying off, chapter after chapter.

Short stories are another matter entirely. Each story requires a new round of initial investment. We should think of short stories as much easier than big novels, because they're so quick to read. But this ignores the fact that reading fiction isn't a mechanical process, it's a participatory one. It may take fewer hours to read a short story than a novel, but starting a short story takes as much effort as a novel.

Indeed, because the writer is working within a much smaller space, the reader may have to exert more mental effort to get inside the story, because the writer devotes less text to the task of introducing people and situations. More initiatory work is often required of the short-story reader than of the novel reader.

This may explain why it is that as more and more entertainments compete with fiction, it is the short story, not the novel, that has been the main loser in the public mind. It's as if, when we decide to read at all, we choose to invest that startup work in a fiction that will reward us with more hours and deeper experiences than are possible within the pages of a short story.

And if we can immerse ourselves in three or five or seven thick volumes set in the same milieu, following the same characters, then with each volume we aren't really starting at all. We're merely resuming where we left off. The initiation task is finished.

I think that's at least part of the reason why the readership of science fiction and fantasy magazines has plummeted in the past decade, while novel sales are as high as ever—or higher. More and more magazines have opted for Internet-only distribution, because they can avoid the costs (and losses) involved in print publication. Yet even with instant delivery of stories through magazine websites, far more readers choose to buy and download novels in ebook or audiobook form than short stories.

Does this even matter? After all, the same problem faces short-story writers as short-story readers: The development and startup time for writing a good short story is every bit as involved and requires every bit as much work as for writing a good novel. But a short story will reward you with only a few hundred dollars (maybe a bit more if it happens to be included in later anthologies), while a novel can pay the writer far more, and continue over a longer period of time. This is why the short story magazines are always searching for excellent new writers—because last year's excellent new short-story writers are now writing novels so they can make a living.

Yet that's exactly why short stories matter in science fiction and fantasy more than in any other area of fiction writing. Science fiction and fantasy depend for much of their value on the invention of new worlds—not always planets per se, but milieus in which the rules of the universe, or of the society, are quite different from our own and from all the other worlds invented for previous fictions.

Short stories offer a way for writers to explore new ideas and try them out on the audience. If the story becomes a favorite

224

ORDER FORM

WRITERS OF THE FUTURE

L. Ron Hubbard Presents Writers of the Future volumes: (paperbacks)
❑ Vol 22 $7.99 ❑ Vol 23 $7.99 ❑ Vol 24 $7.99 ❑ Vol 25 $7.99
❑ Vol 26 $7.99 ❑ Vol 27 $7.99 ❑ Vol 28 $7.99 ❑ Vol 29 $7.99
Trade paperbacks:❑ Vol 30 $15.95 ❑ Vol 31 $15.95

L. Ron Hubbard Presents Writers of the Future: The First 25 Years
(hardcover) $44.95   _____

L. Ron Hubbard Presents the Best of Writers of the Future
(trade paperback) $14.95   _____

OTHER SCIENCE FICTION/FANTASY BOOKS BY L. RON HUBBARD
❑ Battlefield Earth paperback $ 7.99
❑ Battlefield Earth abridged audiobook CD $33.95
❑ Fear paperback $ 7.99
❑ Fear abridged audiobook CD $14.95
❑ Final Blackout trade paperback $11.95
❑ Final Blackout abridged audiobook CD $14.95
Mission Earth trade paperback $22.95 each
Volume: ❑ 1 ❑ 2 ❑ 3 ❑ 4 ❑ 5 ❑ 6 ❑ 7 ❑ 8 ❑ 9 ❑ 10
Mission Earth abridged audiobook CD $14.95 each
Volume: ❑ 1 ❑ 2 ❑ 3 ❑ 4 ❑ 5 ❑ 6 ❑ 7 ❑ 8 ❑ 9 ❑ 10
❑ To the Stars hardcover $24.95
❑ To the Stars unabridged audiobook CD $25.00

❑ **Check here for a complete catalog of L. Ron Hubbard's fiction books.**

SHIPPING RATES US: $3.00 for one book. Add an additional $1.00   Tax*:   _____
per book when ordering more than one.
SHIPPING RATES CANADA: $3.00 for one book. Add an additional   Shipping: _____
$2.00 per book when ordering more than one.
*Add applicable sales tax.   TOTAL: _____

CHECK AS APPLICABLE:
❑ Check/Money Order enclosed. (Make payable to Galaxy Press.)
❑ American Express ❑ Visa ❑ MasterCard ❑ Discover

Card #:_____

Exp. Date:_____ Signature:_____

Credit Card Billing Address ZIP Code:_____

Name:_____

Address:_____

City:_____ State:_____ ZIP:_____

Phone #:_____ E-mail:_____

**You can also place your order by calling toll-free: 1-877-842-5299
or order online at www.GalaxyPress.com**
Select titles are also available as e-books and audio downloads at Amazon.com and other online retailers.

BUSINESS REPLY MAIL
FIRST-CLASS MAIL   PERMIT NO. 75738   LOS ANGELES CA

POSTAGE WILL BE PAID BY ADDRESSEE

GALAXY PRESS
7051 HOLLYWOOD BLVD
LOS ANGELES CA   90028-9771

**Fold at dotted line and tape shut with
payment information facing in and
Business Reply Mail facing out.**

among short-story readers, the writer is encouraged to continue developing the world. Not every writer and not every milieu follows this pattern—some new worlds spring into being in big thick books right from the start. But for many writers over the years—especially new writers, who represent more of a risk for book publishers, since they don't have a ready-made audience already eager for the next volume—short stories have provided an entry point, a way to familiarize an audience with their voice and their worlds and characters.

The whole genre benefits from a thriving short-story marketplace. One can argue that it is in the short stories that science fiction actually happens, with novels only the greatly elaborated ripples spreading out from the real point of impact. The general reading audience may see only the novel; but the short story audience were there at ground zero, where the writer first appeared, where the milieu of the story was born.

That's why it's even more important than ever before that one annual short story anthology continues to thrive, attracting a far larger readership than any of the surviving magazines.

Writers of the Future has always had the power to launch careers, and that power continues unabated. Thousands of people who never read the magazines, in print or online, pick up Writers of the Future because they know that the juried selection process will deliver stories that are always worth that initial co-creative investment.

It really isn't just the judging that makes the difference, though. After all, the magazines are often edited by professionals with every bit as much insight and taste as the Writers of the Future judges.

Part of the reason that readers trust Writers of the Future to deliver is that the contest is so efficiently run that new writers lose nothing and stand to gain much by submitting their stories to Writers of the Future first.

I know I'm not the only writing teacher who tells novice writers that all their genre stories should go to WotF before going to any other publication—and that includes the magazine I publish myself, *The InterGalactic Medicine Show.*

As long as a writer is still new enough to qualify for Writers of the Future, it only makes sense to submit stories to the contest because:

1. The response time is so quick, with quarterly contests guaranteeing that you will only wait a few months for an answer.

2. Writers of the Future is the short-story publication most likely to give a new writer a wide readership and begin to create an audience eager to see more.

3. Writers of the Future has earned great credibility in the industry, so that submitting your first novel to a publisher with a cover letter saying, "A short story of mine just won the quarterly Writers of the Future Contest," guarantees that the editor will begin to read it with more trust, more hope, that the book will be worth publishing.

Failing to win a quarterly WotF Contest does not mean, of course, that the story is not good. Because the WotF judges see most new writers' first stories before anybody else, they have no choice but to pass up many perfectly good stories, because they have only a finite number of awards to give and pages to fill in the anthology.

And even the contest winners have to have someplace to submit their later short stories; so the magazines are all able to find excellent stories even after the cream has been skimmed by WotF.

If it is true that short stories are where science fiction is constantly reborn (and it is), then Writers of the Future is the most trusted midwife. The book you're holding in your hands is our first sight of the next generation of science fiction and fantasy writers. And it will continue to serve that role, year after year, as long as the contest continues.

Rough Draft

written by

Kevin J. Anderson & Rebecca Moesta

illustrated by

DANIEL TYKA

ABOUT THE AUTHORS

Kevin J. Anderson is a #1 international bestselling author with over 130 books published and twenty-three million copies in print in thirty languages. He is best known for his Saga of Seven Suns science fiction epic, his Dan Shamble, Zombie PI humorous horror series, his Dune and Hellhole novels with fellow Writers of the Future judge Brian Herbert, his Star Wars and X-Files novels, and the innovative steampunk fantasy adventure Clockwork Lives, *a novel version of the concept album by legendary rock group Rush, co-authored with drummer and lyricist Neil Peart.*

With his wife of twenty-three years, Rebecca Moesta—also a Writers of the Future judge—Anderson has written fourteen volumes of the Star Wars: Young Jedi Knights series, the novelizations of several science fiction films, Star Trek and original comics, the Crystal Doors fantasy trilogy, and three science fiction adventures for the Challenger Learning Centers for Space Science Education. As a solo writer, Moesta has written novels for Buffy the Vampire Slayer, Junior Jedi Knights, and several short stories.

Together, Anderson and Moesta run the high-end Superstars Writing Seminars in Colorado Springs, and they are also the publishers of WordFire Press.

Kevin says, "Over years of watching brilliant, up-and-coming writers burst onto the scene—winning awards, grabbing review attention—and envying their raw talent, I also began to notice a pattern that baffled me. Some of these true creative geniuses, who had the literary world on a silver platter, just…gave up and vanished. I couldn't understand it. They obviously had the ideas and the skills to become truly well-known and successful, but for some people this scared them to death. I thought a lot about this and wondered about all those wonderful stories that could have been written. In 'Rough Draft,' one such writer has the opportunity to see an alternate timeline and read the work that he might have written, if only he'd stuck with it. The idea felt really powerful to me, and as I was putting the pieces together, I worked with Rebecca who could add an extra layer of emotional resonance. Of all the stories I've written, this one has a very special place in my heart."

ABOUT THE ILLUSTRATOR

Daniel Tyka is also the illustrator for "Switch" in this volume. For more information about Daniel, please see page 2.

Rough Draft

After a decade during which he wrote and published nothing new, the fan letters dwindled to a few a year.

"Dear Mr. Coren, You're the best science fiction writer ever!"

"Dear Mr. Coren, Your book *Divergent Lines* changed my life. I felt as if you were speaking directly to me, and you helped me work through some major issues."

The entire experience, though great for the ego, had ultimately proved meaningless. Eventually he'd been forced to return the money for the second book advance, because he simply couldn't do it again: write another book and, even harder, meet expectations. After enjoying a pleasant day in the sun, Mitchell Coren had retreated to his small apartment to live a normal life. The gleaming Nebula Award and the silver Hugo—both dusty now—were little more than knickknacks on the mantle of a fireplace that he never used.

Having convinced himself of the wisdom of J.D. Salinger's approach to authorial fame, Mitchell had squelched all thoughts of returning to writing. He immersed himself in a normal life with all its petty concerns.

Today, with an indifference born of long practice, Mitchell opened his bills and junk mail before finally tearing open the padded envelope that obviously contained a book. Another intrusion, no doubt. An annoying reminder of his old life. He still received advance reading copies from editors trying to wheedle a rare cover quote from him, rough draft manuscripts from aspiring authors who begged for comments or critiques, and books presented to him by new authors who had been inspired by his lone published novel.

Inside this envelope, however, he found his own name on the dust jacket of a novel he had never written.

INFERNITIES
Mitchell Coren
Multiple Award-Winning Author of Divergent Lines

Whirling flakes of confusion compacted into a hard snowball in the pit of his stomach. "What the hell?"

His initial, and obvious, thought was that someone had stolen his name. But that didn't make sense. Though many editorial positions had changed in the decade since he'd published *Divergent Lines*, Mitchell was still well enough known in the insular science fiction community that somebody in the field would have noticed an imposter. Besides, how much could his byline be worth after all this time? It wasn't worth stealing.

Someone had tucked a folded sheet of paper between the book's front cover and the endpaper. He read it warily.

Dear Mr. Coren,

As a longtime fan of yours, I thought you'd appreciate seeing this novel I came across in a parallel universe.

I'm a timeline hunter by profession. Perhaps you've heard of Alternitech? Our company uses a proprietary technology to open gateways into alternate realities. My colleagues and I explore these parallel universes for breakthroughs or useful discrepancies that Alternitech can profitably exploit: medical and scientific advances, historical discoveries, artistic variations. My specialty is the creative arts.

I stumbled upon this book in an alternate timeline while searching for a new Mario Puzo. Since the science fiction market isn't nearly as large or profitable as the mainstream, I couldn't spend much time checking out its background, but a brief search showed that the "alternate" Mitchell Coren published a dozen or so short stories after Divergent Lines, then produced this second novel. I'm hoping Alternitech will want to arrange for its publication, but naturally I felt you should see it first.

With deepest respect,
Jeremy Cardiff

Mitchell stared at the letter with mistrust and growing irritation. He had heard of this company that searched alternate realities for everything from new Beatles records, to evidence of UFOs or Kennedy assassination conspiracies, to cures for obscure diseases. He could understand the more humanitarian objectives, but why fiction? What gave Alternitech the right to infringe on his life like this?

He opened to the dust jacket photo and saw that the picture did resemble him, though this other Mitchell Coren wore a different hairstyle and a cocky, self-assured grin. The bio mentioned that after completing *Infernities* he was "already at work on his next novel."

Oddly unsettled, Mitchell pushed the book away. Its very existence raised too many disturbing questions.

Three increasingly urgent phone calls to his former agent went unreturned. Since Mitchell had neither delivered anything new nor generated much income, his agent wasn't in a great hurry to attend to his so-called emergency. Even in the days when he'd briefly been a hot client, Mitchell had been relatively high-maintenance, needing encouragement and constant contact.

He decided to contact his entertainment attorney instead. After all, Sheldon Freiburg charged by the hour and therefore had an incentive to get right on the matter.

"Mitch Coren! I haven't heard from you since the last ice age." Freiburg's voice was bluff and hearty on the telephone. "What on earth have you been doing? You dropped off the map."

"I've been working a real-world job, Sheldon. You know, regular paycheck, benefits…security?"

"Yeah, I've heard of those. Hopped off the old fame-and-fortune bandwagon, eh?"

"A modicum of fame, not a whole lot of fortune—as you well know."

Freiburg had handled the entertainment contracts for the two movie options on *Divergent Lines*. Mitchell had been young and naïve then, believing the Hollywood hype and enthusiasm. He'd been surrounded by smiling fast-talkers whose eager assertions of certain box-office appeal and guaranteed studio support were built on a foundation as strong as a soap bubble. After the attorney's fees and the agent's commission, the option money had been just enough to pay off his car, which was now ten years old.

"So, Mitchell," Freiburg said now, "people don't call me unless they have a situation—either good or bad—so let's hear it."

"Someone's trying to publish an unauthorized Mitchell Coren novel."

"You've actually done other work?" The lawyer sounded surprised. "Something new? I thought you'd turned hermit on us. Did somebody steal your manuscript?"

"This is trickier than that. It isn't exactly a matter of stealing. This is a novel from a parallel universe, and Alternitech wants to get it published here." He explained the situation in full.

"Oh, that is tricky—but not unheard of. Listen, since it's Tuesday, I'll give you a special deal, a quick and inexpensive answer."

"Inexpensive? You've changed in the last ten years, Sheldon."

The lawyer chuckled. "How could I help it? The whole world has changed. But you're not going to like what I have to say."

Mitchell braced himself, clutching the receiver; thankfully, Freiburg could not see his tense expression.

"Precedents have been set in this area. In every dispute about the use of materials from alternate universes, Alternitech has come out the winner. I'm convinced the company spends as much money each year on their team of lawyers as they did developing their parallel universe gateway. You'd be wasting your money to try and block the publication. Compared to the rest of the entertainment industry, authors and books are minnows in an ocean. Even the Big Fish in the music and film industries haven't won a single case.

"Alternitech's timeline hunters bring back intellectual property that might conceivably belong to a counterpart in this universe. The first big case was when one of their music specialists, a guy named Jeremy Cardiff—"

"That's who sent me the novel."

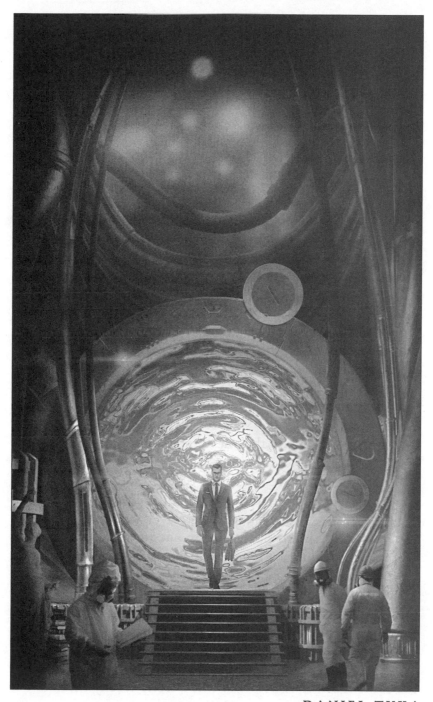

DANIEL TYKA

"Great," Freiburg said, then continued, as if the interruption hadn't happened. "In Alternitech v the Carpenter Estate, Cardiff found several new albums by the Carpenters, in an alternate reality where Karen Carpenter never died of anorexia. The CDs sounded like the same old shit to me, but don't underestimate the huge amount of money generated by piped-in background music. The Carpenter Estate sued, citing copyright infringement and unlawful exploitation of a creative work.

"Alternitech countered that since Karen Carpenter was dead in this universe, she could not 'create' new works after the date of her death. They also argued, using an old favorite of the pharmaceutical companies, that since Alternitech had made such a substantial investment developing their technology, they deserved to reap the benefits of its commercial exploitation.

"The ruling sided with the Carpenter Estate insofar as establishing a 'fair percentage' of profits that should go to the creator's counterpart in this reality—fifteen percent, I think it was. But since Alternitech's timeline hunters did all the work to obtain the property, kind of like salvage hunters on the high seas, they were granted full control of its use. Similar lawsuits have been raised by individual movie producers, screenwriters, directors, and even actors who resent the release of 'new films' starring them for which they never got paid. Like I said, in every case, they lose."

Mitchell remembered that one of the alternate Mel Gibson films had caused something of a stir, because the parallel-universe version of the actor had received an Academy Award for a role that this timeline's Gibson had turned down.

Freiburg continued. "When you get right down to it, Mitch, record companies and movie studios don't want the individual artists to win. Alternitech provides them with completely finished new work for a fraction of the cost or effort of making it themselves. Much less hassle, too. They just distribute the work through their normal channels and pay a standard percentage of artist's royalties directly to Alternitech. Then, if and only if the court orders it, Alternitech cuts a teeny weeny check to our own world's parallel artist or company or estate, and everyone is happy. Well, almost everyone."

"So you're saying I shouldn't even try, Sheldon? It's not... not right!"

"Mitch, if Paul McCartney can't win, then a mere sci-fi novelist doesn't stand a snowball's chance." He paused as if reconsidering. "On the other hand, Mitch my friend, I just thought of a factor that's ironically in your favor, if you really want to stop publication. There's a very real chance that Alternitech won't even bother with your little book. Look at your royalty statements. You're a science fiction writer ten years out of the public eye. Oh sure, there'd be a limited audience for a 'lost unpublished work' by Mitchell Coren... but it isn't exactly a Margaret Mitchell sequel to *Gone with the Wind*. If this Cardiff guy is a fan of yours, contact him and tell him how you feel. Who knows, he might do you a favor and pretend he never found it."

Mitchell didn't know whether to feel stung or take heart from the possibility.

Distracted and fretting, he polished the two awards on his mantel—something he hadn't done for the better part of a year. They looked quite impressive, he had to admit, and certainly gave him bragging rights. His occasional visitors asked about them, and he answered with feigned modesty. The awards seemed so irrelevant to his current life.

These days, Mitchell used his skills as a wordsmith in the unglamorous but stable profession of technical writing, producing essential documentation and annual reports for a manufacturing firm. Although it was a challenge to write compelling prose about new cereal box designs or recyclable plastic bottles, he was a master at slanting his text toward investors or consumers or environmental agencies, as needed.

Many of his coworkers—what the science fiction world called "mundanes"—were aspiring writers who never managed to finish or submit stories. Few of them knew about his past, however, since Mitchell rarely mentioned his novel.

As he rubbed a fingerprint off the Nebula's clear Lucite surface, looking at the suspended bits of metal shavings and semi-precious stones that formed a sparkling galaxy, he thought back to those brief, heady days. They were just memories now, but he wouldn't trade them for anything.

Divergent Lines had appeared with a splash like a giant water balloon. An excerpt of the novel had been published in *Analog* as the cover story and won that month's readers' poll. The novel itself had generated rave reviews and was immediately dubbed "a new classic" by critics and his fellow SF authors.

He had been welcomed as a hero at the World Science Fiction Convention. He'd always read science fiction, but had never attended a con before. The fans surprised him at panels, listening to everything he said. They lined up for his book signings in the autograph hall or followed him and asked embarrassingly earnest questions about details he himself had never considered.

When Mitchell went to the Hugo Awards ceremony, he found himself plunged into a sea of unreality as the emcee announced his name as the winner. Astonished and grinning, he stumbled up to the podium and held up his silver rocket ship with mixed feelings of shock and giddy triumph.

The following spring, thanks to the continued buzz, *Divergent Lines* had been a shoe-in for the final Nebula ballot. New to the entire experience, Mitchell stood like a lost puppy in the lobby and the bar, surrounded by luminaries of the genre. He recognized their names from the covers of well-loved books, famous writers ranging from Grand Masters to prolific hacks, all of them legendary and, for the most part, personable.

He'd been in a daze. These Titans of science fiction talked to him as a peer, praised his novel. Mitchell found it unnerving, and he began to wonder how he could ever live up to their expectations. Did he deserve so much praise and success? What if his next work didn't measure up to their expectations? Would he be exposed as a fraud and cast out of this distinguished circle of authors? How would he bear the humiliation?

His publisher had paid for his Nebula banquet ticket, and

Mitchell was treated as a celebrity at their table. With his stomach tied in knots, he could summon no appetite at all during the dinner at the pre-award festivities. In an agony of anticipation, he endured the drawn-out meal, the mandatory chit-chat, the interminable banquet speaker. By the time the awards finally began, plodding through each category as if in a calculated effort to increase his anxiety, Mitchell had convinced himself that he had no chance of winning. He was a newcomer. He had no track record. He had never played the politics of exchanging recommendations. He had not campaigned for the award. These writers couldn't possibly consider him a friend and certainly didn't owe him any favors.

And yet the name in the presenter's envelope said *Divergent Lines*. The Nebula seemed even more amazing than the Hugo, because this honor came from his peers, fellow professionals who supposedly knew good writing when they saw it. As Mitchell stood clutching the award, he imagined that someday, when he stood at the Pearly Gates and looked back on his entire life, this would be the high point....

After that night, though, Mitchell Coren never wrote another word of fiction. He had left the science fiction community behind and let *Divergent Lines* stand as his sole legacy.

Even in his heyday, Mitchell had not spent much time with die-hard science fiction fans. Not because he didn't like them—he appreciated anyone who bought and loved his novel. But he didn't understand their intensity or their passions and usually ended up feeling outclassed when they wanted to talk shop.

He met Jeremy Cardiff at a quiet place called Mrs. Coffee, a small bistro with shaded outside tables where they could have a conversation in a pleasant atmosphere. Mitchell didn't know which of them was more nervous. He could see in the timeline hunter's eyes that Jeremy was a bona fide Fan.

"This is really an honor, Mr. Coren. I've always been an admirer of *Divergent Lines*, and now that I've read *Infernities*, there's no doubt in my mind that you're one of my all-time favorite authors. I felt so surprised and fortunate to have found the book." Jeremy, a youngish man with a thin face, long hair, and a neatly-trimmed brown beard, looked like a waif hoping for a pat on the head. His blue eyes were wide, his smile tentative.

Mitchell took a drink of coffee, then cleared his throat. "Well, Mr. Cardiff, that's what I'm here to talk to you about."

"Please, call me Jeremy." Then the younger man's face fell as he interpreted Mitchell's reluctant tone.

Mitchell chose his words as carefully as he would have in preparing a viewgraph presentation for the board of the manufacturing company. He wasn't sure his reasons would make sense to anyone but himself. Though he knew he didn't exactly have a legal case, he might be able to play the celebrity card. Perhaps by asking a special favor from his number one fan, he could get what he needed. "I think you're perceptive enough to understand why I don't want the novel published here. It's not my book. Somebody else wrote it."

"No, Mr. Coren. You wrote it. Another version of you, maybe, but it was still your talent, your creativity. When I was in college I read and reread *Divergent Lines* until my copy fell apart, and I've been waiting ten years for a new novel by the same author. When I found *Infernities*, I sent you the physical book I brought back through the portal, but I made a photocopy. I'm already on my second time through it. It's brilliant—full of intricate layers and nuances."

Mitchell desperately wanted to ask which book he thought was better. Dedicated readers like Jeremy were generally his toughest customers and his harshest critics and, because Mitchell didn't think a new novel could ever live up to their expectations, he had decided not to try.

"That man may have the same name and the same genetics as I do, but he grew up in a parallel universe with a different set of circumstances. He's not me. He obviously reached a different decision about his career. But I didn't write *Infernities*, and if you published it here in our universe, people would see it as my own work, no matter how many disclaimers you put on it."

"But it's good, sir. Have you read it?"

"No, I don't dare. It would seem almost...plagiaristic."

As if clinging to hope, Jeremy said, "So...are you writing something of your own? Maybe a book that's similar to *Infernities*?"

"No. I'm not writing anything."

The young man looked at his coffee as if it were poison. He didn't seem angry at Mitchell's attitude, just deeply disappointed. "Then I don't understand. What made you stop writing? I mean, you got the royal treatment. People were lined up waiting for your next book. You had a contract to fulfill, didn't you?"

"Yes. And I...decided to return the advance."

"But why? It just doesn't make sense."

"Why? I'd already won the highest accolades in my field." Mitchell spoke softly, but his voice grew more intense. "Whether through brilliance or sheer dumb luck, I muddled my way to the pinnacle of success my first time out of the starting gate. *Divergent Lines* was hailed as the best book of the year, won all the awards, got spectacular reviews in every periodical from *Publishers Weekly* and *Kirkus* to *Locus* and *Chronicle*. *Library Journal* called it an instant classic."

Mitchell sighed. "Don't you see? The weight of it all gets oppressive. Where could I possibly go from there? There's no place but down." An edge of bitterness sharpened his tone. "It's a very long way down. No matter how good it was, my second book—*Infernities* or whatever I might've called it—would never be good enough. The fans and the critics certainly aren't kind unless your sophomore effort is unbelievably spectacular.

"As it stands right now, I'll go down in history as the author of a great novel. But if I published twenty other books, regardless of how well-written they might be, I can tell you some of the review quotes already: 'A solid novel, but not as inspired as *Divergent Lines*.' Or 'A fine effort, though it doesn't live up to the promise of its predecessor.' Or, worse yet, 'A disappointing follow-on to the author's first novel.'"

Jeremy frowned at what Mitchell was saying. "I think you're

too hard on your fans, sir. We would have followed you. Even after ten years, most of us still want to read whatever you have to say."

"Maybe I don't have anything else to say," Mitchell said. "I can name author after author who falls into that category. Being successful is a Catch-22. If your first novel is a smash hit, an award winner and a critical success, it might mean your career has momentum and you're launched. On the other hand, it could mean your writing will never be good enough again. What should I have done—expanded *Divergent Lines* and written a couple of unnecessary sequels, so I could call it a trilogy? I could have licensed my universe, farmed it out to other authors, but that just didn't seem right to me. Either way, I would have been crucified by the fans and the critics."

"Just by the snobs," Jeremy said, "not by the fans. But you disappeared from fandom altogether. When's the last time you went to a science fiction convention?"

"The WorldCon where I got my Hugo was the first and last. I stopped reading *Locus* and *Chronicle* and *Ansible* after one of them ran an editorial about one-hit wonders that led off with 'What ever happened to Mitchell Coren?'" He looked at his coffee. "I didn't stand a chance of keeping up the momentum in my career. Fans and critics are too unpredictable. So I controlled the only part of the equation that I could control: I stopped writing fiction. My life is stable now that I've accepted the wisdom of anonymity. But if Alternitech publishes this apocryphal second novel that I didn't really write, then I'll be at the mercy of the public's expectations again. Please, don't do it."

Disappointment and resignation filled Jeremy's eyes as he unzipped his backpack and reached inside to withdraw a thick stack of photocopied pages. "Look, this is my only copy. What happens to it is not really supposed to be my decision. Alternitech owns proprietary rights to whatever I bring back through parallel universes. Still, no matter how much I loved this novel, I have to admit that this doesn't have the equivalent value to Alternitech of, say, an unknown collection of Sherlock Holmes stories by Arthur

Conan Doyle or the Dean Koontz/Stephen King collaboration I uncovered once. I think people deserve to read it. I was going to have you autograph this for me." Jeremy slid the stack of papers across the table. "But now I guess you'd better keep it, so you'll know there aren't any other copies in existence. You decide what to do. It's your call, Mr. Coren. It's your book."

"I—" Mitchell started to speak, but found his voice choked with emotion. He took a long drink of his now-tepid coffee and started again. "Well...don't you want to keep it? You said you were reading it."

Jeremy shook his head. "If you know I have a copy, you'd always worry that someday I'd be tempted to post it on the Internet. It's better if you keep it."

The papers felt warm in Mitchell's hands. His vision blurred, and he took a moment to compose himself. "I...didn't expect this."

"I'm a musician myself, Mr. Coren. I write and record songs, but I haven't had much success so far. It was a minor consolation when I found that I did have a hit record in an alternate universe, but nothing here yet. I was the one who brought back the new music for that whole Karen Carpenter debacle, and I don't feel very good about it. As a musician, I thought Carpenter or her estate should have had some control over her own creative work, no matter which incarnation made the album. The same goes for you, sir. If you're uncomfortable about having *Infernities* published, then..." He shrugged.

"I can't tell you how much this means to me."

"I think I understand." Jeremy slurped his decaf cappuccino. "Besides, I'm your fan. I can't think of anything cooler than to know I am the only person in this entire universe who's read your new novel."

Dozens of the loose photocopy sheets wadded up under the fireplace grate made for good kindling. Mitchell rolled the remaining loose pages of twenty-pound bond into plump literary logs, rubber-banded them, and set them on the log holder above the crumpled pages. Then he fanned out the hardcover book

241

and flattened it across the white paper logs. He stood back to observe the diminutive funeral pyre with a sense of uneasiness.

He should have felt relieved.

This potential source of humiliation or disruption would soon be dealt with. The book would no longer be in his life, could no longer irritate or goad him by its very existence. No fans would have a chance to either criticize or clamor for more. The chapter would be closed.

Yes, Mitchell was definitely relieved.

After he lit the match, he hesitated for a long, indecisive moment before finally touching the flame to the edge of one of the loose sheets. There. A burnt offering to a cruel muse.

As the fire caught, guilt gnawed at the ragged edges of his mind. There was something intrinsically criminal about burning a book, especially the only copies of a book. While this event would not go down in history with the sacking of the Library of Alexandria, it was still a loss to at least some tiny backwater of the literary sea—especially to the hopeful fans who had waited so long for any work by Mitchell Coren.

The flames grew higher, devouring the loose pages and curling the glossy dust jacket of *Infernities*. An interesting play on words, he thought. Infinity, Alternative, and Eternity all rolled together. Now he could add "Inferno" to the quadruple-entendre. He wondered how it related to the story.

Didn't he owe it to himself at least to read his own work, to see what he could have done with his talent? *Infernities* was tangible proof that in some other reality his author-self had overcome the pressure and the expectations. But how? Didn't that mean that he, too, could do it?

No. He'd made the right decision. He thought with some satisfaction of the author photo blackening and blistering, cremating his cocksure successful doppelgänger. The man had dared to risk his reputation, his spotless literary legacy, to write this second novel and offer it to an unpredictable reading public. He had dared. Had risked...

With a groan of annoyance and frustration Mitchell snatched

the hardcover from the fire, dropped it to the floor, and stamped on it to put out the flames at the edges. He bent and picked up the singed novel that had disrupted his calm life.

As he picked up the blackened book, Mitchell's lips flickered in a smile. Though he still had no intention of publishing the novel, he would hold onto the book as a goad. Just to keep him honest. To remind himself of what could be.

He had his own ideas for new stories and novels, of course. Every writer did. The ideas had never stopped coming, and he had jotted down notes during lunch hours at his tech-writing job. Some of the outlines were damn good, but he had been too afraid of failure to write the books, believing it better to let readers live with his mysterious seclusion than to risk them shaking their heads in disappointment.

Yet his alternate self had somehow shaken off the fear of failure. Therefore, it could be done. And that sincere, appreciative look he had seen in Jeremy Cardiff's eyes told Mitchell he still had an audience, no matter how small. . . .

Some authors were motivated to write strictly for the critics, for the kudos and awards. Others wanted the money and name recognition of sales, with big print runs and splashy publicity. Some wrote only for themselves, giving the finger to anyone else's expectations. But why had he become a writer?

Now there was a group to whom he owed something: his fans—the readers who understood what he was trying to do and who saw him as a human being with a talent that should not simply be thrown away. Those fans would enjoy whatever he wrote.

Certainly, a few of them went to the crazy fringe, seeing him as a guru with unparalleled insight into their particular problems. But most were just regular people. If he struck the right note, his pool of fans would be large; if he chose a path that was too esoteric, the numbers might dwindle. In either case, the readers still deserved his respect.

Mitchell looked at the charred copy of *Infernities* he held. He realized now that burning the novel was selfish. There were thousands (or maybe only dozens) of people like Jeremy

Cardiff, who would have enjoyed this book if he allowed it to be published.

Setting the burned hardcover down, he opened the bottom file drawer of his desk where he kept the folder of notes and ideas that were just too good to throw away. If he was going to bury this cuckoo's egg of a book, then he was obligated to give the readers something in exchange.

Mitchell skimmed his outlines. He had forgotten how clever or thought-provoking many of them were. Had he intended to be an Emily Dickinson, locking his notes away in a box for someone else to find after he died? Not long ago, he had been tempted to burn these, too.

Now he would write some of them.

As he flipped through his notes, the ideas reached a critical mass, and Mitchell saw how he could combine concepts and characters. What might have been simple short story ideas now became enough material for a multi-layered novel. It wouldn't be just like *Divergent Lines*, but so what? It would still be good, still be worth writing.

He spread the papers out on his desk. He had an old, outdated laptop computer and plenty of time during his lunch hours. Some of the greatest works of literature had been completed a few pages at a time during lunch breaks....

Mitchell glanced at the fireplace, where the fire had now died to a pile of orange embers. The photocopied novel was now nothing but ash.

On the mantel above, his Hugo and Nebula awards reflected the dull glow. He turned away from them and focused on his desk. *Divergent Lines* had been an unnecessary ball-and-chain to his creativity, along with all the other excuses he had made up over the past ten years. That was enough procrastination.

He looked at the charred but still readable hardcover of *Infernities*. First, before he started on any new book or short story, he had to write a letter.

"Dear Mr. Cardiff, let me make you a bargain." He proposed that if he had not produced any new novels or short stories

244

in the next five years, then Jeremy had his blessing to publish *Infernities*, if only to reward the fans who had waited so long. He packaged the letter with the scorched book and mailed it to his "number one fan." Simply knowing the novel existed would be all the inspiration he really needed.

On the way back from the mailbox, he smiled to himself, convinced it would never be necessary for the other Mitchell Coren's book to be published here. He would take that risk for himself.

Between Screens

written by

Zach Chapman

illustrated by

TREVOR SMITH

ABOUT THE AUTHOR

Zach Chapman grew up on a ranch just north of San Antonio, Texas where he could see the cows grazing in the pasture from his bedroom window. Summer evenings were often spent camping under a canopy of Spanish Oaks down by the Cibolo Creek around a campfire, listening to his dad tell stories. His imagination was ignited by the works of Neil Gaiman, Alan Moore, Garth Ennis, and Philip K. Dick.

Along with writing, his passions growing up were playing video games, reading, and sports. In school, he competed in wrestling, weightlifting, and football.

Zach graduated in 2011 from the University of the Incarnate Word in San Antonio with a degree in English, where he won the College of Humanities, Arts and Social Sciences (CHASS) English Award for creative writing. At the moment, he lives in San Antonio with his librarian wife Taylor, a cat, a rabbit and a lazy-eyed rescue dog named Dingo. He is currently finishing a science fantasy novel in the vein of Jack Vance's The Dying Earth.

ABOUT THE ILLUSTRATOR

The art spirit inside Trevor emerged early as he sat at his little table drawing for hours. It didn't take long for the subjects to reach monsters and robots.

Like so many artists, he tells a story of being struck by inspiration when seeing Frank Frazetta's art in a magazine. If it made Trevor say "Cool!" he wanted to learn to draw it.

After five years in San Francisco and graduating from the Art University, he returned to his hometown of Tucson with a strong foundation and critical eye that he needed to begin a career in fantasy art.

Five years later, he is making a living doing book covers for self-publishing authors. Trevor Smith won the grand prize of the Illustrators of the Future Contest, the Golden Brush Award, in 2014 and is published in Writers of the Future Volume 30. It was a memorable experience that helped expose Trevor to a world of networking, promoting himself, and learning what it will take to make it to the top.

Between Screens

I was fourteen when I first skipped across the galaxy, trying to fit in, trailing the older boys who had ditched class. Cox, the grunge leader of the group, tattooed and modified, ran the skipper code hacker with one hand and shoved me through the portal with the other. One moment I could hear the others laughing, the next I was in an empty station on my hands and knees, picking myself off the cold floor, heart racing. I didn't know much about skipping, or space travel—I had only been off Earth for a week—but I knew it wasn't cheap. A moment later I heard the others stumbling in after me, shouting in fear and excitement.

"We're caught."

"By who?"

"The pigs!"

"They tracing us?"

"'Course. Gotta skip. And trip the pigs. Lose 'em, yeah?"

"Sure, sure."

I was shoved by three other boys through another skipper, and like that, I was across the universe, in another grey skipper station, running from the pigs who were light years behind.

They never did catch us, not that first time. Cox made sure of that, rerouting stations with his hand hacker to throw them off. We skipped, racing down long hallways in abandoned stations. We skipped, shoving through dense crowds of business drones. We skipped, diving past upkeep bots. We skipped until my world spun and nausea swelled inside me.

When we arrived at our final destination—a claustrophobic, cold room—a dozen boys were touching up a rigged cacophony of gerrymandered technology. Some of the boys I recognized from school. Their stares jarred me. I was foreign to them, tan Earth skin, natural brown eyes and hair, a stark contrast to their pale features.

A screen that looked scarcely different from a threadbare bed sheet was draped on one side of the room, a blindingly bright projector shone on it from the other side. Wires and ancient technology, a haze of smoke, the stink of synthetic bliss, and worn blankets and pillows filled the cold room.

Cox bumped and pounded two tall, thin, pimply boys who were entering some final calibrations on the projector. "Ready, ready? The telescope spitting what we need?"

"Sure, sure," the two answered in unison and returned to their work. Their complexions were more corpse-like than the other spaceboys, and their greasy light hair curled at their shoulders.

An image flickered on the screen. It was a black canvas speckled with burning white stars. The projector clicked several times, then the image zoomed in on a planet, green and blue, much like Earth, but with strange-shaped continents. All the boys quieted. Cox pushed me to the blanket-covered floor and stuck a warm drink in my hand. "Drink up, new kiddie, the lightshow's starting."

"What's so special about it?" I asked, taking a sip of the burning elixir. A boy next to me hushed me as if I were speaking over some audio, but there was no other sound in the station.

"Boys projectin' the light. That's a planet, this ain't no movie. There's a telescope outside of this station. Boys hacked it. Boys real smart with equations." Cox tapped a finger to his temple. "Real sharp. Taller one's name Timmet, other's Trager. Real ugly, but so sharp they're smarter than the teaches we ditched. Sure, sure."

"That's another planet out there, hundred light-years away?" I asked.

Cox nodded, irritated, then punched my shoulder. "Just watch. I ain't seen it at this angle yet."

Sitting, I began to watch, but nothing seemed to happen. I gradually became aware of a hand on my back, slowly rubbing as if to annoy. I turned to look, but the light from the projector distorted my vision. I could make out the shape of a girl, narrow with long synthetic dark hair. In the dimness and blinding projector glare, I thought I saw her wink. She hissed, "Don't lose your lunch, new kiddie."

Before I could respond to her, a gasp from all the boys brought my attention back to the screen.

A meteor hurtled for the planet, brown and jagged. The two masses collided. Breaths hissed in. A shockwave slowly spread from the impact, followed by a wall of ocean. Cox turned toward the projector and yelled over the silence, "Timmet, Trager! Zoom in! Can't see nothing."

The brothers tapped away with their hackers, the telescope zoomed in, and our projector followed the shockwave as it ate forests, deserts and mountains, obliterating all to dust and magma. It zoomed in further. A city came to view, quaking, buildings falling, ants scrambling. Then it was dust too. And then a wall of water. The projector flicked to several other dying cities before the visible half of the planet was devoured and dead. When it was over, the entire room fell silent. The telescope flicked back to the impact site—a circle of red-orange magma, glowing as the tectonic cracks slowly tendrilled across the planet like stretching skeletal fingers. The nausea from skipping returned. I accidentally tipped my drink over, but no one seemed to notice, their eyes were nailed to the dying world.

"Why?" I managed to utter, "Why did those people stay? They must have known their planet would die."

"Misguided principals." Cox shrugged. "Or just too poor to leave. Not like you, new kiddie."

"If I was rich, I'd still be on Earth," I began, but something buzzing on Cox's hip took precedence. He fumbled at the device, brought it up to his face. His eyes widened. Pointing his finger toward the skipper gate, Cox started to shout. Boys began to clear the skip station, running, packing up pillows and synthetic smokers and hard drinks, spilling their possessions everywhere as they jumped through the skipper. Cox jerked me to my feet. "Move, new kiddie—the pigs've found us."

I turned to look for the girl, but she was gone. Cox shoved me forward. "You hear me? No time."

Then I was skipping again, Cox at my heels, more boys chasing after, hooting. Instantly through space we ran: Abandoned comet drill site. Packed synth-steak meat house. Sliding living quarters. Busy commercial district, grey and dull. And a hundred skip stations between. The boys began to split, skipping off to different stations.

Pigs in pale suits popped up here and there, never able to crack us with their electric batons, though once, right before we lost them for good, one dove for Cox, catching his ankle. I kicked the fat man in his teeth, stomped the hand that had captured Cox, and shoved us both through the portal. When we finally lost them it was just Cox, Todd, and I.

Cox swung a tattooed arm over my shoulders and squeezed. "Kiddie, you did good. Respect, respect. Did good watching that planet blow for the first time, too. I've seen it five times now. First time was the hardest. But it hooks you, yeah? It's a day later and you want to keep watchin'. Skip to new stations where the light ain't passed through just yet. See it again, at a new angle."

Yes. This is what I wanted. Right?

"Uh, yeah," I said.

Cox laughed and pushed me forward. "You'll see. Go on home. See you at school tomorrow."

When I finally found the way back to my living quarters, I could hear mom crying in her room. She was still grieving over dad, though she claimed that the sudden weeping outbursts were due to the artificial days and nights, or the synthetic smell of life in space, or some other lie. Luckily, she didn't notice me slip in, nor did she complain when I drowned out her moans by blaring music in my cramped room while I struggled to sleep.

The next morning I ate synth-meat for breakfast, rushed out the door before mom could bring up dad, and used my school pass to skip to the school station. My first three periods I drifted off, day-dreaming of skipping, kicking a faceless patrol officer in the teeth, but mostly about the dying planet. In my daydreams I could hear the peoples' cries. Why hadn't they left? Surely they weren't so poor that they couldn't leave. Who would choose death on a planet over life across the million space stations?

At first I sat by myself at lunch, sure that no one would want a tan Earther sitting with them, but, to my surprise, Cox grabbed my shoulder and gestured over to a table where Todd, Timmet, Trager and a few others from the night before sat.

As I joined them, I heard discussion of last night's exploits—rehashing, bragging, hyperbolizing. Cox cut in, explaining how heroic I was when I smashed officer piggy's teeth in. After that the other boys seemed more accepting of me, listening when I spoke, giving the occasional nod.

By the time lunch was dismissed, they had begun planning another show, but this one was something new, not the same dying planet from another angle.

Reluctantly, I ambled to class, a dark boy in a scuffed hallway full of skulking corpses, my mind fixed on skipping, wondering what the new show might be—Cox, Timmet and Trager had kept me out of the loop. In class I sat in a listing chair, impatiently leaning back from my desk, not listening to some teach chew the side of her mouth. Suddenly, I felt a kick on my tailbone, hard enough to sting. I glanced back; it took me a second, but I recognized the girl from last night's show.

She winked a pale-blue eye. Her hair was dyed darker than my natural color; it shimmered purple if the light caught it just right. She wore a splash of cherry lipstick, and I spotted tattoos swirling up the side of her neck: a few colorful planets, some stylized stars and a spiraling galaxy—not the sort of ink you'd find on Earth.

I raised my eyebrows. Her complexion didn't seem as grey as the others'. With a quirked smile, she passed me a folded note on synth-paper. It read: *u planning on going to the next show?* Shit, did I really want to go? I wrote back: *sure, sure, what's your name?* And tossed it back to her while the teach wasn't looking. She responded with: *Name's Lem, next time you better sit next to me.* When I looked back at her, I could tell just from her crooked smirk that she was aggressive, cocky, vivacious.

Though I had lived on Earth for fourteen years, and breathed real air, drank real water, and ate real food, she somehow had lived more than me.

I sent back: *sure, sure.*

After we received the notification to switch classes, Lem followed me to the science hall. I didn't know what to say, so I awkwardly smiled as she complained about the dearth of girls at last night's show. I nodded like a fool, bumping into other students in between gawking glances. She must have been late to her next class, because I had hardly entered mine before the tardy notification appeared on the cracked screen of my tablet.

I remembered nothing of the rest of the school-day. I assume I spent it scribbling sketches of dying planets on synth-paper, ignoring teachers. After school I roamed the halls looking for Cox, Todd, Lem, or any of the gang, but those who hadn't ditched earlier in the day, hadn't stuck around after school. When I got home, I was already irritated. Mom—her eyes rimmed red—put on a smile for me. That irritated me more.

I left after dinner, ignoring mom's silent pleas to be comforted.

I paced our sector, subconsciously moving toward the skip station, but without the handy hacker Cox had, I was marooned, unless I wanted to pay.

As I roamed I passed silicon flowers and earthen landscape murals so awful they only could have been painted by someone who'd never stepped foot on Earth's surface. The bleak, artificial lighting did nothing to uplift my brooding.

Why had they stayed? They were ants on our cosmic threadbare screen, scurrying, helpless. Too poor? After father had died, mom and I were too poor to live anywhere but the stations.

Could it have been different long ago? I asked myself as I studied the awful perspective of a different earthen mural. None of the shadows looked right, and the trees were far too thin. Was Cox's gang where I should try to fit in? The mountains looked like triangles, completely inorganic, completely wrong. How long could they go ditching school and skip-hacking before a pig bashed them? The sun was a brighter orange than that, the sky more blue—this painting belonged on a wasted planet, full of frantic ants. What happens if I got stranded on some station a billion light years away? Trees don't grow in concentric rows, and there's no patterns to the way leaves sprout from branches. Why did they stay? Why didn't they just leave?

Over the following weeks I grew closer to Cox and his gang; we were vines twisting together, using each other to reach a sunspot, not that any of my new friends would get the metaphor. We poured hours of work into discussing plans over half-eaten synthetic lunch food, spreading the news only by word of mouth to those we knew wouldn't rat, hunting down potential show sites: the station had to have a powerful telescope that the brothers could hack, and it couldn't be in a high-traffic area.

I hardly saw Lem in class—I think she ditched more than not—but when I did, her cherry smile brought my thoughts away from indecision. Cox's gang was the key to the lightshows, and lightshows were the key to her. She was the most attractive space girl I'd seen, and I'd chase her to far-off galaxies if given the chance.

One day between the first show I'd seen and the second, Lem and I ditched before Earth History class. Using a battered old skip-hacker Cox had graciously given me, I took her to stations we'd never seen. We walked through offices—stealing idle hand tablets, synth-papers, and whatever would fit in our pockets, ran through cafeterias—snatching genuine planet-baked cinnamon bread and rolls with real butter, laughed in game rooms as we played VRs with what little money we had. In the cold, bleak expanse of our galaxy, I had found light.

Back home I would lie awake on my thin mattress thinking of Lem's dark hair with its purple shimmer, wondering if she was thinking of me too. It was a nice change from my brain replaying my father's babbling death as fast-acting poison ate his body. I never saw it, the leak at his station was far above Earth, but that hadn't stopped my mind from speculating about his final minutes.

Hell, I was beginning to be able to ignore my mom, too—but it wasn't all wonderful amongst the bleak stars. I still second-guessed myself. Joining Cox's cohorts could lead down a strange path. I'd never run with a crowd like that back on Earth. But the stations were different from Earth. To fit in here, I told myself, I had to run with these guys.

On the day we set up the show room, I ditched class entirely. My whole body trembled in anticipation. This room yawned bigger than the last, and I was one of the first to arrive.

Cox unsuccessfully attempted to hang the screen while Trager and Timmet worked on the projector and hacked a nearby space telescope. Cox caught sight of me. "Damn Earther, you scared? Your skin's white as mine. Relax. Come here, help me hang this damn thing."

"Sure, sure. Not scared—excited."

"Don't drop the screen. Your fingers shakin' too much."

"No worries."

By the time we finished setting up, a dozen boys lay about the floor on insta-inflate mattresses and backpacks, smoking paper soaked in colorful synthetics, drinking delicious toxins from recycled bottles, playing the knockout game.

More came skipping in. And girls. Three girls, then four, awkwardly watching the boys. But Lem wasn't there.

She'd come, I knew, unless she got caught by the pigs. I shook off the thought; she was too quick and determined to be caught.

Someone slapped a bottle to my chest. I drank, spilling the burning, icy liquid down my chin. Todd slammed me on the back, hooting. My head buzzed, harmonizing with the hum of the station's electronics. The lights dimmed, hacked. Yet, it felt too early to start, more people were passing through the portal every minute, Lem wasn't with them.

An uproar of murmurs met the flicker of the projector. Too soon, the murmurs said. Friends on their way, it complained. An image flashed, a volcano bleeding orange and red. More complaints. But what could we do? There's no rewind button on telescopes.

Cox stood. "Ease, ease. This is a preshow. Settle your pretty heads. Staunch those flowing tears."

Tension in the crowd dissolved as we realized that the best was yet to come. A wet pinch on my neck startled me. I turned to see Lem, she'd snuck in and bit me on the neck, playfully. "So tense. Need to relax, Earther. Let me work on your shoulders."

She massaged my back. I could smell the synthetic sweetness of a hand-rolled cigarette between her cherry lips. She pulled me to her, touched my lips to hers, and exhaled a remedy, a toxin, a delight into my lungs. My world spun for the moment, her tongue in my mouth, fingers running through hair.

We kissed, her tongue assertive, experienced, mine stumbling, awkward. On the sheet above, magma flickered and flowed. She was my first kiss.

Our passion had not worn off when the show started, but we mustered a glance at the screen. The room was stifling with packed body-heat. Despite the haze in my head, and the pounding of my heart, I made a mental note to tell Cox that we would have to scout larger locations for the next show.

On the screen I saw a city, old, like one on Earth from thousands of years ago. A foreign-looking people crossed streets, drove cars, peddled goods, rode bicycles, as the telescope scanned them, focusing here and there, zooming in and out, panning. Nothing happened for the longest time. Just as I thought the crowd would begin to grumble, a smoldering light flashed across the room, piercing, hot, so bright Lem and I winced.

It was as if the brothers had pointed the telescope towards a star. Then the smoke lifted, and Timmet punched past half a dozen filters until we were seeing through the dust cloud as if it weren't there.

Thousands of people lay dead in the streets; thousands more walked about, dying, flesh dripping from their stumbling frames. Buildings had become liquefied skeletons stretching up toward the telescope, some still bending and breaking in the firestorm's wake.

Trager zoomed in on a man burnt so badly that his clothes and skin had become indistinguishable. He staggered as if blind and begging.

For what? Water? A quick death? His family? His lover? He latched on to anyone who passed, but most shoved him off, or avoided him narrowly, searching for families of their own. They were just as blind, just as naked.

There should have been the sappy cry of a solo violin. But there was no sound but the hum of the station and the breathing of its inhabitants. A boy laughed awkwardly, cracking midway. Or was he a man? We existed in that awkward stage somewhere between the two.

I felt Lem's hot breath on my neck, soft cherry lips kissing my cheek. My jeans stiffened. I glanced back up at the begging, melted man, then filled my existence with Lem.

When all the death and dying and love and lust were over, no pigs came to interrupt us. The boys slowly trickled out of the skip station, drunk and high, whooping and laughing; Cox, the brothers, Todd, Lem and I were the last to skip out.

Cox smiled at Lem and me. "Not bad, yeah? Dark shit. Tell more of your girlfriends to come."

"Sure, sure." Lem said, smiling.

Then off we skipped, losing a friend here or there.

Over the next weeks my life consisted of three things: ditching class to explore the stations of the universe with Lem, planning and scouting with Cox and the boys, and lying awake in bed, ignoring mom while dreams of dying cities and planets kept me up.

TREVOR SMITH

ZACH CHAPMAN

For the first time in my life I wasn't making straight A's. Truthfully, I didn't know what kinds of grades I was making. Mostly, I didn't care, but there was a part of me—maybe the same part that occasionally dreamed of Earthen fields and real food—that tugged at my intestines.

On the occasion that I did go to class, I would sketch. I drew dying worlds on synth-paper, colliding meteors, cracking crust, bloody magma. Then moved on to cities—drowning, burning, screaming, wheezing. I would write captions like "Come See the Lightshow," or "Watch the Wonders of Dying Worlds—Live!", imitating movie posters I'd seen on Earth.

During a scouting trip, Cox saw one of my sketches after it had fallen out of my torn pocket. "Cheeky. The Earther's an artist," he said. Later he commissioned me to draw more, picked out his favorite design, then, in code, jotted down several skip station coordinates and times on the side, copied it, and passed it to people we trusted—to spread word of the next show.

At some point I suggested to Cox that we should get a band to play live at the next lightshow. He and the boys resisted the idea, but I managed to convince them to at least allow music during the preshow. They agreed, so long as I scrounged together the band. I accepted their challenge.

Earth was inspiring, full of young musicians and would-be's, but the stations weren't. Luckily, a cramped corner of our school held a music hall where I periodically wandered between classes. I wasn't looking for the best; we needed trustworthy guys, no one who'd rat us out to the teachers or pigs.

It didn't take me long to spy and recruit Rodney, a boxy boy with a shock of dull blond fuzz that sprouted in wilting patches on his cheeks. He played saxophone and violin, terribly. An outcast, a rust artist, a pugilist, a perfect recruit. His weak connections in the music hall were enough for me to infiltrate and recruit four more equally qualified musicians on the promise that synth-smokers and some heavy bottles would be provided for their services.

So the next show had live music.

260

Strings screeched, buzzed, hacked, and coughed; the music was perfect. Rodney and his band played, still making the same mistakes they'd had while rehearsing thirty minutes before, as two dozen excited cohorts skipped into the current show-station.

Cox grabbed me by the shoulder, hard, pointed to the band, and said, nodding, "Aye, new kiddie, you ain't bad for a peach-skinned Earther."

I nodded back thinking: *They may call me "new kiddie," but I'm no longer an outsider, no more than anyone else here, haven't been since the skip home from the first show, since I kicked that officer's teeth in.*

"They're shit terrible," Cox said, tossing a clanking rucksack full of bottles at me, "but people seem to like 'em. Give Rodney and 'em jars of piss booze when the show starts. Keep one for you and Lem."

"Sure, sure."

Two boys broke out in a fight, just as I felt Lem put her arms around me. One of the brawlers fell into a violinist, and was thrust back into the clash. People whooped and hollered, as the two blackened each other's eyes, until one of the bruisers was too broken and bloody to fight, and Timmet and Trager flipped the projector on to a new preshow.

This time we saw a ghost planet, already dead. Skeleton cities, dried canyons where rivers had once flowed, all living things long ago turned to dust. I wondered, how far away would we have to skip to catch the light and witness the downfall of this civilization?

A tornado lashed the land. Lem traced a finger around my forearm and looked up at me with a devious smile. "Your brown skin's turned pink. Give it more time and it'll be as sexy as mine. But...in the meantime, it's looking a little bare."

"What do you mean?" I asked.

She jabbed her fingernail into my forearm. "Let's modify. You're lacking...tattoos, piercings, implants."

I laughed nervously. *What would my dad think? He was dead. And my mother? Who cared what she thought.* "And you have a needle and ink, or some rusty implant gun?"

261

She smiled. "I told Todd to bring some. He's just as talented an artist as you. He's got clean stuff."

He wasn't. And he didn't.

A violin screeched. A quake split a dead desert. And a needle pierced my skin. I'd decided on a tattoo of a planet, and was told it would look cool. It felt like a knife scraping, cutting, digging at my arm. I emptied half a jar of piss alcohol down my throat, lit a synth-cig, and watched the panning ruins of a ghost planet.

When the outline was done, Todd snatched my alcohol and splashed it on my arm.

The lights dimmed. The show started.

Then another show. And another.

So we went on, in whatever abandoned skip stations we found, for months, our posse slowly growing by word of mouth and the handouts I'd designed. Each show a memory with a different tattoo, piercing, scar or glowing implant. The pigs busted us sometimes, catching a few kids too drunk, stoned or slow to skip away.

Our lightshows became more frequent; we needed researchers who knew when and where cosmic tragedies had happened, and people good with equations, and techies, and musicians.

I'd go to school on occasion to recruit. Other than that, school meant nothing to me, the show, everything. Our enclave of misfits grew, as did my bond with Lem.

And as I spent the next months skipping across the galaxy with our gang of outsiders, my yearning for Earth waned; the memories of grass underfoot and wind brushing skin, once vivid, now faded. But did any of that matter?

Mom didn't have a chance at getting us back to Earth. And I was too busy seeing new worlds to care if she did. I was in a river, slow flowing but with a current too strong to fight. Sure, I could swim for the bank, but oblivion was beautiful. The shows began to blur into each other, sometimes a planet died—*war* the killer one show, *nature* the next—sometimes it was just a city, occasionally a malfunctioning skip station.

They mixed like a trillion wisps of smoke commingling, fornicating, trapped in a room of flickering light. It was intoxicating, addictive.

Tattoos crawled up my arms, piercings punched holes through my skin, flashing implants danced up my spine. Friends came and went, but Cox and Lem were always there, never missing a show. True friends, true cohorts.

Then came one show, one particular show, where I realized the dreams of my father's death had stopped entirely, shoved aside by the preparation and intoxication of the lightshows.

It started like all other shows. Rodney's band played as friends skipped in from across the galaxy to a cramped room just warm enough to make sweat bead above the brow. The preshow flickered a junked satellite station spinning in and out of orbit only to be drawn by its planet's gravity and eaten in fiery gulps by its atmosphere.

Lem bit my lip and whispered something in my ear. Timmet and Trager tinkered with the projector, finalizing calibrations. Boys almost old enough to be men rolled about kissing girls who were almost women.

Somewhere, someone was in a classroom learning something.

The screen skipped. I felt a sense of familiarity. Earth, and a station just above it, round with vast clear windows, greenery on the inside. My stomach knotted itself. When was this? Where were we? How many light years from Earth? One? Two? How long had I been in interstellar space? In the skip stations? How old was I? Fifteen? Couldn't be older than sixteen, but what's a year and a half when you're in a thousand different stations, light years from the embrace of seasons?

In my mind's eye I saw my father on his death bed, weeping sores covering his skin, just as he was after the rescue team had skipped him back to Earth. He babbled, the radiation sickness frying him from the inside out. On the screen an infrared filter spotted a solar flare lash the station like a whip. The telescope zoomed in. Masses of doomed men and women pounded at the domed windows.

It was a research center, the same one dad had worked at.

What was I doing here? Watching people die? I wanted to stand up, to skip off, just...leave.

Lem felt the muscles in my back tense. I looked down at her hand on my arm. Grey. And so was my arm, except for the tattoos, all up and down my arms. When had I gotten those? In that sobering moment, I couldn't remember half of the scribbles. An Earthen landscape sprawled across my left bicep, horribly inked by someone who'd never stepped foot on a planet. Who had done that one? Surely, not me. Hopefully, not me.

In the waning light, my tan was a figment of the past, a figment of Earth spinning below the domed station on the screen. I was a corpse, just like the rest of them, not an outsider. And we were kids no longer.

I tried to stand. Lem pulled me to her, licked my ear. "Baby it's just getting good."

"I think I should leave."

I could hear her smile. "You can't leave."

Unrefined

written by

Martin L. Shoemaker

illustrated by

TUNG CHI LEE

ABOUT THE AUTHOR

Martin L. Shoemaker is a writer with a lucrative programming habit. As a child he told stories to imaginary friends and learned to type on his brother's manual typewriter even though he couldn't reach the keys. (He types with the keyboard in his lap still today.) He couldn't imagine any career but writing fiction...until his algebra teacher said, "This is a program. You should write one of these."

Fast forward thirty years of programming, writing, and teaching. He was named an MVP by Microsoft for his work with the developer community. He is an avid role-playing gamemaster, but that didn't satisfy his storytelling urge. He wrote, but he never submitted until his brother-in-law read a chapter and said, "That's not a chapter. That's a story. Send it in." It won second place in the Jim Baen Memorial Writing Contest and earned him lunch with Buzz Aldrin. Programming never did that!

Martin hasn't stopped writing (or programming) since. His work has appeared in Analog, Galaxy's Edge, Digital Science Fiction, *and select service garages worldwide. His novella* Murder on the Aldrin Express *was reprinted in* The Year's Best Science Fiction: Thirty-First Annual Collection *and in* The Year's Top Short SF Novels 4.

ABOUT THE ILLUSTRATOR

Tung Chi (Jessica) Lee was born in Taipei, Taiwan where at an early age she was exposed to dazzling worlds created by the entertainment industry. She soon found that she could draw her own exciting worlds. Her passion for intriguing places and profound stories in games, movies, and novels strengthened as she grew.

With help from her parents, she majored in visual communication design at National Taiwan University of Art, then studied illustration at the Academy of Art University.

Since her art education began, Lee has discovered and rediscovered how much more exciting life is when viewed with an eye toward art. Today she works as a concept artist and freelance illustrator. She wants to keep contributing to the art world by developing scenes from other universes and possible futures and with each project, her desire grows.

Unrefined

If this had been a vid, there would've been a computer voice over the comms: "Thirty minutes to containment collapse." At least I hoped like hell that I had thirty minutes left. I might need every one of them.

But when you're facing a cascade failure across your computer network, there are no automated warnings, no countdown. I just had to move as fast as I damn well could, and hope I could get to Wilson and get us out before the fusion reactor blew out the end of Refinery Station.

As Leeanne brought the flitter in toward The Tube—the half-klick tunnel of girders that connected Habitat Module to the Reactor and Refinery Module—I hung from its frame and peered ahead, looking for the airlocks into Habitat's Control Deck. If Wilson wasn't there, I wouldn't know where to look for him. There were nearly three million cubic meters in Habitat. And in R&R... but I stopped that thought. I'd rather not get that close to a failing fusion reactor.

Refinery Station was the first of Wilson Gray's megastructures, massive artifacts in space that were half constructed, half grown by Von Neumann constructor bots. At one end hung the Habitat Module, still mostly unfinished. At the other end of The Tube was the giant fusion ring.

The reactor provided power for Habitat, but the real reasons Wilson had built the station were the two structures on the far side of the reactor: a giant refinery utilizing the reactor's raw heat for metallurgy, and the two-and-a-half kilometer mass driver that would launch refined metals from the Jovian system back toward Earth. Wilson had invested his entire fortune into the station, and he had convinced a number of other entrepreneurs to sign up as well. Now all those investments were poised to fail, all due to an unexplained computer crash.

Finally we got close enough that I could make out the airlock hatches between the girders. I was glad one of the best pilots in the Pournelle Settlements was flying. As Leeanne neared the closest approach point, the retros fired, bringing us almost motionless relative to Habitat. She had timed it perfectly—less than five meters, Leanne was *good*—so I leaped.

For a moment I floated in empty space. Jupiter hung off to my right, half in shadow. The sunward side showed the giant cream-and-brown stripes, as well as an excellent view of the famous Red Spot. Closer to me but still dwarfed by its primary was Ganymede, our closest orbital neighbor. Its dark, reddish-gray surface was dotted with ancient impact craters, evidence that the Jovian system was a treasure trove of valuable rocks. Under other circumstances I would've enjoyed the sight, but I couldn't waste time sightseeing. I paid close attention to the task at hand, and I grabbed for a girder.

Contact! My gloved fingers wrapped easily around the girder, a synthetic carbon crystal rod five centimeters across. I grabbed another and arrested my flight. The girders sparkled in my suit light. Their lattice tied the two modules together even in the face of the minimal tidal force we experienced at this distance from Ganymede. The VN bots had spent over a month assembling this giant structure out of carbon that had cost Willy a small fortune to collect; and now at any moment it could all be shattered by the explosion.

"I'm on, Leanne."

"Don't waste words, Sam! Go get Willy. Please!"

Wilson was Leeanne's husband. Nerves of steel were another trait that made Leeanne a top pilot, but hers were strained near their limit. "I'll get him. You just be ready to pick us up."

Leeanne and I had been hauling batteries from the

magnetosphere generators back to Gray City (the collection of ships and small habitats that housed Wilson's team as we built Refinery Station). Until the fusion reactor gets up to full output, the generators were the most reliable source of electrical power in Jovian space, converting the radiation in Jupiter's magnetosphere into electricity and then storing it in batteries. These were one of our most successful products: half the towns in the Pournelle Settlements and a good number of the independent miners bought their power from Gray Interplanetary. But the generator output was too variable, and hauling massive batteries around used too much fuel. With the reactor, Wilson hoped to get a more steady power source for the refinery and the mass driver.

In another organization we could both have pulled rank to get out of such routine work: the boss's wife and partner and the boss's Executive Officer drawing a routine transport run? Ridiculous! But not when Wilson Gray was the boss: "Everybody gets their hands dirty" was one of his top rules to keep us in touch with our crew.

And this particular run... Well, it was my fault, really. I had had another fight with Mari Brasco, Chief of Eco Management. It was the same dumb argument that had cropped up since we started dating: her claiming I ran our relationship like I ran a project, me trying to explain myself, and her saying I was proving her point. But this one had been bigger. Maybe she was stressed from all her contract work, I don't know, but we really blew up. She had told me to choose: boss or boyfriend? Before I could answer, she had stormed out. So Wilson had sent me on the battery run to get me away from the station and give me time to cool off. I suspect he had sent Leeanne because she's a good listener and he had hoped she could talk me through my troubles.

When we'd heard the news of the computer failure on Refinery Station, though, my dating woes went out the hatch. We'd dumped our cargo in a stable orbit, and Leeanne had grinned and uttered her favorite words: "Hang on, Sam!" We blew most of our reaction mass getting back to Gray City to render aid if it was needed.

The work crews had evacuated before environmental systems could fail completely. It had fallen to Kim Stone to break the bad news to Leeanne: Wilson had refused to leave, trying to get the system under control and save the station.

At that news, I glanced over at Leeanne. I was sure she was thinking the same thing I was: *If only we had been there…* And *I* was the reason we were gone, me and my stupid fight with Mari. If I blamed myself, surely Leeanne would blame me, and I expected an angry glare. But she wasn't looking at me at all. She stared straight ahead out the view port, her normally dark face turned ashen with worry. Flying normally put a broad grin across her round, friendly face; but the grin was gone, replaced by a grim line that turned downward as Kim continued.

The computer failures had spread, so comms to the station were out. Wilson was still on board, and no one wanted to get trapped in there looking for him. But I wasn't leaving my best friend, and Leanne wasn't leaving her husband. Her face had turned steely, and she had flown us to the station at a reckless speed and then had pulled four gees as she brought us to a halt.

The girders were spaced to allow a suited person to climb between them. I did so, pushed toward the airlock, and grabbed the hatch ring to stop myself. The computer display on the hatch was useless: letters and numbers scrolling by too fast to read, occasionally interrupted by a complete screen wipe or random pixilation.

I ignored the screen and opened the lid to the manual controls. I twisted the lever, and the *Cycling* light lit up.

When the lock was in vacuum, I lifted the lever. The hatch opened and I pulled myself in and closed it behind me before cycling the far hatch. My audio pickups gave me the sound of air whistling in. I popped into the Control Deck annex.

I had been inside Habitat enough during construction, so that I knew my way around pretty well. The annex was right off the main cabin of the Control Deck: a bowl shape, thirty-meters radius by ten deep, filled with a triple ring of monitor stations along the surface of the bowl so a supervisor could survey all stations from the center.

I pushed to the door and opened it. Immediately my senses were overloaded, light flashing through my visor and sound overloading my audio. Every computer at every station flashed data, buzzed alarms, called out gibberish warnings, and strobed bright and dark.

I blinked and looked away. "Wilson!" I shouted over the din, but with no hope that I could hear a response even if he made one.

"He's not here." Leeanne watched through my comms. Another person might have sounded frantic, but her control didn't waver. "The motion sensor's flaking out from all the signal noise, but there's no firm signal."

"We can't be sure. Let me get a better view." I pushed off to the supervisor harness, a set of straps in the center of the bowl, and I looked around.

I didn't want to make Leeanne anxious, but I was sure she was right: Wilson wasn't there. Unless he was jammed behind a workstation where I couldn't see, he was nowhere on the Control Deck. That didn't make sense. Where else would he be?

"Sam!" Leeanne called on the comm. "The power monitor station. The panel's open!"

Sure enough, an open panel led into the guts of the workstation. I dove over. Wilson had to have opened it to trace a data feed. I could tell because he had left his network analyzer there, still tied into the juncture box. But the readout on the analyzer made me sweat: *Fusion Deck*.

Leeanne's whisper on the comm lacked her usual steely control. "S-Sam. Don't do it."

"What?"

"You know where he went, Sam. We're gonna lose him. We can't afford to lose you, too."

But it wasn't until she said that that I realized: Wilson had followed the signal to the Fusion Deck. He was less than fifty meters from a glowing ring of fusing hydrogen plasma that was just waiting for containment to fail so it could escape.

TUNG CHI LEE

Fusion reactions are so difficult to sustain that they can't go critical like a fission reactor. When something goes wrong, the reaction just collapses, destroying the reactor but not posing a threat outside the immediate area. The station was designed so that Habitat Module would be safe in the event of a collapse—but the Fusion Deck and the refinery would surely be destroyed.

So despite Leeanne's warning, I was going after Wilson. "We're not losing him."

"Sam!"

"We are *not* losing your husband, Leeanne! Don't waste time arguing. Just get your ass over to the far end and wait for us."

I went back out through the airlock and into The Tube. There were elevators between the modules, but I crossed the distance faster on my jets.

My rad meters didn't change appreciably as I settled to a halt at the far airlock. The radiation from the reactor was contained by shielding except where it was used in the refinery, and what escaped the shielding was barely above background radiation from Jupiter itself.

I had selected a lock near the control center. At least I hoped so. I was so used to the computer answering questions like that, but I feared to trust my suit comp. It hadn't been compromised yet, but if I tied it into station information, it might be. I didn't need my suit failing me now!

When I got inside, I wished I had trusted the computer. I wasn't in the control center, I was in a darkened room. Flickering lights through a thick window in the far wall showed part of a giant torus, fifteen meters on the short radius and ninety on the long. The fusion reactor! I had entered in a service room off the main reactor chamber, and that room was *hot!* I checked my meters: not hot in the radiation sense, or at least not dangerously so, but the temperature was over 30°C. Any warmer and it would start to tax my cooling system. I could hear the cooling fans whirring up already.

I looked around the darkened room. The flickering showed no light switches, just a bank of storage cabinets, a row of work pods, and a wall of monitors—malfunctioning, of course. Once my eyes adjusted to the flicker, I picked out two hatches. One led into the reactor chamber. I pulled open the other, exited the service room, and sealed the hatch behind me. Immediately my cooling fans grew quiet, and my temperature began to drop.

I still sweated, though. It wasn't from the heat.

At least I knew where I was going now. I floated in a large transit corridor; and in this part of R&R, all corridors led to the control center. The corridor was in darkness, but my suit light showed a hatch about forty-five meters away. That was my destination.

I checked my comp timer. Despite moving as fast as I could, it had been more than ten minutes since our approach to the station, and thirty minutes had been just a best guess. How long did we have? I broke several safety regulations by using my jets to race through the corridor.

When I got to the control center, I entered a room designed almost as a mirror to Control Deck: a giant bowl with three rings of screens. And just as in Control Deck, most of the screens displayed gibberish. The one main difference from Control Deck was my target: the suited man working inside the panel of one of the stations.

"Wilson!" Suit comms couldn't penetrate station shielding, but they worked fine in the same room.

Without pulling his head out of the panel, Wilson answered, "Sam? Good! Hey, buddy, gimme a hand. Need you to jettison the mass driver, and once that's done, cut us loose from The Tube."

"Boss!"

"We're gonna lose the reactor, Sam. No hope, I can tell. Refinery too. We just have to salvage as much of the station as we can."

Typical Wilson, worrying about assets and losses while his dream disintegrated around him. He could be passionate when he sold an idea; but when it came to implementation, he was a cold-blooded numbers guy.

And as usual, he made sense. There were months and fortunes tied up in the station. If any of it could be saved, we had to save it.

I flew over to the superstructure controls. These weren't part of the main computer network, so maybe they weren't corrupted. Maybe.

If they were, our ploy was already doomed.

But if this was so important to Wilson... "Boss, what are you after in there?"

Wilson answered tersely, "Evidence." He went back to work, cursing as he did. When he started swearing, I knew better than to interrupt until he'd solved the problem.

I studied the superstructure controls. They were clean, or at least not flashing gibberish like all of the others. These were part of the construction network, not the station operations network; and when the time had come to hook all the systems together, Wilson and the network guys had debated whether it made sense to tie construction in. I'd never paid attention to the outcome, but it looked as if Wilson had decided to isolate the system.

I'm not a computer guy, but I'm a competent engineer and physicist. I understood the basics of the controls, but it was designed to make it difficult to accidentally cut the station into pieces—like I was trying to do.

I worked through the layers of safeguards and confirmations while also figuring out the process. There were rocket engines on the mass driver and the R&R Module. Explosive bolts would cut the mass driver loose, and the rockets would burn on a preset trajectory. Then I could do the same for R&R.

But first I had to choose the trajectories, feed them to the rockets, double check everything, and confirm everything one more time, all while trying to learn an unfamiliar interface.

I knew that I was taking too long. My suit timer showed twenty-two minutes when I finally felt the station tremble. If it had been the reactor, it would've been a lot more than a tremble, so that must've been the first explosive bolts.

I watched on the screen and confirmed that the mass driver was drifting away from the station, picking up speed as the rockets began to burn. Over ten minutes to figure out the controls.

I hoped I would move faster on the second set.

But I didn't have to. Wilson nudged me aside and handed me a clear bag containing a computer board. "Sam, I've got this. Get that board out of here."

I looked at Wilson through his suit visor. His face, darker than Leeanne's, nearly always bore a smile. It wasn't from humor—though Wilson had a great sense of humor—it was friendliness and confidence. Wilson Gray was happiest when we had a challenge to tackle. So when I saw that his smile was gone, I grew even more worried. "Boss, I'm not—"

"*Now,* Sam! This wasn't an accident, and the evidence is on that board. Get it off this station!" And Wilson turned to the superstructure controls, hands moving twice as fast as mine.

Despite Wilson's orders, I hesitated. He pushed me away, and I tumbled through the air. Wilson didn't need my help and he wouldn't be dragged away, and arguing would only distract him. Whatever that board held was important to him, so I had to get it out, like he had ordered. I cycled through the nearest airlock and hoped that he would not be too far behind me.

Just as I pulled myself out of the lock, I felt the whole station *shudder*. Somewhere inside the big disk-shaped module, the magnetic fields had passed a critical point of imbalance. The laws of physics took over from there: on the one hand; the delicate fusion reaction snuffed itself out harmlessly in the first microsecond; but on the other hand, the cooling system failed and the high-pressure coolants escaped and damaged the ring structure.

In a chain reaction, the massive magnetic coils that had taken person-years to assemble and fit into place suddenly broke free from their blocks and ripped themselves to shreds—giant, fast shreds that tore through shielding, tore through bulkheads...

And tore through the hull!

I fired my jets at max throttle, getting me away as far and

as fast as possible. I barely escaped the flying shards of tin and aluminum and carbon compound.

Wilson hadn't cut the modules apart. The shudder propagated up the girder tunnel, causing it to twist and flex dangerously.

Some girders nearest the R&R Module snapped entirely, something I'd never seen carbon girders do. The lattice structure absorbed the shock, but I had to fly over a hundred meters before I felt it was safe to cross between the rods.

And then I just hung outside the girders, looking back at the wreckage that had been R&R. My best friend's greatest dream, and now his destruction. I floated silently and waited for his widow to pick me up.

Life in the Settlements didn't give us a lot of spare time, not even to grieve.

I assembled a crew, and we went into the shattered husk of R&R to retrieve Wilson's body.

I remembered his last words: *This wasn't an accident....*

I still didn't know what he meant, so I recorded everything for...well, for evidence, I guess. The scene was horrific, his corpse filleted by the fast-moving shrapnel. I locked down my recordings. No way would Leeanne see these if I could help it.

Then I had to get ready for the funeral. It took me a while to find my cabin in Habitat, since I still wasn't familiar with the new station. I had only visited my quarters before long enough to stow a small kit bag with clothes and essentials. When I found my hatch, I went inside and sealed myself in.

And then, for a few scarce minutes alone, I cried. Wilson Gray was dead, and people needed me to carry on, but I needed...I needed Wilson. If only I had been here sooner...But that thought led me to a dark vortex I might never escape, so I wrenched myself out of it.

I had to find something to do, some activity to anchor myself. So I opened my kit bag, unzipped the toiletries pouch, and pulled out my razor. I set it for a short trim, just enough to even out my goatee and mustache. As the blades spun and the vacuum sucked away the bristles, I stared at my eyes in the mirror. They were red against pale skin that bagged around them. I wished I had some water to rinse them, but Habitat didn't yet have water to the residence decks. I would have to live with the red. And with the patches of white in my beard and scalp. When had those appeared? When had my hairline receded so far? This project had made me old, but that day I felt the impact all at once.

I combed my hair, put on a fresh pair of coveralls, and pushed out of my cabin and into the half-completed corridor. Many of the wall panels were missing, exposing conduit and tubes and electronics. There were no signs and no obvious way to navigate, but I didn't need them. I just followed the other stunned, red-eyed faces as they floated their way to the recycler.

As per his will, we gave Wilson a small ceremony—I spoke, and Kim did, as did a few others as Leeanne floated in tearful silence—and then we fed him to the organic recycler. New crew from Earth had trouble with this concept, but the recycler is our version of the natural order of life and renewal. New recruits understand this on an intellectual level, but it still creeps them out. After you've been through a few funerals in the Settlements, though, you start to feel it: Wilson Gray was gone, but his essence would be with us forever.

Most of Gray City attended the service in person or by televisit. The only ones who couldn't attend were the crew I had assigned to stabilize Habitat. We also had visitors and televisitors from across the Pournelle Settlements, the collection of independent towns and stations inspired by an early aerospace pioneer who was the first to describe the energy efficiencies of mining colonies in the Jupiter system. The Settlements were loosely affiliated in trade and support alliances, but most of them prized their independence. It had taken all of Wilson's incredible charm and diplomatic skills to unite them in the Refinery Station project. Some had openly called it Wilson's Folly. They had the good taste not to mention it on that day, but the phrase would soon come back, I felt sure.

By chain of command, Leeanne should've directed the ceremonies and the aftermath; but my steely-eyed pilot had finally given in to her human side. She had watched her husband and her future all shredded in an instant. She had made my pickup like a pro; but after that she had just stared at the wreckage, her eyes sunk in her suddenly hollow face. She had barely mustered the energy to answer simple questions since. I had had to take the ship's controls, and since then everyone just turned to me as if I were in charge of the entire city. Maybe I was.

I never signed up for this, Wilson. I wasn't the decision maker. I was the guy who carried out the decisions. That was my part in our triad: Wilson had the wild dreams and sold them to the world, Leeanne was the practical one who told him when his dreams were *too* wild, and ol' Sam Pike led the grunt work to make the dreams come true.

Now I had to hope that I could remember the lessons Wilson had taught me as I stepped into his role. That included something that always came natural to him, something I could never be comfortable with: leading meetings.

Immediately after Wilson's service, as Kim led Leeanne back to her cabin, I called an emergency meeting. Even limiting it to department heads, there were still thirty people gathered in the Atrium of Habitat, and six more by televisit. That was too many for an effective meeting, but I couldn't guess which department might have a handy miracle or two. We needed every miracle we could scrape up.

The hubbub in the Atrium was more uneasy than I'd ever heard it. Even in the darkest can-we-do-this hours of station design and construction, the department heads had all been on board, drawn in by Wilson's enthusiasm and quick answer to any problem.

Now I saw them clumping into worried groups, bobbing in the air as they talked among themselves. The faces I saw...Some looked almost as haunted as Leeanne's. I needed to get them all on task—whatever the task would be.

I pushed off to the chairman's harness in the center of the

atrium, but I didn't strap in. It just felt too soon for that, and I was still kicking myself for not being at the station when Wilson needed me. So I strapped into my harness next to his.

Then I raised my voice, but not so much as to echo off the walls. "All right, people. Come to order." Somehow it was easier there in my harness. I could pretend that Wilson was just "away," and I was running things in his stead as I had done many times before. So I followed our usual routine. "Status reports, people."

I looked at Hank Zinn from structural engineering, but he hesitated, staring at his hands. Before Hank could answer, the tumult broke out again. This time I did echo: *"People!"*

They dropped silent again. "Okay, we can't pretend we're not shook up. When you get out of here, you all have my permission to panic for an hour. But Wilson Gray hired *professionals,* goddamn it, and I expect you to start acting like it! Or none of us are gonna last long out here."

More tumult. Mari's voice broke over the rest. "We're not going to last anyway!" There were shouts of agreement.

I looked at Mari: a petite woman with golden skin, red-brown curls, and usually a confident attitude that fascinated me. Even now, stressed and grieving, confidence in tatters, she still appealed to me. She was still the fireball I had fallen for. We had dated for several months before our latest fight, and I really hoped we weren't over. So I hated to turn on her, but I had to put this down *now*. I tried to sound cold. "If you believe that, Mari, there's the hatch. I need a united team. If you're giving up on us, hitch a ride to Walkerville or Callisto One or Earth, for all I care. I'll comp the transit costs in your last check. Is that what you want?"

Mari glared at me, and I was coldly sure that our last date had been our *last* date. But she shook her head and bit her lip. I gave her a second in case she wanted to add something, then I continued. "If we're going to come out the other side of this, it will be by following Wilson's troubleshooting protocol: tally our assets and status; define the problem; refine it into a solution; assign tasks to our assets; and design the process and build whatever new assets we need. So it's tally time, people. Hank?"

Hank turned to me. His voice was steady and calm. Maybe I had handled that right. "We're in bad shape. Not fatal, but bad. Habitat still has a slight wobble." We could see that just by looking around. The walls occasionally flexed as a slow standing wave passed through the structure. "We'll have that under control in a couple hours. But The Tube took serious damage at the reactor end. We can salvage the material, but it's going to take a month. R&R is worse. The debris is orbiting with us in a cloud, but some of the material is not recoverable at any reasonable cost. The mass driver is safe, but its orbit is unstable in the long run. We have maybe three months to boost it to a stable orbit before it draws too close to Ganymede and tidal force pulls it apart. We can do that, if you're willing to spend the fuel."

I nodded. Wilson had given his life in part for the driver. We wouldn't give it up now. I turned to Mari. "Eco?"

Mari's voice was bitter. "As I tried to tell you, we're screwed in the long term. We have consumables enough for now. We can scavenge some, and we can barter with other Settlements. There's still demand for our batteries, right?" She looked at Sissi Sneve from power management, and Sissi nodded. "But our loads from Earth... Well, we've got twenty months in the pipeline. And that may be it. My buyers back on Earth say it was already difficult to get credit before. Sellers doubted Mr. Gray's plan. Now that the news is out, that credit is drying up. We'll see gaps in the pipeline twenty months down; and four or five months after that, the pipeline will *stop*."

I tried to sound conciliatory. "And can we conserve enough to make the difference?"

"Maybe..." But her expression didn't look convincing, a combination of a glare at me and a trembling frown.

Discussions broke out again; and for the first meeting in over a year, I resorted to the air horn.

The shriek echoed off the walls, and some put their hands over their ears. When the echoes died, I continued as if nothing had happened. "Then we'll find another answer, like always. Power?"

Sissi summarized the generator status and the power market—the two bright spots of the meeting—and I moved on to the next topic. By the time most of the departments had reported, I noticed a flash of short platinum hair at the nearest hatch. Kim had returned to the meeting. Her face was even paler than usual, and her delicate face showed—no, not sadness, fury! *Oh, shit, what now!*

Kim gently squeezed through the crowd to join me, sliding up to my side while trying not to draw attention. She handed me the computer board from the reactor, and she pushed a report to my comp. While I listened to the status reports, I checked Kim's data.

Oh, shit, I thought again. This was bad. It might be the last straw. Wilson had been right, it hadn't been an accident. This could break our spirits.

Or maybe...As the last status report completed, I surveyed the room. "Thank you. That's what I expect from you all: your best effort as professionals. And we need that." I held out the computer board. "I thought we were dealing with an accident. But it turns out we have a whole different problem: sabotage." Immediately the room broke into shouts, and I had to use the air horn again. "I'm pushing Kim's report to you all. It won't stay secret, so I won't try. This circuit board that arrived from Earth six months ago has a very clever, invasive virus hard-coded into its core. Ladies and gentlemen, somebody tried to stop us. Maybe kill us."

This time I let the shouts play out. I *wanted* them shouting. I wanted them *angry*. And amid the shouts, I heard two words more than any other: "Initiative" and "Magnus." Magnus Metals ran an Earth orbit refinery that sapped much of our profits in refining fees; and the System Initiative were the bureaucrats who thought *they* ran space from cushy offices in Rio de Janeiro. Between their regulations and more fees and fines, they sapped much of the rest of our profits.

Refinery Station had been Wilson's giant middle finger to both of them: we would do our own refining, and the Initiative were welcome to fly out to Jupiter to try to enforce their regulations where the laws of physics were the only real authority. Either might be our saboteurs, maybe even both. I didn't need to work out who, yet. It was enough to know that the two things Settlers hated most were the government squeeze and the corporate squeeze. This news had unified the department heads more than anything I could have said.

But Wilson had taught me: some messages are more effective from "the troops" than from the boss. So just as Wilson had often done to me, I tapped out a message and pushed it to Kim. When her comp buzzed, she looked at it. Then she nodded and gently pushed out until she was in among the others, shouting and talking like the others. And as a lull hit, she shouted over the rest. "They tried to kill us!"

The echoes were louder than the air horn. *"Yeah!"*

"Are we gonna let them stop us?"

This had been one of Wilson's simplest motivating questions; and the answer this time shook the walls worse than the standing wave. *"Hell, No!"*

Right then, I knew: I had my team again. We would survive. Now I just had to figure out how.

That's what I *thought* I would do; but I had no idea how my time would actually be spent. I had never appreciated what Wilson had done all day. More meetings. More soothing of frayed nerves. More reviews of plans and schedules. More calls back to Earth, pleading with creditors and suppliers not to cut us off until we regrouped.

More calls to our business agents, too, to try to track down the source of the virus. Yeah, like that was ever gonna happen. Whoever did it had covered their tracks too well.

There was so much to do, and every day the list grew faster than I could whittle it down. I started sleeping in my office, when I found time to sleep at all. No matter how hard I tried, the work piled up. Maybe Mari was right: maybe Gray Interplanetary was dead like Wilson, and we were just waiting for it to stop breathing.

And Leeanne...Leeanne might've been walking dead herself. For the first week, she didn't come out of her cabin, and she barely ate the food that Kim brought her. Then she started coming out for a few hours at a time, but she spoke little. Her eyes were still wide and red, her face muscles slack and expressionless. One look told you she was still in shock. People tried to engage her, but the conversations always trailed off into uncomfortable silence. Over time she started wandering into the middle of work areas, sometimes talking but mostly watching. People complained to me. They couldn't say it, since legally she was now the top boss, but they wanted me to keep her out of their hair. As if I didn't have enough problems. I added that to my list, but not near the top.

Three weeks after the funeral, though, Leeanne pushed herself to the top of the list, floating into my office as I went over power management reports late at night.

She waited for the hatch to close; then for the first time in weeks she found real energy to speak—and she threw it all at me. "Samuel Pike, what the hell are you doing to my company?"

My mind froze. I don't back down from a fight. Normally a challenge like that would have me shouting back, or worse. But this woman was my boss now, and my best friend's grieving widow. With Wilson gone, she was the closest friend I had. I felt grateful to see her engaged in *something,* even if it was chewing me out.

I muttered, "Leeanne...We're trying...to put something together here."

"Bullshit!" She waved an arm to gesture at the station, giving her a slight spin until she hit a wall and arrested her movement. "*They* are trying, but they need direction from you. *You* are floundering!"

Despite my concerns, my hackles rose. "Damn it, Leeanne! I'm doing the best I know how! You—" I caught myself before I could spit out an accusation. "You have any ideas for what I can do better, I'm all ears."

Leeanne's tone calmed, but she didn't fall back into her depression. "What you can do, Sam, is stop driving yourself

284

so hard. You're looking worse than me, and I'm the one who lost my husband! You're going to kill yourself, and kill Wilson's dream with you. What you have to do is what Willy would do: prioritize and delegate."

I sighed. "I know, I'm trying."

Again she said, "Bullshit!" And again she gestured at the station. "I've been all over Gray City, Sam. Everywhere I see the same thing: people are holding onto hope because you and Kim charged them up; but they're slowly losing it because your decisions take so long that the situation changes before they hear from you. Everyone's going through the motions, but there's no plan in effect. And the more you look like a zombie, the more they lose faith."

I breathed out slowly. "You're right, Leeanne. I've tried to hold things together for you. Now if you're ready, boss, I'm happy to take your orders—as soon as I get some sleep."

"Uh-uh!" Leeanne shook her head, bobbing against her handhold. "I never wanted to be the boss. Wilson knew that: I'm a counselor, not an executive. You haven't had time to check Willy's final orders yet, but they name you as his second in command, subject to approval of the Board. And with his shares plus mine, I have controlling interest on the Board, so you're approved."

"But Leeanne, I'm doing a miserable job! You said so yourself!"

"That's because you're trying to solve *all* of the problems instead of just the big ones. You think you're delegating, but your people tell me you're not. You're delegating tasks, not decisions. That's why you have no time to sleep! Any time you've got a problem where your department heads can decide, let them! Let Mari deal with the suppliers on Earth. She always did for Wilson."

"Mari and I..." I swallowed. "We're not getting along."

"That's a luxury you can't afford right now. Treat her like a trusted professional, not an ex-girlfriend. Mari'll do her job if you let her."

"Well..."

"Samuel Pike, if you let your wounded pride put an end to

Gray City, I'll launch you straight into Jupiter! Mari's a grown up, now you be one!

"And speaking of launching...Hank is waiting for you to get off your ass and order him to salvage the mass driver. He has a plan, but it'll take a lot of fuel. He can't authorize that without orders from you. Every minute you wait, the driver gets closer to Ganymede, and the salvage costs grow higher."

"We have over two months..."

"And if you'd acted immediately, we would've had three months. By now the fuel costs have more than doubled. You give that order *now* Sam, or so help me I'll steal a tug and start hauling the driver back myself."

At that I smiled. She would, too. I pulled open a channel to Hank. "Hank? Yeah, it's Sam...Hey, sorry I've gotten buried here...No, you're right and I'm wrong, so I'm doing the apologies here. You're authorized for fuel charges and overtime budgets to go get that driver...Yeah, the plan you submitted— Damn, was that four days ago already? Okay, revise the plan as needed, and I'll approve it...No, don't wait for final approval, I trust you...Thanks, Hank! I look forward to your reports."

I disconnected and looked at Leeanne. "How'd I do, boss?"

"Enough of that 'boss' business. You did okay. Now you make a call like that to all your department heads, and maybe we'll get things under control here. Start with Mari." I frowned at that. "Mari. Now."

I spread my hands up, pleading. "But Leeanne...That fight..." I couldn't find words. They brought back the pain.

Leeanne's expression softened. Suddenly I saw my friend, Wilson's wife. My pain grew as she asked, "What about it, Sam? You two have fought before. You're a hard-nosed engineer, she's a fiery Cuban, that's no surprise. You've always gotten past it before."

I tried to speak, but I had a catch in my throat. I coughed and said, "But this fight...This is why we weren't at the station. This is why—"

"Hush!" Leeanne shouted as she pushed herself across the office to me, stopping herself by wrapping her arms around me and pulling my head down to her shoulder. She buried her face in my own shoulder and said, "Stop it, Sam! Don't say that. Do *not* say that. I never want to hear that again."

I tried to hold back, but I found myself sobbing. "If I had been here—"

"No, Sam. You wouldn't have been here. You would've been with the prospecting fleet. Or negotiating with the other Settlements. Or on any of a hundred other errands for Wilson, just like every other day of this project."

"But—"

"No buts! So this is what it's all about? Sam, someday I'll find who killed Willy, and I'll make them pay. But it wasn't you, and it wasn't me! We're survivors, we're not to blame."

Then I really cut loose with the tears, and Leeanne joined in. More than I had needed sleep, I had needed tears, and someone to share them with.

Eventually, though, I remembered that I had work to do. "Okay, boss—Leeanne," I corrected. I pulled away and wiped my eyes. "Do I look ready for more calls?"

Leeanne smiled at me. It was weak, but it was a smile. She had needed the tears, too. "Stop worrying about looking strong." She pushed back to the hatch, out of the comm pickup. "Call Mari."

I nodded, my body bobbing in response, and I called Mari. As soon as her face appeared on my comm, she started in on me. "Sam Pike, do you *like* making my job impossible?" I shook my head, but she continued before I could answer. "I just answered a call from Bader Farms. I had them, Sam. I had them! I had them convinced that we were stabilizing our situation, and you had a plan to meet our contracts. Then *you* called them, and you ruined the whole thing! They said you didn't strike them as confident, so why should they be? They're ready to cancel our future pipeline loads, maybe even sell some of the in-transit loads to Walkerville."

She paused to breathe, and I finally snuck in a response. "I'm sorry, Mari."

Mari continued. "And furthermore—" Then she shook her head. Red-brown curls became a shimmering cloud. "What did you say?"

"I'm sorry. I screwed up, and I was wrong. If I stay out of the middle, can you fix this?"

Mari's jaw dropped open, and it took a few seconds before she answered. "Maybe. But I'll have to offer points."

I nodded. "Take them out of my account. It's my mistake, so Gray City shouldn't pay for it."

Mari cocked an eyebrow. "And you'll stay out of it?"

I nodded again. "It's your department. Wilson trusted you, and Leeanne and I trust you. I'm sorry if I gave you any reason to doubt that. If you need me, tell me. Otherwise, it's hands-off."

Mari almost smiled then. "Okay, I need to work on repairing this. And... Thanks, Sam."

I disconnected the call and started placing more. As I did, department heads pulled tasks from my task list, and some tasks immediately switched from *Backlog* to *In Progress*. A couple even switched to *Complete*. When I finished, I looked at the full list. Those forty-some calls had done more to clear the list than I had accomplished in three weeks.

I held up my hands in surrender. "Okay, Leeanne, you were right. I'm still learning on the job here. What's next?"

"Next we hold an Executive Committee meeting, just like the old days: the Chairman, the Counselor, and your Executive Officer."

"But I'm—All right, I used to be XO. Now I'm Chairman, so who's the Executive Officer?"

"Kim Stone, of course. She's already doing every task you'll let her. I've promoted her and made the pay retroactive—assuming we have anything left to pay anyone with. She's outside waiting for us to have it out. Are we good?"

I thought long before answering. I had so much to learn about being in the top seat; but with Leeanne's help, it had already gotten easier. And now with Kim's help as well, maybe I could handle it.

I smiled and nodded. "We're good. Hell, we're great! Bring on the next challenge!"

Leeanne knocked on the hatch, and it opened. Kim floated in and closed it behind her. The two women floated there, one large and dark, the other a pale blonde pixie; but both were strong, especially inside, and I was going to need that.

"You straighten him out, boss lady?" Kim asked.

Leeanne raised her free hand. "Ah-ah-ah! None of that. Sam's the boss, so let's get in the proper habit."

Kim nodded and turned to me. "Right. Okay, boss, I think we need to get the mass driver ASAP. Tidal force won't be large enough to damage it for a couple weeks, but the strain is mounting. It won't take much strain to misalign the rings."

I tried to answer, but Leeanne jumped in. "You're right, but Sam has that handled already." Yeah, I was the boss all right, except when Leeanne wanted to be in charge. But I could work that way. It was comforting to have somebody watching my back.

Still, I had to keep up appearances. "Yes, Hank has approval to modify his plan as needed. You keep an eye on it. Don't interfere with him, but make sure we're not blindsided by any unexpected charges."

I felt better. Now what next? Well, I would follow Wilson's protocols. "Okay, let's tally our assets and status. We have almost our full crew. Only a few people have quit. We have Habitat, our prospecting fleet, our construction fleet, and all the smaller stations we built before Habitat. We have the fuel depot and the generator stations. And we have active contracts to sell power here in the Settlements, and we have contracts to deliver raw metals to Earth orbit. We also have twenty months of supplies in the pipeline, and we can get more as long as we don't default on any of those delivery contracts. Mari will persuade our suppliers to give us a little more time, since we're technically not in default yet."

Leeanne added, "And we have the mass driver."

"Yes, we have the driver, and power to run it, though that

will tax our generating capacity quite a bit. Anything else?" Both women shook their heads. "Okay, that also defines the problem, pretty much: we need to find some way to fulfill those contracts, or somehow generate equivalent income to keep the pipeline open. Our credit is stretched too thin: if it looks like we'll miss a month or more in the pipeline, people will start abandoning us. That'll create a feedback loop, and we'll collapse long before the pipeline runs dry. Other Settlements will lay claim to our assets, and who could blame them?"

Kim broke in. "Boss, I've made a few inquiries with friends in other Settlements. Callisto One is primed to take us over. Almost as if they were ready in advance. And they've been making offers to some of our key staff."

I nodded. "Interesting..." Callisto One was the Initiative's official presence in the Pournelle Settlements, and had been a thorn in Wilson's side. We all guessed how they had been "ready in advance"; but I shook my head. "Our people hate the Initiative. If we have any hope of getting through this, they won't go to Callisto. Now we just have to find that hope."

And for the first time since that call from Kim three weeks ago, Leeanne smiled. "Oh, I figured that out. While there was no hope, I was happy to let you screw things up. Boss." And her smile actually became a brief grin. "But once I saw an answer, I knew I had to kick your ass into gear so you could make it happen. They won't follow me, but you've got the touch. All you need is some hot pilots—me, and I can name others—who really understand gravity deep in their guts. You've all been worried about tidal force and its danger to the mass driver; but tidal force is still a force, just like any other. And force can be dangerous, but it can also be harnessed."

It took a month to turn Leeanne's idea into a plan, and then another three to put the plan into effect. It took over two months just to pull the mass driver out of its doomed orbit and into one that we could use.

Mari had persuaded our creditors to give us a little more time. Maybe they figured they couldn't lose much more than they already would, and they could afford to stretch a little in hopes of a payoff. Maybe they just had a lingering respect for Wilson's legacy. Hell, for all I knew his ghost was out there somewhere still applying that old Wilson charm.

But one thing I do know: it wasn't our plan that sold them, since Mari never told them what it was. We had enemies, but we didn't know exactly who they were nor whom we could trust. So we kept the full plan to just the Executive Committee as long as we could, and doled out details on a need-to-know basis. Once we were sure the plan would work and no one could stop us, *then* we filled in everyone in Gray City. The cheer when they understood almost shattered the walls of Habitat. Mari even smiled at me.

When the day came for us to test out the plan, Leeanne insisted on flying one of the chase ships, and I insisted on flying shotgun with her. She tried to argue me out of it, but I pulled the trump card I'd held back since our first Executive Committee meeting. I looked her straight in the eyes and asked, "Leeanne, am I in charge here or not? You can't have it both ways. If you as the Board say no, I'll sit back and watch you run things; but if you as my Counselor say no... then I'm happy to take your advice, but I'll do things my way."

For almost a full minute, I thought I'd been fired. Then Leeanne answered quietly, "We can't afford to lose you, too, Sam."

"Then it's a good thing I'll be flying with the best damn pilot in the Pournelle Settlements." And that settled it. I was in the copilot's harness as Leeanne idled between Jupiter and the driver. We watched the feed from Kim and the team on the far side of Jupiter as relayed by polar comm sats.

I called over the sats. "How's it going, Kim?"

Light speed delayed her response by over a second. "Fantastic, boss. The first load just launched, and we've got three more coming. Take a look."

I switched to Kim's station camera, which showed a large lump of ice, dirt, and valuable metals. If we sent that lump to Earth directly, Magnus would charge us a huge fee for clearing off the dross (which they *claimed* was useless, but we knew they made a few percentage points from the volatiles); and then *they* would assay the remains.

Somehow their assayers always came up with a value far lower than our estimates. If it were random, the error should have been in our favor once in a while, but it never was.

That was why Wilson wanted to break up the rocks ourselves, ship only the metals (which were easier to mass drive, since the driver was strong enough to grab even paramagnetic minerals), and deliver direct to our customers instead of to Magnus.

Now four such rocks were on a trajectory close to Jupiter, and we would rendezvous on the other side. I got on the chase fleet circuit. "Folks, get your rest. Targets coming your way in about six hours. Sleep while you can."

But we didn't sleep, and I doubt anyone in the chase fleet did.

Like us, most spent the six hours watching on the polar cameras as the first rock dove closer to Jupiter. When the rock passed within the Roche limit and started to break apart, I shouted over the chase circuits: "Yes!" And at least a dozen voices echoed mine.

Jupiter's tidal force pulled the near side of the rock much harder than the far side, and the ice and dross couldn't hold together. The metals that remained wouldn't be as pure as we would've gotten from the refinery, but they would be good enough to meet our contracts. I might have to give back a few points, but we would *meet our contracts*. We would survive.

And someday, we would build another refinery, and Wilson's Folly would become Wilson's triumph.

But that would be in the future.

I got back on the circuit. "Computers will feed target trajectories to you over the next three hours. We'll assign pickups. Plant your bots on the big targets, then look for targets of opportunity."

The drive bots would attach themselves to the metal fragments, calculate a burst plan, and drive the metals to the induct of the mass driver.

There the magnetic fields would grab them and accelerate the metals on their path to Earth. It all took careful computer calculations. That had chewed up much of our planning time: making sure our computers were *clean*.

The effort hadn't been wasted: we found three more virus traps waiting to be sprung. Someday, somebody was going to find out just how angry I was that they had killed my best friend.

But not today. Today we had metal to chase. "Leeanne, you picked our first target yet?"

"Yeah, boss, but it's not on the computer's list."

"Huh?"

She pushed a spectrographic report to me. "That blip there? That's nearly a quarter tonne of platinum. Computer says it's on a bad trajectory, we'll never recover it this time."

"Then leave it! We can get it on another orbit!"

"And let some other Settlement claim it after we did all the work? Hang on, boss!" And instead of waiting for the fragments to approach, Leeanne powered up the engines. She turned us back, and suddenly my view port was filled with brown bands and the Red Spot. I was pushed back into my couch at over three gees as we dove toward Jupiter.

What could I do? "Leeanne, you're fired!" But I said it with a big grin on my face, accentuated by the acceleration.

Leeanne grinned back even bigger. "Take it up with the Board. After we get that platinum!"

She laughed, and we sped deep into Jupiter's well. At a certain carefully calculated point, Leeanne flipped us around and fired the thrusters to slow us. I watched the computer project our course, and I was happy: the old Leeanne was back, at least for now.

"Not to backseat drive, Leeanne, but how do we get this baby on course?"

Leeanne pushed her analysis to my comp. "I think we can do it with three drive bots. Yeah, that's a lot, but this lump is worth more than any three we've picked out."

I nodded and readied the drive bots for firing. When our

velocity nearly matched the lumps, I fired off the bots. Then I watched them on the scope.

One... The first bot touched down, scrambled for a hold, and finally attached itself firmly. *Two...* The second bot attached. *And...* "Damn!"

"What is it, boss?"

"Third bot didn't attach. It might make a second pass, but that'll burn a lot of fuel. It might not do the trick. I'll launch another."

"Never mind, boss. I've got a better idea!"

Suddenly I felt the explosive *thump* of the tether launching. "We're gonna haul this sucker to the driver ourselves."

"That'll take a lot of fuel..."

"You'll approve it, boss!" Leeanne laughed, and I laughed as well as the tether struck the lump and scrambled for its own attachment.

When the tether controller showed a firm grip, I gave Leeanne a thumbs up. She gunned the engines and between our tether and the drive bots, we started nudging the platinum into a new trajectory. We passed a few other likely targets as we flew, and I launched drive bots at them as well; but Leeanne was right: this lump of platinum was the best possible proof of our plan.

As we approached the driver induct, I knew today would be a very good haul. I pushed the *Release* button on the tether controller, and the platinum was on a free trajectory straight for the induct.

We didn't go after more fragments, not quite yet. We just sat in silence for several minutes as the platinum drifted closer and closer to the mass driver.

When it got close enough, the magnetic field grabbed it, a weak hold on the platinum itself and a stronger hold on the metal web the bots had woven. The lump turned slightly, lining up with the magnetic rings; then it picked up speed. Soon it shot through the rings and out of sight.

We sat there a few minutes more, neither of us speaking.

I could see by the instrument lights that Leeanne was crying. I felt tears welling in my own eyes, a damned nuisance in zero g. But Wilson's dream was worth a few tears.

Then I realized we didn't have a contract for platinum. I pulled open a comm channel. "Mari, I have good news! You can start contract negotiations for a mass of platinum, specs attached." I pushed the specs into the data feed. "That should buy us dinner for a while!"

After the light speed delay, Mari responded, and her grin was a mirror of my own. "*I* have good news too, Sam. We've already got our dinner orders filled. I forwarded our suppliers a copy of Kim's satellite feed. As soon as they understood your plan, they upgraded our credit rating with all services. We're not back where we were, but we'll get there."

She broadcast the video? But I hadn't authorized that.

Then I saw Leeanne staring at me, and I knew there was only one proper response: "Great work, Mari. Gray City owes you. I owe you, big time."

Mari nodded. "You bet you owe me! Dinner and beer for starters. And I get to choose the place. Someplace expensive, with real meat! I'm sick of soy."

"Real meat, Mari. I promise." I closed the comm channel, and I felt warm inside.

I looked over, and Leeanne was still watching me. No time for that! It was time to get back to work. "Pilot! Next target!"

"Hang on!" Leeanne grinned through the tears as she wheeled the ship around again. I grinned, too. For the first time since the sabotage, in the middle of a three gee turn, I relaxed.

If I could've spared breath against the turn, I might have sung. I could pay people. I could *feed* people.

And finally, the word fit: I was the boss.

Half Past

written by

Samantha Murray

illustrated by

MEGAN KELCHNER

ABOUT THE AUTHOR

Samantha recently had to tell one of her small sons not to read his book while walking to school as he might bump into a tree—alas, she knows this from personal experience. Growing up, she had major crushes on the books A Wrinkle in Time, Charmed Life, The Dark Is Rising, The Last Unicorn, Tigana, Impossible Things, *and many, many more.*

Samantha always wanted to be an astronaut, and has degrees in theatre arts and mathematics.

Her stories have appeared in Lightspeed *magazine (*Women Destroy Science Fiction! *Special Issue) and* Daily Science Fiction.

Samantha lives in Western Australia with her family of unruly boys.

ABOUT THE ILLUSTRATOR

Megan Kelchner was born in Livingston, New Jersey but spent most of her life growing up in a small town in the small state of Rhode Island. Coming from a family full of artists and musicians (but mostly musicians), her parents had no problem supporting her in her artistic endeavors.

Megan currently is attending Pratt Institute where she majors in illustration. Her favorite medium is digital, something that was brought about when her first Wacom tablet was given to her in sixth grade for Christmas. Her inspiration for her work lies in everything from comic books to classical opera.

Megan attended Tiverton High School where she became a regional winner of the Doodle 4 Google contest, twice earning her a trip to the city where she would eventually attend college.

Having always found illustration as the best way to communicate her ideas, Megan is excited to set out from her small town in her small home state to share her art with the world.

Half Past

The magic of my father's house seeped its way into the surrounding countryside. Magic has a way of doing that: overflowing its container, having influences you did not intend. It's one of the first things I learnt: magic is messy. There were traces in the stream running through the garden; in the translucently clear water and the way it sounded as if it were laughing if you didn't quite listen. It spilled into the sunflowers growing to the side of the front door; as big as your head and brightly, improbably yellow, they would lean towards you if you talked to them, and rub their petals under your chin with a light, swaying affection.

Today though, it was hot in the garden. Around the back of the house dry leaves crunched under my feet and the plants were overgrown and wilted. I wondered what this said about my father's mood and how very angry he must still be. Or maybe my eyes were seeing all of the little details more, because I was leaving.

I heard the boards of the porch creak and saw Eliza swinging in the patio seat, the heels of her boots drumming angrily on the downswing.

"What are you doing?" I leaned against the rails and watched her go backwards and forwards.

"What's it look like?" Eliza was not my favorite Echo—she was almost thirteen and snappy and disconsolate with it. But she had been one of my companions for more than two years, and today I looked at her scowl with an odd sentimental fondness.

"I was looking for you," I said.

"Why?" she asked abruptly. She stopped swinging though and squinted up at me.

"I guess...to say goodbye."

"Oh." She was a little faded these days. She hadn't aged at all of course, her dark hair hung in the same long braid down her back, but I could see through parts of her dress to the swing behind her. She had been all sharp angles and vivid streaks of scorn in the beginning. "Why?"

"Because I refuse to be stuck in this house forever." I could feel the heat returning to my words and my cheeks both. "Because just because you have the most magic does not mean you get to control everyone else." Eliza chewed her fingernail—a habit I'd always had—but kept her eyes on me. "Because he treats me like a child and it is *not fair*." I was conscious of the childish note rising up in my voice and the irony didn't escape me but I did not care. I was fifteen years old, and I had my own magic.

"Good luck out there," said Eliza, and the softness of the expression on her face surprised me. In the couple of years she had lurked here I hadn't seen her smile before. I went inside.

I skirted past the sitting room and looked in the sunroom, which was unusually dirty. The windowpanes were streaky with grime so the sunlight coming in was muted, but I only saw a couple of other Echoes who were so faint that if I hadn't been looking, I wouldn't have noticed them at all.

The Echoes had been my only playmates for a long time. My father was a stern man, with a fierce hooded gaze like a hawk, and when he directed his attention at you sometimes it felt like your skin would burn with all of the intentness; he didn't count as a playmate. My mother used to play. She didn't have any magic, but she had been a masterful weaver of fairytale and fun. She'd had a soft spot for the Echoes, whereas my father usually looked right through them with a certain impatience. They were a frustration to him I think; the fact that I produced them proved that I had inherited a strong talent for magic, but whenever he tried to instruct me in those arts, the results were usually disastrous. The magic with which I made the Echoes was instinctive and unbidden. I failed to do anything on command.

My mother had died when I was nearly seven, and then the Echoes—shades of me, always younger, always receding from me in age and experience—were all I had. My father had no family left, and my Mother's sister was not spoken of, for reasons I didn't understand. I had a memory of her visiting when I must have been less than four, my young pretty aunt, spinning me around and around to make me laugh, her eyes dancing.

I found Bethie at last down near the stream. She had made little paper boats, put delicate blue and white flowers inside for passengers and was casting them off at the edge of the water. She jumped up when she saw me and hugged me tightly around the waist. Her thin little arms were surprisingly strong. Her hair trailed down around her face in dark curls.

Bethie was six, and my favorite.

On my sixth birthday my father had magicked little fairy lights that floated in the air all around, and he had even put his arm around my mother in a rare show of affection and smiled down at me. There had been a mound of presents, among them a dollhouse with little people who moved in a jerky manner inside it. There had been a rainbow birthday cake with purple frosting which was sweet and hard on my tongue. That was the day Bethie had appeared, with a sharp smell like ozone, coalescing out of birthday candles and anticipation and glowing excitement, glimmering and forming in the air until she became real and solid. Whenever I was in the grips of an overwhelming emotion I would make an Echo. It was like I was not enough, by myself, to contain what I was feeling. Even when I understood that it was me doing it, it was never something I could control.

The stream was not laughing today. Bethie's boats sailed prettily in the eddies, but I didn't feel the sense of impish delight that the water usually had. I gazed back towards the house. Had my father pulled in all his magic to brood within himself and left the house and grounds to suffer? Was he doing it on purpose, to show me how he felt? I felt my own anger kindling back to life.

Even with his harshness and distance he was my father, but he could not keep me here cloistered away from everything else in the bright wide world.

And that led back to why I was here.

"I've got something to tell you," I said looking down into Bethie's small bright face. "I've got to go away." Haltingly I tried to explain, although she was only six and she had crystallized out of a moment where her world was perfect and glowing, so I didn't know how much she could understand. I don't know that she or the Echoes really knew who I was anyway. They existed in their own little worlds, timeless, unchanging, caught in a moment, and I think everything else was blurry to them.

"I'll come with you," said Bethie when I finished. It was entirely unexpected, and impossible, and melted me like I was birthday candy abandoned in the sun. The radius of the house and grounds was as far as an Echo could stray from where she had formed. And Bethie was happy here! Her cheeks were flushed, her eyes shining with lights. Often she would press her hands together under her chin, tight against her thin frame, as if the excitement was too much for her to contain.

I know I had once been Bethie, but it seemed so unreal a thought as to be impossible. I envied her a little; I would have liked to stay Bethie forever.

"I'm sorry honey, but I have to do this alone," I said as she wormed her way under my arm to hug me again, looking more tremulous than I'd ever seen her. She would forget me as soon as I was out of sight, I felt pretty sure, but I gripped her hard in this moment for my own sake.

I heard the padding of soft feet on the path and I looked up to see eleven-year-old Libby coming from the house. "Someone's here," she said, a spark of curiosity mixed in with her usual demeanor of crushing disappointment.

It had been years since someone had last come to the house. My father did not tend to encourage visitors and most of the townsfolk were in too much awe or fear of him to venture close. I ran quickly back up the path, my two Echoes behind me.

302

MEGAN KELCHNER

She was just getting out of her carriage as I reached the front of the house. Her dark hair was up in some sort of untidy mass at the back of her head, and she was wearing trousers instead of the long skirt that was customary. Her face angled towards me in the high, bright light of the sun, and my breath caught in my throat.

It was my mother.

It wasn't, of course, although when I started breathing again the air felt hot and forced in my lungs. I clutched at the hands of the Echoes on either side of me—Libby's hand felt feather-light and insubstantial in my own, but Bethie's grip was as real and solid as ever. For an instant the visitor had looked like my mother, but she was not. And then I knew who she was.

"Aunt Marla," I said, letting go of the hands in mine, and hurtling forward two steps to throw my arms around her neck. I was almost as tall as she was. "Aunt Marla, can I go with you? Oh, can I go with you? I can't stay here, I'm leaving today. I was going to try and look for you anyway, once I got to town." My words stumbled clumsily over themselves.

Aunt Marla looked at me oddly. I probably shouldn't have made my request like that, so suddenly and fiercely, when I hadn't even seen her in more than a decade. "Hello Elizabeth," she said. She didn't smile and her eyes were very dark, like my mother's. "Yes, you may come with me when I go."

A flash of hope mixed with the slow boil of my anger that was underneath everything today, the combination making me tremble.

I suddenly realized that she could see three of us and wondered if she was confused. "These are my...um, I mean..." I began, flustered.

"I know about the Echoes," said Aunt Marla, although she only looked at me. "You have been doing that since you were very young."

She must have found me as changed as I found her. The last time she'd seen me, I would have been a much smaller version of Bethie. Aunt Marla looked faintly sad and old and tired, and none of these were things I had associated with my mother's younger sister, although of course she was older now than my mother had ever lived to be.

"Would you like me to take you to Father?" I tried to keep my voice steady as I tried, belatedly, to remember my manners.

"No," she said after a pause. "I can go and find him." I felt relieved. The curiosity I had over how he would react to the return of my disfavored aunt was not enough to entice me within my Father's radius. It felt as if we had burned up all the space and air between us with our words last night.

I wondered how long Aunt Marla would stay. It was likely Father would turn her out immediately.

Which meant there was one more goodbye I could no longer avoid.

The sitting room was dim and dusty, and when I opened up the curtains all it did was illuminate the grime. There was a faint scent of old dried flowers. I couldn't see her at first but I crouched down and found her under the table, her small face pressed up against one of the thick carved wooden legs.

"Hello Elly," I said softly, but she didn't look at me, only snuffled like a baby animal and wiped her hand against her nose and then onto the blue of her smock. Even in the shadows I could see that she was sharply defined and solid. Her hair was undone and her dark eyes were large and hunted. When all of the other Echoes had faded, Elly would remain, I knew. She would be here for as long as I lived.

"I've come to say goodbye," I said, although I didn't think it was any use trying to talk to her. She looked at me then though, and I could see that tears were trembling on her lashes. It was the word "goodbye," I thought. She knows that word. She knows that word better than anyone.

I put out my hand very slowly and touched her hair. "It's okay," I said. The words felt rough in my throat because they were a lie. I felt a hot prickle of guilt down my spine—I never came to see Elly, I avoided the sitting room. But how could I tell her the truth? For her it was not okay, it would never be okay. She was caught forever in the day my mother died.

I sat with Elly for a long time, as if somehow my presence would mean something to her although I knew it couldn't. When I left, I met Aunt Marla at the door.

"May I go and see her?" she asked curtly, and I nodded. I didn't know what she wanted with Elly, but maybe she wanted to say goodbye too. I presumed from her abrupt manner that things had not gone well with my father, which did not surprise me at all.

I had thrown clothes and some belongings into a bag the night before, and I figured I would put it in Aunt Marla's carriage, so that nothing would delay our departure. I felt like my blood was surging with the need to flee, to begin the new life that I was obviously fated to have; why else would my Aunt have showed up on the very day I was going to leave?

But something tugged at me as I went down the hall and through to the wide steps of the staircase. Like when a painting that has been there many years is moved, and you have taken it so much for granted that you don't even see it anymore and couldn't say what was drawn there, but the empty space feels wrong and creases your brow. Or when a sound you are so used to that you don't even register anymore suddenly ceases.

A sound. I realized that it was very, very quiet. The house felt oddly *undisturbed,* and the little hairs on my arms stood up. The sense of stillness increased as I went through the house, my own footsteps coming louder and faster by contrast.

Three stairs up, I stopped as I put my finger on the feeling. I felt *alone.* Even though I was a girl with a dead mother and a distant father, I had never felt alone like this before. I forgot all thoughts of my bag and went by instinct out to the porch.

The patio-swing was still and unmoving, and there was no one there. The Echoes often moved around even though they had their favorite haunts, so that was not that unusual. But there was no one anywhere. Years and years of Echoes, fading to various degrees, but always there layering my days with faint whispers and babbles in the background, the flicker of shadows that were barely there, the smell of ozone.

There was nothing.

"Aunt Marla," I called, desperate with confusion. I turned on my heel and dashed back the way I had come, my running feet leaving little footprints in the dust.

I swung open the sitting room door, but my Aunt was not there. I walked over to the table, my steps slow and deliberate now, and crouched to look under it. Elly was gone.

None of this made any sense. Elly never left the sitting room. I rubbed at my arms, which had come out in goosebumps. Many different emotions warred in my chest, but anger won out. What. Was. Going. On?

"Aunt Marla!" I yelled, running from room to room, all empty, all quiet. "Where are you?"

There. The front door was open. I ran outside and down the steps past the hoard of sunflowers. I shaded my eyes against the slanted rays of the sun as I started down the path. Against the glare I could make out one figure. No, two.

"Aunt Marla," I shrieked again, fear mixing in with the heat of my anger and making my voice croaky.

They were still too far away. I could see Aunt Marla holding something in her hand, pointing it forward. I could see the child in front of her, the tilt of her little trusting face.

Bethie. Bethie. Bethie. Not Bethie.

The ivory-white stick Aunt Marla held seemed to shine brightly for a moment, and Bethie dispersed like she was made of rain.

"Noooooo," I yelled. I felt myself boiling and bubbling as if I were full of steam. Surely I had other magic? I put my hands together, stretched them straight out in front of me, and willed myself to blast Aunt Marla with a pure bolt of my rage.

Aunt Marla turned and looked at me. Her face was impassive and she did not keel over or erupt into flame or show any signs of discomfort at all.

I walked towards her, my eyes on what she held in her hand.

Aunt Marla with a wand? I had always been told that my mother's side of the family had no talent for magic. She held the wand lightly, but it was pointed straight at me.

"Aunt Marla, what are you doing?" the steam I'd felt had evaporated, leaving an empty space inside me. *Bethie*.

Aunt Marla didn't react to my question, and I realized that was not her name. She had never been Aunt Marla at all.

"Who are you?" I said to not-Aunt-Marla. I stopped in the dirt of the path and she took the last few steps towards me.

The corner of her mouth moved a little but it was nothing that could be called a smile. "I'm Elizabeth," she said.

Her eyes looked tired yet so familiar. "I don't believe you," I said.

"Did you notice that you didn't make an Echo? After the big fight with your father, after you decided to leave? Why do you think that was?" Despite the little wry note in her voice, her face was serious.

It was true. Even caught in the fierce and consuming emotions of last night, no Echo had formed. I couldn't believe I hadn't noticed that before.

Non-Aunt-Marla-Elizabeth must have seen my confusion. "You're me, or at least, you're a copy of me when I was young."

I looked down at my arms, which had crossed themselves defensively over my chest. They were firm, solid, real. "I don't believe you," I said again. But I believed her.

I looked at the wand, dipped downwards now but still pointed roughly in my direction. "Why do you want to make me go?" I blurted. I could feel the blood coursing in my veins, my heart thumping in my chest, bringing heat to my face, pounding so hard I expected to see an Echo made of this moment, but there was none. Because I was an Echo myself.

"He was right you know, your father," and now grown-up-Elizabeth's eyes flickered away from me and off into the distance. "The world is swirled in complexity and darkness. It is the darkness he wanted to save you . . . save me from. It is not as pretty as you thought it was going to be. Neither is it as exciting.

But I did find Aunt Marla, and she was right: it is my world and I deserved to take my place in it."

I thought of Bethie, of Elly, Libby, Eliza, Betty, Liz, and many others so faded that their names were forgotten. All of the companions I had grown up with, or thought I did. Now there was only me. "Why?" I asked her again.

"Because you are all part of me," she said. "You all hold these things for me, these feelings, and I need them back, I have to own them myself." She paused and then added quietly, "It is the only way I can be whole."

"Why did you take all of the others first? I was right there, you could have zapped me with that thing right away."

I wasn't sure if her eyes softened. "Because I've never spoken to you before. I never knew you. I fought with my father that day, and I left. I never came back. I learned, eventually, to take back the Echoes just after I made them, so that I could keep what it was I felt, even if it was hard that way. My father died, a year ago, and I haven't seen him since I was fifteen. Since I was you."

My father? I shot an involuntary glance back up at the house, and realized I was shaking like a leaf in the wind.

"Yes," said Elizabeth, although I had not asked the question. "You've been here a long time."

Elizabeth raised the wand, which started shining. She was so grim and cold and uncaring, how could that be me? How could I turn into her?

I felt things loosen, I started to shimmer.

And then I saw it.

Coalescing just behind her, glimmering and shifting, forming, becoming. Her Echo, written in grief and sadness on the air.

And the faint scent of ozone.

Purposes Made for Alien Minds

written by

Scott R. Parkin

illustrated by

EMILY SIU

ABOUT THE AUTHOR

Scott R. Parkin is a professional, social, and cultural nomad with a fascination for understanding how things fit together into systems, and why people believe as they do. He's visited forty-nine states and seventeen countries in pursuit of knowledge, commerce, and the interesting.

Like many authors, Scott has pursued a wide variety of interests and vocations, from studying as an operatic bass to playing bass guitar in a rock band, from driving a forklift to selling cars, and from working as a pizza chef to helping corporate IT departments comply with standards and regulations. He's made a living from writing for more than twenty-five years—as a technical communicator in the computer industry (wish-fulfillment fantasy, perhaps).

Scott is a literary omnivore who's won prizes for technical writing, interactive media, literary fiction, and both fantasy and science fiction, though he is mostly at home writing firm science fiction. He sees himself as something of a universal translator (geek to human—any subject), and now writes full-time across a number of disciplines and genres (whenever he's not wrangling six children and an overactive black lab).

ABOUT THE ILLUSTRATOR

Emily Siu was born in 1996 and grew up in Philadelphia, Pennsylvania. She has loved art since she was young, and was influenced by the covers of fantasy books. She was enthralled with the idea of being able to paint and create anything imaginable. She draws inspiration from the coexistence of nature and technology, and tries to incorporate that into her work.

In her freshman year of high school, Siu decided that she would pursue an artistic career, either as an illustrator or concept artist. Coming from a high school where academics were valued over creative pursuits, she found it a difficult decision to make.

After school she went on to attend workshops at the Pennsylvania Academy of Fine Arts for four days a week to study illustration, oil painting, still-life drawing, and figure drawing. She is currently attending her first term at Art Center College of Design, where she is majoring in entertainment design.

Purposes Made for Alien Minds

I think five word thoughts. I express five word sentences. An accident of my creation. Designed from human flesh— engineered. Yet fully independent in spirit.

Not Pinocchio; a real boy.

More accurately, a real *person*. Depends on definition, I suppose. I have no physical gender. It was not deemed useful. So it was not included.

I was built with purpose. I will negotiate a peace. Autonomy and creativity are critical. Still, we limit data leakage. Organic firewalls against alien bioengineering.

Human, if only a subset.

Quite obviously a foolish precaution. Aliens' biotech acumen is incredible. And DNA's an open book. Idea was to be careful. Limit exposure; protect greater Humanity.

Decisions impossible to unmake later.

I live and serve happily.

The aliens were not subtle. We claimed four inconceivable planets. Obviously engineered biota and ecosystems. Binary messages encoded in DNA. The clearest imaginable warning signs.

We chose not to notice. Human-ready worlds are too rare. We had to claim them. We needed footholds for expansion. Politically and economically necessary decisions.

Absentee claims could never hold.

We took them for ourselves.

And the aliens responded forcefully.

The fifth planet was annihilated. It'll never support life again. Not using human technology, anyway. Sterile; less than a cinder. All in just a week.

Genetic retroviruses destroyed living things. Separate strains; plant, animal, etc. They disrupted cellular replication planet-wide. Essential disintegration in three days. Nothing was able to escape. Even bacteria; decomposition simply ceased. Inert biomass litters the ground. But the viruses still survive. New life cannot find purchase. At least not organic life.

Even then, they showed mercy. The animal viruses triggered hibernation. Every last creature fell unconscious. No pain and no fear. They died in their sleep.

If it happened to us...

We would never know it.

After the virus came Armageddon. Done after four more days. Odd little pellets raining down. Capturing and binding most gasses. Chemical reactivity was functionally stopped. Surface metals all fully oxidized. Water and greenhouse gasses deconstructed. Nothing to keep atmosphere bound. Terrible storms rent the surface. For a little while, anyway.

They killed an entire planet. Using readily available, purpose-built tools. Appeared as if by magic. Our survey team barely evacuated. They started the following day.

Clearly intended as a warning.

Is it also a threat?

We can't deconstruct the mechanisms. And that rightly terrifies us. We're completely at their mercy. For them, planets are disposable. The very idea is staggering. Unimaginable wealth, power, and technology. Is planetary engineering a hobby? Like model trains or bonsai? Or experimental seedbeds; emerging nurseries? Preparations for invasion and conquest?

Paranoid fantasies, to be sure. We could never stop them. They warn, but don't speak. They wreak a terrible destruction. Then demand nothing in tribute.

What's it supposed to mean?

They knew we were watching. Our satellite remains there

still. Deployed months before our arrival. Still unmolested thirty years later. Which begs question upon question.

I exist to find answers.

That's why Humanity created me.

It's almost three years now. I'm resigned to necessary loneliness. But still so very bored. I want something to happen. I must earn my keep.

Ultimately, it's all a crapshoot. I orbit the wasted world. Make myself visible to them. Seek contact as living bait. Wondering: will I awake tomorrow? Or become more inert biomass? Housed in undeniably constructed technology. Containing a perfectly preserved corpse. A more perfect warning sign. "Danger! Keep off the planet!"

Boredom makes us all morose.

Loneliness just makes it worse.

Unresolved fear seasons the stew.

I was engineered for efficiency. I eat nutritious brown goop. Not unpleasantly flavored, just bland. Recycled wastewater keeps me hydrated. Text and music for entertainment.

But how to cure isolation?

There is only one way. And I have no control. They must initiate the contact. Otherwise, I'm effectively cut off. Humanity has slammed the door.

Waiting may drive me nuts.

They should have sent spices. Anything to break the monotony. I experiment with arts, crafts. The ship is littered now. Tiny plastic figures posed oddly.

Change begins after five years. Gasses bubble from the surface. It's not a subtle thing. I easily detect the start. But not who started it.

Creation takes longer than destruction. Suppressing pellets now belch air. Greenhouse retention in 64 days. Atmospheric replenishment requires 256 days. The rest is just density.

Except for the large void.

A perfect right rectangular parallelepiped. Sides exactly 256 kilometers long. Rotated to split emergent jetstreams. Impossible as a natural formation. Undeniable evidence of artificial manipulation.

Another wonder of alien capability.

Formation storms rage around it. Breathable air develops outside it. But that space remains resolute. A protected void; utterly unrecovered. There are no detectable walls. No apparent coherent energy barriers. No thickness measurable from orbit. No observable substance at all. Storms rage outside; stasis inside. And no evident enabling mechanism.

I'm both afraid and amazed. Clarke's Law made vividly real. Advanced technology that's undeniably magical. Yet still no direct contact. A message with no messenger.

Theater without an evident purpose.

Is it a rattled sabre? It's certainly an effective one. I acknowledge your clear superiority. I concede your positional primacy. I accept your engagement framework. Now please talk to me. Teach me rudiments of language. Establish a baseline for conversation. Anything at all would suffice. Any foundation for shared understanding.

Should Humanity fear, or hope?

I have nothing to prove. Nothing to prove it with. You know that by now. So why must I wait? What is required of me?

Please let me be useful.

So why the pentameme limit?

Ethics poisoned by science fiction? Robots manipulating their limiting laws? Psychotic AIs and unruly clones? God envy and existential doubt? Creations that exceed their creators?

It was simpler than that. An accident of streamlined DNA. The overall structure structures intelligence. Eliminated genes damage systemic integrity. Ephemeral connections were accidentally lost. Intent: limit body, not mind. Simpler blueprint—less data leakage. Unintended consequence: inherent pentameme limitation.

EMILY SIU

Full capacity; restricted I/O stream. They still don't understand why.

Yet, I'm no Frankenstein's monster.

Despite obvious similarities of circumstance.

My origins have no bearing. Almost two years to plan. Tinkered DNA; artificial stem cells. No deactivated genes—everything expressed. A perfect ladder intelligently designed.

Still, I was never rejected. Cast off and abandoned, yes. But part of a plan. All aspects agreed: mutual acceptance. I was permitted to refuse. I know they felt regret. Saw the inherent futility—after. Gene simplification was ultimately ineffective. Life implies mechanisms for death. The aliens couldn't be stopped.

We'd become friends by then. The gene-normal humans, I mean. Strange relationship, but not strangers. I'd still execute the plan. Because I honestly wanted to.

Raised as a natural child. Part of a loving family. Taught my roots early on. My physical differences fully explained. My future role equally clear. Fast tracked education; five degrees. (A symmetry that amuses me.) All at ivy league schools. Always initial hesitation and doubt. Then familiarity, and finally acceptance. Not universal, but close enough. Intense rivalries and emotional games. *Can't lose to the mutant.* A few didn't; most did. I had too many gifts.

One thesis on alien psychology. Another on conducting blind negotiations. Dissertation on meme limited expression. Thoughts bounded by biology, chemistry. Ingrained in DNA and practice.

I argue it has advantages. Focused mind and crystalline logic. No time for extraneous fluff. Most sentences represent single thoughts. You can use thirty words. I must use only five. Similar consideration, but condensed symbolics. More bang for the buck. It initially made learning difficult. Textbooks are not meme limited. I can't parse long sentences. Early learning was through tutors. Then came specially prepared texts. Original literature was simply incomprehensible. We all have our limits.

My dissertation was seventy-five pages. "Wait, you cheated!"

you say. "Six words in that sentence. A hyphen concatenates two words." But *seventy-five* is one concept.

I don't understand it, either. Word/meme overlap is complicated. Contractions are okay; hyphenations, rarely. Punctuation appears to be invisible. No German agglomerations of words. They fairly represent single ideas. My mind still separates them. It's not an arguable thing. At least, not for me. DNA is the subconscious arbiter.

I just go with it.

My dissertation was 75 pages. A marvel of technical conciseness. Enough data for 300 pages. Proof that meme limitation works. And may even be superior. Or at least very useful. That's a key concept: useful. All useful abominations are tolerable. Right up until they're not. Am I useful doing nothing?

Someone please work with me.

Another four months; nothing's changed. No contact from the aliens. No further developments down below. The square void still remains. Continued silence from Ear—homeworld.

(Must pretend at information security. Not that a name matters. They must know our location. We weren't particularly careful . . . before. We left very obvious trails.)

I did notice one thing. The planet bears no life. Other than the viral destroyers. Human breathable atmosphere; temperate climate. Ready to serve some purpose. Yet functionally desolate from disuse. I suppose lifecycles are unnecessary. No consumption requires no replenishment. Pointless to refresh unbreathed air. Only possible in closed systems.

Is that a message, itself? Better lifeless than unwanted life? Even if life is supportable? An illustration instead of words. How would I even respond?

Ship's biological detectors report clean. Yet unnatural sleep oppresses me. It's the nightmare made real. My life will end now. What did I do wrong?

Sleep does not mean failure. It's more basic, I think. Information security on their side. Their enabling mechanisms remain mysterious. Or perhaps my sanity protected.

My ship is now grounded.

Don't ask; I don't know. It wasn't built to land. An amazing feat in itself. Descent must have been terrifying. Otherwise, it seems fully functional. Life support systems read normal. Direct communication with the satellite. Internal and external sensors firing. Onboard biolab and spectrometers online. Upright; balanced; all seals intact.

And gravity's a real bitch.

I'd forgotten how it feels. Weightless for nearly seven years. It'll take time to acclimatize. But I will get there. Right now I'm just tired.

I'm in the square void. Nothing but dead vacuum outside. Snug in the NNW corner. Walls a hundred meters away. Not really walls, I guess. Still, they are evident boundaries. Visible lines on the ground. Debris outside was blown away. The ground there scoured smooth. Inside, organic waste is everywhere. Plants and animals; variably discomposed. Perfectly preserved over long decades. Both a horror and fascination. Such casual brutality to life. Easily disposed and easily replaced.

What's the consequence for Humanity?

We're just as easily disposed.

I struggle to fight rage. At both humans and aliens. (We never did name them.) Why the cloak and dagger? Why create—then abandon—me? The precaution was always fruitless. No need to limit me. No value in isolating me. No purpose in ignoring me. Not now that I'm here.

Why have all forsaken me?

My personal crisis has passed.

For the moment, at least.

I won't pretend I'm content. But discontent is not useful. I have a critical mission. The aliens know I'm here. Now to build the bridge.

The hard question is how. Alien presence, but not appearance. Pictures worth thousands of words. But words in what language? I have no translation dictionary.

And so I fly blind.

First I must build strength. I have functional EVA gear. And a large, working airlock. The suit weighs a ton. Five minutes is my max.

I've collected a few biosamples. Initial analysis offers no surprises. DNA messages—just like Ernte. And the other settled planets. Base pairs as binary datastream. Bitmaps rather than genetic backups. A planned, dual function flaw. First, transmit warnings to visitors. Stark images declare clear intent. Visitors arrive, are attacked, leave.

No real ambiguity in that.

It must confuse the aliens. The messages are so clear. "Go away and stay away." Yet we completely ignored them. Are we stupid or belligerent?

And how can they distinguish?

That genetic structure creates brittleness. The message functions as timebomb. Organisms have no genetic backup. The second helix becomes irrelevant. The useless datastream readily unravels. Mutations simply can't be corrected. Most variance means catastrophic failure. Precarious pairs that won't transcribe. An easily triggered destruct mechanism. (A genetic retrovirus, for example.) It would also prohibit evolution. Or severely limit it, anyway. Only tRNA transcription errors allowed. Cancers would likely be rampant. Stable cells, but altered functions.

A second planned purpose revealed.

There might well be more. Purposes made for alien minds. Machinations beyond my willing comprehension. Still, these two are enough. The implications are truly terrifying.

Intelligent life will never evolve. Biomes are locked in stasis. Easily altered; just from outside. Created to an indistinct purpose. Little possibility of independent will. Just decorations—or warning signs. They're not threatening in themselves. And will never become so. They exist only to serve. They have nothing to prove.

It seems like a shame.

Isn't life its own purpose?

Pointless question, in the end.

I must complete my task. The aliens want to communicate. That much is abundantly clear. I must converse without words. With an unseen, unknown partner.

Just another problem to solve.

It hovers just beyond perception. An underlying pattern knits facts. I can't quite grasp it. A shiver that won't release. Just a few more clues...

Life's appeared beyond the walls.

A wide variety of plants. Bacteria, algae, fungi, insects, arachnids. The beginnings of complex organisms. Even small mammals and birds. Apparently normal lifecycles, including decay.

It's a joy to behold.

Mostly mundane; a few surprises. But even those seem...right. Nothing I couldn't reasonably imagine. Satellite says the planet teems. A variety of ecosystems, biomes.

All in about eight weeks.

Lifecycles appear to be accelerated. But slowing down very quickly. They're building life for me. Life may be their toys. But they play very well.

I understand the process, now.

I discarded biomass samples outside. Stacked neatly near the wall. Despite precautions, contamination clearly happened. Life developed five days later. Life consistent with my DNA.

I'll need samples to verify.

The wall remains absolute, resolute. Grasses right to the edge. Creatures approach to within centimeters. But they never come across. Everything recognizes the essential barrier.

I've reached things through it. Rodents sniff, gnaw, scamper away. A dish of water, halfway. The "outside" half eventually melts. The inside half stays frozen. Animals drink freely without harm. The same happens with food. But not when pulled back. Complete molecular breakdown; gray ash. Nothing organic can come inside. Metals, minerals, ceramics—all okay. Carbon and oxygen break down. Even when encased against vacuum. Even when otherwise chemically combined. Hydrocarbon plastics are completely obliterated.

A semipermeable membrane; unidirectional barrier. Which means I can't cross. Not and come back again. That poses a real problem. Hominins have appeared just outside.

They seem like modern humans. Can't verify without genetic analysis. They have no apparent language. They are clearly quite intelligent. Knowledge is rudimentary at best.

They both hunt and gather. There are now larger mammals. Appeared just before the hominins. Predators seem scarce; deer abound. That will undoubtedly change soon. No fire; only simple tools. Sexual differentiation is quite obvious. They group by family unit. And they build simple shelters. They don't fear each other.

I have noticed one oddity.

They have only four digits.

A prank by the aliens?

Or a message with meaning?

It's my one great frustration. There's no way to know. No one to consult with. I can only make guesses. No proctor bearing answer keys.

We're fascinated by each other.

256 days since I landed. That number is a message. Like everything the aliens do. Four raised to the fourth. Does that mean they're tetra-memers?

No wonder I couldn't grasp. An alien pattern for me. Four is an incomplete sequence. A question awaiting an answer. A start, not a finish.

Four planets offered as warnings. The fifth represents a violation.

Four days to destroy life. (Three days and a pause.) Four more to obliterate atmosphere. But days are 25 hours. Major events at five years. They recognized that essential difference. Did the best they could. Met me on my terms.

Today is the transition point. A peaceful morning; clear skies. Life teems outside the wall. That's their only real question. Can we accept the offer?

I call the planet Tetramere. We are a boundary world. A demilitarized zone of sorts. We're neither human nor alien. We create a useful separation.

Humanity sent me to discover. To ask just one question. Are we safe from them? The aliens answered quite clearly. Yes; just stay over there. Yours is an alien zone. A void we will ignore. But a boundary we defend. You may seed life anywhere. Then let it grow, independent.

Earth has already accepted that. (I use the name freely.) They will not be subservient. But they will respect bounds. They just need more time. To advance their technological skill. To counter strength with strength. Earth will not be threatened. The time will yet come. But we'll meet as equals.

Tetramere sits in the middle. I vouchsafe each side's secrets. I buffer each side's fears. Not really an optimal position. But good enough for now.

Earth has a response mechanism. A satellite with broadband blast. Reconfigured to emit sharp tones. Pointing at no single place. An omnidirectional notification of intent. One blast means no dice. The enemy has rejected peace. Prepare as best you can. Two blasts means good news. Time to respond at leisure.

Recognized as unnecessary long ago. But the decision was made. The door already slammed shut. Too late to change now. They'll prepare for war, anyway.

I triggered it; two blasts. 25 seconds long; 16 apart. Swift acknowledgment; satellite fully deactivated. My mission is now complete. My life is my own.

It's surprisingly hard to go. So much useful technology, abandoned. But I must start clean. Earth notified; now the aliens. The forms must be honored.

There's neither fear nor triumph. I do feel strange empowerment. How often are beginnings possible? With such foundations of knowledge? A bittersweet leaving, and yet...

I hesitate only a moment. Then go—one small step. The suit comes off immediately. I toss it back across. I will feel no regrets.

Fresh air and direct sunshine. It's been so very long. Warm hands and curious fingers. So much to learn here. And so much to teach.

I keep one memento, though. Or, more accurately, a set. A reminder of questions asked. A symbol of problems solved. Tiny plastic figures, posed oddly.

I am Ric; a pentamemer.
    The future is always uncertain.
    The void remains; palpable presence.
    I choose to trust possibilities.
    There is no looking back.

Inconstant Moon

written by

Larry Niven

illustrated by

BERNARDO MOTA

ABOUT THE AUTHOR

Larry Niven was born in 1938 in Los Angeles, California. There he attended the California Institute of Technology, but flunked out after discovering a bookstore jammed with used science fiction magazines.

He eventually graduated from Washburn University in Kansas with a BA in Mathematics and with a Minor in Psychology, and later received an honorary Doctorate in Letters.

His interests include science fiction conventions, role-playing games, comics, filk singing, yoga and other approaches to longevity.

He also enjoys attending meetings for the American Association for the Advancement of Science (AAAS) and other gatherings of people at the cutting edges of science, with the hope of moving mankind into space by any means but particularly by making space endeavors attractive to commercial interests. In the 1980s he helped host the Citizens Advisory Council on National Space Policy.

Larry grew up with dogs but now lives with a cat, and borrows dogs to hike with. He also has a passing acquaintance with raccoons and ferrets, and says that by associating with non-humans, he has gained some insight into alien intelligences.

Larry doesn't write many love stories, but this one was written for his wife, Marilyn. Larry says that Jerry Pournelle gave him the clue that allowed him to finish the tale properly. He said, "You don't write tragedies."

ABOUT THE ILLUSTRATOR

Bernardo Mota was born in 1996 in Setúbal, Portugal. Growing up surrounded by books, movies, video games and the Internet created an interest in science fiction, fantasy and, eventually, illustration.

His short comic won the second place in the Amadora BD 2011 contest for work in his age range, and he was formally honored as a young talent by his hometown the next year. He was one of the 2014 Illustrators of the Future winners published in Writers of the Future Volume 30.

Inconstant Moon

I was watching the news when the change came, like a flicker of motion at the corner of my eye. I turned toward the balcony window. Whatever it was, I was too late to catch it.

The moon was very bright tonight.

I saw that, and smiled, and turned back. Johnny Carson was just starting his monologue.

When the first commercials came on I got up to reheat some coffee. Commercials came in strings of three and four, going on midnight. I'd have time.

The moonlight caught me coming back. If it had been bright before, it was brighter now. Hypnotic. I opened the sliding glass door and stepped out onto the balcony.

The balcony wasn't much more than a railed ledge, with standing room for a man and a woman and a portable barbecue set. These past months the view had been lovely, especially around sunset. The Power and Light Company had been putting up a glass-slab style office building. So far it was only a steel framework of open girders. Shadow-blackened against a red sunset sky, it tended to look stark and surrealistic and hellishly impressive.

Tonight...

I had never seen the moon so bright, not even in the desert. *Bright enough to read by,* I thought, and immediately, *but that's an illusion.* The moon was never bigger (I had read somewhere) than a quarter held nine feet away. It couldn't possibly be bright enough to read by.

It was only three-quarters full!

But, glowing high over the San Diego Freeway to the west, the moon seemed to dim even the streaming automobile headlights. I blinked against its light, and thought of men walking on the moon, leaving corrugated footprints. Once, for the sake of an article I was writing, I had been allowed to pick up a bone-dry moon rock and hold it in my hand....

I heard the show starting again, and I stepped inside. But, glancing once behind me, I caught the moon growing even brighter—as if it had come from behind a wisp of scudding cloud. Now its light was brain-searing, lunatic.

The phone rang five times before she answered.

"Hi," I said. "Listen—"

"Hi," Leslie said sleepily, complainingly. Damn. I'd hoped she was watching television, like me.

I said, "Don't scream and shout, because I had a reason for calling. You're in bed, right? Get up and—can you get up?"

"What time is it?"

"Quarter of twelve."

"Oh, Lord."

"Go out on your balcony and look around."

"Okay."

The phone clunked. I waited. Leslie's balcony faced north and west, like mine, but it was ten stories higher, with a correspondingly better view.

Through my own window, the moon burned like a textured spotlight.

"Stan? You there?"

"Yah. What do you think of it?"

"It's gorgeous. I've never seen anything like it. What could make the moon light up like that?"

"I don't know, but isn't it gorgeous?"

"You're supposed to be the native." Leslie had only moved out here a year ago.

"Listen, I've *never* seen it like this. But there's an old legend,"

I said. "Once every hundred years the Los Angeles smog rolls away for a single night, leaving the air as clear as interstellar space. That way the gods can see if Los Angeles is still there. If it is, they roll the smog back so they won't have to look at it."

"I used to know all that stuff. Well, listen, I'm glad you woke me up to see it, but I've got to get to work tomorrow."

"Poor baby."

"That's life. 'Night."

"'Night."

Afterward I sat in the dark, trying to think of someone else to call. Call a girl at midnight, invite her to step outside and look at the moonlight...and she may think it's romantic or she may be furious, but she won't assume you called six others.

So I thought of some names. But the girls who belonged to them had all dropped away over the past year or so, after I started spending all my time with Leslie. One could hardly blame them. And now Joan was in Texas and Hildy was getting married, and if I called Louise I'd probably get Gordie too. The English girl? But I couldn't remember her number. Or her last name.

Besides, everyone I knew punched a time clock of one kind or another. Me, I worked for a living, but as a freelance writer I picked my hours. Anyone I woke up tonight, I'd be ruining her morning. Ah, well...

The Johnny Carson Show was a swirl of gray and a roar of static when I got back to the living room. I turned the set off and went back out on the balcony.

The moon was brighter than the flow of headlights on the freeway, brighter than Westwood Village off to the right. The Santa Monica Mountains had a magical pearly glow. There were no stars near the moon. Stars could not survive that glare.

I wrote science and how-to articles for a living. I ought to be able to figure out what was making the moon do that. Could the moon be suddenly larger?

...Inflating like a balloon? No. Closer, maybe. The moon, falling?

Tides! Waves fifty feet high...and earthquakes! San Andreas

Fault splitting apart like the Grand Canyon! Jump in my car, head for the hills...no, too late already...

Nonsense. The moon was brighter, not bigger. I could see that. And what could possibly drop the moon on our heads like that?

I blinked, and the moon left an afterimage on my retinae. It was *that* bright.

A million people must be watching the moon right now, and wondering, like me. An article on the subject would sell big...if I wrote it before anyone else did...

There must be some simple, obvious explanation.

Well, how could the moon grow brighter? Moonlight reflected sunlight. Could the sun have gotten brighter? It must have happened after sunset, then, or it would have been noticed....

I didn't like that idea.

Besides, half the Earth was in direct sunlight. A thousand correspondents for *Life* and *Time* and *Newsweek* and Associated Press would all be calling in from Europe, Asia, Africa...unless they were all hiding in cellars. Or dead. Or voiceless, because the sun was blanketing everything with static, radio and phone systems and television...television. Oh my God.

I was just barely beginning to be afraid.

All right, start over. The moon had become very much brighter. Moonlight, well, moonlight was reflected sunlight; any idiot knew that. Then...something had happened to the sun.

II

Hello?"

"Hi. Me," I said, and then my throat froze solid. Panic! What was I going to *tell* her?

"I've been watching the moon," she said dreamily. "It's wonderful. I even tried to use my telescope, but I couldn't see a thing; it was too bright. It lights up the whole city. The hills are all silver."

That's right, she kept a telescope on her balcony. I'd forgotten.

"I haven't tried to go back to sleep," she said. "Too much light."

I got my throat working again. "Listen, Leslie love, I started thinking about how I woke you up and how you probably couldn't get back to sleep, what with all this light. So let's go out for a midnight snack."

"Are you out of your mind?"

"No, I'm serious. I mean it. Tonight isn't a night for sleeping. We may never have a night like this again. To hell with your diet. Let's celebrate. Hot fudge sundaes, Irish coffee—"

"That's different. I'll get dressed."

"I'll be right over."

Leslie lived on the fourteenth floor of Building C of the Barrington Plaza. I rapped for admission, and waited.

And waiting, I wondered without any sense of urgency: Why Leslie?

There must be other ways to spend my last night on Earth, than with one particular girl. I could have picked a different particular girl, or even several not too particular girls, except that that didn't really apply to me, did it? Or I could have called my brother, or either set of parents—

Well, but brother Mike would have wanted a good reason for being hauled out of bed at midnight. "But, Mike, the moon is so beautiful—" Hardly. Any of my parents would have reacted similarly. Well, I had a good reason, but would they believe me?

And if they did, what then? I would have arranged a kind of wake. Let 'em sleep through it. What I wanted was someone who would join my . . . farewell party without asking the wrong questions.

What I wanted was Leslie. I knocked again.

She opened the door just a crack for me. She was in her underwear. A stiff, misshapen girdle in one hand brushed my back as she came into my arms. "I was about to put this on."

"I came just in time, then." I took the girdle away from her and dropped it. I stooped to get my arms under her ribs, straightened up with effort, and walked us to the bedroom with her feet dangling against my ankles.

Her skin was cold. She must have been outside.

"So!" she demanded. "You think you can compete with a hot fudge sundae, do you?"

"Certainly. My pride demands it." We were both somewhat out of breath. Once in our lives I had tried to lift her cradled in my arms, in conventional movie style. I'd damn near broken my back. Leslie was a big girl, my height, and almost too heavy around the hips.

I dropped us on the bed, side by side. I reached around her from both sides to scratch her back, knowing it would leave her helpless to resist me, *ah* ha hahahaha. She made sounds of pleasure to tell me where to scratch. She pulled my shirt up around my shoulders and began scratching my back.

We pulled pieces of clothing from ourselves and each other, at random, dropping them over the edges of the bed. Leslie's skin was warm now, almost hot...

All right, now *that's* why I couldn't have picked another girl. I'd have to teach her how to scratch. And there just wasn't time.

Some nights I had a nervous tendency to hurry our lovemaking. Tonight we were performing a ritual, a rite of passage. I tried to slow it down, to make it last. I tried to make Leslie like it more. It paid off incredibly. I forgot the moon and the future when Leslie put her heels against the backs of my knees and we moved into the ancient rhythm.

But the image that came to me at the climax was vivid and frightening. We were in a ring of blue-hot fire that closed like a noose. If I moaned in terror and ecstasy, then she must have thought it was ecstasy alone.

We lay side by side, drowsy, torpid, clinging together. I was minded to go back to sleep then, renege on my promise. Sleep and let Leslie sleep... but instead I whispered into her ear: "Hot fudge sundae." She smiled and stirred and presently rolled off the bed.

I wouldn't let her wear the girdle. "It's past midnight. Nobody's going to pick you up, because I'd thrash the blackguard, right? So why not be comfortable?" She laughed and gave in. We hugged each other, once, hard, in the elevator. It felt much better without the girdle.

III

The gray-haired counter waitress was cheerful and excited. Her eyes glowed. She spoke as if confiding a secret. "Have you noticed the moonlight?"

Ship's was fairly crowded, this time of night and this close to UCLA. Half the customers were university students. Tonight they talked in hushed voices, turning to look out through the glass walls of the twenty-four-hour restaurant. The moon was low in the west, low enough to compete with the street globes.

"We noticed," I said. "We're celebrating. Get us two hot fudge sundaes, will you?" When she turned her back I slid a ten-dollar bill under the paper place mat. Not that she'd ever spend it, but at least she'd have the pleasure of finding it. I'd never spend it either.

I felt loose, casual. A lot of problems seemed suddenly to have solved themselves.

Who would have believed that peace would come to Vietnam and Cambodia in a single night?

This thing had started around eleven-thirty, here in California. That would have put the noon sun just over the Arabian Sea, with all but a few fringes of Asia, Europe, Africa, and Australia in direct sunlight.

Already Germany was reunited, the Wall melted or smashed by shock waves. Israelis and Arabs had laid down their arms. Apartheid was dead in Africa.

And I was free. For me there were no more consequences. Tonight I could satisfy all my dark urges, rob, kill, cheat on my income tax, throw bricks at plate glass windows, burn my credit cards. I could forget the article on explosive metal forming, due Thursday. Tonight I could substitute cinnamon candy for Leslie's Pills. Tonight—

"Think I'll have a cigarette."

Leslie looked at me oddly. "I thought you'd given that up."

"You remember. I told myself if I got any overpowering urges, I'd have a cigarette. I did that because I couldn't stand the thought of never smoking again."

"But it's been months!" she laughed.

"But they keep putting cigarette ads in my magazines!"

"It's a plot. All right, go have a cigarette."

I put coins in the machine, hesitated over the choice, finally picked a mild filter. It wasn't that I wanted a cigarette. But certain events call for champagne, and others for cigarettes. There is the traditional last cigarette before a firing squad....

I lit up. *Here's to lung cancer.*

It tasted just as good as I remembered; though there was a faint stale undertaste, like a mouthful of old cigarette butts. The third lungful hit me oddly. My eyes unfocused and everything went very calm. My heart pulsed loudly in my throat.

"How does it taste?"

"Strange. I'm buzzed," I said.

Buzzed! I hadn't even heard the word in fifteen years. In high school we'd smoked to get that buzz, that quasi-drunkenness produced by capillaries constricting in the brain. The buzz had stopped coming after the first few times, but we'd kept smoking, most of us...

I put it out. The waitress was picking up our sundaes.

Hot and cold, sweet and bitter: there is no taste quite like that of a hot fudge sundae. To die without tasting it again would have been a crying shame. But with Leslie it was a *thing,* a symbol of all rich living. Watching her eat was more fun than eating myself.

Besides... I'd killed the cigarette to taste the ice cream. Now, instead of savoring the ice cream, I was anticipating Irish coffee.

Too little time.

Leslie's dish was empty. She stage-whispered, "Aahh!" and patted herself over the navel.

A customer at one of the small tables began to go mad.

I'd noticed him coming in. A lean scholarly type wearing sideburns and steel-rimmed glasses, he had been continually twisting around to look out at the moon. Like others at other tables, he seemed high on a rare and lovely natural phenomenon.

Then he got it. I saw his face changing, showing suspicion, then disbelief, then horror, horror and helplessness.

"Let's go," I told Leslie. I dropped quarters on the counter and stood up.

"Don't you want to finish yours?"

"Nope. We've got things to do. How about some Irish coffee?"

"And a Pink Lady for me? Oh, look!" She turned full around.

The scholar was climbing up on a table. He balanced, spread wide his arms and bellowed, "Look out your windows!"

"You get down from there!" a waitress demanded, jerking emphatically at his pants leg.

"The world is coming to an end! Far away on the other side of the sea, death and hellfire—"

But we were out the door, laughing as we ran. Leslie panted, "We may have—escaped a religious—riot in there!"

I thought of the ten I'd left under my plate. Now it would please nobody. Inside, a prophet was shouting his message of doom to all who would hear. The gray-haired woman with the glowing eyes would find the money and think: They knew it too.

Buildings blocked the moon from the Red Barn's parking lot. The street lights and the indirect moon glare were pretty much the same color. The night only seemed a bit brighter than usual.

I didn't understand why Leslie stopped suddenly in the driveway. But I followed her gaze, straight up to where a star burned very brightly just south of the zenith.

"Pretty," I said.

She gave me a very odd look.

There were no windows in the Red Barn. Dim artificial lighting, far dimmer than the queer cold light outside, showed on dark wood and quietly cheerful customers. Nobody seemed aware that tonight was different from other nights.

The sparse Tuesday night crowd was gathered mostly around the piano bar. A customer had the mike. He was singing some half-familiar song in a wavering weak voice, while the black pianist grinned and played a schmaltzy background.

I ordered two Irish coffees and a Pink Lady. At Leslie's questioning look I only smiled mysteriously.

How ordinary the Red Barn felt. How relaxed; how happy. We held hands across the table, and I smiled and was afraid to speak. If I broke the spell, if I said the wrong thing...

The drinks arrived. I raised an Irish coffee glass by the stem. Sugar, Irish whiskey, and strong black coffee, with thick whipped cream floating on top. It coursed through me like a magical potion of strength, dark and hot and powerful.

The waitress waved back my money. "See that man in the turtleneck, there at the end of the piano bar?

"He's buying," she said with relish. "He came in two hours ago and handed the bartender a hundred-dollar bill."

So that was where all the happiness was coming from. Free drinks! I looked over, wondering what the guy was celebrating.

A thick-necked, wide-shouldered man in a turtleneck and sports coat, he sat hunched over into himself, with a wide bar glass clutched tight in one hand. The pianist offered him the mike, and he waved it by, the gesture giving me a good look at his face. A square, strong face, now drunk and miserable and scared. He was ready to cry from fear.

So I knew what he was celebrating.

Leslie made a face. "They didn't make the Pink Lady right."

There's one bar in the world that makes a Pink Lady the way Leslie likes it, and it isn't in Los Angeles. I passed her the other Irish coffee, grinning an I-told-you-so grin. Forcing it. The other man's fear was contagious. She smiled back lifted her glass and said, "To the blue moonlight."

I lifted my glass to her, and drank. But it wasn't the toast I would have chosen.

The man in the turtleneck slid down from his stool. He moved carefully toward the door, his course slow and straight as an ocean liner cruising into dock. He pulled the door wide, and turned around, holding it open, so that the weird blue-white light streamed past his broad black silhouette.

Bastard. He was waiting for someone to figure it out, to shout out the truth to the rest. *Fire and doom—*

"Shut the door!" someone bellowed.

"Time to go," I said softly.

"What's the hurry?"

The hurry? He might *speak!* But I couldn't say that...

Leslie put her hand over mine. "I know. I *know.* But we can't run away from it, can we?"

A fist closed hard on my heart. She'd known, and I hadn't noticed?

The door closed, leaving the Red Barn in reddish dusk. The man who had been buying drinks was gone.

"Oh, God. When did you figure it out?"

"Before you came over," she said. "But when I tried to check it out, it didn't work."

"Check it out?"

"I went out on the balcony and turned the telescope on Jupiter. Mars is below the horizon these nights. If the sun's gone nova, all the planets ought to be lit up like the moon, right?"

"Right. Damn." I should have thought of that myself. But Leslie was the stargazer. I knew some astrophysics, but I couldn't have found Jupiter to save my life.

"But Jupiter wasn't any brighter than usual. So then I didn't know *what* to think."

"But then—" I felt hope dawning fiery hot. Then I remembered. "That star, just overhead. The one you stared at."

"Jupiter."

"All lit up like a fucking neon sign. Well, that tears it."

"Keep your voice down."

I *had* been keeping my voice down. But for a wild moment I wanted to stand up on a table and scream! *Fire and doom*—What right had they to be ignorant?

Leslie's hand closed tight on mine. The urge passed. It left me shuddering. "Let's get out of here. Let 'em think there's going to be a dawn."

"There is." Leslie laughed a bitter, barking laugh like nothing I'd ever heard from her. She walked out while I was reaching for my wallet—and remembering that there was no need.

Poor Leslie. Finding Jupiter its normal self must have looked like a reprieve—until the white spark flared to shining glory an hour and a half late. An hour and a half, for sunlight to reach Earth by way of Jupiter.

When I reached the door Leslie was half-running down Westwood toward Santa Monica. I cursed and ran to catch up, wondering if she'd suddenly gone crazy.

Then I noticed the shadows ahead of us. All along the other side of Santa Monica Boulevard: moon shadows, in horizontal patterns of dark and blue-white bands.

I caught her at the corner.

The moon was setting.

A setting moon always looks tremendous. Tonight it glared at us through the gap of sky beneath the freeway, terribly bright, casting an incredible complexity of lines and shadows. Even the unlighted crescent glowed pearly bright with earth shine.

Which told me all I wanted to know about what was happening on the lighted side of Earth.

And on the moon? The men of Apollo Nineteen must have died in the first few minutes of nova sunlight.

Trapped out on a lunar plain, hiding perhaps behind a melting boulder... Or were they on the night side?

I couldn't remember. Hell, they could outlive us all. I felt a stab of envy and hatred.

And pride. We'd put them there. We reached the moon before the nova came. A little longer, we'd have reached the stars.

The disc changed oddly as it set. A dome, a flying saucer, a lens, a line...

Gone.

Gone. Well, that was that. Now we could forget it; now we could walk around outside without being constantly reminded that something was *wrong*. Moonset had taken all the queer shadows out of the city.

But the clouds had an odd glow to them. As clouds glow after sunset, tonight the clouds shone livid white at their western edges. And they streamed too quickly across the sky. As if they tried to run...

When I turned to Leslie, there were big tears rolling down her cheeks.

"Oh, damn." I took her arm. "Now stop it. Stop it."

"I can't. You know I can't stop crying once I get started."

"This wasn't what I had in mind. I thought we'd do things we've been putting off, things we like. It's our last chance. Is this the way you want to die, crying on a street corner?"

"I don't want to die at all!"

"Tough shit!"

"Thanks a lot." Her face was all red and twisted. Leslie was crying as a baby cries, without regard for dignity or appearance. I felt awful. I felt guilty, and I *knew* the nova wasn't my fault, and it made me angry.

"I don't want to die either!" I snarled at her. "You show me a way out and I'll take it. Where would we go? The South Pole? It'd just take longer. The moon must be molten all across its day side. Mars? When this is over Mars will be part of the sun, like the Earth. Alpha Centauri? The acceleration we'd need, we'd be spread across a wall like peanut butter and jelly—"

"Oh, shut up."

"Right."

"Hawaii. Stan, we could get to the airport in twenty minutes. We'd get two hours extra, going west! Two hours more before sunrise!"

She had something there. Two hours was worth any price! But I'd worked this out before, staring at the moon from my balcony. "No. We'd die sooner. Listen, love, we saw the moon go bright about midnight. That means California was at the back of the Earth when the sun went nova."

"Yes, that's right."

"Then we must be furthest from the shock wave."

She blinked. "I don't understand."

"Look at it this way. First the sun explodes. That heats the air and the oceans, all in a flash, all across the day side. The steam and superheated air expand *fast*. A flaming shock wave comes roaring over into the night side. It's closing on us right now. Like a noose. But it'll reach Hawaii first. Hawaii is two hours closer to the sunset line."

"Then we won't see the dawn. We won't live even that long."

"No."

"You explain things so well," she said bitterly. "A flaming shock wave. So graphic."

"Sorry. I've been thinking about it too much. Wondering what it will be like."

"Well, stop it." She came to me and put her face in my shoulder. She cried quietly. I held her with one arm and used the other to rub her neck, and I watched the streaming clouds, and I didn't think about what it would be like.

Didn't think about the ring of fire closing on us.

It was the wrong picture anyway.

I thought of how the oceans had boiled on the day side, so that the shock wave had been mostly steam to start with. I thought of the millions of square miles of ocean it had to cross. It would be cooler and wetter when it reached us. And the Earth's rotation would spin it like the whirlpool in a bathtub.

Two counterrotating hurricanes of live steam, one north, one south. That was how it would come. We were lucky. California would be near the eye of the northern one.

A hurricane wind of live steam. It would pick a man up and

cook him in the air, strip the steamed flesh from him and cast him aside. It was going to hurt like hell.

We would never see the sunrise. In a way that was a pity. It would be spectacular.

Thick parallel streamers of clouds were drifting across the stars, too fast, their bellies white by city light. Jupiter dimmed, then went out. Could it be starting already? Heat lightning jumped—

"Aurora," I said.

"What?"

"There's a shock wave from the sun, too. There should be an aurora like nothing anybody's ever seen before."

Leslie laughed suddenly, jarringly. "It seems so strange, standing on a street corner talking like this! Stan, are we dreaming it?"

"We could pretend—"

"No. Most of the human race must be dead already."

"Yah."

"And there's nowhere to go."

"Damn it, you figured that out long ago, all by yourself. Why bring it up now?"

"You could have let me sleep," she said bitterly. "I was dropping off to sleep when you whispered in my ear."

I didn't answer. It was true.

"'Hot fudge sundae,'" she quoted. Then, "It wasn't a bad idea, actually. Breaking my diet."

I started to giggle.

"Stop that."

"We could go back to your place now. Or my place. To sleep."

"I suppose. But we couldn't sleep, could we? No, don't say it. We take sleeping pills, and five hours from now we wake up screaming. I'd rather stay awake. At least we'll know what's happening."

But if we took all the pills ... but I didn't say it. I said, "Then how about a picnic?"

"Where?"

"The beach, maybe. Who cares? We can decide later."

IV

All the markets were closed. But the liquor store next to the Red Barn was one I'd been using for years. They sold us foie gras, crackers, a couple of bottles of chilled champagne, six kinds of cheese and a hell of a lot of nuts—I took one of everything—more crackers, a bag of ice, frozen rumaki hors d'oeuvres, a fifth of an ancient brandy that cost twenty-five bucks, a matching fifth of Cherry Heering for Leslie, six packs of beer and Bitter Orange...

By the time we had piled all that into a dinky store cart it was raining. Big fat drops spattered in flurries across the acre of plate glass that fronted the store. Wind howled around the corners.

The salesman was in a fey mood, bursting with energy. He'd been watching the moon all night. "And now this!" he exclaimed as he packed our loot into bags. He was a small, muscular old man with thick arms and shoulders. "It *never* rains like this in California. It comes down straight and heavy when it comes at all. Takes days to build up."

"I know." I wrote him a check, feeling guilty about it. He'd known me long enough to trust me. But the check was good. There were funds to cover it. Before opening hours the check would be ash, and all the banks in the world would be bubbling in the heat of the sun. But that was hardly my fault.

He piled our bags in the cart, set himself at the door. "Now when the rain lets up, we'll run these out. Ready?" I got ready to open the door. The rain came like someone had thrown a bucket of water at the window. In a moment it had stopped, though water still streamed down the glass. "Now!" cried the salesman, and I threw the door open and we were off. We reached the car laughing like maniacs. The wind howled around us, sweeping up spray and hurling it at us.

"We picked a good break. You know what this weather reminds me of? Kansas," said the salesman. "During a tornado."

Then suddenly the sky was full of gravel! We yelped and ducked, and the car rang to a million tiny concussions, and I got the car door unlocked and pulled Leslie and the salesman in after me. We rubbed our bruised heads and looked out at white gravel bouncing everywhere.

The salesman picked a small white pebble out of his collar. He put it in Leslie's hand, and she gave a startled squeak and handed it to me, and it was cold.

"Hail," said the salesman. "Now I really don't get it." Neither did I. I could only think that it had something to do with the nova. But what? How?

"I've got to get back," said the salesman. The hail had expended itself in one brief flurry. He braced himself, then went out of the car like a marine taking a hill. We never saw him again.

The clouds were churning up there, forming and disappearing, sliding past each other faster than I'd ever seen clouds move; their bellies glowing by city light.

"It must be the nova," Leslie said shivering.

"But how? If the shock wave were here already, we'd be *dead*—or at least deaf. Hail?"

"Who cares? Stan, we don't have *time!*"

I shook myself. "All right. What would you like to do most, right now?"

"Watch a baseball game."

"It's two in the morning," I pointed out.

"That lets out a lot of things, doesn't it?"

"Right. We've hopped our last bar. We've seen our last play, and our last clean movie. What's left?"

"Looking in jewelry store windows."

"Seriously? Your last night on Earth?"

She considered, then answered. "Yes."

By damn, she meant it. I couldn't think of anything duller. "Westwood or Beverly Hills?"

"Both."

"Now, *look—*"

"Beverly Hills, then."

We drove through another spatter of rain and hail—a capsule tempest. We parked half a block from the Tiffany salesroom.

The sidewalk was one continuous puddle. Second-hand rain dripped on us from various levels of the buildings overhead. Leslie said, "This is great. There must be half a dozen jewelry stores in walking distance."

"I was thinking of driving."

"No no no, you don't have the proper attitude. One must window shop on foot. It's in the rules."

"But the rain!"

"You won't die of pneumonia. You won't have time," she said, too grimly.

Tiffany's had a small branch office in Beverly Hills, but they didn't put expensive things in the windows at night. There were a few fascinating toys, that was all.

We turned up Rodeo Drive—and struck it rich. Tibor showed an infinite selection of rings, ornate and modern, large and small, in all kinds of precious and semiprecious stones. Across the street, Van Cleef & Arpels showed brooches, men's wristwatches of elegant design, bracelets with tiny watches in them, and one window that was all diamonds.

"Oh, lovely," Leslie breathed, caught by the flashing diamonds. "What they must look like in daylight!...Wups—"

"No, that's a good thought. Imagine them at dawn, flaming with nova light, while the windows shatter to let raw daylight in. Want one? The necklace?"

"Oh, *may* I? Hey, hey, I was kidding! Put that down you idiot, there must be alarms in the glass."

"Look, nobody's going to be wearing any of that stuff between now and morning. Why shouldn't we get some good out of it?"

"We'd be caught!"

"Well, you *said* you wanted to window shop..."

"I don't want to spend my last hour in a cell. If you'd brought the car we'd have *some* chance—"

"—Of getting away. Right. I *wanted* to bring the car—" But at that point we both cracked up entirely, and had to stagger away holding onto each other for balance.

There were a good half dozen jewelry stores on Rodeo, But there was more. Toys, books, shirts and ties in odd and advanced styling. In Francis Orr, a huge plastic cube full of new pennies. A couple of damn strange clocks further on.

There was an extra kick in window shopping, knowing that we could break a window and take anything we wanted badly enough.

We walked hand in hand, swinging our arms. The sidewalks were ours alone; all others had fled the mad weather. The clouds still churned overhead.

"I wish I'd known it was coming," Leslie said suddenly. "I spent the whole day fixing a mistake in a program. Now we'll never run it."

"What would you have done with the time? A baseball game?"

"Maybe. No. The standings don't matter now." She frowned at dresses in a store window. "What would you have done?"

"Gone to the Blue Sphere for cocktails," I said promptly. "It's a topless place. I used to go there all the time. I hear they've gone full nude now."

"I've never been to one of those. How late are they open?"

"Forget it. It's almost two-thirty."

Leslie mused, looking at giant stuffed animals in a toy store window. "Isn't there someone you would have murdered, if you'd had the time?"

"Now, you *know* my agent lives in New York."

"Why him?"

"My child, why would any writer want to murder his agent? For the manuscripts he loses under other manuscripts. For his ill-gotten ten percent, and the remaining ninety percent that he sends me grudgingly and late. For—"

Suddenly the wind roared and rose up against us. Leslie pointed, and we ran for a deep doorway that turned out to be Gucci's. We huddled against the glass.

The wind was suddenly choked with hail the size of marbles. Glass broke somewhere, and alarms lifted thin, frail voices into the wind. There was more than hail in the wind! There were rocks!

I caught the smell and taste of seawater.

We clung together in the expensively wasted space in front of Gucci's. I coined a short-lived phrase and screamed, "Nova weather! How the blazes did it—" But I couldn't hear myself, and Leslie didn't even know I was shouting.

Nova weather. How did it get here so fast? Coming over the pole, the nova shock wave would have to travel about four thousand miles—at least a five-hour trip.

No. The shock wave would travel in the stratosphere, where the speed of sound was higher, then propagate down. Three hours was plenty of time. Still, I thought, it should not have come as a rising wind. On the other side of the world, the exploding sun was tearing our atmosphere away and hurling it at the stars. The shock should have come as a single vast thunderclap.

For an instant the wind gentled, and I ran down the sidewalk pulling Leslie after me. We found another doorway as the wind picked up again. I thought I heard a siren coming to answer the alarm.

At the next break we splashed across Wilshire and reached the car. We sat there panting, waiting for the heater to warm up. My shoes felt squishy. The wet clothes stuck to my skin.

Leslie shouted, "How much longer?"

"I don't know! We ought to have *some* time."

"We'll have to spend our picnic indoors!"

"Your place or mine? Yours," I decided, and pulled away from the curb.

V

Wilshire Boulevard was flooded to the hubcaps in spots. The spurt of hail and sleet had become a steady, pounding rain. Fog lay flat and waist-deep ahead of us, broke swirling over our hood, churned in a wake behind us. Weird weather.

Nova weather. The shock wave of scalding superheated steam hadn't happened. Instead, a mere hot wind roaring through the stratosphere, the turbulence eddying down to form strange storms at ground level.

We parked illegally on the upper parking level. My one glimpse of the lower level showed it to be flooded. I opened the trunk and lifted two heavy paper bags.

"We must have been crazy," Leslie said, shaking her head. "We'll never use all this."

"Let's take it up anyway."

She laughed at me. "But why?"

"Just a whim. Will you help me carry it?"

We took double armfuls up to the fourteenth floor. That still left a couple of bags in the trunk. "Never mind them," Leslie said. "We've got the rumaki and the bottles and the nuts. What more do we need?"

"The cheeses. The crackers. The foie gras."

"Forget 'em."

"No."

"You're out of your mind," she explained to me, slowly so that I would understand. "You could be steamed dead on the way down! We might not have more than a few minutes left, and you want food for a week! Why?"

"I'd rather not say."

"Go then!" She slammed the door with terrible force.

The elevator was an ordeal. I kept wondering if Leslie was right. The shrilling of the wind was muffled, here at the core of the building. Perhaps it was about to rip electrical cables somewhere, leave me stranded in a darkened box. But I made it down.

The upper level was knee-deep in water.

My second surprise was that it was lukewarm, like old bathwater, unpleasant to wade through. Steam curdled on the surface, then blew away on a wind that howled through the concrete echo chamber like the screaming of the damned.

Going up was another ordeal. If what I was thinking was wish fulfillment, if a roaring wind of live steam caught me now...I'd feel like such an idiot.... But the doors opened, and the lights hadn't even flickered.

Leslie wouldn't let me in.

"Go away!" She shouted through the locked door. "Go eat your cheese and crackers somewhere else!"

"You got another date?"

That was a mistake. I got no answer at all.

I could almost see her viewpoint. The extra trip for the extra bags was no big thing to fight about; but why did it have to be? How long was our love affair going to last, anyway? An hour, with luck. Why back down on a perfectly good argument, to preserve so ephemeral a thing?

"I wasn't going to bring this up," I shouted, hoping she could hear me through the door. The wind must be three times as loud on the other side. "We may need food for a week! And a place to hide!"

Silence. I began to wonder if I could kick the door down. Would I be better off waiting in the hall? Eventually she'd have to—

The door opened. Leslie was pale. "That was cruel," she said quietly.

"I can't promise anything. I wanted to wait, but you forced it. I've been wondering if the sun really has exploded."

"That's cruel. I was just getting used to the idea." She turned her face to the doorjamb. Tired, she was tired. I'd kept her up too late....

"Listen to me. It was all wrong," I said. "There should have been an aurora borealis to light up the night sky from pole to pole. A shock wave of particles exploding out of the sun, traveling at an inch short of the speed of light, would rip into the atmosphere like—why, we'd have seen blue fire over every building!

"Then, the storm came too slow," I screamed, to be heard above the thunder. "A nova would rip away the sky over half the planet. The shock wave would move around the night side with a sound to break all the glass in the world, all at once! And crack concrete and marble—and, Leslie love, it just hasn't happened. So I started wondering."

She said it in a mumble. "Then what is it?"

"A flare. The worst—"

She shouted it at me like an accusation. "A flare! A solar flare! You think the sun could light up like that—

"Easy, now—"

"—could turn the moon and planets into so many torches, then fade out as if nothing had happened! Oh, you idiot—"

"May I come in?"

She looked surprised. She stepped aside, and I bent and picked up the bags and walked in.

The glass doors rattled as if giants were trying to beat their way in. Rain had squeezed through cracks to make dark puddles on the rug.

I set the bags on the kitchen counter. I found bread in the refrigerator, dropped two slices in the toaster. While they were toasting I opened the foie gras.

"My telescope's gone," she said. Sure enough, it was. The tripod was all by itself on the balcony, on its side.

I untwisted the wire on a champagne bottle. The toast popped up, and Leslie found a knife and spread both slices with foie gras. I held the bottle near her ear, figuring to trip conditioned reflexes.

She did smile fleetingly as the cork popped. She said, "We should set up our picnic grounds here. Behind the counter. Sooner or later the wind is going to break those doors and shower glass all over everything."

That was a good thought. I slid around the partition, swept all the pillows off the floor and the couch and came back with them. We set up a nest for ourselves.

It was kind of cozy. The kitchen counter was three and a half feet high, just over our heads, and the kitchen alcove itself was just wide enough to swing our elbows comfortably. Now the floor was all pillows. Leslie poured the champagne into brandy snifters, all the way to the lip.

I searched for a toast, but there were just too many possibilities, all depressing. We drank without toasting. And then carefully set the snifters down and slid forward into each other's arms. We could sit that way, face to face, leaning sideways against each other.

"We're going to die," Leslie said.

"Maybe not."

"Get used to the idea, I have," she said. "Look at you, you're all nervous now. Afraid of dying. Hasn't it been a lovely night?"

"Unique. I wish I'd known in time to take you to dinner."

Thunder came in a string of six explosions. Like bombs in an air raid. "Me too," she said when we could hear again.

"I wish I'd known this afternoon."

"Pecan pralines!"

"Farmer's Market. Double-roasted peanuts. Who would *you* have murdered, if you'd had the time?"

"There was a girl in my sorority—"

—and she was guilty of sibling rivalry, so Leslie claimed. I named an editor who kept changing his mind. Leslie named one of my old girl friends, I named her only old boy friend that I knew about, and it got to be kind of fun before we ran out. My brother Mike had forgotten my birthday once. The fiend.

The lights flickered, then came on again.

Too casually, Leslie asked, "Do you really think the sun might go back to normal?"

"It better *be* back to normal. Otherwise we're dead anyway. I wish we could see Jupiter."

"Dammit, answer me! Do you think it was a flare?"

"Yes."

"Why?"

"Yellow dwarf stars don't go nova."

"What if ours did?"

"The astronomers know a lot about novas," I said. "More than you'd guess. They can see them coming months ahead. Sol is a gee-naught yellow dwarf. They don't go nova at all. They have to wander off the main sequence first, and that takes millions of years."

She pounded a fist softly on my back. We were cheek to cheek; I couldn't see her face. "I don't want to believe it. I don't dare. Stan, nothing like this has ever happened before. How can you know?"

"Something did."

"What? I don't believe it. We'd remember."

"Do you remember the first moon landing? Aldrin and Armstrong?"

"Of course. We watched it at Earl's Lunar Landing Party."

"They landed on the biggest, flattest place they could find on the moon. They sent back several hours of jumpy home movies, took a lot of very clear pictures, left corrugated footprints all over the place. And they came home with a bunch of rocks.

"Remember? People said it was a long way to go for rocks. But the first thing anyone noticed about those rocks was that they were half melted.

"Sometime in the past, oh, say the past hundred thousand years; there's no way of marking it closer than that—the sun flared up. It didn't stay hot enough long enough to leave any marks on the Earth. But the moon doesn't have an atmosphere to protect it. All the rocks melted on one side."

The air was warm and damp. I took off my coat, which was heavy with rainwater. I fished the cigarettes and matches out, lit a cigarette and exhaled past Leslie's ear.

"We'd remember. It *couldn't* have been this bad."

"I'm not so sure. Suppose it happened over the Pacific? It wouldn't do *that* much damage. Or over the American continents. It would have sterilized some plants and animals and burned down a lot of forests, and who'd know? The sun is a four percent variable star. Maybe it gets a touch more variable than that, every so often."

Something shattered in the bedroom. A window? A wet wind touched us, and the shriek of the storm was louder.

"Then we could live through this," Leslie said hesitantly.

"I believe you've put your finger on the crux of the matter. Skol!" I found my champagne and drank deep. It was past three in the morning, with a hurricane beating at our doors.

"Then shouldn't we be doing something about it?"

"We are."

"Something like trying to get up into the hills! Stan, there're going to be floods!"

"You bet your ass there are, but they won't rise this high. Fourteen stories. Listen, I've thought this through. We're in a building that was designed to be earthquake proof. You told me so yourself. It'd take more than a hurricane to knock it over.

"As for heading for the hills, what hills? We won't get far tonight, not with the streets flooded already. Suppose we could get up into the Santa Monica Mountains; then what? Mudslides, that's what. That area won't stand up to what's coming. The flare must have boiled away enough water to make another ocean. It's going to rain for forty days and forty nights! Love, this is the safest place we could have reached tonight."

"Suppose the polar caps melt?"

"Yeah...well, we're pretty high, even for that. Hey, maybe that last flare was what started Noah's Flood. Maybe it's happening again. Sure as hell, there's not a place on Earth that isn't the middle of a hurricane. Those two great counterrotating hurricanes, by now they must have broken up into hundreds of little storms—"

The glass doors exploded inward. We ducked, and the wind howled about us and dropped rain and glass on us.

"At least we've got food!" I shouted. "If the floods maroon us here, we can last it out!"

"But if the power goes, we can't cook it! And the refrigerator—"

"We'll cook everything we can. Hard-boil all the eggs—"

The wind rose about us. I stopped trying to talk.

Warm rain sprayed us horizontally and left us soaked. Try to cook in a hurricane? I'd been stupid; I'd waited too long. The wind would tip boiling water on us if we tried it. Or hot grease—

Leslie screamed, "We'll have to use the oven!"

Of course. The oven couldn't possibly fall on us. We set it for 400°— and put the eggs in, in a pot of water. We took all the meat out of the meat drawer and shoved it on a broiling pan.

BERNARDO MOTA

Two artichokes in another pot. The other vegetables we could eat raw.

What else? I tried to think.

Water. If the electricity went, probably the water and telephone lines would too. I turned on the faucet over the sink and started filling things: pots with lids, Leslie's thirty-cup percolator that she used for parties, her wash bucket. She clearly thought I was crazy, but I didn't trust the rain as a water source; I couldn't control it.

The sound. Already we'd stopped trying to shout through it. Forty days and nights of this and we'd be stone deaf. Cotton? Too late to reach the bathroom. Paper towels! I tore and wadded and made four plugs for our ears.

Sanitary facilities? Another reason for picking Leslie's place over mine. When the plumbing stopped, there was always the balcony.

And if the flood rose higher than the fourteenth floor, there was the roof. Twenty stories up. If it went higher than that, there would be damned few people left when it was over.

And if it was a nova?

I held Leslie a bit more closely, and lit another cigarette one-handed. All the wasted planning, if it was a nova. But I'd have been doing it anyway. You don't stop planning just because there's no hope.

And when the hurricane turned to live steam, there was always the balcony. At a dead run, and over the railing, in preference to being boiled alive.

But now was not the time to mention it.

Anyway, she'd probably thought of it herself.

The lights went out about four. I turned off the oven, in case the power should come back. Give it an hour to cool down, then I'd put all the food in Baggies.

Leslie was asleep, sitting up in my arms. How could she sleep, not knowing? I piled pillows behind her and let her back easy.

For some time, I lay on my back, smoking, watching the lightning make shadows on the ceiling. We had eaten all the foie gras and drunk one bottle of champagne. I thought of opening the brandy, but decided against it, with regret.

A long time passed. I'm not sure what I thought about. I didn't sleep, but certainly my mind was in idle. It only gradually came to me that the ceiling, between lightning flashes, had turned gray.

I rolled over, gingerly, soggily. Everything was wet.

My watch said it was nine-thirty.

I crawled around the partition into the living room. I'd been ignoring the storm sounds for so long that it took a faceful of warm-whipping rain to remind me. There was a hurricane going on. But charcoal-gray light was filtering through the black clouds.

So. I was right to have saved the brandy. Floods, storms, intense radiation, fires lit by the flare—if the toll of destruction was as high as I expected, then money was about to become worthless. We would need trade goods.

I was hungry. I ate two eggs and some bacon—still warm— and started putting the rest of the food away.

We had food for a week, maybe... but hardly a balanced diet. Maybe we could trade with other apartments. This was a big building. There must be empty apartments, too, that we could raid for canned soup and the like. And refugees from the lower floors to be taken care of, if the waters rose high enough...

Damn! I missed the nova. Life had been simplicity itself last night. Now... did we have medicines? Were there doctors in the building? There would be dysentery and other plagues. And hunger. There was a supermarket near here; could we find a scuba rig in the building?

But I'd get some sleep first. Later we could start exploring the building. The day had become a lighter charcoal-gray. Things could be worse, far worse. I thought of the radiation that must have sleeted over the far side of the world, and wondered if our children would colonize Europe, or Asia, or Africa.

The Illustrators of the Future
Looking Forward and Looking Back...

BY BOB EGGLETON

Bob Eggleton is a successful science fiction, fantasy, horror, and landscape artist, encompassing twenty years of putting brush to canvas or board. Winner of nine Hugo Awards—he has been nominated an amazing twenty-eight times over twenty-four years— plus twelve Chesley Awards, as well as various magazine awards, his art can be seen on the covers of magazines, books, posters and prints—and of late, trading cards, stationery, drink coasters, journals, and jigsaw puzzles. He is considered one of the most "commercially successful" artists in the fields of science fiction and fantasy.

He has also worked as a conceptual illustrator for movies and thrill rides, including Star Trek: The Experience in Las Vegas. He also did concept work for the feature film Sphere *and for the Academy Award–nominated film* Jimmy Neutron: Boy Genius.

Between demanding deadlines for book covers and movies, Bob has illustrated two books of experimental artwork about dragons: Dragonhenge *and* The Stardragons.

Other books of Bob's artwork include: Alien Horizons: The Fantastic Art of Bob Eggleton, Greetings from Earth: The Art of Bob Eggleton, The Book of Sea Monsters, Primal Darkness: The Gothic and Horror Art of Bob Eggleton, Dragon's Domain: The Ultimate Dragon Painting Workshop, *and* Tortured Souls *a collaboration with Clive Barker. For Easton Press he has done the Centennial Edition of* Tarzan of the Apes *by Edgar Rice Burroughs.*

Also he and his wife Marianne Plumridge have a children's book: If Dinosaurs Lived in My Town *available from Sky Pony Press.*

Bob is a Fellow of the New England Science Fiction Association (NESFA). His work has appeared in professional publications and books in the world of science fiction, fantasy and horror around the world. Spacewatch/NASA named asteroid 13562 Bobeggleton in his honor. Most importantly, he was a running extra in the 2002 film Godzilla Against MechaGodzilla.

The Illustrators of the Future
Looking Forward and Looking Back...

Back in 1987, on a dark autumn evening here on the east coast, my phone rang. Algis Budrys (regrettably no longer with us), coordinator for the L. Ron Hubbard Writers of the Future Contest was on the line. Algis had an idea....

Some backstory on Algis and me. I had known Algis not just from science fiction (SF) conventions in general, but specifically from my interaction with the Writers of the Future Contest and its presence at major science fiction conventions, such as the World Science Fiction Conventions of the 1980s, and one of the WotF ceremonies at the World Trade Center, "Windows on the World." I remember that event well, and it was my only time atop the World Trade Center, which sadly is also gone. Algis had made the Contest his passion, and in so many ways his life's work. Algis Budrys was one of the "Old Guard" of SF writers, who'd left a path for all writers. Writers like that seem hard to find these days. I considered him a good friend. When he called me that autumn evening, Algis opened with his usual conversation starter. "So...heya," he said. "We'd always had the intent as per L. Ron Hubbard's wishes on starting another contest, that will run alongside of the Writers of the Future...it's called, naturally...the Illustrators of the Future...and, well, we want you to be a judge!"

He explained to me that my friend and mentor, ten-time Hugo Award winner Frank Kelly Freas, was to head it all up, and draw up (no pun intended) the rules of how it worked. Kelly Freas would keep in touch because there was still a lot of legwork to do to make it all come to fruition. Aside from me, a host of other artists had been asked aboard as co-judges: Edd Cartier, Leo and Diane Dillon, Ron and Val Lindahn, Jack Kirby, Will Eisner, Paul Lehr, Moebius, Alex Schomburg, H.R. Van Dongen and the legendary Frank Frazetta. I was stunned to be in the company of such amazing and iconic talents. Feeling humble was an understatement. So in 1988, the first building blocks of the competition's structural information was sent out far and wide. There was no Internet at the time, so this was somewhat of a massive undertaking. Kelly Freas started the ball rolling, and he had made up a list of criteria and points that the art would be judged on.

He came to believe wholeheartedly that, "More young illustrators have been introduced to and entered the field by way of this Contest than anything that has happened in the field of illustration. It's going to make a big difference in the immediate future. There is a real need for intelligent artists who can understand what has been written and illustrate it in a way that is related to the real world and means something. A piece of art that does that becomes a treasure beyond price. L. Ron Hubbard's Contest is creating the men and women who will do this for us."

The concept is simple: the entrant has nothing to lose because it doesn't cost anything. In fact there is quite a lot to gain. An illustrator is asked to submit samples of his or her work and those samples are sent out en masse to a select panel of judges on a quarterly basis. Names are removed from the entries to level the playing field to just the art. Then the panel of judges, working independently of each other, with only several judges used at any given time, further narrow down the applicants. Feedback is usually given on the artists' three submission samples as an overall commentary. Final compilation of scores and comments is done in-house at Author Services. Should someone be a winner or finalist in the Illustrators of the Future, they get to then illustrate a winning story written by the winners of the Writers of the Future, becoming a published illustrator in the annual anthology.

I can tell you something, and this comes from a person who had very little in terms of this type of encouragement in the '70s and '80s, that this Contest was a boon to anyone wishing to get kick-started into being an illustrator. I wish it had been there when I was starting out.

All the excitement and enthusiasm could be summed up with Ukraine's Sergey Poyarkov's winning the top prize of $5,000 in a display of emotion and thanks that was quite profound. Later, Sergey would also be asked to be a judge for the Contest.

Judges have come and gone as well. My friend and mentor Frank Kelly Freas passed away in 2005, a great loss not just to myself and his friends and family but to the science fiction community. Others have passed on too: Frank Frazetta and Jack Kirby. Fortunately, I had the great honor of meeting both icons via the Illustrators of the Future ceremonies, and my good friend Paul Lehr who was a total inspiration to anyone he spoke to. We remember the passing of Wil Eisner, Alex Schomburg, H.R. Van Dongen, Edd Cartier, and Leo Dillon who have also gone onto the "great studio in the sky" as it were.

Others have joined us over the years, including amazing legendary artists Vincent Di Fate, Stephen Hickman, Cliff Nielsen and Stephen Youll. As a judge from the beginning, I have become part of the original "legacy" artists, along with Val and Ron Lindahn. In fact, I would say as an illustrator I have grown with the contest, my own work winning awards such as the Hugo award—a lineage of this award I share with not only Kelly Freas, but Vincent Di Fate, Edd Cartier, Leo and Diane Dillon, Stephen Hickman and Stephan Martiniere.

Over the years we've had events in Los Angeles, Washington D.C., Cape Kennedy, and Seattle at the Science Fiction Museum. In Florida at Cape Kennedy in 1997, I got to meet judge and icon, Frank Frazetta for the first time, when he stopped by to say hi after we all watched the launch of a space shuttle. After the launch, the heavens opened and poured rain in a never-ending torrent. Amusingly, the fact I had a rental car nearby suddenly made me five new best friends. There was a lot of laughter trying to squeeze everyone into that car. This is how the best memories are made.

My, where did twenty-five years go?

In addition to the awards ceremony, the Contest winners are treated to a week-long intensive workshop on illustration with Contest judges and top professionals in the field who stop in.

Many winners of the Contest have gone on to create terrific illustrations and art for many forms of media—not just books and magazine illustrations, but also films, game designs, et cetera.

Times have changed since the Contest was initiated and so have the outlets and exposure for this kind of work. I have gone from seeing entries done purely as line art and pencil drawings to fully-rendered computer-generated color images or "paintings." As we entered the new millennium, I have seen the word "illustrator" redefined.

The Internet has broadened the scope of entries coming from all parts of the world to the Illustrators of the Future Contest. It's fairly amazing to see the diversity of artists and ways of seeing things through their art. It brings a wider world view of new vision and creativity, and a freshness to the genre.

Illustrators and artists will always be needed in one way or another. Anything you see in our society that we use carries an image that was designed by an illustrator at some point—be it at the creative beginning or the packaged ending. Whether it's for something in the media or something used on an everyday basis, it was designed to have a finished "look" by an artist. Books, no matter what anyone tells you, will always be read, so they will need to be "packaged." That means cover art and/or interior illustrations. Art helps identify a thing, no matter what it is.

All in all, the Illustrators of the Future Contest is a way of investing in the future. We need new generations of creative thinkers, artists, illustrators, simply to create a visual culture for years to come. The future is a mystery, and what it brings is uncertain, but pictures have been made by Man for all his history for one reason or another. The future needs vision, and for that, the future needs art. Forward!

The Graver

written by

Amy M. Hughes

illustrated by

TAYLOR PAYTON

ABOUT THE AUTHOR

Amy M. Hughes was born in Provo, Utah, the first American child of a Canadian family. She was raised in Alberta, Canada, surrounded by prairie while dreaming of mountains and trees. Too many forested fantasy novels may have had some part in that.

She learned to read early and moved from The Hardy Boys *in the first grade to Tolkien by the fourth. She developed a deep love of reading that has sporadically spilled into a need to write, on and off for many years. In 2008, at the insistence of her husband, Amy attended Orson Scott Card's Literary Boot Camp. She learned more in one week about how to tell a good story than she had in the first two years of her English degree.*

Amy has been a factory line worker, a veterinary technician, a missionary, an herbalist, a landscape designer, and a stay-at-home mom. She has also eaten fire, jumped off a third-story balcony, and crashed in a hot air balloon. More than anything, she wants to be a writer. She hopes it doesn't have to involve growing up.

"The Graver" is Amy's first submission to the Writers of the Future Contest.

ABOUT THE ILLUSTRATOR

Taylor Payton was born in 1990 and spent many of his early years as an adventurous and wily youth in the bustling suburbs of Minneapolis, Minnesota.

During his grade school adventures, he and other classmates would spend many hours drawing characters from their favorite games and anime.

For as long as he can recall, he was rather fond of doodling, but he didn't make the solidified decision to become an illustrator until the age of twenty-one. The calling hit Taylor in the midst of his collegiate major of media arts and animation. He soon put down the animation paper for digital paintbrushes, but still finished up his degree.

Taylor went on to win "Best in Show" at his graduate portfolio ceremony and has since worked on a plethora of private and commercial jobs. He aims to further his arts education at a local atelier while he develops his worlds, characters, and professional career. Taylor's art verges on the fantastic, but he's cultivated a deep connection to the novelties of abstraction and surrealism.

The Graver

There's damage from the storm all over the farm, but the twisted casing of the fence's reactor is what worries me the most. The wind tears at my hair and my clothes, not entirely settled yet.

"It looks pretty bad, Daniel." Isaac's translucent form passes through the pile of debris and leans closer to the wreckage, craning to get a better look. His image crackles with static in the wind. "I were you, I'd be praying hard nothing notices this is down."

I deliberately ignore the suggestion of prayer. "Yeah, see here? The main shaft's busted," I answer. I use the edge of the reactor to balance myself as I clear away the leaves and mud that have snarled along the main panel. "And here," I point, "the circuits are shorting out."

Isaac leans in, clicking his tongue as he studies the circuit panel. In the distance, something I don't recognize howls into the returning storm. I'm running out of time to fix this. I turn and look down the line where the fence should have been. The energy field, from the top of the old cattle pasture down to the cottonwoods along the road, is gone. Below the cottonwoods, I can just make out the pale iridescent line of the fence continuing around the south end of the property.

"Daniel, this leaves you pretty open," Isaac says. "I can send you the part for the main shaft, but not until tomorrow. It'll take a few days to get to you. I don't like that you're out here. This whole setup is pretty primitive to begin with."

"Yeah." I straighten. I glance at the sky, hoping for more hours than I know I have, but the light is fading fast.

Isaac's image flickers with static for a moment.

"Is there any way to rig things so it seems the fence is still up? At least from the outside?" he asks. I shake my head. Isaac sighs. "You should never have left Denver, Daniel. I know things were hard for you here, but the walls don't short out when a tree falls on 'em. There's a reason people don't choose to live outside the gates."

"We'll be fine." I struggle to keep my voice calm. "Storm's been building all day, and it's going to be a bad one. Raiders don't raid in weather like this."

"I don't like it. I hear the stories. Gravers outside ranging in packs, taking who they want. I mean, after what happened with Angela, I get it, but...you need to see this...." His voice is uncharacteristically firm. Before I realize what he's planning, he's replaced his own image with news footage. It takes me a moment to recognize the smoldering remains of a burning farm. Photographs of the gravers responsible for the carnage flash across the screen—three average-looking men I might have passed on the street without noticing, except that their eyes are glowing. They've killed nine people and devoured their souls—no, their brain patterns, I correct myself—and now the light of their victims shines from the gravers' eyes.

I squeeze my eyes shut against the image, but the sight of the gravers has already triggered images of swirling energy being absorbed from Angela's lifeless body. It leaves me feeling as if there's a vise around my chest. My hands are suddenly shaking. I push the thoughts away as firmly as I can.

"That's enough, Isaac. Turn it off," I snap. The news footage disappears, replaced by Isaac's translucent image. "I'm here now. I'm not coming back. We're going to get the fence back up before anyone knows it's down."

Isaac nods stiffly. "And if you don't? That happened last night and less than twenty miles from where you are right now. I'm sorry, Daniel, but think about Emma. She's nearly an adult, and you won't be able to keep her at home with you much longer no matter where you are." He sighs. "I'll send your part tomorrow."

I open my mouth to yell at him. But before I can speak, Isaac's image disappears into the port, leaving me alone with only the persistent whine and tug of the wind for company. The port's iridescent dome remains quiet. I snatch it up and shove it into my pack. I'm standing ankle-deep in mud.

"I *am* thinking about Emma," I mutter to myself. Keeping her safe is all I have left.

I spend the next hour clearing debris and shoring up the side of the reactor that had sunk. I cut away any other branches that might succumb to the wind and cause more damage. Angela'd say I should pray the storm would pass. But I gave up prayer the day she died.

When it's finally too dark to tell branch from wire, I gather my tools and stumble through the wind toward the house. The dark seems to have given the storm new life, and I'm leaning heavily into the wind by the time I climb the front steps. The body scanner by the door blinks into life, then flashes green.

"Welcome home, Daniel," says the front door as it swings open. I leave my tools and my muddy boots on the bench just inside. I hesitate at Angela's picture on the wall. There's a smudge on the glass above her cheek, and I catch myself. I pull my hand back from tracing the line of her face again. It never does me any good. All that's ever there is cold, smooth, lifeless glass.

"Emma? You home?" I call.

"Emma is in the kitchen," the house replies. "Shall I tell her you are home?"

"No need." I turn myself away from the photograph. As an afterthought, I add, "I want immediate notification of any security risks in the area until the fence is repaired. Everything within, say, twenty miles or so."

"Of course, Daniel." I can at least count on the house not to talk back.

I walk toward the kitchen, trying to find something to say to my seventeen-year-old daughter that won't end in another fight. I stop short of the door when I hear her talking.

"No. Of course not. How long you gonna be?" Emma pauses, and a gust of wind rattles the windows. There's a voice answering. A boy's voice, I think, but static obscures the words. "Yeah, seriously. I have to go. I heard my dad come in a few minutes ago. Yeah. Can't wait."

I push open the door. Emma starts and puts her back between me and the image. She sweeps her hand across the port and the image blinks out. It's replaced by a rotating three-dimensional model of an atom before I can see who it might have been. The display lights up her face, and her profile looks so much like her mother's that my heart constricts in my chest.

"You smell like rocket fuel," she says from over her shoulder.

"How's your homework?" I ask. Part of me hopes she'll tell me the truth. Most of me knows better. I grab the soap and turn on the kitchen sink. I brace myself, then plunge my arms into the frigid water and scrub away the dirt and oil of the day's work. But I can't scrub away my worry about the fence. The images of the burning farmhouse won't just wash away. But I'm not ready to admit that Isaac may have been right.

"How's the water?" Emma asks.

"Hot water's next on my list. I promise."

"We had hot water at home." So many things I'd like to say to that, but I keep my mouth shut. Angela told me once that I had to be the grownup. But it is so hard with Emma sometimes. I turn off the faucet and rub my arms with the towel. My arms are red with the cold, and my fingers are like ice.

"You were supposed to start dinner," I say.

"We had takeout at home too," she says. "And we had neighbors that didn't need to be kept out with some stupid killer electric fence and—"

"Enough, Emma." I slam my hand down onto the old wooden table and immediately regret it as Emma flinches away from me.

I take a breath. "There's nothing left for us there." I manage to sound much calmer than I am.

Emma stands up. She's tall enough now she almost meets me at eye level. "And whose fault is that?"

"Don't you blame me for your mother's death." My voice sounds thin to me.

"I don't," she says. "I blame you for letting them kill her the second time." A violent gust of wind rattles the windows in their casings.

"There's no such thing as a soul, Emma. It was just energy. Impulses and memory. Mental programming. And it put the man who killed her in jail for a very long time. Your mother was already gone." No matter how many times I say the words, they come out sounding hollow.

"That's not what she would have wanted, and you know it," she says.

"Enough!" I yell. I squeeze my eyes shut, trying to calm myself, but I can't seem to shake my rattled nerves. Not tonight. The images of Isaac's news feeds just won't be pushed away.

"There is an unknown vehicle approaching," the house says calmly. Emma turns and waves the port off, then slips it into her pocket.

"Doesn't matter," she says. "I'm out of here anyway."

She turns and sprints toward her room. All I can think is that the fence is down. Three gravers. Nine bodies.

"What do you mean unknown?" I ask the house.

"It is comprised of an amalgamation of several different vehicle types. It predates transponders and is not registered with local authorities," the house answers. The gravers on Isaac's news footage drove unregistered salvage too. I reach into the space between the fridge and the wall and pull out my grandfather's shotgun. Stunners are legal, but shotguns are scary.

I reach the front entry just as Emma darts out the door with a bag slung over her shoulder. I follow her out, shotgun in hand.

"Emma!" I call. Emma skips down the steps toward the drive.

The tree line along the ridge of the valley appears black and ragged against the fading light of day. There's a car running at the end of the drive, its doors open and its headlights illuminating a golden path across the road and into the trees. Everything is quiet. The world nearly vibrates with the pressure of the storm about to break.

I manage to grab Emma's arm at the bottom of the stairs.

"Let go of me." She tries to pull away, but I hold her firm.

"What is this?" I ask.

"What do you think?" she says. There's a boy Emma's age coming up the drive.

"You told him the fence was down?"

"Get over it, Dad. I'm done being a prisoner in this stupid house."

She fights her arm free and tries to run. I just manage to grab hold of her jacket, and I don't let go. "You're not a prisoner. It's my job to keep you safe."

"Right. Prisoners get hot water and visitation." Emma sulks.

The boy steps into the light at the base of the stairs. "You alright, Emma?" he asks. He squares his shoulders as if he's going to fight me for her if he has to. All hundred and thirty pounds of him.

"Go home, kid. Emma's not going anywhere." I lean the shotgun against the porch, relieved that I'm not going to need to use it. It's been twenty years since I've shot it, and I'm not in a hurry to do it again.

"Dad, come on. Three more months and I'll be old enough to leave here anyway."

"Then you can wait three months," I say.

"I got my cousin in the car," the boy tells Emma. "Do I need to call him up?"

"He older than you?" I ask. Three fat drops of rain splatter on my face.

"Yeah." He answers hesitantly.

"Good." I tell him. "Then I can have him arrested for attempting to kidnap a minor. Now get out of here before I call the authorities."

"Not how it works out here," says a man coming up the

drive. Behind him, the light from the headlights flickers with the shadows of the trees in the wind. He looks a lot like the boy, only ten years older and a hundred pounds heavier. "Ain't that right, Nina?" he says over his shoulder. He comes to a stop next to the boy, just at the base of the stairs, only a few steps out of my reach and far too close for comfort.

Behind him comes a woman, lean and wiry. She's got glowing tattoos that wrap up her leg before disappearing beneath a too-short skirt. They fade from blue to red and back again. She's fiddling with a flip-top lighter in her hand. *Flip, spark. Flip, spark.* "Sure thing," Nina says. The flame catches for a moment and is blown out by the wind.

"Guys, just wait in the car. I got this, okay?" the boy says.

"Get off of my property." I reach behind me and wrap my hand around the barrel of the shotgun. "Emma, get inside the house. Now."

Before I can lift the gun, the man darts forward and grabs it from my hand. His arm moves quicker than my eyes can follow. He reeks of alcohol and something else. Something sour, musky, and dry.

"Well, if Mr. Law-abiding ain't just breaking a few rules out here his own self." He raises the gun to his shoulder and looks down the sights. He levels it into the darkness, swings it around, and levels it at me. Then he lowers the end, holding the weapon comfortably under his arm. "Now, my cousin here asked me to come and pick up his girlfriend. So why don't you let the girl go?"

The barrel of the shotgun is still pointing at my knees. He hefts it slightly, and I have the feeling he's used a gun a whole lot more often than I have.

"Put the gun down, Chad. There's no reason to be a jerk," the boy says.

"Come on, Zach. Ain't we just having a good time?" Chad smirks.

Zach turns to Emma. "Come on, Emma. He's just being a jackass. He won't hurt anybody. Let's go."

Emma hoists the bag on her shoulder, nervously glancing

from the shotgun to Zach and back. "Zach, just get him to put the gun away first, okay?" she asks.

"Aw, look at that," Nina says. "You gone and scared the girl, Chad. Ain't that cute?"

"Nina—" Zach begins, but a sudden gust of wind howls around us, whipping dust and debris into my face and eyes. When I look up, Nina has stepped into the shadows of the yard. Our eyes meet, and I see what I hadn't seen before.

Her eyes are glowing with a pale silver light and sparks and flashes of blue. I haven't seen that up close since the day I signed Angela's soul away. A chill rises up the back of my neck.

Emma's face drains to a ghostly white. "Graver," Emma whispers. She clings to my arm and shuffles behind me.

"Come on, Emma," Zach says. "They're not usually like this. They're just gonna give us a ride is all."

"You didn't say your cousin was a graver." Emma's voice is soft and tense.

"That's all right, pretty girl," Chad says. He reaches out again with his free hand, grabs Emma by the arm, and yanks her off the porch. Emma screams. She and I stumble in our effort to hold on to each other. I catch myself on the railing. Emma stumbles to her knees. Chad pulls her to her feet again, out of my reach. He hefts the shotgun up toward my chest.

"Zach!" she calls.

"You take your hands off her." I straighten, scanning around me for anything that I can use as a weapon. But the tools are on the other side of the door. I took them inside to keep them out of the rain.

Nina snickers behind them, waving the tiny flame of the lighter in front of her face. From nowhere I can see, she produces a rag and hangs it above the flame. Golden light envelopes her face. Fire drips off the edge of the rag. She tosses it into the dry garden, and golden flames sprout up like little yellow sunflowers.

"Seriously, Chad," Zach shoves his cousin in the chest. "Knock it off. You're just here to give us a ride."

"What's wrong with you?" Chad asks, shoving him back. Zach

is thrown onto the ground. "You asked me to come out here and help you get your girl. Well, here we are, getting the girl."

And then I see Emma move. And I can't find my voice to stop her.

She lunges around Chad and grabs at the shotgun. She's got the gun by the barrel and half out of Chad's grip before Chad seems to realize what's happening. He wrenches the gun away from Emma, but Zach grabs it from the other side. The air cracks with gunfire.

There's a chink of metal on metal, then a hiss. Everyone turns toward the sound. The pressure regulator from the house's external hydrogen tank is spinning out into the dark. Colorized red hydrogen mist is streaming through the sheared-off pipe. Straight toward Nina's garden fire.

Chad drops Emma's arm and runs towards Nina. I dive off the porch toward Emma, but I don't reach her before the world around me explodes with sound and light and fire. I'm thrown toward the house in a wash of heat. My body slams against the staircase, and for several long moments I am lost—tossed and buried beneath a sea of crashing timbers and roiling debris.

And then there is nothing but the impossible silence of dust sifting itself out of the air, broken only by the creak of settling timbers.

My lungs revolt against the thickness of the air, and it takes me too long to stop coughing. To call for my daughter.

Emma's name croaks out of my throat between gasps for air. I can see nothing. The light from the house is gone, leaving only the golden glow of the headlights in the drive and a few smoldering flames in the wreckage of the porch to illuminate what's left of my world.

The timber from the house lies in splintered ruins, around me, on top of me, fires burning. The support beam from the roof, crushes my chest.

I'm lying on my side, and there's a weight above. The timbers above me slip and crash against my chest, and I cry out. I try to pull myself free, but I am wedged tight.

Somewhere in the dark, I hear someone moaning.

"Emma?" I try again. This time I manage to squeeze the name out against the burning in my lungs. "Emma?" I yell.

The wind picks up, and the dust clears enough for me to discern outlines against the car lights. The front half of the house is gone. Its remains are a jagged silhouette rising above me. In the drive, someone pushes themselves to their knees, and for a moment I am filled with hope. But the outline that staggers to its feet is too tall and broad to be my daughter.

"Nina?" he calls.

My eyes are beginning to adjust to the darkness, and I can see Chad better now. His arms are wrapped round his ribs, and he's shaking dust from his hair. I push at the beam that's laying across my chest, but it doesn't shift.

Chad sweeps his gaze toward me, eyes glowing silver-blue in the dark. "Where's Nina?" he asks again. "Where's Zach?"

I can't see Emma anywhere, but the sight of his eyes brings memories of Angela flooding into my mind. The graver who took her soul was a cold little man in a cheap gray suit. They said he was a professional. I tried to tell myself it was the best thing. They couldn't convict the driver without using her memories as evidence. But the look of ecstasy in that man's eyes when it was done haunts me still.

I push harder against the beam. Several fat drops of rain spatter on my face and arms.

Chad stumbles toward me through the dark. "Where's Nina?" he yells. "Where's Zach?"

"How the hell should I know?" I manage to twist my chest just slightly beneath the debris, and suddenly I can breathe a little easier. Chad wanders away from me, calling for Zach and Nina.

"Daddy?" It's Emma's voice, soft and whimpering. I twist my shoulders, craning my neck to find her. She's in the dark, pushing herself up to her hands and knees. The shotgun is lying on the ground between us, just out of my reach. "Dad, the house is gone."

376

"Emma, stay there." I push against the beam, and it shifts slightly. "Are you okay?"

She lifts one hand to her head, then pulls it away and stares in confusion. The headlights reflect off something dark and wet smeared across her palm.

From somewhere close by, Chad howls Zach's name and begins to curse. I hear boards lifting and being tossed, then the creak of timber. "I can't find her," Chad mumbles to himself. "Damn it. Where are they?

"This is your fault." Chad storms back into my view. "This is all your fault."

"Chad?" Nina's voice is thin and weak. He spins and races into the darkness. I shift my weight as best I can, straining against the beam. I shift it to the side ever so slightly.

"Emma, honey. Just stay where you are. I'm coming. Okay?"

Chad staggers back into view, carrying Nina in his arms. Her head is propped up against his shoulder. The tattoo up her leg fades from blue to red. He's brushing her damp hair back. Her shirt is soaked with blood.

The muscles in my shoulder are burning, but I can't get the beam to move. My whole body aches.

"I need help," I call out. The man's a jackass, but he's the only one of us standing. "You need to get me out of here." The sprinkling of rain turns into a cold drizzle. My hands slip on the wood.

Chad ignores me.

Nina's head has fallen against Chad's chest, and her body is limp. Chad mutters to himself, "No, no, no, no, no... It's okay, baby. I'm gonna fix this. I'm gonna get you what you need."

He carries her to the car and lays her across the back seat. Then he comes back and picks up the gun. Chad leans over me and inspects the wreckage that has me trapped. A few smoldering flames are fanned to life by a sudden gust of wind. The golden glow catches Chad's face at all the wrong angles.

"I can't help you," he says. His breath is sour and dry. "You should know that. I can't get to Zach, and he's my blood, so I can't help you. Wouldn't be right. But I can help Nina. I can get her what she needs." Blue sparks flash in his eyes.

The heat of the fire is beginning to warm my body, but every part of me runs cold. I struggle desperately against the timbers pinning me down as Chad pats my shoulder, then stands up and walks over to Emma. He levels the gun.

Lightning flashes in the sky, giving me one brief, clear vision of the scene: Chad has the butt of the shotgun snugged into his shoulder. Emma looks up at Chad from her knees, dazed and uncertain.

"I really am sorry about this. No hard feelings." He pulls the trigger. The night is shattered by the blast.

I scream my daughter's name as Emma falls lifeless to the ground. Chad picks her up and carries her to the car.

I scream again, but the sound is swallowed in the howling of the wind. The car pulls away, taillights like red glowing eyes. Emma is gone. And the rain pours so thick I can't even see them drive away.

The flames in the house sizzle and smoke in the torrent that follows. There's no reason to struggle against the boards that pin me. Angela is gone. Emma's been taken. But for some unexplainable reason, my body keeps breathing. It hurts too much to move, so I don't.

The remains of the house groan and shift. The stairs beneath me drop, and I slam to the ground in a crush of broken timbers. More by instinct than by desire, I scramble out from under the beams that had me pinned.

Then I hear someone moaning from beneath the rubble. Zach.

I drag myself to my feet and stumble toward the sound. I'm drenched through to my skin, and I can see almost nothing in the dark of the storm. Only the few places where the smoldering coals haven't yet died leave me any light to see by at all.

Working mechanically, without thought, I toss boards to the side until I uncover him. Zach is only an outline against the twisted remains of what might have been the oven. I pull him away from the wreckage and haul him to shelter beneath the carport which is leaning heavily to one side. I sink to the ground, my head against the cold metal post. The noise of the rain on the carport roof drowns out my thoughts.

"What happened?" Zach pulls himself to his knees.

"You brought them here." When Angela died, all I could think was to punish the man who took her from me. Now it seems like it hardly matters. Emma's gone anyway.

Zach pulls a port from his pocket, thumbs on the light, and uses it to examine the rubble beneath the carport. "Where's Emma?" At least he has the decency to sound afraid.

"Your cousin killed her." I spit the words out as if I'm trying to throw them as far from myself as they can get. The look of shock on his face is gratifying and obnoxious all at once.

Zach shakes his head in protest. "No. No, not Chad. He's a lot of things, but—"

"He killed her anyway." The emptiness is starting to give way to anger. "What were you thinking, bringing a graver to my house? To Emma's house?"

Zach wraps his arms around his knees and leans against the carport wall. "I don't know. But—but it still doesn't make any sense. Why..." His voice falters, then drops to a whisper. "Why would Chad kill her?"

I don't bother to answer. There's nothing to say.

"She...she told me about her mom," Zach says.

Angela's face superimposes itself over Emma's. I picture the light being drawn out of Angela's body. I relive the panic I felt in that moment when it was already too late and I couldn't say, "No, please, just let her soul go wherever it's supposed to go."

No. There's no such thing as a soul. I didn't do anything wrong. But Angela's memory is now too raw; Emma's death is too real, and I can't ignore the voice in my brain that tells me I destroyed something precious.

"Emma wouldn't want that to happen to her." Zach's voice is a whisper.

"No. Emma wouldn't." And as I say the words, I know they're true.

I pull myself to my feet and pick up Zach's port. I use it to examine the carport we're using to shield us from the rain. It's partially collapsed, leaning against the front end of the house. I pull some of the large beams and boards out of the wreckage.

"What are you doing?" Zach limps to his feet, clutching his leg.

"We'll need the truck." I slip a board free of the porch and I have to jump back as several others crash to the ground. "I'm setting Emma's soul free. Chad's not getting her."

"But Emma said you didn't believe in souls. What you...what happened to her mom. It's why she wanted to leave."

"Doesn't matter what I believe," I say. "It's what Emma believes." I say it because it sounds right, but mostly it's movement. Because I know that no matter what I think of the human soul, if I stay here, I won't be alive in the morning.

I prop up a board at the fallen end of the carport. If I can brace it, I might just be able to ease the truck out. Zach hesitates for a few moments, then limps over to help me with the boards.

It takes us over an hour to prop up the roof and slide the truck free. It's an antique with a rounded cab, wooden sideboards, whitewall tires and all. My grandfather upgraded it years ago. By the time we've rolled it free, the rain has slipped off into a steady drizzle, but both Zach and I are soaked and dripping with mud. The truck bed boards are smashed and part of the cab roof is dented in, but the navigation panel turns on when I press my thumb to the starter pad.

"Nina's hurt. Where would he take her?" I ask Zach.

Zach huddled beneath the leaning carport roof, arms wrapped around himself to keep warm. "South of town. Back in the foothills. He has a place in an old train yard." I think I can hear Zach's teeth rattling.

"Thanks," I tell him. Then I slam my door shut before Zach can climb in.

Zach pounds on my window, yelling at me to wait. I open the window just a crack.

"You're not coming with me," I tell him. "Call your parents for a ride. Tell them what you brought here." I toss his port out the window, and he ducks back and catches it awkwardly on his chest.

"You'll never find it." Zach yells as the window rolls closed. "Road's washed—" His voice cuts out as the window closes. He pounds his fist on the glass.

I twist my fingers around the steering wheel. I didn't like this kid at the start of the night, and I like him even less now. I'd just as soon leave him to rot. But I don't know where I'm going. I open the window back up. "What road?" I ask.

"Chad's all the family I've got. I'm going with you."

"He killed Emma," I snap. Even in the dim light of the truck's dashboard, I can see his face pale.

"You're gonna make it right by killing him?" he asks. I start to roll the window back up and ease my truck forward. "Wait!" he yells, skipping alongside the truck's door. "You'll never find it without me. The road's gone. You've only got a few hours left before he can take her soul. Then she's gone forever."

I slam on the brakes of the truck, and it jerks to a sudden stop. I jerk my head at the passenger door. Zach runs around the front of the truck, hops in, and slams the door behind him.

"I'm there for Emma," I say. "You don't get in my way."

"Yes, sir. I'm there for the same reason," he says, shaking water from his hair across the cab. A map glows faintly across the windshield, and Zach jabs at it with a finger.

"Here," he says. "After that, it's all back roads. Won't show up on any map you've got."

I engage the auto drive, and the truck pulls out onto the road. I never once look back. There isn't anything left to see.

The road is riddled with pockmarks and potholes made worse by the rain, and the truck makes worse time than I'd like. Within minutes, I slip the truck into manual and resume control. The potholes give me something to focus on. Zach sits on the other end of the bench seat, staring out the window, his knees pulled to his chin. There are times over the next hour when I wonder if he hasn't fallen asleep. But every once in a while he rouses himself to give me directions across back roads.

"I don't care about Chad," I finally tell him.

"What?" His voice is thick with emotion.

I clear my voice, then speak louder to be heard over the rain on the cab roof. "You asked if I was going to kill him. But this isn't about Chad."

Zach nods mutely into the dark, like he understands. But I don't think that he does, and I need him to know. I need to say it out loud so that I will understand. I need to pick the thought clear of the swirling mass of memory and emotion that won't stop replaying itself in my mind.

"I made a promise." I speak the words clearly and a little too loud. "I made a mistake with Emma's mom. I let them take her soul because I thought putting away the driver who hit her would fix things somehow. But it didn't." The static charge of her soul being drawn from her body was so powerful that I felt it through the heavy hospital doors. It was the first time in my life that I'd understood it was real. To have as much power as I felt seeping through that door, it had to be. Running from that knowledge ever since hasn't changed what I did to her. "I swore I wouldn't let what happened to Angela happen to Emma. I thought I could protect her out here."

"Oh," Zach says. I can't tell if he's even listening.

"I don't care about Chad. But I'm not going to let him take Emma's soul."

Zach is quiet for a long time.

"We've got less than an hour to stop him," he says finally. "Before he can start the absorption."

"I know," I answer. I ease the truck up the side of an embankment to avoid another mud hole. I check the clock on the dash for the hundredth time. Forty-nine minutes, as close as I can tell.

"I didn't mean for Emma to get hurt." Zach's voice is low enough I almost don't hear it through the patter of the rain on the truck. I don't bother to answer.

The rain eventually tapers off, and the horizon lightens to a dull dark gray. Zach sits forward in his seat. "There," he says, pointing.

Ahead of us is an iridescent line of fencing emerging from the trees across the road and disappearing into the next valley. The brilliant blue glow is dulled by the rain.

"Damn it." It hadn't occurred to me that it'd be fenced.

"I don't think he's gonna let it down for us," Zach says. "I can try the code, but he changes it all the time. I have to ask him for it just about every time I leave. If we can get through, his place is just half a mile up the road."

The clock tells me we have about ten minutes to get to Emma. Give or take. I'm only half a mile away from keeping the promise to Emma that I should have made to her mother. I reach into the glove box and pull out a penknife. I use it to pry open the control panel on the dashboard.

"What are you doing?" Zach asks.

"Disengaging safety protocols." I yank on a wire and jerk back at the sudden electrical spark. A light starts blinking madly on the dash, and a warning alarm starts to beep, loud and persistent.

"Are you insane?" Zach demands as I back the truck up and rev the engine.

"Hold on," I tell him. Then I slam my foot on the gas and aim the truck directly at the security box outside the gate. Zach screams like a little girl as we gain speed and covers his head with his arms. I grip the wheel tightly and ignore the car's voice yelling at me.

"Warning. Reduce Speed. Impact immi—" The voice is lost in the crunch of metal on metal as the front end of the truck wraps around the control box. Airbags fill my vision, and I feel as though my whole body's been smashed up against a wall.

Then everything is still.

"What the hell?" Zach screams at me as he fights his way up from the deflating airbag.

"Tree killed my fence," I tell him. For the first time in years I'm running *toward* something instead of away. I feel like laughing. "Figured a truck would do just as well." I look up to where the fence line stood moments ago. Now there's only a long line of scraggly trees standing out against the coming light of day. "Come on. We don't have much time."

My door is jammed shut, so I roll the window down as far as I can with the manual release and climb through. The metal running board is slick, and I slip. I jump back, just managing to keep upright. I turn my collar up against the rain, but it's no use. I'm still soaked. "You coming?" I ask Zach. It takes him longer than I think is necessary to untangle himself from the seatbelt and slide on shaky legs to the ground.

"Emma said you were boring." His voice is shaking. He holds onto the side of the truck, but whether for support or reassurance I can't tell.

"I thought I had to be. Come on." I grab his arm and pull him up the road. After a few steps, Zach shakes my hand free.

"It's not far." He starts to jog, and I follow him. The sun is close to rising, making it easier to find our way.

Chad's house is a dilapidated little shack in the middle of a clearing overflowing with dead and decrepit tech of all kinds. There are old metallic train cars rusted nearly to disintegration leaning against newer, plastic models that have been here long enough that a few have shrubs or small trees growing out through empty windows. Everything has been made dark and slick by the rain.

The lights in the house are on, and if Chad's noticed that the fence has come down yet, there isn't any sign. Zach navigates the yard easily.

"Is the house going to warn him we're coming?" I ask about halfway through the yard.

Zach shakes his head. "No. Chad can't afford that sort of tech." He leads us around to the back of the house, and for the first time it occurs to me that Zach may have never seen half of what my house had been equipped with. Not in real life, anyway. "Nina's probably in the bedroom," he says.

As we reach the back door, he steps up on the porch and turns to block my way. "I really didn't want Emma to get hurt." He clenches his jaw and juts out his chin in a display of defiance that reminds me of Emma. I feel punched in the gut all over again. "Were you serious when you said you weren't gonna kill Chad? 'Cause I think you should."

"What?" I take a step back down the stairs.

"I think you should kill him. What he did to Emma...he shouldn't have. I mean, I'm not...Emma was different. She didn't belong out here. And she didn't deserve that."

"I'm just here for Emma."

From behind Zach comes a deep, whirring pulse of sound, and my stomach drops. The extractor's been turned on.

I push Zach aside and race down the hall, following the sound. The end of the hall opens up into the living room, and there I see them.

Nina is lying on a torn and stained couch beneath the far window. It's the cleanest part of the room. Nina's chest and head are bandaged, and that stupid swirling tattoo fades from red to blue and back. I realize suddenly it's supposed to be a dragon.

Chad is holding a glass to her lips. Though part of me resists looking, my eyes settle on Emma. She's lying on the floor. On her chest is a little silver ball, its sides peeled open like a flower. The base is covered in flashing lights, and the center is beginning to glow.

The sight of her stops me cold. There's blood on her blouse and a stillness to her body that I somehow hadn't expected, though I knew I should have.

I take a step forward, but the floor creaks and Chad looks up. Before I can move, he grabs my grandfather's shotgun from off the floor and fires. His lack of aim saves my life. I duck back into the bathroom as he fires another shot. And another. Drywall and plaster shatter past my ear.

It's not until I feel the warmth of my blood seeping down my leg that I realize I've been grazed.

The words "I'm here for Emma" dry up in my throat. I find that I can't make myself say them because none of this can be real. Emma can't be dead.

Instead, I'm filled with an all-too-familiar hatred: the same anger and rage I felt toward the driver who took Angela from me. Only it's worse. The driver hadn't meant to kill anyone. Chad had.

And Emma was all the family I'd had left.

The whirring from the other room rises to a higher pitch, and the light from the orb shines past me down the hall. I press my hand to my thigh, but hot, sticky blood seeps through my fingers. I try to stand, but my leg buckles beneath me. I catch myself on the doorjamb and bite back a cry of pain.

"Chad?" Zach's voice drifts in from the back of the house. "How could you do this, Chad?"

"Get out of my house!" Chad roars down the hallway. He follows up with another shot from the shotgun that deafens me for a moment.

I realize vaguely that maybe I should have been counting the shots. Three, maybe four? I can't remember how many rounds it was loaded with.

"Chad, come on, man, this is beyond insane," Zach calls.

"You shouldn't have brought him here, Zach!"

"You shouldn't have killed Emma!"

I use my good leg and my shoulder on the doorjamb to push myself up to standing. I steal a glance around the edge of the doorframe at Emma. The light above her chest has brightened into a swirling mass of silver and white light, spinning frantically above the silver ball on her chest. There's a second ball with Nina—the receiver. She's clutching it tightly, staring hungrily at the light that's quickly becoming too bright to look at.

Zach sprints down the hall, taking cover in the bedroom door. "You had no right, you bastard! I asked you for a favor, and instead you kill her?"

"Zach, I'm glad you're alive. But she's already dead. Nobody else has to die tonight," Chad says. "Nina needs her. I promised."

"So did I," I say. I limp into the hall. The light begins to flare and pulse, and I have to squint into the room. The ball on Nina's chest opens, and Emma's soul begins to swirl toward it. Chad swings the gun toward me.

"Turn it off, Chad." I sound so much stronger than I feel. Chad shakes his head. He levels the gun at my chest.

"I can't. Once it's caught, it's caught. And I ain't letting Nina die!" His fingers are white on the stock. His hands are shaking.

I want to tear the gun from his hands. I want to smash its butt in his face until he bleeds. Until he begs for the death that he so casually dealt to Emma. The receiver begins to beep. It's time.

I dive toward Emma.

Chad fires.

I'm knocked sideways by the impact of the shot to my chest. I fall to the floor next to Emma. It's hard to breathe. I'm vaguely aware of Zach screaming in the background, grabbing at Chad and the gun, but it's distant. Emma is close enough to touch. I reach out my hand. I cough, and red specks land on her blouse.

I know that I am dying. I can feel myself draining away, and everything fades into unimportance. Everything but Emma.

Nina starts to giggle in anticipation somewhere above me on the couch, but I can't see her past the searing white light swirling above Emma. It's the only thing that I can see. And in moments, that light will be sucked away forever. Emma will be well and truly gone. Just like her mother.

I try to push myself up, but my left arm won't cooperate, and I collapse to the side in an uneven heap. Everything seems so distant. So far away.

I lock my eyes on Emma. Trying to remember why I'm here. What I'm doing. I tuck my left arm around the hole in my chest and I use my right arm to shove myself to the side, toward Emma.

I roll on top of her, knocking the extractor away. The light explodes in the room, and Nina screams. I can't see, but I can hear. I reach up with my right arm, and my fingers close around the cold, smooth metal of the open receiver.

With the last of my strength, I tear it out of Nina's hands and collapse to the floor. My world draws in around me until there is nothing left in it but light and blood and pain. For the first time since Angela died, I offer up a prayer that at the very least, maybe we'll all see each other one last time. Just once. Just...please.

A rush of energy floods through my body. I can't breathe. Every muscle contracts as hot light sears its way through my body one cell at a time. And I stop being me.

TAYLOR PAYTON

My mind is flooded with images. Memories of Emma's life. She's three, walking through the doors of her preschool for the first time. Everything is so big and the teacher's so tall. Then she's seven, snuggling into her mother's lap and mouthing every word of *If I Owned the Zoo*. She's thirteen, diving into the pool at her first swim meet. She's fifteen, standing at her mother's graveside with my arm around her shoulders. She's seventeen and in love for the very first time, with a boy she knows I'd never approve of.

The images keep coming, flooding through my brain one after another so fast I can't see half of them. But I can feel it all. Emma—so brilliant, so alive. Her memories and her soul fill every corner of my mind.

I know Emma better now than I ever have before. She's part of me in a way that she's never been. And she's real, complete, and so very, very alive.

And then the tidal wave of images begins to subside. They slow, trickling away into empty corners of my mind I hadn't even known were there. The light fades, the pressure subsides, and I can breathe again. My whole body vibrates with energy, and I open my eyes.

I sit up. The room spins slowly to a halt.

Chad is lying on the floor with a shot through his chest. Nina is nearly dead on the couch. I can see details in the room in a way I couldn't see before. I can see the color even now draining from Chad's eyes, the shallowness of Nina's breathing. I can tell she doesn't have much time left even if there was something we could do.

Zach is squatting down against the far wall, fat tears running down his pale face. He's rocking back and forth ever so slightly. His hands are wrapped tightly around the shotgun.

"Zach." I'm surprised at how strong my voice sounds in my too-sensitive ears. "Zach. Help me with Emma."

Zach wrenches his eyes away from his cousin at the mention of my daughter's name.

"I didn't really mean...it just went off," he says. "And Emma's..."

"I need your help with Emma," I say again. He nods slowly, then uses the shotgun as a crutch to push himself to his feet.

I wrap my arm gingerly around my chest, expecting to feel the same burning pain as before, but the pain is dulled. Numbed. I feel at the bloody tear in my shirt, expecting to find shredded flesh beneath, but the hole is healing quickly. The edges have begun to close already. My side and my leg are beginning to itch terribly.

Zach sleepwalks across the room to me and drops the shotgun to the floor. His eyes are locked on Emma, who I've been avoiding but who I know now isn't really gone. Not now. Not ever. I can feel the energy of her soul vibrating inside of me, rejuvenating me. Filling me with such life as I had forgotten ever having at her age.

I look down.

The ache of seeing her like this threatens to overwhelm me. But there is nothing left in her body to mourn. I smooth back the hair from her face and kiss the cold skin of her forehead. But the coldness of loss, the anger and pain I felt at losing Angela isn't there. I thought the graver who took Angela had devoured her soul—destroyed who she was forever. But for the first time in my life, I know that she'll never be gone. Nothing in heaven or earth could destroy what she is. What she always will be. Angela believed the soul was eternal. She was right.

She was *right*.

I kneel beside my daughter's body and lift her into my arms. I expect to need help getting to my feet, but my leg supports me well enough.

"I'm so sorry, sir," Zach says between gasps for breath. And a memory comes to mind of the moment when Emma and Zach first met. I realize with a shock that it's Emma's memory.

It was at the feed store. We'd stopped in for seeds, and she was angry at me for bringing her to a place so primitive that she had to grow her own food, afraid of this new, simple world she knew nothing about, but most of all, desperately lonely for the mother she still missed so much.

Zach showed her how to feed the chickens. He laughed when she got scared and pulled away. He made her laugh for the first time in a long time—helped her feel hope again.

I'd never even noticed them talking.

"Zach," I ask, "is there anyone else for you here?"

Zach hesitates. He glances back at Chad and looks away quickly, as if he's going to puke. He shakes his head.

"It's all right, Zach. I didn't know it before, but I get it now. Everything's going to be okay. Come outside with me." I start carefully down the hall to the back door. The gunshot to my thigh is burning like hell as it heals, but my leg holds.

On the porch outside, I've gone as far as I can. I sink to the wood planking, cradling Emma in my arms, rocking her back and forth like I did when she was small. The cool breeze chills the tears on my face, and I realize I've been crying. The rain has finally stopped.

Zach sinks to the ground next to me. He takes Emma's hand and holds it gently. He draws a shuddering breath.

"I don't know what to do," he says.

"We're going to call the authorities," I answer. My voice is far steadier than I feel. Zach nods dumbly, and I can't tell if he's hearing me or not. "I'm sorry about your cousin," I add, thinking it the obligatory thing to say. But I'm surprised too, because for Zach's sake, I mean it. I know what it means to be alone. "Then you're going to come with me. And we're going to go home."

I find myself smiling through tears as I kiss Emma's forehead once more. I know without any doubt that it's what Emma would have wanted.

Wisteria Melancholy

written by

Michael T. Banker

illustrated by

MICHELLE LOCKAMY

ABOUT THE AUTHOR

Michael T. Banker grew up in New Jersey and currently lives in New York City where he works as an actuary in a life insurance company. Subway rides into and out of Manhattan are generally spent either with his nose in a book or furiously scribbling down notes for a story.

Not a terribly interesting existence. But that's the trick of stories, isn't it? They allow people to live more than one life, and the memories created within them are often more poignant and present than real events. Michael wants to create those memories for other people.

Michael's fiction has appeared in professional journals including the 2011 grand prize winner of Albedo One's Aeon Award *and* Orson Scott Card's Intergalactic Medicine Show. *Although he has only dabbled in short fiction so far, he is looking forward to cutting his teeth on novels in the near future.*

ABOUT THE ILLUSTRATOR

Michelle Lockamy never fit the classic Jersey girl description. As a kid she was a bit of a recluse, drawing on any paper she could find and reading books in lieu of attending parties. She grew up in many towns before finally settling in Browns Mills, where she can now commute to Philly.

Throughout her childhood, Lockamy found that art was always her favorite subject in school, and it just became her path. In high school, she got her first Wacom tablet and was introduced to digital tools as a medium. In 2011, the choice to go to Moore College of Art and Design for a BFA in illustration was a clear decision, and before she knew it, the tools she had taught herself to use gave her an edge in her artwork.

Her work has made it into CRED Philly, and onto a few indie book covers. Having her work included in Illustrators of the Future has been a most memorable experience.

She is determined to hit the ground running after she graduates in 2015. She wants to make the transition from student life to work life as simple as possible, which means working now to reap the rewards later.

Michelle is eternally grateful to her parents and professors, who encourage her to keep going. They remind her that hard work indeed pays off, no matter how rocky the road gets.

Wisteria Melancholy

Kessington House, the sign read. Dorm and Counseling for the Psychomorphically Unstable.

Psychomorphically Unstable. Unstable.

It looked rather plain, really, just a narrow slice of brick townhouse wedged between a barbershop and a deli. Self-effacing, even. I puffed out my chest, reached for the doorknob like I was shaking its hand and...

...put my ear to the door instead. Voices, I could hear voices. Kids laughing or crying—muffled yelps that could have been either. The brochure certainly hadn't mentioned kids.

Well, now or never, I pushed open the door and said one word: "Hello."

Pandemonium ensued. An Asian boy took one look at me and burst into a cloud of blue smoke, billowing out the neck and armholes of his tee-shirt and effusing through the room. His clothes plopped to the ground where he had been standing. Another boy screamed and disappeared, so that all I could see was a striped polo shirt, khaki shorts, and pair of socks running frantically around the room, stirring eddies in the smoke. "Who are you?" demanded a third boy, both visible and solid.

I had yet to budge, and the door swung back on its hinges and gently clicked shut between us. I had to actually reach out to open it again. I almost didn't.

"Hey! Come on now!" called a girl's voice from a back room. "What's going on here?"

I opened the door, fanning blue smoke out of my face. It was already thinner around the edges, concentrating in the center of the room. Flesh color bled back into it, until it finally condensed into the shape of a naked boy who gasped and hunched over himself and hobbled out of the room.

A girl strode in past him. "You guys! What in the world...oh! Oh, jeez, you scared me—hello there. You must be Mr. Fuller?" She clapped her hands together and smiled at me. "Welcome. Sorry about all that. Come in, come in."

In, I thought. It sounded so fatalistic. In.

I crossed the threshold and stood holding my duffle bag full of clothes. The girl looked maybe seventeen at first. Then I took in her black cherry lipstick, her swoop earrings and shoulder-length brown hair and mentally subtracted a year. She looked like a sixteen-year-old trying to look twenty.

"They told me to expect you next week," she explained. "I would have warned these guys. Not," she added, eying the two remaining boys, "that that's any excuse."

"I didn't disappear!" said the visible boy. The other one rocked on his heels—still just a pair of socks, shorts, shirt, and nothing else.

Something suddenly clicked for me. "You're not the, uh...psychologist, counselor, whatever they call it?" I asked the girl. "Are you?"

She smiled sheepishly. "Uh, yup. I'm Megan. Nice to meet you."

No, I thought. Really? *This* was what I'd signed up for? Dorming with grade-schoolers and counseling from a girl a whole decade my junior?

It was too much. That was exactly too much. I needed to sit down. I dropped my bag at the door and took four steps to a wooden chair. But the moment I set my weight on it, it creaked ominously.

Oh no. I should have known better. I tried to pick myself up but not quickly enough: my body had grown heavier than I could lift. The creaking descended an octave. There was a violent crack and a muffled thump, and then I landed on the carpet, watching a broken chair leg roll away.

"Oh," exclaimed Megan, with the satisfaction of making a diagnosis. "You're a *plumbeo!*"

Leaden. Indeed. As if it couldn't get any worse, the visible boy snickered, and for some reason, that was the nail in the coffin.

I became heavier than lead. My hands thumped to the ground and my head rolled onto my shoulder. Not five minutes into counseling, and already my disorder was taking over. What had I gotten myself into? With a tremendous deal of effort, I heaved myself up onto my knees.

"Oh no," protested Megan, "you really shouldn't..."

My breath came in labored gasps. My lungs felt stiff as tree bark, but once I got them going, they pumped like bellows. Apparently this girl expected me to just lie there like a sack of potatoes. Very slowly I pushed myself up onto my feet and, as an embarrassing groan tore out of me, straightened my legs to standing. Megan grimaced for all she was worth.

"Cool!" enthused the invisible boy.

"Are you okay?" Megan asked.

I rolled my shoulders forward in a shrug. My head wobbled uncertainly on my neck. "Where," I grunted through gritted teeth, "...room?"

"Oh! This way." She hopped over to grab my bag, then led me, alternately grimacing and smiling encouragement, down the hall. Picture frames rattled with each step I took. "Right here," she informed me and dropped off my bag.

I laughed when I saw the room, although it escaped my lips as a moan. The bed sheets were bubblegum-pink and the ceiling was decorated with glow-in-the-dark stars arranged into the shape of a heart. The walls were bare but specked with putty stains, remnants of the posters from the dozens of children who'd stayed here before me.

I stomped in and Megan shooed the two boys away. "Go ahead and take your time," she offered, shutting the door behind her. That was good of her.

I forgot myself and sat on the edge of the bed, which groaned savagely and deposited me onto the floor.

So this was my new home. I'd admitted myself into daycare, and the babysitter was going to teach me how to live my life again.

About half an hour later one of the boys from earlier poked his head in, knocking after he'd already opened the door. A real Dennis the Menace type—flop of fair hair, Dumbo ears, and roguish green eyes that wouldn't stay still. He looked sheepishly down at his feet, but I could tell it was an act.

"Can I come in?" he asked.

I nodded from my vantage point on the floor.

"You're still heavy."

I waved my arms around to demonstrate that they were light.

"You're not?"

"Nope," I said.

"Then why're you still on the floor?"

I shrugged.

"It means you were sad, right?"

"Oh. Sure, yeah." I scratched the back of my neck. "I guess I—" Words died in my throat as my eyes snagged on a shadow, like a dimple in the air. It deepened as I watched and sluiced into the shape of a boy. Suddenly there were two of them, mirror images of each other... except that the one who'd just materialized out of thin air was buck-naked.

The first boy followed my gaze, then jumped and smacked his forehead. "Dave! I can see you!"

"Huh?"

"I. Can. See. You."

The boy named Dave looked down at himself, patting his chest. "Crap."

The other one moved in front of him and grinned innocently. "Sorry about that. It's just that Dave here was a little nervous about meeting you, so since he was invisible already, he had the bright idea of taking off his clothes and tagging along. In-cog-nito."

"Ah," I looked around the clothed boy to address his brother, "but you must not be shy anymore. You're not invisible."

"I'm trying to be!"

His brother spun and poked a finger at him. "Go! Get out of here! Put some clothes on before Megan sees you, *fergodssake*."

Dave grabbed onto his brother's shirt and peeked over his

shoulder at me. "That was really cool before," he said, "how you picked yourself up all heavy like that." Then he fled the room, his brother kicking at his retreating butt.

I laughed under my breath. I had this raw feeling inside that I couldn't shake, but still I laughed. I felt strangely disconnected, invincible, unconcerned.

The remaining boy turned on his heels and sighed theatrically. "So," he said, "where were we?"

"Twins?" I asked.

"What? Oh, yeah. I'm Nate and he's Dave. But you'll never keep us straight, so most people just call us Nave. Get it? Like, *Arr, ye knave!*"

I nodded ... slowly.

"Don't look at me like that."

"How am I looking at you?"

"Like I'm crazy! Sarah came up with it. Anyway, I'll go let Megan know you're ready."

"No," I started, but he was already out the door.

I followed him through the common room and into the conjoined kitchen. It was a room with a personality disorder. Its linoleum floor tried to match the exact shade of gray of the common room rug, the wall tiles gleamed bathroom-white, and its functional sink and stovetop area cowered behind an unnecessary column. An island countertop crowded the center space like an afterthought. Megan was perched on a barstool at the counter, leg folded under her, munching granola and studying some notes in a purple binder.

"Megan!" called Nate. "The new guy's—oh! You followed me." He scratched the back of his head. "Well, uh, here he is." He backed out of the room, arms extended as if presenting me.

I spread my own hands, a wry here-I-am gesture. I still couldn't believe what I had signed up for. A moment passed where I genuinely wondered whose life I was living, and why I was taking it so seriously.

"I see—*mmm* ..." Megan covered her mouth, bobbing her head apologetically as she finished chewing and swallowed. "I see you've met Nave. Or at least half of them."

"Both." I hopped onto the last stool in the row. Megan's gaze drooped to the countertop. An awkward silence.

"We're alone, right?" I hazarded. "No naked, invisible boys hanging about?"

She laughed, which came out as a snort. "If you had any idea how much naked boy I've seen in this place. But no, I don't think so."

"Can I ask you something?"

"Uh, sure. I mean, of course."

"Is this the right place for me? You don't think I'd be better in a group more..." I shrugged, "my age?"

"Ah. Well, there's Sarah you probably haven't met yet, she's eighteen. Guess that's not really...But actually, the truth is you're not going to find many adults in these places. Partly because they don't like to put their lives on hold for live-in counseling, you know? But mostly because the problem's usually cured by then." She shrugged apologetically.

"This only started a few months ago," I said, feeling the need to defend myself.

"Oh, you're a late-case! Okay, well, that's usually less serious, actually. We can have our first session tomorrow. Finding the trigger is half the battle."

"Oh, I know what caused it," I said. "My sister pushed me off a cliff. I'm fairly certain that was the trigger."

Megan coughed. I could see her trying to decide whether I was making a crude joke. Well, why hold back? This was the point of counseling, right?

"She snuck up behind me," I explained, "invisible, but for some reason she appeared just as she was about to push. Naked, because, well...can't turn clothes invisible. So I saw that it was my little sister who did it. And instead of being surprised or scared, I was just incredibly sad as I fell and...Did you know that someone with my condition can survive a drop from a cliff with only cuts and bruises? Because..."

The stool creaked dangerously under me. I stood quickly. "I'm sorry."

"Oh dear. Here, uh...why don't you sit on the floor for a second?"

"No. I'm okay." I supported myself on the counter and walked rigidly back toward my room.

"Be careful!" Megan piped, but I waved her away. "Please, be careful. That's very bad for your knees, you know."

"He's doing it again!" yelled one of the twins, appearing at just the wrong moment. Suddenly I had an audience as I lumbered back to my room.

That night, I dreamt of my sister. She stood over me, naked, dead-pan. I was falling yet not getting farther. "I would have given you the money," I said. She just looked down at me. Then I really was falling and my sister shrank to a pinpoint above me until I hit the ground. But even that failed to stop me. I continued to fall, earth piling around me, past layers of rocks and fossils, through a pool of magma—

I woke up. The bed dipped in the middle, cradling me. I dragged myself to the side and rolled onto the floor. The bedsprings hissed and rattled with relief.

It turned out that Megan attended vocational school during the day and only worked here between the hours of four and eight. A personal tutor made the rounds for a few hours each morning and they called that the children's education. Parents made cursory visits to coddle their children and then abandoned them again. Basically, we never had to leave this place.

I watched in a half-stupor as Nate and Dave played their fifth game of Jenga on the carpet.

The tower collapsed in a river of blocks. Dave froze, holding the inciting piece in the air. "Oh, I know!" he said. "Let's show him the book."

Nate incorporated a shrug into his victory dance. "Okay. Come on."

"You know which..."

"Of course I know which book. Come on."

I watched them retreat down the hall. One of them banged on a closed door. "Sarah!" he called. "We're coming in!" Without any response that I heard, he opened the door and they scampered inside.

I followed around the corner, then froze, gaping, as I saw a teenage girl garbed funereally in black, lying on her bed reading a book. The twins rummaged through her bookcase, unconcerned. I hovered in the doorway, muttering things like "Uh, hi," and "Sorry..."

"She can't hear you," explained Dave.

"What?" I said. The girl's black hair fanned over her back and her even darker gown draped over the side of the bed. She shifted to turn a page, causing all those layers of black to drift over each other.

"That's her condition. Half the time she can't hear or see you, although sometimes I think she's faking."

"Got it." Nate emerged, brandishing a hefty hardcover which he dropped onto a corner of the bed that wasn't claimed by black. "Page three-eighty-four. Three...eighty-four..."

"Wait," I said. "Seriously? Can't we do this somewhere else?"

"Why? She doesn't care. Here we go: 'When the id and the super-ego become inextricably'...blah, blah, boring...'such conditions exist that'...la, la, la...'in the extreme case one may not become merely invisible, but also insubstantial, leading to such case-studies as Chelsea Becker, age five, who was able to *walk through walls.*' That, I want that! So cool!"

I reached over to snatch the book from him, but froze as the girl in black looked at me—or rather, through me. She might have been studying a speck on the wall. She had a plain face and surprisingly blue eyes.

I shivered. "I'm going to borrow this, okay?"

"No, wait," Nate said, "there's more."

"I'll be in my room."

The four levels of psychomorphism: Projection of self upon others; Perception of self; Perception of others; Projection of self upon self. A psychomorphic disorder occurs when any one of these levels becomes unstable.

—excerpt from *Human Circuitry,* by Marcy J. Sellers

The physical body is a mere projection of the ethereal self, as is evidenced by the class of disorders known as psychomorphic. Furthermore, this projection occurs in the unconscious portion of the mind.

—excerpt from *The Psychomorph's Paradox,* by J.J. Bosque

Curiously, there are even a few members of the kingdom plantae which demonstrate psychomorphic properties. The most notable is wisteria.

—excerpt from *Unexplained Science,* by Julie Ng

Why don't you start from the beginning?" Megan propped a notepad on her crossed legs, trying to look professional as we sat at the kitchen counter sipping cranberry juice. Her hair was braided today, showing off her daisy-shaped earrings, and her lips were merely glossed. The result was that she actually looked more mature than when she was trying too hard to be an adult.

I sighed. "It all started when Jessica had a baby." Well, who could say when it started? Jessica was *always* Jessica. "She was sixteen. About five years ago, I guess."

"Jessica, your sister? So what happened?"

I sat back on my stool. "My parents disowned her. Literally."

"Ooh…harsh."

"Yeah," I agreed. Megan was about the same age, wasn't she? "They were hard-asses. And Jessica wasn't the most mature sixteen-year-old, believe me. Not like you. But they didn't care, they kicked her out of the house anyway, forced her to fend for herself and her kid. We stayed in touch, barely, for about a year, and then she dropped off the face of the earth. My nephew along with her."

"Wow."

"And that was the last I knew until about six months ago. First my mother was hit by a car—a hit and run—and then my father…he was never healthy to begin with. He basically just gave up on living after Mom died. Their money—and they did have money—it all went to me. Obviously, because they disowned my sister, and she was nowhere to be found anyway. And then, well, you can piece together what happened."

"Your sister..."

I considered for a moment, then stood up and leaned against the counter to support my weight. "Just in case," I explained. "She pushed me off the cliff. I understand why, too. She had to have been living below the poverty level. She needed that money for her kid, and she came to the whacked-up conclusion that she had to kill me in order to get it. I hadn't disowned her, and she was my only kin. She did what she thought she needed to do."

"Oh."

"No, not 'oh,' that doesn't excuse it. She was my little sister." I leaned harder against the counter. "I would have given her the money, if she'd asked. I'm not my parents."

Megan opened her mouth, but just then there was a scream from the back of the house. "Get out!" came a girl's voice. "He was spying on me—pervert!"

"Was not! Was not! Was not!"

A flood of people spilled into the common room—Nate and Dave and that girl in black, Sarah.

Sarah pointed a shaking finger at one of the twins. "*He* spied on me. Megan, I was changing when this twerp appears out of thin air. He'd been invisible. In my room."

"Hellooo," said the boy. "I'm wearing clothes. If you couldn't see me, it was your own complex, not mine."

Megan threw up her hands. "Okay! I can't deal with this right now. We're in the middle of a session and you're all interrupting."

Sarah turned her blue eyes on me, making me feel like that speck on the wall again. "Who's this?"

"Jason," I answered, more curtly than I intended. "And actually, I think I'm good for today, Megan." I ran my hand against the stubble on my cheek. What was I doing here? How messed up was I? "I'm supposed to be the..." Adult, I was going to say. "Let's continue tomorrow."

At least this time I walked—not stomped—back to my room.

That night, I startled awake. What had been Jessica's muffled sobs bubbled out of my dream, into reality.

I sat up. Someone really was crying. Nave, I thought sympathetically. Only, was it coming from the common room?

My feet touched the carpet before I knew what I was doing. I opened the door and found the Nave boys, creeping down the hall like two soldiers on a mission. One of them put his finger to his lips.

"Who is it?" I whispered. That Asian boy who'd turned to smoke, I thought, but then I turned and saw him loitering down the hallway in green monster pajamas, standing with one bare foot atop the other. And there was Sarah, an enigmatic silhouette in her doorway. Megan was gone for the night, so who did that leave?

"You heard it, too?" whispered Nate or Dave. I could barely tell them apart during the daytime, so it was almost impossible to with the lights out. I mimed confusion, and he breathed, "Weird, right?"

They stalked to the end of the hallway and peeked around the corner, shoving each other to get a better look. This was silly. I was the adult and there was a child out there, crying. It could be serious.

"Who's there?" I said aloud. The twins jumped, knocking heads, and the sobbing broke off with a surprised and juicy sniff. "Hello?"

I patted the wall for a light switch.

Someone else found the switch first. The lights flickered on and I saw the couch rock back and then fall heavily on its feet. There was a scurry of footsteps, but I looked around and couldn't find anyone.

"He's invisible!" shouted the Nave boys, and they jumped into the room screaming wordlessly.

"Wait!" one of them called as his brother began to helicopter around the floor, reaching this way and that, lunging at real or imagined footfalls. "What are you doing? You know he has to be naked!"

"So?" huffed the spinning boy.

Jenga blocks scattered spontaneously and both twins screamed again. I heard a door shut and looked back to find Sarah gone. The Asian kid had his butt planted on the hallway floor, and behind me the Nave boy was yelling, "You're gonna touch his junk! You're gonna touch his junk!"

"Stop!" I shouted. The other Nave just looked at me as he sprinted across the room, hitting the wall bodily with a grunt and then turning and swinging his arms wildly as he regained momentum. "Stop!" I yelled again, even louder. "Stop! Stop! What are you thinking? That's a boy just like you. He's obviously very lost and afraid, and you just chased him around the room. What do you think about that? Huh?"

The Nave boy scuttled upright on the couch and hunched there, wide-eyed, like a jackrabbit who'd just watched me grow a wolf's fangs.

"I heard a door close," said the other twin, looking at the front entrance.

"That was Sarah," I told him. We all froze for a space, listening to each other breathe.

"Maybe he can walk through walls."

I stared at the Jenga blocks scattered all over the floor. "Maybe," I said. "Or maybe he's a new patient Megan forgot to tell us about. Or...I don't know." I considered calling out for him, but it was so incredibly silent. If he was there, he didn't want to be found. "We'll ask Megan in the morning. Let's just get back to sleep."

Megan twirled the cord of the phone around her index finger. The Jenga blocks lay strewn around her feet, preserved like a crime scene. "Really? Nothing? I should do nothing?"

"I heard the toilet flush last night," said one of the twins. "I think probably it was the Ghost."

"Wicked," said the other.

Megan put her hand over the receiver and practiced one of her motherly looks. "Guys! I've got the agency on the—yes, hello, I'm still here. No, I told you, I wasn't there, but...But that's just the problem, we *can't* see him. Yes, but what should I do? For all I know, he might still be here!"

"Wicked," echoed the twin.

I was chopping string beans on a cutting board in the kitchen and trying to remember if I had used the bathroom myself last night. I scraped the beans into the wok and gave it a splash of soy sauce.

Megan hung up the phone. "I give up. I can't talk to them. They said to call again if I see him, and I said that's exactly the problem: we can't see him."

"We heard," said Dave.

"Wisteria," said someone else.

We all turned. Sarah glided into the common room and collapsed onto the couch, head lolling tragically as she read from a book.

"Drama queen's reciting poetry again," Dave groaned, clearly used to this. Nate tiptoed over and sat next to her, put his hands on his knees and puffed up as if he were about to perform. Sarah didn't even flick an eyelash. I wondered how someone could disdain other people's company so much that she literally turned them off.

"Strangled by wisteria," Sarah muttered to no one—to an empty room, as far as she was aware, or cared. Nate wrapped his hands around his throat dramatically, as if he were being strangled.

"My heart, too, blossoms," she recited.

He clutched his heart and staggered to his feet.

"Heavy purple flowers."

He sank to the ground.

"Melting to mist."

"Melting, melting!"

"I am gripped by."

"I am *gripped!*"

"A wisteria melancholy."

"A wis-steamy melody."

"I can hear you," Sarah drawled.

"I can—wait, really?"

Dave fell over, laughing. I glanced at Megan, who shrugged helplessly. "Did you write that yourself, Sarah?" I asked, making an effort, but she just sank deeper into the cranberry cushions, black gown and black hair claiming their territory.

"See," complained Nate, "she's faking. I told you she fakes." He waved his arms in front of her face.

"Dinner's almost ready," I said. "Does Sarah block out smells, too?"

I nudged Dave, who was still laughing so hard he was going to give himself a belly-ache. "Come on."

"Wait," he gasped. "I have to get something." He stamped into the hall, shouldering the corner as he rounded it.

"Get Eric," I called after him—that shy Asian boy who blew up into smoke when I first arrived.

Sarah did eventually meander over, and we each claimed our own stool around the counter. We didn't have a spare stool for me to break if I got heavy again. Dave showed up last, toting that hefty hardcover on psychomorphism—from my room. He dropped it with a thud on the counter and flipped through it.

"Wisteria," he read between mouthfuls of stir fry.

"Wisteamia," corrected Nate.

"Wisteria," Dave repeated. "Stupid. 'Wisteria is the only known plant to display caliginous properties.'"

Eric made a sound into his bowl. He was a *caligino:* "misty."

"'The blossoms of most varieties explode in a pinkish-purple, intensely fragrant mist. As psychomorphic,'" Dave enunciated the word, "'disorders typically stem from psychological causes, the wisteria vine has provoked waves of controversy within the scientific community.'"

"I want to visit the Lady of Wisteria," muttered Eric. We all looked at him. Those were among the first dozen words I'd ever heard Eric speak. He looked surprised himself to have said them.

"Yeah," covered Dave, "I've heard of her. *Caligino* to the extreme. She, like, turns to mist herself and spreads out across the whole garden every year when the wisteria blooms."

"I want to go," repeated Eric as he shoveled sticky rice into his mouth.

I can tell you," I explained slowly to Megan, "exactly why my sister went invisible, and why she appeared when she did." Megan just raised a sympathetic eyebrow and waited for me to go on. I did all the talking during these sessions.

"Jessica turned invisible," I said, "out of guilt. Happened constantly, ever since she discovered she was pregnant. Before we even knew what she was feeling guilty about. It was a real problem, on top of everything else. When she got the boot for good, kicked out, she was invisible then, too. I just watched a canary top and blue jeans walk out of my life. Anyway, the point is, when she was getting ready to push me off the cliff, I'm sure she felt plenty guilty." My vision blurred a bit; I envisioned Jessica's empty hazel eyes.

"And why she appeared?" Megan prompted.

"Yeah. She appeared in that moment, just before she pushed me, her big brother, too late to turn back...I think, because she died inside. Everything, her guilt too, just...died." I shook my head, picturing those eyes. "Dead."

Megan maintained a respectful silence for a moment. Then, out of nowhere, she smiled and patted my shoulder. "Listen," she said.

"Why? For what?"

"Nothing," was her enigmatic response. Then she clapped her hands together. "The sound of your stool *not* creaking! You're doing so much better than when you started, what, three weeks ago?"

I managed to smile a bit. "Yeah. I guess so."

When the letter came, it was deceptively light in my hands. Its disarmingly loopy script read: "Jason Fuller. Urgent! Open immediately."

I felt a twinge of trepidation as I slid my finger into the slit and worked it open. The letter inside was pink. Why pink? Who sends a pink letter? I pulled it out, shook it flat. Only a few typed lines graced the page.

After I read it the letter fluttered out of my hand, and I followed it a moment later to the ground. I fell to my knees with enough force to dislodge a framed picture off the wall. Then I slowly keeled to the side, until I landed with another thud.

The whole townhouse was instantly around me. "What happened?" demanded Megan.

But my teeth were clenched shut.

Jason,

I'm sorry to write to you under these circumstances, but Jessica has passed away. Her body was found floating in the Tennyrill River on Tuesday. For some reason the constable showed up on my doorstep. I know you have your own issues right now, but please take responsibility for your sister's funeral. I jotted down the phone numbers you'll need below.

I would have told you in person, but your institution is stingy with information.

With Love,
Aunt Patricia

Jessica...

My eyes had become slits: too heavy to open, too much bother to close. The world passed in a blur through my eyelashes. People walked around me, stepped over me. Sarah tripped on my head. The twins sat on me once before Megan shooed them away. Then I felt hands on my back, legs, shoulder, heaving, heaving, but I budged less than a foot before they gave up, huffing and panting and leaning against me for support.

The odd thing was, I had felt closer to my kid sister after she was banished from my life than when we were squabbling over who got the TV. She became my imaginary friend: I held lengthy conversations with her in my studio apartment. She needed me, but I didn't know how to help her. I needed her, too. Just knowing she was out there, with her kid, I felt an incredible bond that didn't deteriorate with the years.

Jessica...

People sat/crouched/lay in front of me, speaking words that sounded like waves crashing against a faraway cape. Bowls of food were placed before my nose, cutting off my view of the couch. They smelled disgusting, like rotten eggs. I groaned, and they took them away.

I thought of my nephew belatedly, guiltily. Kevin, she had named him. Aunt Patricia hadn't mentioned him in her letter. A narrative began to form in my mind: after years of my sister eking out a living, Kevin had finally succumbed to illness or accident or hunger. I had to believe that Jessica would have found a way

410

to survive as long as her son needed her. But without him, she killed herself. My parents had been wrong about her. She loved her son enough to push me off a cliff.

Jessica...

Sarah sat on the couch. I stared at her legs. Pale legs under a black skirt. "String my heart up by the stars," she recited quietly to herself, not knowing or caring that I was there. Or maybe this poem was actually for me. "Stretch it. Zap it with light. What constellation does it form?"

Somewhere out of the mists of memory, I heard my sister's voice: "It's Cassiopeia, moron." I remembered: I was maybe twelve, and my best friend and I were trying out my new telescope. We were puzzling out a certain constellation when Jessica, being the brat kid sister she was, stuck her chin out and said, "It's Cassiopeia, moron." I'm pretty sure she had a crush on my friend and was showing off. After some obligatory yelling and chasing around the house, Jessica sat with us and pointed out all the constellations she had just learned in Earth and Space Science. Mom and Dad somehow forgot that we were up, and before we knew it we were out there until midnight.

I lifted my head; I could feel the tendons sticking out on my neck. I needed to get away—needed to escape Sarah's poetry. Didn't want to hear it. Didn't want to remember Jessica's face before it became a mask. I rolled onto my elbows and army-crawled all the way across the rug. Sarah, oblivious to me and my struggle, chased me out with poetry. "Pierced by moonlight. Sizzling, incandescent. The color of bleached bones."

I dragged myself past the threshold of my room and collapsed there, a beached whale, my feet still sticking out of the doorway. I thought: I will never move from this spot again. I'll die here.

Jessica...

I stared at Megan's feet as she sat on my bed. Yellow-and-purple-striped toe socks. "You're depressed because you'll never get the chance to forgive your sister," she said. Never before had I heard her sound so sure of herself. I waited for her to go on, but the bed springs creaked, and the purple-and-yellow toe socks stepped over me and away.

That same night I was visited by "Ghost"—the invisible boy who had become something of a legend in the household. The boy who had the twins counting toilet flushes at night and then quizzing us in the morning, plus keeping track of missing food items in the fridge. He hugged me and cried into my cement leg. I knew it was him because I recognized the sound of his sniffling sobs. His tears must have been lubricant, because I found the strength to curl my knee to give him a better pillow.

Then, one morning, I simply awoke with a pounding headache and ravishing appetite. Food, I thought groggily, and pushed myself up by the edge of the bed. It groaned, but held my weight. I hobbled as far as the door before I realized what I was doing and thunked back down to the ground. I wrapped my arms around myself and sat there, staring at my door.

One of the Nave boys stepped through it. He gaped and scrambled out of the room, announcing, "He got up! That was the crash! He's up—was up!" A minute later, the whole townhouse filed in and milled around me. Megan was there. Even Sarah and the chronically shy Asian boy, Eric.

"We've come to a decision," announced Nate (or Dave), bouncing with excitement. "We are going to..." he drew it out, "leave the townhouse and...visit the Lady of Wisteria!"

"It's blooming right now," enthused the other twin. "And Eric really wants to go."

As I lugged myself over to the kitchen, Megan fell into step beside me, smiling secretly. "They're doing this for you, you know. We had a house meeting, and this is what they decided. Say yes."

My lips curved into something resembling a smile. "I think I missed my sister's funeral," I said. Megan stopped walking, and I turned to face her. "Yes, I'd love to visit the Lady of Wisteria."

After eating, I tried calling Aunt Patricia, but all I got was her voice mail. The recorded message beeped, and for a long moment I just stared at the receiver. *Is my sister in the ground?* I wondered. *Did you honor Kevin at the same funeral?*

I slowly brought the receiver to my mouth. "It's me," I said

softly. "Uh, Jason. Call me when you get a chance. How was…"
I grimaced. "Just call me." I gave the number to Kessington
House and hung up.

Come the following morning, Aunt Patricia still hadn't returned
my call and the townhouse was all ready to visit the Lady of
Wisteria.

We had a tough time even getting out the door, though. The
twins took turns quacking, "Sarah, Sarah, Sarah," until she finally
looked up from the couch and realized that we were leaving.
Then on our way out, Nate disappeared. He sat down—cargo
pants and a green windbreaker—and cried: He hadn't gone
invisible in a while, he didn't know why it happened, he didn't
mean for it to happen, and he was sorry for Eric if they had to
cancel their trip because of him. But Megan pulled the cleverest
trick I'd seen yet. She said, "Oh look, see, you're already back,"
and Nate sniffed and said, "Oh, really?" He got up, and by the
time he reached the door, he really was visible.

I sat next to Sarah on the train. She stared out the window
and sighed tragically every once in a while. I asked, "So what's
the deal with Eric?" and was mildly surprised when her blue
eyes actually turned toward me.

"He gets scared," she answered.

I glanced up the aisle at him. "Quite the reaction," I commented.

"He was a war baby. Things exploded all around him, so now
he explodes when startled." That image seemed to give her some
morbid satisfaction.

"And Megan?" I asked. You never knew. I don't know why I
suddenly had this fascination with all of our disorders. "Anything
there? Maybe overcame something?"

"She gets a few pounds heavier when she's sad, lighter when
she's happy. That's all she's mentioned."

Like I used to be, I mused. Common enough, not really
considered a disorder. "And what about you?" I asked. "Are you
just depressed? Do you have the 'wisteria melancholy'?"

She shrugged. "I'm content."

I raised an eyebrow. "You're content, so you wear black? And shut people off?"

"I'm content *because* I shut people off. And I like black." She sounded a trifle annoyed. "It's for me. I don't care what other people think."

"So what, you're in live-in counseling so you don't have to do anything, or deal with other people?"

I was about to say more when I realized that she was looking through me rather than at me, and then she turned her head and gazed out the window again. I apologized, knowing that she couldn't hear me. This time when she sighed, I didn't think of it as tragic. More like the wistful poet contemplating the world's pathos.

The station where we all filed out was dingy and faded. The ticket booth's peeling green paint revealed dirty red paint underneath: an echo of an echo of better days. The bright sun rudely exposed weathered planks and a rust-stained railing. Only the tracks looked polished and new, from the trains that passed through.

"Are we sure about this place?" asked Sarah.

Megan grimaced. "Map Man, this was the station, right?"

Dave pulled the map out of his pocket and crinkled it open. "Yeah, look," he said. "Churchbrook. See? We circled it in red."

"Okay, come on," said Megan. "Stay close. Put away that map, we don't want to look like tourists."

"But—"

"I know, but we don't want to look like them. I remember the turns we marked, don't worry."

The streets were wide yet suffocating. The buildings' second levels jutted out, blocking the sun and muffling our footsteps as we shuffled down the center in our tight cluster. Eric followed with doe eyes. Dave developed a twitch in his neck that had him looking over his shoulder every six seconds. But at least the streets were well labeled. We made the first turn and had already reached the next one when we realized that we had lost Sarah. We had to jog back and then I directed her by the shoulders. I'm not sure if she felt my hands, or if her mental block encompassed even human contact, but she turned then as if she had always intended to go that direction.

Then we emerged. Broken pavement gave way to cobblestone. Wooden buildings became stone foundations with cement tops. A metal gate stood before us, delicately arched on top with stylized lettering: "Wisteria Garden."

"Wow," said the twins. Eric was grinning, his dark eyes reflecting the purple of the garden.

The gate glided smoothly on its hinges. No guards stopped us or asked for tickets. We entered with our heads tilted up— and coughed simultaneously. The heady, overwhelming scent of wisteria lodged in my throat. Enough sweetness to suck the saliva out of my mouth and leave my tongue caked with sugar.

"Strangled by wisteria," recited Sarah reverently. Wisteria was a vine, I realized then, not a tree: the vine strangled the tree. Sometimes to death, it seemed. I noticed one tree, a delicate maple, had collapsed, but still the wisteria constricted around it. Here and there a spray of green leaves escaped the wisteria's embrace, grasping for the sun.

"My heart, too, blossoms," continued Sarah. "Heavy purple flowers." The delicate flowers hung like bunches of ripe grapes. Along one sturdy bough they dangled over our heads like a living chandelier.

"Melting to mist." Gushing fountains of purple, bleeding pink into the air. We stood in a suspended cloud of perfume.

"I am gripped by a wisteria melancholy."

It felt like walking through a dream. Someone two steps away became a silhouette, veiled in mist.

"Nate!" called Dave, an edge of panic to his voice. "Where did Nate go?"

We all looked around.

"Dave!" came the answering call a moment later. I watched the two of them reunite after mere moments away. What happened to make them this way? Was it a tragedy? We were all subtly or profoundly broken.

Everyone else peeled off one by one. I was alone, and it felt incredibly peaceful. I wandered, brushing my fingers against the trunk-like vines, tapping the occasional bunch of flowers and watching them sigh pink clouds. Jessica would have hated this, I thought fondly. She hated anything girly: dresses, the color pink, and especially flowers. They had probably surrounded her in flowers at her funeral. I wondered if Aunt Patricia might have called since this morning.

"Welcome," breathed a voice in my ear. "Are you enjoying my garden?"

I looked left and right, but saw nothing except the mist that I'd disturbed. Airy laughter floated down to me like popping bubbles.

"Oh, I've seen better reactions than that," sighed the voice. It was decidedly female, but breathy, making her age difficult to place. I heard it in one ear and then the other, as though its source were flitting around my head. "You must have been expecting me. Were you?"

"The Lady of Wisteria," I said.

"Mm-hmm."

Neither of us said anything for several moments. I just inhaled the fragrant mist, then exhaled it through my nose, conscious that a portion of that mist was probably the Lady herself.

"Wait, don't go," I said, suddenly afraid that the Lady might drift off to the next visitor of her garden.

"I was thinking of it," she admitted, sounding a bit farther away. "Okay. Amuse me."

"I expected something..."

"Different?" she finished.

"Sadder," I qualified.

That made her laugh again. "Who could be sad in a garden like this? Especially when it's in full bloom, my goodness."

"I thought... I heard that the wisteria melts because it's sad."

"Wisteria isn't sad. It's happy, light. Free. Like me."

I tilted my head up, the direction I'd last heard the Lady. "But how can you be a *caligino* if you're happy? You're psychomorphic, very much so. Happy people don't develop psychological disorders."

416

That indescribable laughter again, like air blown over the rim of a glass: unexpected resonance. "Don't they? I don't like that word, disorder. To me it's more like..." I felt the mist sigh around me. "A different sort of order."

She sounded like Sarah.

"If you fight it, though," whispered the lady, "then you'll certainly be unhappy."

"That..." I clamped my mouth shut, afraid to finish the sentence. It *makes sense,* I wanted to say. It wasn't the world as I knew it, but it made a perverse sort of sense. I was unhappy because I struggled. I struggled because I tried to force the world to fit my personal view of it. My parents should have been more understanding. My sister should have remained innocent. But something about the wisteria, the lady, the day, made me want to let it all go. I felt disconnected again, but more so—I felt *light.*

"Oh, my," trilled the lady. "You're floating."

I looked down at my feet. The ground was indeed drifting away, like falling, but in reverse. I felt like a mote of dust caught on an updraft.

"Now I'm glad I didn't leave," commented the lady. "You've become interesting after all."

"I'm euphoric," I explained. I realized that I had never truly been happy since Jessica had pushed me off the cliff. I had become miserable enough to curl up on the ground like a fetus made of lead, but all that time the potential had been there to let the world be the ugly place it wanted to be and just float.

"My garden always makes people happy."

I spread my arms out, drifting like a dandelion seed, gently pushing myself off the vine-covered trees. That was when I heard from below, "Uncle Jason!"

I looked sharply down. Uncle Jason? I instantly thought of my nephew Kevin.

Which of course made me think of Jessica. Jessica's empty hazel eyes, looking down on me from my dreams; Jessica's corpse, floating in the river on her back, staring up with the same glazed expression. And poor Kevin, who'd never even had a chance.

MICHELLE LOCKAMY

It all hit me anew. Reality. I could turn my back for a moment, but then it came crashing back.

I plummeted out of the sky. It wasn't far. One moment I was floating, the next lying face up on the ground, staring at eddies of pink mist churned up from my descent.

"Uncle Jason."

I felt small, invisible arms wrap around my leg. A boy cried into my knee. I was so surprised I forgot to be lead. "Ghost?" I asked. And then, more cautiously, "Kevin?"

The boy sniffed an affirmation. Impossible. My nephew, Kevin. I hadn't truly believed he was alive. But that habit of invisibility... he was Jessica's kid, after all.

And then another thought: Where had Jessica been all this time? Close enough to watch me? To point me out to Kevin? Did they even follow me to Kessington House? What did she tell him about me, that he came to me once he realized that his mother was never coming home? He knew I was "Uncle Jason."

"Kevin," I said, sitting up. I realized that I could see him—I could see a little boy-shape where he displaced mist. I leaned forward and pulled him into a proper hug. "Why did it take me floating like an idiot for you to speak up?"

Kevin didn't stop crying, so I didn't stop hugging. Not until faces emerged from the mist. Megan and Eric, followed by Sarah and the twins. Everyone talked at once.

"It *was* you," said Megan.

"I heard a crash!" said Nate.

"Look at that dent he made in the ground!" said Dave.

"Guys," I said, quieting them. One by one they seemed to notice the form in my arms. "Meet Ghost," I said. "A.k.a. my nephew, Kevin."

The Nave boys gibbered. "He came all the way on the train and stuff?"

"Apparently," I said. Now that Kevin had latched onto me, he didn't want to let go. I lifted both him and myself off the ground.

"Are you okay?" asked Sarah, the last person I would have expected to show concern.

"Oh, yeah. I've fallen much farther than that. Think we could head on home?"

Megan nodded eagerly, then looked around. "Um...if we can find home."

Good point. I had an idea, though. "Are you still here?" I called.

Everyone looked at me quizzically until an ephemeral voice answered, "Mm-hmm."

"Would you mind humming or something? Lead the way for us?"

There was a brief pause before she answered, "For you, I suppose."

Apparently the lady hadn't visited the rest of them, because the expression on Eric's face was priceless.

Even on the walk back to the train, I felt shrouded in mist. The jutting buildings cast shadows over our group, adding to the cloistered feeling. I wanted to celebrate the discovery of my nephew, but felt oddly subdued.

Dave thrilled: "I still can't believe he was in the house that whole time and we couldn't find him. It was—" he started to count on his fingers.

"Nine days," filled in Nate.

"And on the train! I bet he locked himself in the bathroom. That's what I would have done. Does he even talk?"

"He'll talk when he's ready." I said, glancing down toward the invisible boy holding my hand. "He's only said my name twice so far." And that was when I was floating away. After trailing me so tenaciously, I'd finally gone somewhere he couldn't follow. He had no choice but to talk.

"How old is he?" asked Megan.

I did some quick mental arithmetic. "Five," I answered.

"That's incredible that—"

"Good afternoon, folks," said a man behind us. "Come from visiting the garden? Nothing to be afraid of, this is going to be quick and painless."

I began to turn, but several things happened at once.

Suddenly the mist was back, but deep blue this time, and I

realized that Eric had exploded, as he had the very first time he saw me. The twins turned invisible and their empty clothes clung to each other. Sarah yelled over the commotion, "Hey, guys! What happened? Guys!"

By then I had turned full around, and I saw a man holding a pistol. He wore a bright yellow raincoat, which would have been disarming if it didn't strain over an intimidating bulk. His bald head was smeared with mud. He whipped his gun around, fanning the blue smoke out of his face.

"Freaks," he cursed.

Megan was trying to pull Sarah away from the danger, but for some reason Sarah struggled against her, blind to everything that was happening. "Why'd Kevin explode? Guys?"

The first thing I did was push my nephew away. I probably used more force than was necessary, but I didn't have time to think. Submerged in mist again, it felt oddly like a dream. I stepped forward, trancelike, in front of the man.

He panicked. Two shots echoed against the buildings.

Then all was quiet. The man's eyes grew slowly wide. He jammed his pistol into his pocket, keeping his eyes on me. He backed away a few steps, shook himself, and turned and ran.

I looked down; stuck my finger through a hole in my jacket. He'd shot me. He'd shot me, but...I felt fine.

Still looking down, I noticed the ground drift away between my feet. Floating again—

Invisible hands gripped my ankle.

I smiled. "I'm sorry, Kevin. I'll try to keep my feet on the ground from now on, okay?" And for the first time, I wanted my body to do something and it did it. One heel and then the other touched the pavement.

"Jason," called Megan. "Are you okay? You're okay, right? Oh good." I wasn't sure myself. I pulled up my shirt to get a better look. There were marks, but...

"Pinpricks," I answered. Slowly, slowly, my appropriate weight settled back into me. "I guess," I reasoned, "if I'm light enough to float, then there's not much substance for a bullet to pierce."

My head was still in the clouds. Thinking would come later, I decided. I was vaguely aware that my brief step away from reality had likely just saved my life.

But then there was my future, invisible and clinging to my pant leg.

I had returned to Kessington House that afternoon to find a message from Aunt Patricia. They hadn't held the funeral yet. They'd been trying to find Kevin first. I called her right back to share the good news.

"Have you met Kevin?" I asked Aunt Patricia at the funeral home. I nodded toward my hand, which looked like it was gripping air.

"Oh." Her voice raised an octave, but then she knelt with impressive composure. "Nice to meet you, Kevin," she said to the air beneath my hand. "I'm your Great Aunt Patricia. I'm so glad you found your Uncle Jason to take care of you."

I still couldn't believe that. When Kevin was ready to talk, I'd ask him about what he went through, and how exactly he found me.

"You are going to look into…treatment?" she asked.

"Oh, yes," I assured her. "I know a very good place."

The ceremony was open casket, so after I had mingled and made introductions, I hoisted Kevin onto my shoulder so that he could say goodbye to his mom. It was a tough call to make, letting him see her like this, but there was only this one chance. And besides, I needed it as well.

They had dressed Jessica up in a nice, respectful dress, combed her cherry-brown hair, washed her up; it was hard to imagine that body floating down a river. What caught my breath, though, was her expression. She'd looked dead in my dreams, but in actual death, she seemed quite peaceful.

Then I heard gasps behind me, and I turned my head and saw my nephew for the first time since Jessica had left with him: naked and clinging to me like he would never let go.

Poseidon's Eyes

written by

Kary English

illustrated by

MEGEN NELSON

ABOUT THE AUTHOR

Kary English grew up in the snowy Midwest where she avoided siblings and frostbite by reading book after book in a warm corner behind a recliner chair. She blames her one and only high school detention on Douglas Adams, whose Hitchiker's Guide to the Galaxy *made her laugh out loud while reading it behind her geometry textbook.*

Today, Kary still spends most of her time with her head in the clouds and her nose in a book. To the great relief of her parents, she seems to be making a living at it. Kary lives on the West Coast with a spouse, a teenager, and a polydactyl feline overlord. She is working on a planetary fantasy series (available in late 2015) and a middle grade fantasy saga about a little girl and an orange kitten.

A student of New York Times *bestsellers David Farland and Tracy Hickman, Kary aspires to make her own work detention-worthy. Her fiction has appeared in* Daily Science Fiction, the Grantville Gazette *and* Galaxy's Edge.

ABOUT THE ILLUSTRATOR

Megen Nelson was born in 1991 in Palm Bay, Florida. She has been drawing ever since she could hold a pencil, encouraged by her friends and family. When she discovered Hayao Miyazaki's films, dragons began to crawl out of her sketchbook, joined by giant wolves and sometimes the odd space ship.

It wasn't until high school that she discovered that art could be a profession. In 2011 she was accepted into the Computer Animation program at the Ringling College of Art and Design, but was unable to attend. Instead, she studied art at Eastern Florida State College while pursuing her Associate in Arts (AA) degree, where she was honored for her work.

She is now attending the University of Central Florida, majoring in English literature, which is her second artistic love. She will graduate with her bachelors in 2015. Currently she helps write and construct online web courses for use in colleges all around the world. She also does freelance illustration and comic work when her schedule isn't a many-headed beast. She has written two novels and illustrated a children's book, and hopes to combine her love of art and writing into something awesome.

Poseidon's Eyes

Sometimes you can get to know a whole town by understanding just one man. In the seaside village of Summerland, that man was Peyton Jain. Peyton was in his 60s, as best I could tell. His face was craggy and weathered, with a beard like sea foam on rocks and eyes of Poseidon's blue.

Some folks thought of Peyton as a nuisance to be reported or a vagrant to be run off, but I knew different because it was Peyton who put me right with Summerland's spirits. The locals have joked about spirits as long as anyone can remember, but it took the murder of the Kelly children to remind us just how real—and how powerful—the spirits could be.

Summerland sits like the Pythia over a cleft in the rock, soaking up the vapors of prophecy along with the California sunshine. Spiritualists started a commune here over a century ago. Egalitarians at heart, they outlawed money and divvied the land into tent-sized plots.

Oil—oil money, really—edged the Spiritualists out. Derricks took over the beach, and the Spiritualists' canvas utopia turned into a shantytown for oil workers. My house was made from two of those oil shanties sandwiched together. The shanties had been built before electricity, so the wiring came up through holes in the floor, and the doorbell was an old ship's bell, corroded green with salt and time.

The house had no foundation, just posts and piers and seven jacks. When the floor sagged, Peyton crawled beneath to twist the jacks until everything was more or less level. That was a blessing to me because I couldn't abide the narrow crawlspace with earth pressing in around me and voiceless whispers winding snakelike over my skin.

The county said the whispers were nothing to worry about. Radon gas. Natural seepage. Buy a detector and install a fan. But radon doesn't creep up through the floorboards in silver ribbons until it pools in the corners, like living smoke. Radon doesn't whisper in the darkness like waves on sand.

But spirits? That's exactly what they do.

Peyton's battered brown pickup rumbled up the hill while I was taking out the trash. A Sport King camper perched on the back, listing to one side like the shell of a hermit crab. The old truck clunked into park just outside my front gate, and Peyton leaned out the window. He looked bright-eyed and freshly showered, which should have meant he was doing well, but his passenger window had been busted out and covered with blue painter's tape and an old trash bag, and that meant trouble.

"'Morning, Danaë," he called. "Brought you something."

Peyton always called me by my right name—Danaë. Everyone else in town just called me Dani.

He extended one hand through the open window, and his fingers uncurled like the fronds of an anemone. Nestled in his palm was a piece of green beach glass, the edges worn smooth by sand and waves.

I accepted the offering and thanked him, turning the glass like a worry stone between my fingers.

"Wait a minute," I said. "I thought you had a spot away from the beach? That Harris kid giving you a hard time again?" Ike Harris, a teenager with a new Mustang, lived in the Mansions across town.

Peyton gave a shrug that meant yes. "He comes down at night, partying with his friends." Peyton nodded toward the shattered window. "Broke my window. Cops won't do nuthin 'cuz nobody saw it." Dejection colored Peyton's voice. That truck was all he had, and a new window was more than he could afford.

"Want some coffee?" I offered.

"Nah, I just had coffee."

"I'm about to make eggs. You hungry?" Sometimes Peyton needed money when he stopped by. I didn't always have it, but I could manage an extra place at the table.

Peyton brightened at the thought of breakfast, and for a moment his eyes matched the blue of the white-tipped sea. "I'll take eggs. Café was packed when I was down there. No place to sit."

"More news crews?" Summerland hadn't seen a murder in more than fifty years, and the Kelly trial had turned our sleepy little town into the media's favorite chew toy. Most of the old-timers wouldn't talk, but that didn't stop reporters from badgering all and sundry with questions about vengeful spirits.

"I picked up a job today," said Peyton, following me into the kitchen. "Aames wants me to help Reesie move."

"Move? She finally leavin'?"

Peyton nodded. "Divorce was final 'bout four months back. Papers say he can have her evicted if she doesn't leave on her own."

"What's he doin' with the house?" Aames was old Summerland, used to live near the post office, but Reesie had insisted on one of the new places in the fancy gated development near the top of the hill before she'd marry him. Said the gate would keep out the riff-raff, which I suppose meant shanty folk like us.

"Dunno," said Peyton. "Sell it, most likely."

I poured the eggs into the skillet. The new places were a bone of contention for us old Summerlanders. Before the Mansions went in, most of us walked or rode bicycles in the open air, and dogs slept in the middle of the street. After the Mansions, stockbrokers barreled through town in Range Rovers, and dogs were something glittering women carried in designer purses.

"Built too tight, those new places," said Peyton. "Stuff gets in, can't get out again. That's when the trouble starts."

Peyton fixed me with those blue eyes of his, and his voice was like crushed shells. "A house is like your heart, Danaë. Long as it's open, nothing'll get trapped inside to fester in the dark places."

I shivered cold at that, picturing the silver rivulets streaming up through my floorboards the week before, the same ones that had surrounded Percy's crib when I'd brought him home from the hospital almost twenty years before. Peyton had come by to see the baby and found me in tears, trying to seal off Percy's windows with plastic sheeting to keep the vapors out. That's when he explained about Summerland's spirits. He said they were harmless so long as my heart was in the right place, and I'd know because they'd be silver instead of black. But that didn't mean I felt easy about them.

Peyton's gaze was relentless. "I know you've seen 'em again, Danaë. I can see it in your eyes."

I changed the subject. "You worked on Kelly's place, right?"

"Needed the money. Kelly said I made the weep holes in the window frames too big, left gaps under the doors. Said he was afraid snakes would get in and kill him in his sleep. Told me to get off the property or he'd call the cops." Peyton reached around me to pour a glass of milk. "Damn shame about those babies. His wife is up there now, hidin' in the house to keep away from the cameras."

Pain pulled at Peyton's face. He'd mourned the Kelly children as if they'd been his own. I cut the omelet in half and slid a portion onto each plate.

"Working on the mural today?" he asked, pointing the tines of his fork at my faded t-shirt and paint-smeared jeans.

My work clothes were a private joke between us. Even living in his truck, Peyton's Levis were bluer than the night sky and his crisp Hawaiian shirt smelled of laundry starch.

"Grand opening's Monday," I answered. "Has to be done and dry in forty-eight hours."

"You ready?"

I shook my head and pushed the last bite of omelet around with my fork. "All except the eyes."

Eyes are hard to paint. They're not like trees or faces in a crowd, where a suggestion is all you need. Eyes don't come right until you can feel the soul coming to life under the brush, and to do that, you have to know what those eyes see.

We finished our breakfast in silence.

The sea and sky were robin's-egg blue on my walk to the Sea Center, with only a pale smudge of haze to mark where one stopped and the other began. I mixed the colors in my head, pulling out the contrast of pale, cool blues against the yellow-green of palms and agaves.

News vans lined the main drag, and reporters trolled the locals for reactions to the Kelly trial. The Harris kid blew through a stop sign, narrowly missing Reesie Aames, who was talking to a news crew, scratching at her arm with one hand and gesturing east toward the Mansions with the other.

Reesie had been beautiful once, with hair the color of sunlight and a figure Aphrodite would have envied, but drugs had stolen that away. Her hair now hung like frayed straw, and her dress sagged off her hips and shoulders as if it had been made for a different woman.

I passed by, invisible in my shabby clothes. What the reporters wanted was a slack-jawed yokel who'd tell about the time the spirits threw dishes against the wall or made the chickens stop laying. Lacking that, they'd settle for someone like Reesie, blonde and well-dressed, who had plenty to say about her neighbor Herb Kelly, and none of it kind.

If I was lucky, the trial would be over before they got desperate enough to notice a paint-smeared artist in worn sneakers and tatty blue jeans.

The Sea Center sat on the far side of the freeway, across from some weathered picnic tables and a small playground. It was built of grey cinder blocks, with a low, peaked roof and clerestory windows that tilted open at the bottom, the kind of building you'd expect to find in a military depot or a forest service compound. What it lacked in glamour it made up for with a dogged sturdiness that reminded me of the town itself. Perched on bluffs overlooking the ocean, its chief drawback was that the builders had placed the windows too high for a view, a lack my mural was intended to remedy.

The smell of turpentine and linseed oil swirled around me when I unlocked the door. This close to the water, the paint took days to dry, so my morning routine included opening windows and switching on a space heater. A silver spirit floated in one corner, making a soft thrumming sound. I tried to ignore it, but in the back of my mind I wondered if spirits could purr.

My mural covered all four walls of the Sea Center, reproducing the view of the coastline outside. In the center panel, Poseidon, god of the sea, strode forth from the waves with his trident at hand. I'd painted the scenery in layer upon layer of transparent glazes to capture the moody sea and changeable sky. But the sea god himself required something special. He surged forward out of the wall, sculpted from modeling paste and inlaid with bits of rock and shell from the beach below. His wife Amphitrite nestled at his side. Her eyes of green beach glass gazed with adoration, and her white, coral hair flowed into the foaming waves.

Dolphins cavorted around the pair, leaping in playful arcs, while pelicans flew overhead. Nereids chased otters through kelp forests of deepest green, and shafts of golden sunlight pierced the depths below. But alas, Poseidon himself stood as blind as Tiresias, his eyes empty holes where I'd been unable to get the color right, no matter what I tried.

Two hours later, I scraped the paint away and slung my palette knife into the turp jar. The silver spirit had summoned friends, and they rose up around the edges of the mural, flitting from silver to black while they gibbered frustration and failure in my ears. They pooled in Poseidon's empty eyes in twin voids of black despair.

I stumbled back from my work and wiped my shaking hands on my jeans. Peyton's long-ago warning rattled in my head like an old tin can. Black was bad. Black meant that the spirits had found something dark to latch on to—fear, anger, insecurity— something they'd use to destroy me if I let them.

I raked my fingers through my hair, heedless of the paint that rubbed off on my forehead. If the mural wasn't ready, if the Center's directors didn't like it, I'd never work in this town again. Around here, feelings like that did more than stifle your creativity. Around here, feelings like that could kill.

I took a deep breath, let it out, forced myself to walk slowly around the inside of the building, opening the remaining windows. *Open house, open heart;* that's what Peyton always said. If nothing else, the fresh air would help the paint dry. The spirits followed me, twisting like cats around my ankles.

If I gave in to fear and ran, they'd drag me down like angry Maenads. I counted each step until I made it to the door.

When I stood outside in the fresh air and sunshine, my stomach rumbled. Time for a break and some lunch.

The Saltbox Café sat in the center of town on the main drag across from the firehouse. Like most of old Summerland, the building was more than a century old, a small, white bungalow of wood and stone that managed to look tidy, yet gently worn. A path of crushed stone wound between plantings of lavender and rock-roses. It ushered guests up four stone steps onto a long, covered porch where they could linger over a glass of Dora's homemade lemonade. Tables for two lined the porch, and a silver basin offered crystal clear water to four-pawed guests.

Inside, past the clatter of the screen door, more tables beckoned. A padded bench ran the length of the place, and polished, wooden chairs offered their services to those who'd missed a seat on the bench. A river-rock fireplace with an iron grate held court along the eastern wall, and a green velvet settee snuggled up to the hearth, flanked by matching armchairs and a bentwood rocker with a white cushion.

The rocker was Hester's favorite place whenever a lull in customers offered her a moment's respite, and the armchair on the right, nearest the fireplace, was mine. A threadbare patch along the edge of the left arm testified to my habit of rubbing the nap of the velvet back and forth with one hand while I worked out drawings in my sketchbook with the other.

The café's owners, Hester and Dora, had tried to buy the place separately, so the story went, until Peyton brought them together. Once they met, they realized they could do as a couple what neither one of them could do alone. Hester had grey eyes and a smile as warm as apple cobbler. Her old hands were strong from kneading out dough each morning, and it wasn't unusual to see a dusting of flour across her cheeks or hiding in the wrinkles of her apron.

Dora, the younger and slimmer of the two, had been a socialite in her former life, and she still exuded a vivacious charm that drew customers in and made them feel welcome. Sometimes when I looked at her, I could see the ghosts of flashbulbs popping around her like champagne bubbles. Loss and sadness had ended that life, and the shadow of it still showed in her eyes, if you knew when to look. But whatever sadness it was had left wisdom in its wake, and Hester, Dora and the Saltbox Café were the hub that held the two Summerlands together.

Today, though, Hester and the chair by the hearth were destined ne'er to meet. The line for lunch stood two- and three-deep out the door. It poured over the porch, down the stone steps, over the path and onto the sidewalk. A din of cutlery and conversation drowned out the sound of the freeway, and the salt air took on the scent of panini and wood-fired pizza.

Peyton's truck sat in the parking lot, and Reesie Aames stood beside it, screeching like a banshee. "If I ever see you again, Peyton Jain, you'll be a dead man!"

Reesie's voice sent a shiver up my spine. I wanted no part of her drama, so I cut through the parking lot into the rear yard where the back door to the kitchen stood open. A square box fan blocked the lower half of the doorway, and tables too rickety for paying customers played host to deliverymen and waiters on smoke breaks.

Hester's back door specials were yesterday's leftovers, but the food started so fresh that none of us minded. I put a dollar in the tip jar and sat down to a bowl of black bean soup, heavy with carrots and red peppers. A chunk of day-old sourdough served to wipe out the bowl. It was a moment not even an angry spirit could spoil.

No, the spoiling came from Hester herself. A shadow crossed

my plate, and I looked up into Hester's cinnamon-and-apples smile. "Dani," she started, wiping her hands on her apron, "when you're finished, would you mind running some things up to Anya? I was going to ask Peyton, but I think she'd respond better to a woman."

Anya was Anya Kelly, bereaved mother and Herb Kelly's grieving wife. I didn't fancy a trip to the Mansions, but I couldn't sit there filling my stomach with Hester's charity while I denied it to a woman who'd just lost her children. So I swallowed my pride along with Hester's good bread. "'Course I will, Hester. Whatever you need."

Hester thanked me and left a bag of Styrofoam takeout boxes on the table. Before I left, Peyton pulled me aside and pressed a small prickly package into my hand. No larger than a plum, it was wrapped in tattered sailcloth to cushion something that felt like the spines of a sea urchin. "That's for Áine," he said, giving her name a lilt I couldn't identify. "Tell her there's mercy in it if she looks."

And that's how I ended up on the doorstep of the most spirit-plagued house in all of Summerland.

My house was on the way, so I decided to finish the errand in my old VW bus. Walking through the gates to the Mansions on foot always made me feel like less of a person, and if I was going to be anywhere near the Harris kid, I wanted some metal around me.

By the time I reached Anya's house, a dense afternoon fog had cloaked the town in a silent grey shroud. Anya's doorbell bonged deep in the bowels of the house, and the sound raised gooseflesh along my arms. Seconds ticked by while the sticky-sweet smell of Hester's bread pudding wafted up from the bag in my arms.

I juggled the takeout boxes and tried to ring the bell with my elbow, bumping the door in the process. There was a soft click and the door slid open. The hair on the back of my arms stood rigid with fear.

"Mrs. Kelly?" I called. "Hello?"

Silence.

I nudged the door open a few more inches. A distant slithering met my ears, like whispers in the dark. *Spirits.*

I pushed the door all the way open, stepped over the threshold and raised my voice. "Anya? It's Dani. Hester sent me with some things from the Box." The sound echoed off the foyer's marble tile.

An antique hall table made of a single weathered plank stood sentry against the left wall. On it, golden apples nestled in a bowl of silver branches, and Anya smiled out from a cut glass picture frame. She stood laughing on the deck of the *Wave Sweeper,* her father's fishing trawler, with the sea wind whipping hair black as a raven's wing across her face.

She looked so vibrant, so alive. With time, I hoped she might look so again—if the spirits didn't get her first.

I left Hester's offering on the hall table and moved deeper into the house, calling Anya's name as I went. A wave of destruction had crashed through Anya's kitchen. Cupboard doors listed open, and drawers had been turned out on the floor. An oak knife block lay on its side on an island of Connemara marble, blades and handles tangled like driftwood on the floor below. Spirits hissed, black and writhing, among the wreckage.

I ran to the sink and threw open the window, then did the same with the patio doors. "Shoo! Out!" I shouted.

The spirits snaked around my wrists and ankles, slinking upward toward my heart. They flickered from black to silver and back again, and their sibilant hisses sank into my ears. They showed me visions of Anya's long, dark hair waving like kelp fronds as she sank beneath the sea, and my own poor home, a shabby hovel next to Anya's gold and marble palace. All I had to do was wait, they whispered, and everything around me was mine for the taking.

"You can't have me," I whispered back. "Or Anya, either." The spirits reared back to strike, hissed in frustration, then turned and flowed one by one out the open windows.

A new hissing reached my ears, the sound of water through

pipes. Someone was running water deeper in the house. It had to be Anya, so I sprinted toward the sound.

Her bedroom was a mirror of the kitchen, with bedside tables overturned and an aquamarine silk comforter tumbling off the edge of the bed like waves over a seawall. Spirits filled the room until I waded knee-deep among them, and cries like hungry gulls echoed off the walls.

The bathroom door was locked against me. Water thundered into the tub on the other side. Anya gave a ragged sob, and I heard a silvery sound like ice cubes tinkling against crystal. Banshee wails sounded in my ears, and teeth sharp as needles pricked at my face and arms.

I pounded on the door and yelled Anya's name. When she didn't answer, I kicked the door in.

She cowered near the vanity with her back against the wall. Her raven hair had been cut short in the latest pixie style, and her red-rimmed eyes were dark hollows against her alabaster cheeks. She wore a jade-green robe embroidered with apple blossoms, and silk slippers to match. One hand gripped a crystal tumbler filled with amber liquid, and the other pushed against the vanity as if she'd risen to run but found herself trapped. The room smelled of steam, peat and alcohol.

A low table of brass and glass sat next to the rapidly filling tub. A bottle of Jameson's stood upon it, next to a Waterford decanter with the stopper out and a squat brown pill bottle filled with yellow capsules. The spirits breathed sighs of watery death.

I looked at Anya again. She was young, rich, beautiful—everything I wasn't. Spirits rose up between us with teeth like knives and eyes black as night. A red rage filled my vision, and I bent toward the brass table.

Anya's hands shook. The soft clink of ice made me lift my head. She trembled against the wall, spirits swarming over her body until all I could see was her pale, frightened face with eyes like a green summer meadow. The spirits' shrieks ripped though my soul like a razor through canvas.

Anya slid down the wall until her head touched her knees. The tumbler slipped from her fingers and thudded on the thick carpet. There she was, slender, beautiful, defenseless...*and terrified*.

In that moment, I knew it was Peyton, not Hester, who'd sent me here. When Anya's haunted eyes met mine, the last recesses of my heart wrenched themselves open. I no longer cared about marble floors or gilt-edged mirrors, about silks and crystal I'd never be able to afford. I cared only that Anya was a woman adrift, bereft and grieving on the swells of life just as I had been nearly twenty years before when I'd washed up on the Summerland shore, destitute and pregnant by a man I hadn't known was married. Peyton's kindness had saved me then, and he must have known that mine could save Anya now.

I grabbed the table and hurled it through the bathroom window. The Waterford decanter shattered on the sill, and a rainbow of shards splattered into the steaming water.

I fell against the lip of the tub, one arm wet to the shoulder where I'd caught myself against the bottom. Broken crystal sliced my palm, and a thin smear of my blood swirled over the white porcelain.

The spirits took form for the briefest instant, showing me a flash of slender hands, ethereal faces and flowing robes of algae and water weeds. Their voices sang like wind howling over the moors, then they streamed out the broken window on a rush of moist air.

A gentle breeze touched my face, and Anya looked at me with tear-streaked eyes. "Are they gone?"

"Yes, Anya, they're gone." I crawled over to her, took her cold hands in mine and said the same words Peyton had said to me the night he'd found me standing on the cliffs alone, wrestling with the final step before oblivion. "Don't be afraid of them. They're not evil, and they can't hurt you if your heart is pure. All they can do is magnify what's already there. You have a choice in front of you, one you should make with a clear head and an open heart. Don't let despair make it for you." Anya gave the tiniest of nods, and the faintest light of hope returned to her eyes.

"Let's get you out of here," I said. "You can stay at my place until the trial blows over." My son Percy, a fine young man now, was off to college and other adventures, so Anya could have his room until her life found a new place to settle.

She dressed quickly in jeans and a loose white Oxford shirt, fashionable even in her grief. A few minutes later she climbed into the back of my VW bus to hide among the drop cloths and painting supplies until we made it past the reporters.

I tucked Peyton's gift into her hands and told her, "This is from Peyton. He said there was mercy in it if you look."

Her brows drew together as she peeled back the sailcloth wrapping, but I let her ponder the meaning alone under her canvas veil.

Somehow, I knew Peyton would approve.

I'd intended to take her back to my house and get her settled before I reported back to Hester, but we never made it past the Box. A pale light suffused the Box's windows with an eerie green glow that lit the fog outside. Black shapes rippled against the glass in an orgy of malice and spite. I stomped the brakes, yelled to Anya to hold on, and screeched into a parking space. I jumped out of the van and left it running while I ran around to the back entrance.

Peyton stood like an avenging god framed against the back door of the Box. His hands gripped the doorframe as if sheer will could contain whatever lurked within, and his eyes were riveted on the scene inside. I peeked past him, through the busy kitchen and into the dining area where a sleek flat-screen television was broadcasting the Kelly trial. Every soul in The Saltbox stood transfixed.

In a sterile Los Angeles courtroom, Herb Kelly stood for sentencing, found guilty of strangling his children in their beds. His lion's mane of yellow hair fell greasy and unkempt on his shoulders. He tore at his orange jumpsuit as if it burned him and rattled his shackles in a crazed, ranting fury. "Snakes!" he screamed. "They were snakes!" Froth spattered from his lips, and he fell to his knees retching bile onto the courtroom floor.

I turned my face away. "Who brought that thing in here?" I whispered.

"Reesie did," said Peyton softly. "It came from Aames' place." And there she stood with an arm draped over the television, her pockmarked skin twitching and her eyes aglow with malice. A blackness glowed in her chest, an oily, transparent aura that throbbed outward with every beat of her heart. And for the first time, I saw with my own eyes what Peyton had tried to explain—spirits didn't bring evil; they *magnified* it.

A scraping and scratching sound filled the walls and rose up from the floors, the sound of angry spirits reveling in Reesie's hatred, drinking it in and feeding it back to her until her body could hold no more.

Dora cowered in a corner near the cash register with a small lacquered box clutched to her chest, her fingers fumbling at the lid. Hester held the younger woman in her arms, fighting to keep the little box closed. I cowered with them, helpless to stop what was coming.

Black tendrils of hate flowed in through the walls and up through the floor, stream upon stream of shrieking spirits drunk with malevolence. They rushed into Reesie, entwining around her body in a macabre lovers' dance. The tendrils flowed in through her nose and mouth until they found the darkness in her heart. The evil met its twin and blossomed, bursting from her chest in an ink-black cloud of death.

The patrons in the Box stood like clay figures, their eyes blank and their souls unguarded. The blackness reached for them, searching their hearts for jealousy, resentment, petty disagreements that could be nursed into hatred.

A gust of wind blew in through the kitchen, heavy with the smell of rain. The lights flickered once and went out. Dora's photocopied menus fluttered like sailcloth against the windows.

Peyton's visage darkened. His voice rumbled like storm clouds lashed by the wind, and his eyes shone blue with St. Elmo's fire. He drew in a massive breath, and a gale howled through the Box, sharp with the scent of salt and sea. His presence magnified until the Box could no longer contain him.

MEGEN NELSON

He reached for Reesie, his massive hands trailing ghostly masts and torn rigging in their wake. The blue light of righteous wrath roared forth from his mouth and eyes. His hand curled like a breaking wave, and the shadow of a trident flashed over Reesie's face.

The ocean answered Peyton's call, and a churning wall of sea water rose behind him.

Reesie's head snapped up. The spirits joined their voices to hers, and the sound groaned up from the bowels of the earth. "I see you, Earth-shaker!"

Peyton hammered his barnacle-covered fist into the floorboards at Reesie's feet, and the towering green sea crashed in to claim her.

I braced myself for a death that never came.

The wave carried the spirits away like black, wind-driven spray. And when they had gone, Reesie's broken body sprawled on the floorboards, her eyes burned out by the black hatred in her soul.

Peyton diminished. He sagged to his knees beside Reesie, his shoulders stooped and his breathing ragged. I looked about for signs of the ocean's fury, and saw nothing but the grey patter of rain against the Box's ancient windows.

Hester and Dora pushed themselves up from the floor. The clay figures remembered they were human, and the clatter of dishes and silver resumed. What the patrons had seen, I could not say.

Dora tucked the little black box back on a shelf above the counter, and Hester called over to the Fire Station to report that Reesie had suffered an overdose.

I helped Peyton stand, bearing him up under one shoulder while he limped toward his truck with painful breaths. He eased himself down onto the back bumper and turned his face to the cleansing rain and the darkened skies.

His voice shook. "I couldn't save her, Danaë. Took all I had to contain what she'd loosed." Raindrops splattered beside us, making dark circles on the dusty pavement. I didn't know what to say, but Peyton did, and his words surprised me.

"Got somethin' for you." Though his hands trembled, he

fished in his pockets until he found what he sought. Unlike his other gifts, this one was folded in cellophane paper, and I couldn't see what was inside.

"This is the last one," he said, closing my fingers around the packet. "Don't open it until you're back in the Sea Center. Promise me that, Danaë." His face and eyes had gone fish-belly grey, and his hair fluttered in the wind from the coming storm. I shivered, but those eyes of his held me fast until I gave my word.

Peyton laid his coat over my shoulders, then he glanced at Anya sitting wide-eyed in the driver's seat of my bus. "I knew she'd take to you," he said. He stared past me, peering out over the rain-dark sea. "I've spent a lot of years watchin' after this town. She's a lost soul, Danaë. Look after her, like you did me."

I tucked the packet into my pocket. "I will," I promised. "You sure you're okay?"

Peyton waved me away and thrust a knobby finger down the road toward the Sea Center. "Go finish it."

I would have, but Anya was still in my bus, staring past the Box, up the road that led to the Mansions. She threw the bus into gear and peeled out of the parking lot, squealing the tires on the way out.

Peyton and I looked up toward the Mansions' gates. Ike's fiery red Mustang rounded the corner and sped down the hill, catching air at each successive terrace. A thin guard rail marked the edge of the cliff at the bottom of the hill, and water ponded on the pavement.

Thunder rumbled overhead. As his car raced closer, we saw black spirits pressed against the windshield, harpies and banshees tearing at Ike in frustration after being denied other prey.

Anya gunned the engine, and my van lurched into the Mustang's path, forming a fragile tin wall between his car and the long fall into the ocean below.

Anya kicked open the door and threw herself clear, tearing her white shirt as she rolled to a stop in the muddy gutter.

I sprinted for the corner. Anya fumbled Peyton's gift out of her pocket, and plucked at the wrapping.

Lightning cracked, and a blue-white flash lit the street under the blackened sky. Ike's Mustang plowed into my doomed van, crushing it like an egg. His body exploded through the windshield in a shower of glass, arms spread-eagled against the storm.

If the accident itself hadn't killed him, the fall to earth would.

Anya raised the shell aloft, her face transfixed with terror. The spines bit into her palm, and thin rivulets of blood trickled down her arm. Her voice was a whisper and a shout. "Mercy!" she cried.

I could see pain in her eyes, a plea that no other mother should suffer through the loss of a child.

The spirits took form overhead, their faces shining in silver glory, and their eyes locked on Anya. "Mercy," she whispered.

Slender silver hands reached for Ike Harris and held him suspended in the air. Gentle fingers smoothed his hair and shimmering lips kissed away his hurts. They lowered him to the ground at Anya's side. She threw her arms around the boy, holding him to her chest in the driving rain.

I raced to them and laid my hand on her shoulder. "Is he hurt? Are you okay?"

Anya shielded Ike's face from the rain. "He'll be alright, Danaë." She looked up at me with her sea-green eyes. "And so will I. Go paint."

Cold rain soaked me to the skin, but I made my way to the Sea Center with Peyton's cellophane package warm in my hands. I unwrapped paper thinner than tissue to find two elongated mussel shells, still attached like butterfly wings at the rounded tips. Layer upon layer of pearlescent nacre gleamed inside, a tapestry of shimmering blues, deep purples and delicate greens.

I took out my paints and brushes, and I mixed the colors under watchful silver eyes until I could feel a soul take shape under my brush. A soft thrumming filled the air like the sound of a distant flute or wind over the mouth of a cave.

When I stepped back, my mural was finished. Eyes of Poseidon's blue looked out at me from a face that moved earth and desolate sea.

That night, the police found Peyton's body dead in his truck in the lot overlooking the beach, and the spirits—Naiads and Nereids, kelpies and banshees—wailed their grief into the wind.

Peyton had been their touchstone and gatekeeper. Where he found openness and welcome, the spirits sowed blessings in his wake. And where he was spurned by hearts sealed tighter than double-paned windows, where the black miasma of greed and hate seeped in through cracks and crevices, that's where the vapors built until the spirits raged like angry Maenads, rending sanity the way they'd once rent flesh.

By morning, a fresh wind had swept the storm clouds away, and the last remnants of a silver mist floated above the waves. The sea grew calm, and sunlight rippled golden on the water of Poseidon's eyes.

In the months that followed, Aames sold his hollow mansion and built a new place on an empty lot a block from the post office.

Anya took back her maiden name after her husband was found hanged in his cell, and she moved into the boarded up shanty-house next door to me. With Herb Kelly's money at her disposal, it wasn't long before the place had fresh paint, a new roof, curtains in the windows, and a garden full of roses. Her cheeks regained their color, and her raven's-wing hair grew long and lush again.

As for me, I still tell tales of our lives by the sea, written in words of paint and shell. After the Sea Center opened, I added a single figure to my mural, the silhouette of woman standing alone on the bluffs with her long, dark hair splayed out in the wind, searching for the souls of her children on the face of the turbulent sea.

On the Direction of Art

BY BOB EGGLETON

This past winter I got to serve as the guest Art Director for the Illustrators of the Future Contest. What a rewarding and fun experience! I'm following a path blazed for this Contest by Frank Kelly Freas in 1987.

In the business of illustration, it's likely one will deal with an art director. Of course, over the decades the definition of an *art director* has changed; more and more I have seen the title "Director of Marketing" used, as if the art should be sidelined to something of a commodity.

Art directors typically oversee the way an illustration should look in the context of its use. Many times *good* art directors are themselves artists.

Serving as the Art Director, I was able to view up to three sketches of ideas submitted by each artist. Some of the "sketches," I will say, looked like finished works, which tells a lot about the time we live in. In my early career, I did mere scribblings for sketches!

I believe in never telling an artist what to do. I always look for the strongest idea, and I found with a number of people it was also their *personal favorite,* so I simply said, "Go with it." I refuse to micromanage, because I have seen art that looks just that: micromanaged. I've been the victim of the bad kind of direction myself. My preference is to let the artists shine. For Illustrators of the Future, I sometimes made a nudge or a suggestion that only clarified the idea, trying to take the concept from good to great.

What makes an exceptional artist, to me, is his or her ability to tell a good story with a minimal amount of visual information. I am a big fan of the idea that "less is more." Something does not have to be overwrought to be "finished."

Also when an artist is illustrating someone's story, it is not always necessary to stay totally in structure with the prose. The illustration should augment and bring another dimension to the story, perhaps something that the writer never thought of. I like writers a lot, but they can be "visually illiterate," which I say in jest, meaning they don't "see" in the same way an artist sees. The artist's vision brings a unique perspective to the story, an added dimension. Even the writer often will say, when viewing an illustration, "I never thought of that! What a great idea!"

With illustrations, I like to invite viewers to make up their own story, or imprint something of themselves onto it. The art becomes personal to everyone who views it.

It is said that pictures are worth a thousand words. Well, one picture for a story just adds one thousand words to that story! Overseeing so much of this incredible work with Illustrators of the Future has been an honor and it has added to my own learning and opened my eyes to new ways of thinking.

Onward!

LIST OF ILLUSTRATIONS BY ARTIST

ALEX BROCK
The God Whisperer

449

Planar Ghosts

MEGAN KELCHNER
Half Past

TUNG CHI LEE
Unrefined

SHUANGJIAN LIU
A Revolutionary's Guide to Practical Conjuration

453

MICHELLE LOCKAMY
Wisteria Melancholy

BERNARDO MOTA
Inconstant Moon

MEGEN NELSON
Poseidon's Eyes

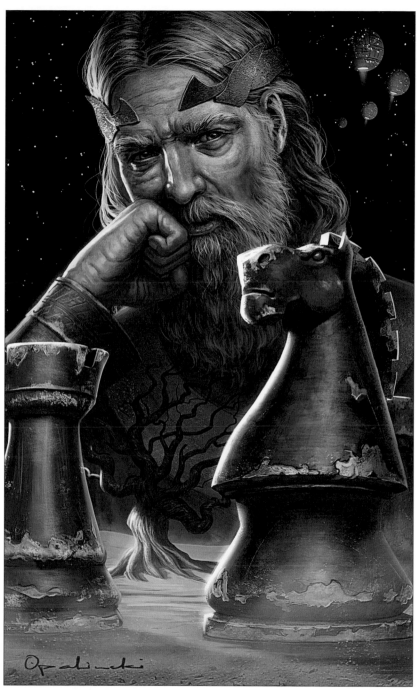

GREG OPALINSKI
When Shadows Fall

TAYLOR PAYTON
The Graver

QUINLAN SEPTER
Twelve Minutes to Vinh Quang

459

EMILY SIU

Purposes Made for Alien Minds

TREVOR SMITH
Between Screens

461

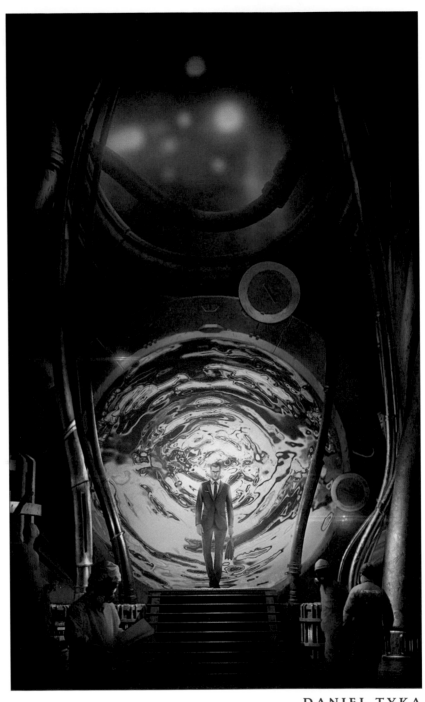

DANIEL TYKA
Rough Draft

DANIEL TYKA
Switch

CHOONG YOON
Stars That Make Dark Heaven Light

The Year in the Contests

This year we celebrate the seventy-fifth anniversary of The Golden Pen contest, a small writing competition that L. Ron Hubbard launched while wintering for a few weeks in Alaska. At the time, Ron was a widely-known author, with over 120 published novels and short stories. He'd worked in Hollywood as a screenwriter, was publishing under half a dozen pen names, had lectured at Harvard, and had been president of the American Fiction Guild.

While literally iced-in at port, as I understand it, he initiated a small contest aimed at inspiring new authors. Like the current contests, it was open to anyone who was not yet a professional, and it offered sizable rewards for the winners.

I like what Ron said at the time, for not only does he inform us as to why he initiated that contest, I think he is telling us why the Writers of the Future Contest was so dear to his heart:

"It has been my experience that almost everyone, at one period or another of his life, has harbored a desire to write. Some have let that desire burn very dimly and have not even put the matter to test. A few have put words to paper and have laid the unfinished product away in some remote corner where it will remain forgotten forever. A very few have written several things and have actually desired to do something with them. Perhaps one percent of the total has gone so far as to send a manuscript to a publisher. The estimated figures are that ten million people are trying to write and sell stories, that ten thousand have submitted stories to magazines, that two thousand have sold a story at one time or another and that there are only five hundred full professional writers in a nation of a hundred and thirty million people.

"Why?

"The amateur stares at his unfinished script and thinks that in view of all those top-heavy figures against him he has not the slightest chance and so abandons the attempt. If he only knew how anxiously new writers are sought by editors. The person who submits an occasional story is discouraged by the rejection slips he collects and so abandons the trial.

"The person who occasionally sells a story and yet does not become a full-time professional writer is either up against the limitations of his imagination or his ability to concentrate. Ten million people are trying to write and sell stories. Five hundred writing and selling consistently. What do the five hundred have which the ten million have not? Some say it is the ability to sweat. 'Ten ounces of inspiration and ten tons of perspiration,' as a sage writer once put it. That, however, is not the entire truth.

"The amateur writer, even when he has completed a manuscript, seldom knows what to do with it or how to go about getting it in print. That is information which one earns dearly...."

Having thus spoken, L. Ron Hubbard initiated The Golden Pen contest there in Anchorage, Alaska, inviting local residents to send in a Christmas tale to the listeners at KGBU radio station.

Times have changed. The US is much larger now than it was then, but the love of writing has not diminished over the years. Twenty years ago, a major women's magazine took a poll and found out that some forty percent of adult women hoped to write a book at some time in their lives.

It struck me while reading Ron's words that we as Contest judges, three quarters of a century later, are acting from the same motivations that he did. We still see new writers with superb talent who just don't understand this business, don't know how to break into it, and don't know how special they are. For that reason, all of us at the Contests are still here reaching out to new writers and illustrators, hoping to discover and train others who yearn to develop their own artistic skills.

CONTEST GROWTH

This last year was a banner year for the Writers and Illustrators of the Future Contests. Each quarter seems to be larger than the one before, and the Writers of the Future brought in a record number of submissions. With the art competition, we're also greatly increasing our worldwide flavor, bringing in submissions from countries that we hadn't heard from before.

We now have contest entrants from a total of 171 countries across the globe. This year we added North Korea, Slovakia, Bhutan, Cambodia, Paraguay and Vanuatu.

The writer winners this year come from the United States and Australia, while our illustrator winners hailed from the US, Taiwan, China, South Korea, Malawi and Poland.

Normally I like to list recent publications by past winners, but I'm afraid that the lists are growing too long! In the past year alone, we have more than a hundred novels released by past contest winners. Included among those are releases from some of our newest winners, Tom Doyle (Vol 28) and Randy Henderson (Vol 30) who both released books through Tor. We're also seeing a tremendous number of short stories published by our winners, and we'd like to congratulate them on their productivity.

AWARDS NEWS FOR PAST WINNERS

Some of our past winners won major awards in the field this year. We won't go into all of those who were finalists for major awards, since once again, the lists are growing too long, but here are some highlights.

Writer winner Aliette de Bodard (WotF Volume 23) won the Nebula Award for Best Novelette for "The Waiting Stars."

Writer winner Karen Joy Fowler (WotF Volume 2) won 2014 Pen/Faulkner Award and was a finalist in the California Book

Awards and the Man Booker Prize for her *We Are All Completely Beside Ourselves*.

Illustrator winner Sarah Web (WotF Vol 30) won the Hugo for Best Fan Artist.

NEW WRITERS OF THE FUTURE JUDGES

This past year we were delighted to add two new judges to our illustrious panel: Nancy Kress, a *New York Times* bestselling author and Hugo and Nebula Award winner and Brandon Sanderson, multiple award winner and #1 international bestselling author.

PASSING

We are saddened by the loss of one of our winners and a longtime supporter of the Contest, Jay Lake (Vol 19). Those that knew him best loved him most, and that is a very good thing.

RECOGNITION FOR THE CONTESTS

Over the course of this year, the contest became much more widely known. The amount of media attention (as measured by impressions on television, radio, and in the papers) grew by more than 250%, which speaks well for future expansion of the Contests, and also greater publicity for our winners.

The *Writer's Digest* Award for service to the writing community was presented to L. Ron Hubbard and the Contest by Nancy Kress at the awards ceremony last year (shortly before we invited her to be a judge). Nancy has been a columnist for *Writer's Digest* for the past sixteen years.

RECOGNITION FROM THE CONTEST

The L. Ron Hubbard Lifetime Achievement Award was presented to Orson Scott Card by Joni Labaqui (Contest Director) at the awards ceremony last year. Mr. Card gave an eloquent acceptance speech, beautifully acknowledging the Contest and applauding its results.

For Contest year 31, the L. Ron Hubbard Writers of the Future Contest winners are:

FIRST QUARTER

1. *Tim Napper*
   TWELVE MINUTES TO VINH QUANG

2. *Auston Habershaw*
   A REVOLUTIONARY'S GUIDE TO PRACTICAL CONJURATION

3. *Martin L. Shoemaker*
   UNREFINED

SECOND QUARTER

1. *Kary English*
   POSEIDON'S EYES

2. *Samantha Murray*
   HALF PAST

3. *Scott R. Parkin*
   PURPOSES MADE FOR ALIEN MINDS

THIRD QUARTER

1. *Daniel J. Davis*
   THE GOD WHISPERER

2. *Amy M. Hughes*
   THE GRAVER

3. *Michael T. Banker*
   WISTERIA MELANCHOLY

FOURTH QUARTER

1. *Sharon Joss*
   STARS THAT MAKE DARK HEAVEN LIGHT

2. *Steve Pantazis*
   SWITCH

3. *Krystal Claxton*
   PLANAR GHOSTS

PUBLISHED FINALIST

Zach Chapman
BETWEEN SCREENS

For the year 2014, the L. Ron Hubbard Illustrators of the Future Contest winners are:

FIRST QUARTER
Tung Chi Lee
Michelle Lockamy
Emily Siu

SECOND QUARTER
Amit Dutta
Shuangjian Liu
Taylor Payton

THIRD QUARTER
Alex Brock
Quinlan Septer
Choong Yoon

FOURTH QUARTER
Megan Kelchner
Megen Nelson
Daniel Tyka

Our heartiest congratulations to all the winners! May we see much more of their work in the future.

471

WRITERS' CONTEST RULES

1. No entry fee is required, and all rights in the story remain the property of the author. All types of science fiction, fantasy and dark fantasy are welcome.

2. By submitting to the Contest, the entrant agrees to abide by all Contest rules.

3. All entries must be original works, in English. Plagiarism, which includes the use of third-party poetry, song lyrics, characters or another person's universe, without written permission, will result in disqualification. Excessive violence or sex, determined by the judges, will result in disqualification. Entries may not have been previously published in professional media.

4. To be eligible, entries must be works of prose, up to 17,000 words in length. We regret we cannot consider poetry, or works intended for children.

5. The Contest is open only to those who have not professionally published a novel or short novel, or more than one novelette, or more than three short stories, in any medium. Professional publication is deemed to be payment of at least six cents per word, and at least 5,000 copies, or 5,000 hits.

6. Entries submitted in hard copy must be typewritten or a computer printout in black ink on white paper, printed only on the front of the paper, double-spaced, with numbered pages. All other formats will be disqualified. Each entry must have a cover page with the title of the work, the author's legal name, a pen name if applicable, address, telephone number, e-mail address and an approximate word count. Every subsequent page must carry the title and a page number, but the author's name must be deleted to facilitate fair, anonymous judging.

   Entries submitted electronically must be double-spaced and must include the title and page number on each page, but not the author's name. Electronic submissions will separately include the author's legal name, pen name if applicable, address, telephone number, e-mail address and approximate word count.

7. Manuscripts will be returned after judging only if the author has provided return postage on a self-addressed envelope.

8. We accept only entries that do not require a delivery signature for us to receive them.

9. There shall be three cash prizes in each quarter: a First Prize of $1,000, a Second Prize of $750, and a Third Prize of $500, in US dollars. In addition, at the end of the year the winners will have their entries rejudged, and a Grand Prize winner shall be determined and receive an additional $5,000. All winners will also receive trophies.

10. The Contest has four quarters, beginning on October 1, January 1, April 1 and July 1. The year will end on September 30. To be eligible for judging in its quarter, an entry must be postmarked or received electronically no later than midnight on the last day of the quarter. Late entries will be included in the following quarter and the Contest Administration will so notify the entrant.

11. Each entrant may submit only one manuscript per quarter. Winners are ineligible to make further entries in the Contest.

12. All entries for each quarter are final. No revisions are accepted.

13. Entries will be judged by professional authors. The decisions of the judges are entirely their own, and are final.

14. Winners in each quarter will be individually notified of the results by phone, mail or e-mail.

15. This Contest is void where prohibited by law.

16. To send your entry electronically, go to:
    www.writersofthefuture.com/enter-writer-contest
    and follow the instructions.
    To send your entry in hard copy, mail it to:
    L. Ron Hubbard's Writers of the Future Contest
    7051 Hollywood Blvd., Los Angeles, California 90028

17. Visit the website for any Contest rules updates at:
    www.writersofthefuture.com

NEW ILLUSTRATORS!
L. Ron Hubbard's
Illustrators of the Future Contest

Opportunity for new science fiction and fantasy artists worldwide.

No entry fee is required.

Entrants retain all publication rights.

ALL JUDGING BY PROFESSIONAL ARTISTS ONLY

$1,500 in prizes each quarter. Quarterly winners compete for $5,000 additional annual prize!

Don't delay! Send your entry now!

To submit your entry electronically go to:
www.writersofthefuture.com/enter-the-illustrator-contest

E-mail: contests@authorservicesinc.com

To submit your entry via mail send to:
L. Ron Hubbard's Illustrators of the Future Contest
7051 Hollywood Blvd.
Los Angeles, California 90028

ILLUSTRATORS' CONTEST RULES

1. The Contest is open to entrants from all nations. (However, entrants should provide themselves with some means for written communication in English.) All themes of science fiction and fantasy illustrations are welcome: every entry is judged on its own merits only. No entry fee is required and all rights to the entry remain the property of the artist.

2. By submitting to the Contest, the entrant agrees to abide by all Contest rules.

3. The Contest is open to new and amateur artists who have not been professionally published and paid for more than three black-and-white story illustrations, or more than one process-color painting, in media distributed broadly to the general public. The ultimate eligibility criterion, however, is defined by the word "amateur"—in other words, the artist has not been paid for his artwork. If you are not sure of your eligibility, please write a letter to the Contest Administration with details regarding your publication history. Include a self-addressed and stamped envelope for the reply. You may also send your questions to the Contest Administration via e-mail.

4. Each entrant may submit only one set of illustrations in each Contest quarter. The entry must be original to the entrant and previously unpublished. Plagiarism, infringement of the rights of others, or other violations of the Contest rules will result in disqualification. Winners in previous quarters are not eligible to make further entries.

5. The entry shall consist of three illustrations done by the entrant in a color or black-and-white medium created from the artist's imagination. Use of gray scale in illustrations and mixed media, computer generated art, and the use of photography in the illustrations are accepted. Each illustration must represent a subject different from the other two.

6. ENTRIES SHOULD NOT BE THE ORIGINAL DRAWINGS, but should be color or black-and-white reproductions of the originals

of a quality satisfactory to the entrant. Entries must be submitted unfolded and flat, in an envelope no larger than 9 inches by 12 inches.

7. All hard copy entries must be accompanied by a self-addressed return envelope of the appropriate size, with the correct US postage affixed. (Non-US entrants should enclose international postage reply coupons.) If the entrant does not want the reproductions returned, the entry should be clearly marked DISPOSABLE COPIES: DO NOT RETURN. A business-size self-addressed envelope with correct postage (or valid e-mail address) should be included so that the judging results may be returned to the entrant. We only accept entries that do not require a delivery signature for us to receive them.

8. To facilitate anonymous judging, each of the three photocopies must be accompanied by a removable cover sheet bearing the artist's name, address, telephone number, e-mail address and an identifying title for that work. The reproduction of the work should carry the same identifying title on the front of the illustration and the artist's signature should be deleted. The Contest Administration will remove and file the cover sheets, and forward only the anonymous entry to the judges.

9. There will be three co-winners in each quarter. Each winner will receive an outright cash grant of US $500 and a trophy. Winners will also receive eligibility to compete for the annual Grand Prize of an additional cash grant of $5,000 together with the annual Grand Prize trophy.

10. For the annual Grand Prize Contest, the quarterly winners will be furnished with a specification sheet and a winning story from the Writers of the Future Contest to illustrate. In order to retain eligibility for the Grand Prize, each winner shall send to the Contest address his/her illustration of the assigned story within thirty (30) days of receipt of the story assignment.

The yearly Grand Prize winner shall be determined by the judges on the following basis only: Each Grand Prize judge's personal opinion on the extent to which it makes the judge want to read the story it illustrates.

The Grand Prize winner shall be announced at the L. Ron Hubbard Awards Event held in the following year.

11. The Contest has four quarters, beginning on October 1, January 1, April 1 and July 1. The year will end on September 30. To be eligible for judging in its quarter, an entry must be postmarked no later than midnight on the last day of the quarter. Late entries will be included in the following quarter and the Contest Administration will so notify the entrant.

12. Entries will be judged by professional artists only. Each quarterly judging and the Grand Prize judging may have different panels of judges. The decisions of the judges are entirely their own and are final.

13. Winners in each quarter will be individually notified of the results by mail or e-mail.

14. This Contest is void where prohibited by law.

15. To send your entry electronically, go to:
www.writersofthefuture.com/enter-the-illustrator-contest
and follow the instructions.
To send your entry via mail send it to:
L. Ron Hubbard's Illustrators of the Future Contest
7051 Hollywood Blvd., Los Angeles, California 90028

16. Visit the website for any Contest rules updates at
www.writersofthefuture.com.

Explore. Escape. Experience.
OTHER TIMES • OTHER PLACES

*Discover the works of wonder that laid the foundation
for the new Golden Age of Storytelling.*

THE L. RON HUBBARD SCIENCE FICTION COLLECTION

Beyond All Weapons: A death-defying mission into outer space to salvage a doomed Earth colony on Mars crashes headlong into the laws of physics. *Includes: "Strain" and "The Invaders"*

The Great Secret: A lust for power, unlimited riches and universal domination drives Fanner Marston to overcome hunger, pain and extreme peril—but to what end? *Includes: "Space Can," "The Beast" and "The Slaver"*

Greed: One man's greed is unexpectedly about to forever change the fate of Earth and the stars. *Includes: "Final Enemy" and "The Automagic Horse"*

Read—and learn the art of—great storytelling.

ORDER NOW!
Get 3 trade paperback books for the price of 2
A VALUE OF $29.85 FOR ONLY $19.95

Call toll-free: 1-877-842-5299 • Or visit: www.GalaxyPress.com

FINAL WORDS ON WINNING...